THE
DICK

THE
DICK

BRUCE JAY FRIEDMAN

ALFRED A. KNOPF
NEW YORK
1970

FOR

Steven Vinaver

AND

Harvey Breit

PART
ONE

◎◎◎◎◎

IN A SOMEWHAT EASYGOING WAY, THE TWO
lookalike Greek detectives began to rib each other with familiar nationalistic-style insults. Ordinarily, this might have
tapered off into a friendly shoving match, but it was a sullen,
pent-up time in the homicide bullpen. Not a single "fresh
one" had come in all day. Somehow, neither Greek could put
on the brakes; before long they had made deep slices in each
other's pride and flown at one another with nonregulation
bone-bangers, generally kept out of sight in personal lockers.
These were angry, heavy-headed little rubber chunks capable
of slapping small craters into flesh, giving it the surface of
expensive, hotly-bid-for *Life* Magazine lunar shots. In their
fury, the two let it be known that they required more room
so that they could really get at each other. Watching the
brawl was Medici, a Negro detective who wore more guns
than anyone in the department, two at the shoulders, a pair
in the crotch. Assigned to Sex Patrol, he was known as the
Dean of Child Molestation and had great, heavy-socketed
eyes which he could never close completely, even in deep

sleep. Medici accommodated the Greeks by bowing from the waist, saying, "Freedom, brothers," and opening the bullpen door. Out they rolled, locked together in a single ball of delphic crime-fighting fury, pinwheeling down the hall until they approached the partitionless office of a large, comfortable-looking man who sat at his desk arranging homicide clippings. A thin, nervously drawn line ran the length of his face, from forehead to chin, giving his pleasant features a curiously divided look, as though they had once been boundaried off by jealous, back-stabbing diplomats. On his desk was an empty silver holster in which he kept his pencils and glue brush; pinned to his large chest was a "baby badge," an exact replica of the real thing, though scaled down to half the standard size. Although he had come east only two weeks before, his desk had a lived-in look to it. He took great pride in his clipping displays, always making sure to give them some slant or focus so that homicide chiefs, at a single glance, might get the drift of the week's slaughter. In this particular layout, he had placed the suicide of a video kingpin in the center of the page and then bordered it with what he considered an ironic, point-making fringe of vicious little fruit stabbings. He had been about to finish the job, but then the bone-banging Greeks rolled in, and the tall, boundaried-off newcomer had to move his legs to let them by.

"This is some violent place," he said to himself. "This may be my worst yet."

◉

He was Kenneth LePeters, a clippings expert for homicide bureaus, who for seventeen years had lived in polite and hearty towns of the Midwest, then sensed a storm coming up in his life and come back east to face it. He had enjoyed being in America's heartland, yet in a sense it had been like pacing back and forth in outer hallways; he had always known that one day he would have to march into some main section of the house and face the music.

He was slipping up on forty now and scared to death about it. The first part of his life had been bumpy, but tolerable. Lord knew what was coming up in the second and final section. Through the years, he had developed a comfortable, yet oddly contradictory body. A massive rib cage was his best feature. When he peeled off his shirt and huffed it up, he could make it look like the ruined prow of a newly unearthed Viking ship. Yet his arms and legs were thin and sensitive. LePeters enjoyed his powerful rib cage, yet it saddened him that there was little he could actually do with it. On occasion, he heaved it about ominously, but he knew in his heart there was no way, for example, to actually use it for beating up people. His hair was a puzzle; he wore what he had in tangled, deceptive swirls, but if you put a gun to his head he could not actually tell you whether he was bald. At times it seemed his hair had cleared out forever; then, when he had abandoned all hope of seeing it again, it would make spine-tingling recoveries, rolling back in, like Allied troops, in fierce new junglelike waves. Girls, looking at his divided face for the first time, would rub their eyes as though confronted with a slightly out-of-focus film.

He was not so much angered as curious about his scar and, as a child, had often pressed his mother for some answers. She fed him vague stories—a fall from a New England cliff; a powerful runaway zipper; a knife-wielding Negro in the night. He had not seen his widowed mother for many years. A scout for an employment agency, her job was to prowl the southern states, talking muddled Negro girls into coming up north as poorly paid domestics. Someday he would get

around to pinning her down; he would make her tell him
exactly how he had become a Boundary Face.

◉

Years back, he had been Kenneth Sussman, a young lieutenant in Army grain supply. One morning, prompted by no
one, and after polishing off a barley requisition, he had
turned himself into Ken LePeters, taking the name of a
magic boy who had appeared long ago to his old New Jersey
neighborhood, rallying a scraggly, thin-chested corner football team to thrilling, towering victories over richly equipped
monster Catholic squads—then vanished, as though in
smoke, at season's end. Immediately after tacking on the
new name, LePeters could have sworn there had been a
global Sussman breakthrough. Each time he picked up a
newspaper, it seemed a Sussman had rocketed to the top of
an international cartel, smashed a record at Grand Prix, become a leading fashion photographer, seized the reins of a
sensitive government bureau handling tricky inter-American
trade relations. Somehow it was difficult for LePeters to reverse his field; he kept the new name loosely sutured to him,
a poor toupee he would get around to adjusting one day.

  He was going to get around to a great many things. For
forty-five years, his father, William Sussman, had worked like
a dog in badger pelts, his goal a massive career's end bonus
that had been promised to him by company higher-ups. At
home, LePeters and his mother would sit around and smack
their lips over the future payoff, speculating on its size,
dreaming about the marvelous things they would do with it
once it tumbled in. One morning, before he had collected a
dime, the easygoing old furrier quietly succumbed to occupa-
tional fur fumes. At the time, LePeters had been doing

public relations for a small, kill-crazy homicide bureau in Montana. When he got the news he actually bought a ticket east, but somehow the thought of confronting the fur tycoons had frightened him and he never got on the train. His mother, Nan Sussman, bitterly took the first job in her life, as a Negro maid hustler. As LePeters curled his way across the nation's homicide bureaus, he rarely passed a night without envisioning his vengeance trip to the fur tycoons. He felt no urgent responsibility to his mom; he would take care of her when she was old. But she was no chicken now. How long could she continue to parade through Dixie, selling a bill of goods to confused black teen-agers?

The Midwest had been ideal for putting things off. Living in neat, measured-off, barracks-style homes, he might just as well have remained in the Army. His wife, Claire LePeters, bought blondewood furniture that smelled of the PX, dinette sets of a type favored by hard-drinking service families who were always being shipped to Wiesbaden. On weekends, along with other crime-busting families, they attended volleyques, acted in raucously thrown-together police versions of *Most Happy Fella*. LePeters let it be known that he missed deeper cultural stimulation, but secretly he wolfed down the combination volleyball games and charcoal cookouts, loved dancing on stage in detectivey musicals. Still, he knew he had been treading water, splashing around in the temporary. Age forty loomed up, just around the corner. He longed to pay a visit to Frickman Furs, in memory of his dead dad, even if it meant just standing across the street and glaring at it. For years he had been unable to find his wife's lips. He lay in ambush for them, leaped across to nail them as she slept, but generally had to settle for lipless sex. His pasted-on name began to itch at him, too. He felt somehow that it was pulling the boundaries of his face farther out of line.

◉

One day, Bruno Glober, his boss for all seventeen years, told him of a large, violent, but somehow conscience-stricken homicide bureau in the East that needed a public relations team to repair its grim and tawdry image. For trivial, microscopic shifts in policy, Glober had a way of summoning LePeters, his one-man staff, and addressing him with enormous ceremony, as though he were the entire population of Madrid. LePeters enjoyed the phony pomp and hoped one day to use it on a one-man team of his own. Because the news of the eastern shift was major, Glober dropped it casually, as the pair sat stall to stall in the detective john. Too embarrassed to be forthright, LePeters took his time in answering, shuffling his feet, whistling, scribbling a few clandestine penis-guns in a rosette about the dehumidifier. Finally, he lofted his reply over the partition.

"All right then, count me in," he said, as though he had come to the end of a massive conscience struggle. "I've got a few things I have to tidy up back there."

◉

Timid about plunging right into the center of eastern life, LePeters stuck in one toe by selecting a home in a cordoned-off suburb, two hours' drive from the city. A parched and barren place that seemed to have no connection with the East Coast, it might have been picked up during a storm and blown in whole from Wyoming. Bruno Glober had told him about the house, a modern job situated in a section once favored by retired police chiefs and called "Detectives' Hill." All the ex-dicks lolling about made it fiercely law-abiding, rape-free, and aside from an occasional indecent exposure, the most crime-starved little community in the hemisphere. Arriving east, LePeters took his family out to the house in a police squad car, driving tensely, with exquisite care, as though he had heads of state in the back. Earlier that day, Sergeant Cartney of the Motor Pool had told him yes, as a homicider he was entitled to drive a squad, but warned him about stepping out of line with it. "It will go much harder with you than with your average citizen," Cartney said. "We step in and really crush your nuts." The car was rigged up with twin police radios and there was no way to turn off the crime calls. LePeters enjoyed listening to Negro rhythm and blues music. He turned up the regular radio, trying to drown out the robbery alerts, and as he drove toward Detectives' Hill, he got a strange new kind of soul-crime sound. His wife was a hell-for-leather driver, born in a state that was anxious to get people out on the road as soon as possible; it issued special pre-teen licenses, catapulted its tots from the nursery to the wheel; LePeters was proud of her recklessly confident style and more than once had said. "She's the only broad I know who drives like a man." Impatient now, Claire Le-Peters asked him if he could go a little faster.

"I'm down on the floor already," he answered, but he kept the needle glued to twenty.

LePeters's daughter was along, a ten-year-old boy–girl with great fascinated eyes and a fierce passion for skating-rink hamburgers. The two loved each other to an almost painful degree and took outrageous care not to hurt one another's feelings. As they inched along, LePeters combed both sides of the road, searching for rinks.

"If it's hard for you, Daddy, just forget it," the child said.

"It's not hard," LePeters said, straining his eyes. "I love doing things for you."

"But if we find a hamburger place, think of the money it will take away from you."

"What if it takes every dime," said LePeters. "It kills me when you talk that way."

◉

The house itself was a furiously handsome puzzle of wood and glass owned by a trio of Croats who had been forced by some unmentionable tragedy to hack the price down to a ridiculous level. It was perched not so much on a normal hill but on more of a peak. Let a snowflake or two fall and you could forget about getting a car up to it. LePeters parked his squad below and then helped his family toward the house; radio calls for armed, white-sneakered Negroes in black leather jackets snaked out after them as they fought for the summit. Claire LePeters had gone through a stage in which she refused to move four steps without a taxi. Now she trudged up the sheer Everest-like driveway.

"What about packages?" she asked, out of breath, yet gamely clawing her way forward. "How would we get them up?"

"You put in some sort of a pulley arrangement," said LePeters, the last fellow in the world for installing such a system.

At the door, LePeters decided to flash his baby badge at the waiting Croats. "LePeters of homicide and his family," he said, giving them a quick look and elbowing his way inside. He tended to use the badgette only on underprivileged groups, foreigners in particular. At one short-handed bureau in the Midwest, he had actually gone out on the homicide investigation of a murdered fruit merchant. When he flashed it at the clerk in charge, the man said, "This is shit," and

LePeters had been forced to stand behind the overripe avo-
cado bin while his teammate, an authentic detective, looked
for bloodstains. Attractively futuristic, the house inside was
contradictory, filled with sad, cabbagey tenement smells.
While LePeters looked around, the husbandless Croat mom
and her two daughters hovered close by, weeping bitterly,
their lips fiercely stitched together by some dark Slavic curse.
LePeters was terribly anxious to know the secret of the preposterously underpriced house, yet he could not bring himself to say, "Out with it. What's the deal?" He was not good
at asking that type of question. For years, he had speculated
on the exact amount of his dad's salary, yet could never bring
himself to come right out and grill the mild-mannered furrier. Had he ever queried his wife on her hidden lips? He
wanted to say, "Do you really love me?" to certain people.
Out of the question. LePeters shook off the grief-stricken
Croats momentarily and went below, determined to root out
the reason for the minuscule price. Always, he had been gunless, without real power in a world of violent men. Asked his
profession at parties, he would say he was "sort of a detective." Yet sometimes, particularly when he was alone, he felt
like an authentic homicider, able to rip off tough questions,
dig for clues. He prowled the basement now, making intense, crime-fighting faces. Through a basement window, he
spotted the trickily concealed edge of an enormous golf
course that bordered the house on one side. Muscular drives
pumped past the ninth hole might easily slash six huge modernistic windows a day. A teen-age Croat who had stealthily
tailed him downstairs sucked in her breath when he made his
discovery. The jig was up. LePeters did some quick calcula-
tions. Even with a towering glass-replacement bill, the house
remained a steal. Patting the frightened Croat on the head,
he waltzed upstairs to say he would phone the real estate

agency and come up with a binder. Upon hearing the news, the woman and her two daughters broke into tantalizing gold-toothed Gypsy smiles.

His first day in the new bureau, LePeters met Chief Guster, head of Homicide, a kindly man who wore his sleeves rolled up to the elbow and had huge, furred, crime-busting fore-arms, much like those of LePeters's expired dad. Up to his ears in aggravated batteries, the gentle top-kick put his arm around the new man's shoulders, led him to the door, and dismissed him with a single word: "Compassion." The second syllable shot through a gap in the elderly man's teeth, encased in a small wet cloud, and reminded LePeters of a blind money-lender his father had had to deal with during the depression. The shylock, who conducted his business outside of luncheonettes, had only one condition for loans: that he be allowed to roll the money in a little ball and spit it contemptuously in the borrower's face. Tickled to death to get the money any way he could, William Sussman had stopped more than one wet blast with his head. He would thank the blindie, pocket the balls, and run home to dry them out on radiators. One day, after watching his dad take one in the eyes, LePeters asked him if he got to repay the loans by spitting them back. "That's all I'd need," the furrier had said, patiently raking his fingers through his son's hair. "I'd be dead in an hour."

Now, years later, when Chief Guster spit "compassion" at him, LePeters's first instinct was to check the carpeting for a damp fifty.

Next, LePeters took a homicidal psychiatry test, designed to put the finger on queers and flush them out of the department before they took root. The test was administered by a psychiatrist named Worthway, who had to be called "Doctor-Detective" since otherwise there would have been no fiscal procedure for siphoning funds over to his department. Held in low esteem around the bureau, the psycho-homicider had no actual office and did his testing in a corner of the detectives' bullpen beneath a giant "Cleanliness is what it's all about" poster. As LePeters plunged into the first question, Detective Flamoyan, department rakehell, howled out the first of a series of simulated police sirens, while Gibney of Petty Vice, feigning official duties, took his regular morning riffle through the sex-crime photo files. A pushover for common-law wife mutilations, Gibney could not resist holding one aloft now and then, and hollering, "Here's a lulu." Just outside the door of the bullpen, Lieutenant Riggles of Polygraph had strapped himself into the lie-box and could be heard asking himself general questions to test the equipment. *Are you a sweet guy? Would you describe yourself as being on the sneaky side? Have you ever stolen so much as a kiss?* A polygraph pioneer, Riggles claimed that in twenty years he had never been able to put one over on the machinery, to beat his box. LePeters was peculiar about noise. During the credits on Antonioni films, he had been known to climb over seats in order to shush down movie mumblers nine aisles away. Yet once his mind was actually hooked into something, the grip of his concentration was like iron. LePeters had good luck with the first half dozen questions, easily spotting the fruit snares and belting them out of the park. From that point on, he was able to ignore his surroundings. In the chair beside him, Doctor-Detective Worthway squeezed in a catnap. He had been halfway out the door when he had spotted LePeters, and was still fully dressed, a fedora hooded low on his face, only his ears preventing it from covering his entire head. LePeters, meeting him for the first time, had wondered if he wore it in this style because of complexes. As LePeters barreled ahead with the test, Flamoyan crept close to the dozing shrink, slipped two fingers into his ribs, and said, "This is a stickup," then finished him off with a lonely, wailing fake siren in his ear. "Schmuck," said the psychiatrist, rubbing his eyes.

"I suppose you're wondering how I got into homicide psychiatry," he said to LePeters, "the asshole of the profession."

"Now?" said LePeters. "During my test?"

"I'll take it into account," said Worthway.

Worthway said he had spent much of his life studying in Europe, receiving a wonderful formal education, sponging up the best Heidelberg had to throw at him. Nearing forty, he had returned in triumph to the States, crammed with the latest psychiatric know-how, ready to begin a howlingly successful practice. His first patient had been a distraught though heavy-chested young waitress and the kick-off session went smoothly. But midway through the second, he suddenly lost control of himself, threw off all professional moorings, and whisked the troubled wench off to Cuernavaca for a swinging month in the sun, instantly getting himself disbarred from normal practice for all time.

"What could I do?" he said, leaning back in his chair, eyes moist, still reveling in the month of Mexican madness. "I had the hots for the kid."

LePeters never passed up an opportunity to listen to psychiatrists. If one were pointed out at a party, he would sidle as close as possible to the man and strain his ear for a few droppings. A fragment here, a few dribbles there—they all added up, and it was his feeling that through a lifetime he might in this manner pick up a free though choppy analysis.

"I'm enjoying this conversation," he told the discredited Worthway, "but perhaps I'd better return to the test." LePeters found the final section much trickier.

What would you rather be, a ship-builder or a florist specializing in white gardenias?

You are Detective Jones, called in to search a homicide victim for pellets. Where do you look first, mouth or rectum?

The questions were not really that straightforward. Perhaps only a non-fag, sure of his masculinity, would be confident enough to dive in immediately for rectal bullets. After all, it was a dead ass they were talking about. What was the great harm. LePeters agonized over each question now, certain he would be drummed out of the new bureau as an incipient though flaming pansy. Finally, he handed the test over to Worthway, who scanned it quickly and said, "Borderline. I'll slip you through."

"I thought I did better than that," said LePeters.

"What do you think all these guns around here represent?" he asked LePeters in a lightning change of subject.

"Oh, I don't know," said LePeters. "Phalluses, I guess." Actually, he had dipped into a textbook or two and was taking a not-so-wild shot.

"Not bad," said Worthway, lifting one crafty finger in the Heidelberg style and making ready to leave. "But some of them are pussies, too."

"And don't you ever forget it," he said, cramming LePeters's test into his overcoat pocket and racing out of the bullpen.

◎

Next on LePeters's itinerary was the armory where he was issued a pearl-handled Smith and Wesson .38. On one wall of the entrance, arrayed under glass like trophy fish, was a massive collage of ingenious weapons that had been wrested from captured criminals after hell-for-leather gun battles. The police sergeant in charge was a stout, motherly looking man wearing an apron and giant metal earmuffs that covered the sides of his head like cymbals. Handing over the weapon, the sergeant said, "Heft your new baby around so's to get the feel of 'er."

LePeters found the gun surprisingly heavy and wondered how much damage it would do if he were to obey an impulse and fling it at the matronly sergeant's forehead. Suddenly nervous, he asked if he actually had to carry the weapon about and the sergeant said no, it was merely a question of having one officially assigned to him. It would be kept in a footlocker and only in the event of an enormous crime wave blanketing the city would a public relations detective be pressed into emergency action.

In his seventeen years as a quasi-dick, LePeters had been issued many guns but never expected to carry one on his person. Only at his last bureau had he been required to qualify in "mad dog" shooting, a style in which you whipped out your gun, fell to your knees, and without taking time to aim, got off volleys of crazed, yelping, animal-like shots at a human silhouette. LePeters dreaded the four-times-a-year tests; as each one loomed up, he had stifled terrifying, gun-metal-colored dreams in which he kept shooting off his own toes. He knew little of weapons or marksmanship and was always amazed that he was able to hit the targets at all. Yet before each session, a snarling, unknown section of himself would boil to the top, smoking his eyes, putting froth on his lips, enabling him to get off enraged bursts of fire with demoniacal accuracy. Though he racked up few "certain kills," he got more than his share of "maimers," a much-desired kind of shot that passed up the heart and lungs to clip off ears, elbows, and pelvic bones. Abrezio, the midwestern range man, would often mock up each target with the satirically drawn face of an actual detective who was still on the force. On one occasion, he tacked up a likeness of LePeters, who then had to blast off his own chin, to fill the stomach he loved with holes. The pistol tests were one reason he had been anxious to leave the last bureau; he prayed he would never have to mad-dog it again.

Now the sergeant stuffed six shells into the chamber and passed it along to LePeters. "See how she feels after a meal," said the sergeant. LePeters took the weapon with two fingers, the chamber fell open, and the shells dropped out, tinkling across the armory floor like a pocketful of change. Daintily adjusting his apron, the sergeant dropped to his knees and went looking for them.

"How come the muffs?" asked LePeters, joining him on the cold floor.

"In case one of m'babies goes off," said the sergeant. He then made a sour Scottish nanny face, as though he smelled cooking that had begun to burn. "And so I don't have to hear a brilliant move like the one you just pulled on me."

◉

Bruno Glober then showed LePeters to his office, a partitionless affair just outside Glober's own fully walled, sumptuously carpeted number.

"It's just till we get settled in," said Glober, a tall, blocked-off man without a single curve to his body. Scratching the back of his neck, he got up on the points of his toes and

seemed to peer out over an invisible fence, then dove back
into his office to "polish off a few items." LePeters knew exactly what those "items" were. Once inside, Glober would
slap on a variety of colognes, then strip down to get the feel
of the carpeting on his back and spend an hour on his leather-
bound collection of *Skirts Ahoy* magazine, every now and
then dictating a loud, false memo to throw possible outer-
office listeners off the scent. After seventeen years of being
strapped to his side, LePeters knew every one of Glober's
tricks; his ingenious cover-ups for unquestionable nose-
picking, his way of stuffing socks with holes in them deep
into his shoes so that observers couldn't really tell. The two
had teamed up in the Army, LePeters (then Ken Sussman)
reporting in to Lieutenant Colonel Glober as a mint-fresh
lieutenant in base grain supply. After a single glance at the
newcomer, Glober insultingly called Base Personnel and
said, "Why are you doing this to me?" But LePeters had
begun to doodle with a soybean requisition, tightening up its
syntax, peppering it with "aforementioneds" and "hither-
tos." Once Glober got a look at the spruced-up com-
muniqué, he became instantly and almost sickeningly de-
pendent on LePeters and had been ever since. It had been
Glober's idea that there was big postwar money to be made
in homicide public relations, and indeed, the tall tiptoer had
become mysteriously rich at it. Although he, too, had lived in
neatly parceled PX-style homes in the Midwest, Glober's
walls began to crowd up one day with daring pointillist art of
dizzying cost, his neat FHA-sponsored driveway to bulge
with late-model Maseratis. A mysterious, chauffeured Vien-
nese named Otto, wearing mammoth cufflinks, would roll in
regularly in a wash of expensive colognes to check on where
Glober intended to "water" that year. LePeters had no idea

how his boss had gone from an underpaid military man to a fellow who watered, yet somehow he was not the least bit envious. Even in the Army, Glober had been good to him, handing over extra amounts of money each week, above his Army pay, a different amount each time. He still shelled out the surprise money packages, and even though LePeters had always been the one man on Glober's team, the fractionally older man supplied plenty of action, dreaming up new titles for LePeters, giving him promotions that would leapfrog him over the heads of imaginary execs, one place closer to some mythical top slot. Mainly, Glober acted as a buffer zone between LePeters and the frightening, unknown world of higher-ups. For all of his weaknesses, many of them fetishistic, Glober was the advance scout in LePeters's life, going up ahead to draw off fire and beat down impending trouble.

Now, on his first day, LePeters neatened his desk and arranged his scissors assortment and glue pot, feeling quite satisfied, as though he were hungry and knew that a sumptuous meal was on the way. He was very proud of his skills and at times felt he might be better at arranging crime clips than any other homicider in the country. LePeters admired people who could do things better than anyone in the world. He still thought fondly of the Gregory twins, champion junior-high-school urinators, whose record for lofting their twin, golden rainbow-arced streams high against building walls would go unmatched for all time. A short blond man with a fixed smile came by and said he was Detective Hortham of Micro-Analysis, just down the hall. He kept one hand behind his back, and after he had used the other for shaking hands, he suddenly flung a pair of evidential panties in LePeters's face, saying, "Sniff these. They just come off a dead broadie."

LePeters handed them back, saying, "It's not my bag."

"Airline stewardess," said Hortham, stuffing the undies into his apron pocket. "Cute little biscuit with some ass on her."

Le Peters had a fatal weakness for stewardesses and wondered if Hortham would give him another try, yet he was too embarrassed to ask.

"Hey," said Hortham, in a sudden reverie, "you know the time when you've finished in the upstairs crapper and your old lady's calling you from downstairs and you stare out through the window wishing you could be back on the beach, laying in the sand with a wet bathing suit and guzzling beer and salt pork until your belly feels like it's ready to explode. You know the time?"

"I don't know it," said LePeters. "I've frankly never had that set of sensations."

"Or when you've just nicked yourself with a razor," Hortham went on, "and you wish you had a pet corn snake you could keep around your neck to suck up the blood so you wouldn't have to use the styptic pencil on your neck and have it break out for a goddamned week.

"Tell the truth," said Hortham, eyes shining with nostalgia. "How many times have you felt that way?"

"You want the truth," said LePeters. "The truth is, never. Not once in my life. I don't want to hurt your feelings or anything, but it's just not a typical situation for me."

Hortham stood alongside LePeters's desk for a long time as though debating whether to rearrange his smile; finally, he simply drew it wider, winked, and said, "You're a humdinger," then waltzed off to the lab.

◉

An old-timer now took a seat beside LePeters and said he was
Detective Gus Flamoyan, bureau jokester and general wise-
guy. "However," he said, "if you ever kid me back or insult
me in any way, I'll tail you all over the United Snakes and
shoot you like a dog."

He was a huge, once powerful man whose massive chest
seemed to have slipped and become a giant stomach. He said
that in the old days he had been fabled as a great elevator
man and that no criminal in the world could stand up against
him once the doors of one slid closed. "They'd put him and
me inside on the top floor and by the time we got down to
the lobby and he'd been introduced to my big thirteens I'd
have your Mr. Won't-Say-A-Word ready to rat on the Holy
Mother." Flamoyan said that quite frankly he had not been
beyond chaining an occasional man to a radiator to loosen his
tongue.

"Oh, why dainty it up," he told LePeters. "I give more
than one head a little toilet soak, too, if I thought it would
speed the cause of justice a little."

But things had changed, said the cone-bellied dick. "One
day I lost my Kay Kyser oomph and now if I see a Puerto
Rican minority kid swipe a meat pie I have no urge to beat
him about the head. I've gone over to kidding and joking
around. For example, I give everyone in the department a
nickname. I called Gibney 'Ears' and if you take a look at the
set on him you'll see what I'm driving at. Vlatipopolis I just
come right out and nail him with 'Greek' and I stuck 'Bosco'
on Medici, although frankly your typical nigger dick don't
take kindly to nicknames. Anyway, it's all good-natured hors-
ing around and the whole trick in interpreting it is to read
between my lines. I'm here now to say I haven't come up
with one for you yet."

LePeters was fascinated by Flamoyan's oddly shaped

stomach and wondered if the old-timer had swallowed a small Cong artillery piece.

"How about 'Pete,' " said LePeters. "That's what I usually go by."

"That ain't it at all," said Flamoyan. LePeters had the feeling his face would have been exactly the same if you held it upside down. "It don't have the class I'm looking for. When I nail you, you'll know it soon enough. I was thinking of 'Double-Header' for a while, but that ain't the ticket either. There's something about you, but the idea hasn't quite walloped me yet."

"I don't see the humor in taking a guy's physical characteristics," said LePeters, who was easily angered when someone commented on his facial boundaries.

"Guess what," said Flamoyan, shifting his stomach as though it were a heavy infant. He seemed not to have heard LePeters at all. "All the time I been sitting here getting acquainted—two guys taking a little afternoon tea—I've had my heater out, right under my coat where you can't see it. I developed that technique from years of habit and being slipped up on a few times. So I'm just sitting here diddling it under my coat, pretending to pay attention to your discourse, and guess where I had it pointed all along?"

"Where's that?" asked LePeters.

"Right at your family jewels."

After Flamoyan left, LePeters wondered what that "certain thing" about himself was. And would the sharp-bellied dick be able to pin it down. LePeters, too, was dying to know. But what kind of way was that to welcome a new man into the bureau—training a concealed pistol on his pecker? Some-

what unnerved, LePeters almost failed to notice the thin
particle of a man who sat at a desk beside him, his flake of a
body almost totally lost in the cushions of a specially made
chair. This was the intricately contraptioned Teener, who was
to serve as LePeters's assistant, a once great detective whose
body had literally been trimmed down by gunfire in a major
shoot-out. Gadgets whirring and ticking, Teener introduced
himself and then told LePeters of the celebrated battle in
which his body had been drastically reshaped. Cut to ribbons himself, he had killed eight of a nine-man gang and
was about to polish off the ninth when he had blacked out,
later to be discovered half-conscious, still snarling, trying to
load his gun with one nostril, the only part of his body that
had escaped injury. In the hospital he had been completely
fitted out with dozens of science's latest contraptions, some
guaranteed to outperform your workaday internal organ. "I
got one inside me that only a dog ever wore," said Teener,
but he wouldn't give LePeters a look at it. In the hospital, at
some point during his mechanical fittings, Teener said the
snarl had finally leaked out of him.

"I became nice, easygoing, a liberal like yourself."

"How do you know that about me," said LePeters, a little
insulted. "Just by looking? Sometimes I am, sometimes I'm
not. On certain issues you'll find me remarkably conserva-
tive."

As though to damp down the possibility of an argument,
and to demonstrate his new nastiness-free style, Teener slid
close to LePeters and asked him how he would like to have
two dozen white-on-white shirts for just nickels and dimes.
They belonged to his brother, Philly Teener, a comedian
who had been working nightclub outer lounges for twenty
years and who had ordered them when he mistakenly
thought he was getting a shot at a main room.

"I don't know," said LePeters. "I've got a big chest, out-sized. What about the fit?" What he really wanted to say was, Forget the haberdashery; show me one of your tickers. Teener placed a stunningly clean hand on LePeters's shoulder, then got to his feet, and in a surprisingly resonant, perhaps gadgeted voice, thundered out, "I fear I must go to the dentist." This was for Glober's sake; LePeters heard a strangled but assenting "Um-hum" slip through Glober's door and wondered what outrageous fetishistic activity the team leader was up to on the carpeting now.

An hour after Teener left, Mailroom Sal came by with a telegram. A sinister-looking fellow with a troubled, hunted face, he resembled the man on every Wanted poster; people were always making citizens' arrests of him, beating him to a pulp, then hauling him down to the station in triumph only to discover he worked there and had the most spotless record on the East Coast. The many arrests and false accusations had made him edgy, and after handing LePeters the telegram, he slunk off, collar pulled up, as though he were about to be nailed unjustly again. Thinking the telegram might be from his touring mom, LePeters slashed it open quickly. The message said:

Couldn't pull it off. Sick with embarrassment. Brother wouldn't part with nary a one. Still thinks he'll crack the big time. Don't know how I got involved. Just wanted to do something nice, I guess. Will you ever forgive me. Answer collect wire.

Cordially,
Det. Teener

LePeters immediately dashed off a reply, paying for it him-self, and telling Teener for Christ's sake of course he could come back and not to take it so seriously. He had all the shirts he needed and it was ridiculous to make such a big deal about it. He sent it to the draperies department of a suburban branch of Abraham and Straus where Teener was hiding out; in three quarters of an hour, the little sliver of a detective was back at his desk, shamefaced but grateful.

"Look," he said, "I know you're going to think I'm pulling another stunt, but how about watches? Truthfully, how are you fixed for them? I *know* I can deliver on them, three skin-diver ones. They look attractive as hell and can be worn for dress or everyday. Will you give me a chance to redeem myself?"

"Look," said LePeters, who had been hit in a vulnerable spot again—undersea equipment of any kind—"if you want to get me a discounted watch, fine. If you don't, don't. The important thing is that you don't have to do anything for me. I like you for yourself, as a person. You don't have to shower me with gifts."

But Teener had not heard him at all. His eyes jiggled uncertainly in his immaculately scrubbed head. "I'm getting you the watches," he said. "I just want to prove that I can come through on just one thing." Teener evidently could not see anyone loving him for himself. He no longer considered himself a person. As far as he was concerned, he was just a flesh-covered little network of scientific wonders. How could he know that was exactly the kind of thing that fascinated LePeters.

LePeters wondered why the little fellow kept himself so ridiculously dirt-free. Was it to wash away all traces of his angered, snarling past or was it simply a precaution against rusting up. When he knew him better, he would ask him, too, how he had fared on the fag test. Perhaps they had given him an honorary high grade in deference to his heroic past. He wondered about Mrs. Teener, too, imagining her as a great-spigoted, voluptuous type, calmly accepting her husband's whittled-down predicament, each night nestling the little dick close to her in order to get the spin-off benefit of his finely tooled ticks and throbs. At 16:00, just before the end of LePeters's shift, Sissy Glober breezed in to make a quick pass at helping out around the office and then to whisk her dad home for dinner. A dead ringer for her towering, blocked-off parent, she was nevertheless a subtly rearranged version, with long, restless legs, a great spill of barn-yellow hair, and green devil's eyes, slightly drugged, a little deranged. As her father became mysteriously homicide-rich, the teen-age Sissy had taken to mingling with the famous, enticing them to frenzied peaks of tumescence and then slipping off to proudly notify her dad that she had failed to come across for a single one of the celebs. With bra straps flying, she had made a virginal escape from the pad of a famed World War II flying ace, left a world-renowned physicist and Enrico Fermi protégé with his pecker hanging. Nobel Prize winners had vainly chased her across Biarritz yacht decks, and she had slipped erotically through the fingers of key State Department undersecretaries with family lineage dating back to early settlers in Vermont. Posing as a fan, she had sexually stimulated a famed octogenarian percussionist, let him soak up a standing ovation for the first real Mahler breakthrough of the fifties, then cannonballed out of his hotel suite when the celebrated senior citizen feebly stripped down to claim his real prize. One day her dad, sensing hang-ups, had taken the name of a Portuguese family therapist out of the restaurant ads of a small sexology bimonthly. A fly-by-night shrink with faked degrees, the dark-complexioned shyster had nevertheless been amazingly effective in hacking away at the parched and flinty family structure of the New England-born Globers; within a month, he had them sexually at ease, amiably kicking fellatio around the breakfast table, farting *en famille*, trading pedophilia anecdotes about the office. Overnight, Sissy Glober had become an authentic chandelier-swinger, racing off each weekend with lowly, callow, non-celeb vibraharp players.

Her father, Bruno Glober, was delighted, though at first he had been a little shaky about it.

Tiny-skirted now, thinly bloused, Sissy Glober vainly tried her father's door, then wheeled toward LePeters and said, "What's he doing in there, whacking off again I'll bet."

"Your dad's a busy guy," said LePeters, tidying his desk, end-of-day style.

"What do you think of these?" she asked, tossing a sheaf of contact prints in LePeters's lap. "I brought them in for Dad's perusal. Don't look at C-8, which I think, frankly, is too risqué."

LePeters scanned the shots, bathtub nudes of Sissy Glober doing coy winks, over-the-shoulder hair tosses, contrived vamping poses of the thirties, possibly stolen from her dad's favorite monthly, *Skirts Ahoy*. C-8 was a wondrous accident, taken by a photog who had to be stretched out on the bathroom tile to get it, the kind of "mistake" LePeters had been searching for since puberty, vainly going through tons of pix to find one. Forcing himself to breathe evenly, LePeters took a professional look at them, as though they were just another batch of homicide clips, returning again and again to C-8. He was amazed that the greatest thing to happen to him since childbirth should show up so casually, with no trumpeting advance ceremonies, simply tossed on his desk like the morning mail.

With elaborate, Japanese Noh theater gestures, Sissy Glober flipped a dial-a-pill birth control tablet into her mouth and said, "The photog frankly wanted to groove me, but I lied, telling him 'bloody battlefield' and on we went with the session, although from that time on I allowed him hornier shooting privileges."

"What was the guy's name?" LePeters asked, eyes still glued to C-8, casual, yet dying to know. At that moment, he heard some machinery begin to hum, as though a generator had been switched on, and saw Teener, fully overcoated, sheepishly grinding his way to the door. Sissy Glober stood up on her toes, wet-mouthed, delighted, and waved him off. Could it have been Teener who had taken the naked lip-smackers, Teener craftily sprawled out on the tiles, who had conned her into posing for C-8? And here LePeters had foolishly kissed him off as a harmless though finely tooled little bundle of gadgetry. Perhaps he had some curious, electronic, world's end appeal to girls who had tried everything else. The prospect made LePeters sad and nervous in equal doses.

"Perhaps you'd like to study them at your leisure," she said, reviewing the pictures with him, her bosom's edge touching his head.

"Maybe I would," he said. With that, he got to his feet, stuffed them into his pocket, and raced off to Detectives' Hill, giving her no chance whatever to change her mind and snatch back his prize.

◉

LePeters's first month east, in the new bureau, was pleasant, tranquil, no doubt about it, something of a winner. He wondered why he had spent seventeen years being apprehensive about it. He could see twelve, but seventeen had been foolish. Perhaps he would round the bend of his life and slide past age forty in the same smooth manner. Maybe he would keep sailing along, calmly, relatively trouble-free and—hope of all hopes—one day breeze through death's door without batting an eyelash.

Being east was like being west, like being anywhere. The twain did meet after all. But during that first month, sometimes a doubt slipped through. His body was east, so was his family and his home, but in spite of this tangible evidence, perhaps he wasn't east after all.

In this bureau, possibly because of its eastern cosmopolitan air, the dicks came close to accepting LePeters, if not as a full-fledged member of the homicide family, at least as some kind of third cousin by marriage. Which is more than he could say for any of the other bureaus. Through the years he had learned to play it close to the vest, not to fall all over men in the death game. In earlier, more self-conscious years, he had tried smothering dicks with love and more than once been kicked in the head. He was cooler now and let the dicks make the first move. Some did, some didn't. His tangential slot, in the detective bureau yet not really in it at all, made him a reasonably good bet as an impartial voice, a confidant, particularly for spillover, nonhomicidal issues. One day, Medici, the heavily gunned Negro dick, and a hypochondriacal Auto Thefter named Kuens, fell into a lunch-hour dispute and dragged it before LePeters who was eating a tuna on rye at his desk. "He says he don't want to contract syphilis," said Medici, "and I been telling him 'What you worried about, man, they got the goddamned thing cured now.'"

"I don't care," said the pill-gobbling Kuens, "I don't want it anyway. Don't want anything to do with it."

"You crazy, man," said Medici, disgustedly. "You get a dose, they got you cured in three days flat."

"Not certain strains," said Kuens.

"Name your strain, babe," said Medici. "Go 'head. Name me one strain they ain't got under control."

"I can't right off the top of the head," said Kuens. "But there are plenty, take my word for it."

"You see what I'm up against," Medici said, throwing up his hands. "You see the shit I got to take. Go ahead," he said to LePeters. "You the intellectual. Arbitrate that."

Stalling for time to reflect, LePeters dabbed some tuna from his lips, then said, "I'm with the side that says you can do without it." In a Seattle bureau, he had seen a similar argument end with one dick blowing off the other's kneecap. Respectful of Medici's artillery, he quickly added, "I also take the position that they've got a pretty good headlock on the disease."

"That's what I said," said Medici. "What did I just say? That they whomped it out of business. That's exactly what I been saying to the man."

"You won't catch me getting a dose," said Kuens, but possibly in deference to Medici's celebrated itchy finger, he used a low voice.

Thickly spectacled, breathing carefully as if to slow down the intake of possible cold germs, Kuens stayed behind and told LePeters he was convinced his hypochondria had something to do with his stern, all-powerful dad. All through Kuens's childhood, the father had held fierce competitions with his son, giving him no quarter, arm-wrestling the thin-wristed youngster to the ground, breezing fastballs past him, slashing him to ribbons at the Ping-Pong table, disgracing

him in the quarter mile. He made it a point to read with
more expression, to take longer steps during casual nighttime
strolls, to beat the boy at everything in life except inadequacy. Just before young Kuens's wedding, the father had
lured the bride-to-be away for a weekend in the Poconos.
"Why are you doing this to me?" the weeping Kuens more
than once had asked his all-powerful dad. "Because someday
you're going to whip me at all these things," said the vision-
ary older man. "And when you do, by God, you're going to
know that you did it entirely on your own." Being filled in on
his dad's long-range child-rearing scheme always cheered
young Kuens. But unfortunately, the day of reversal never
came. When Kuens turned forty, his spry and wiry dad was
still slashing him to ribbons on the tennis court, leaving him
in the dust in the 440 low hurdles, whisking new girls away
from him with a fascinating new septuagenarian charm.

Kuens got off a fusillade of nervous sneezes. "To this day,"
he told LePeters, "the old coot can still beat the shit out of
me at anything. I guess that's why I take pills and am so
afraid all the time," he said, breaking into an unnatural
sweat.

"I sympathize with you, believe me," said LePeters, "but
it's not something I can really understand since, frankly, I
had a loving dad." For the first time in weeks LePeters remembered his beloved father and the visit he had to make to
Frickman Furs. Tears collected in his eyes as he thought of
how hard the gentle old furrier had worked, how he had put
his blood into every Frickman pelt only to be snatched from
on high before he got to sample his promised—though finally
mythical—payoff. LePeters had to look up a certain Uncle
Fabe, too, who he understood from his mother had eaten
bales of coleslaw after his father's modest funeral. What
kind of behavior was that, LePeters wanted to know, even if

it was a long-established Hasidic custom. He could have understood coffee, a donut at the most, but to stuff yourself to the gills in honor of a brother's death was the height of insensitivity. Uncle or no uncle, if he had been at the restaurant, LePeters thought, and not bogged down in Far West homicide, he would have rammed the coleslaw bowl down Fabe's throat, the bastard.

◉

Other dicks took sniffs at LePeters and ended up sidling fairly close. One was Gibney of Petty Vice, a lisping, high-hipped Irishman, tallest in the department, whose waist leveled off at the height of most men's eyebrows. Using his height to full advantage, Gibney had ankle-grabbed second-story voyeurs by the dozen, leaned through transoms to break up many a fag-blackmailing. One day, flushed with success after a series of classic Aggravated Incest pinches, Gibney relaxed a little and told LePeters he came from a family of dicks, but that even though they all still lived together in the same house, somehow it was not as safe and crammed with law enforcement as you would think. Word had gotten around that the house was a pushover, and as a result, Gibney's mom and sister had both been mugged and raped, beaten and buggered with a higher frequency than any other women in the neighborhood. "They've been screaming to high heaven to us guys to do something about it,"said Gibney, "but what happens is that when I hear Mom scream I assume Pop is taking care of it or one of the guys. Actually they're sacked out in the attic or guzzling beer nuts somewhere, assuming that I'm taking care of it. And all the while some spade is jamming a broomstick up poor Mom's cooze." Gibney chuckled softly and shrugged his shoulders. LePeters felt sorry for the ironically defenseless Gibney girls, sitting ducks in a sea of crime-fighters, and told Gibney to get on the ball, to make sure someone was always on the alert. "I don't care how tough a neighborhood it is," he said. "Work shifts if you have to, so that someone's always responsible. It's a rotten shame to let your womenfolk go unprotected that way."

Gibney seemed angered for a moment, instinctively dropping a hand to his gun, but then realized that the new clippings man was on his side. "You're right," he said finally. "We sure as hell got to do something and do it fast. I'm getting sick and tired of seeing Mom and Sis get the business like that.

"They're squawking about it plenty," he said, almost two detectives, as he rose to his full, giraffelike height, "and they got every right to."

One of LePeters's favorite treats in the new bureau was the taking of after-hours sauna baths in the handsomely equipped detective gym. Tough as lead pipes around the bureau, the dicks were men whose very breath was sour with violence; yet in the baths, gunless, stripped down, some of them many-bellied, they seemed harmless and a little silly. They might have been clubhouse politicians or even a group of haberdashery salesmen. Only Medici held out against the no-gun rule. In twenty years as a crime-fighter, not once had he removed his pistols, having devised a method of washing beneath the weapons while taking showers. Once he had to be forcibly restrained from crashing the sauna, admittedly nude but with holsters bulging. He blackballed the baths for a while, but was dying to try them and capitulated one day, depositing his guns on a hook just outside the sauna door, within easy access in case of a sudden crime wave. As he resignedly entered the sauna for the first time, Medici walked with a peculiar weighted-down gait and LePeters wondered whether the sleekly muscled Negro hadn't concealed a tiny weapon in some bodily orifice.

In the democratically nude saunas, the perspiring dicks were somehow neutralized, violence-free, and as a result, LePeters enjoyed their company more than ever, felt much closer to them. Hortham plunged in each day at 17:30 on the dot. The glistening Micro-Analysis man would parade before LePeters, saying, "I'm one eighty-seven now. How do you like me at it?"

"Not bad," said LePeters.

"At one sixty-six most of my friends think I'm too gaunt. But you should have seen me at one seventy-three."

Hortham regaled LePeters with stories of great sweats he had had during the past, his best being an absolute classic post-depression years' one he had worked up one afternoon in a bath that had been set up for jobless and distraught Polish welders.

"What are some of yours?" he asked LePeters.

"I've had a couple," said LePeters, "but I tend not to keep them on file."

Hortham seemed annoyed and stuck a finger-gun into LePeters's armpit. "You been on my back for a long time," he said. "I'm telling you now, either climb off or suffer the consequences."

LePeters thought Hortham was probably kidding, but in the wash of steam he could not tell whether the lab man had his fixed smile on or not.

LePeters also got to know a broken-nosed General Assignments man named Casters, who was mildly concerned about his wife's possible adultery. "Many times I wake up," he said, "and peer across the room and can swear I see her in bed with another man. It's too dark to really tell. I think it may be my own kid brother, because of his hair style, which I can make out in silhouette. I used to arrange it for him in that very style when we were boys and close as kittens. Anyway, so far I've said nothing to Bertha."

"How come?" LePeters asked.

"I'm building up a good case. Then I'll hit them both with it."

"I think you ought to say something right away," LePeters advised. "As fast as possible. Otherwise you'll find the situation running away from you."

On occasion, particularly during citywide robbery outbreaks, LePeters would find he had the baths all to himself. At these times he liked to spit at the sauna equipment and listen for the resulting hot sizzle, always pleasing. On one such day, after checking to make sure he was alone, he hoisted one across the baths and out rolled Teener, who had been taking a heavily sheeted doze beneath a bench.

"Caught you," he said, with a rare, off-center smile, "but don't worry, I won't say a word."

"What was my great crime," said LePeters. "You'd think I was farting or something."

"Even if you were, I'd still keep mum."

For a moment, LePeters thought of asking Teener if he had taken the bathtub nudes of Sissy Glober; if so, how had he managed to grab C-8! But suddenly he realized it was no time to be casual, that the little dick was probably taking a tremendous risk in hanging around sauna baths. God alone knew what would happen if the dampness got into some of his precisely made little contraptions. Where would you take such gadgets for repairs—and would Teener have to go along with them or be able to ship them off by mail? Beneath his sheets, Teener's body seemed angular, totally lacking in smooth contours.

"What in the hell are you doing in here, you fool," LePeters suddenly shouted.

"Probably taking my life in my hands," said Teener, with a pitiful quaver in his voice. "But what the hell, I've got to do a few things in life. Otherwise, what's the point of it all? I can't just throw in the goddamned towel."

◉

Although LePeters had made a few casual friends in the new department, he never kidded himself for a second. This was no social club. Chuckling, affable around the bullpen, such men as Gibney, Medici, even the frightened, pill-popping Kuens were hell on wheels once you got them involved in a crime. Still basically terrifying men in the world's most violent game, the idea of kindness, even fleeting samples of it, was alien to their nature. He kept remembering the episode of the bone-banging Greeks pinwheeling past his clipping desk. Going down in the elevator one night, LePeters met Flamoyan, his arm around a buddy. "New guy," said Flamoyan, "just breezed in from the L.A. bureau." LePeters shook hands with the lethargic newcomer and saw instantly it was a dead man. With all his experience in homicide, he had run into remarkably few stiffs. This one seemed in good condition, all things considered, not a bad-looking guy. Flamoyan said he had checked him out of the morgue as a gag for the annual Homicide and Aggravated Battery party.

"Lot of red tape involved?" LePeters asked.

"Naw," said Flamoyan, giving the stiff a friendly chuck on

the chin. "Just tell them it's for a dick party and they'll give you all you want. Listen, if you go over there, take a look at a little schoolmarm just come in with a shiv up her pretty little keister. I tried to nail her but they handed me a story m'lady's still a little fresh."

The elevator reached the lobby floor. Flamoyan hoisted the victim over one shoulder and said, "Instead they give me my friend here, Russ Colombo."

◉

The dicks in this bureau went along with a custom LePeters had never come across before—posting the number of men they had killed on a little corkboard inside their personal footlockers. There were plenty of shockers in the totals: Gibney had four, but the mild-mannered Kuens had racked up a surprising nine. Medici, perhaps expectedly, rang in with an even dozen. One week after LePeters joined the bureau, the heavily gunned Negro went into his "teens," slaughtering an unarmed Mexican hophead in the back row of a movie theater as he slept through a newsreel about Ghanaian border feuds. To celebrate, Medici blew the entire bureau to delicious spareribs and thick chocolate shakes.

Hortham, too, kept one oar dipped in the violent tide. Balanced and rational around the lab, some kind of man of science, Hortham was also on a one-man campaign to win public approval for the Spanish garrote. Each night, in front of the Micro-Analysis Coke machine, he gave silk handkerchief demonstrations to show it was neater than the noose and got LePeters to edit a series of pro-garrote broadsides to be distributed at tense moments during summertime race riots. After setting up the first few and slipping a "Give the

Garrote a Chance" editorial into *Bullet-In*, the homicide monthly, LePeters finally stood his ground and absolutely refused further involvement.

In its own silken, well-mannered East Coast way, it was probably the most violent place LePeters had ever worked. There was not a single totally Christ-like figure in the entire department. Even the balanced, constitutional Riggles of Polygraph had been known to lose his temper and begin karate-chopping a strapped-in suspect he believed to be pouring baloney into his beloved lie-detector. Immediately remorseful, realizing he had overstepped his bounds, Riggles would do his best to revive the unconscious wrongdoer and get him back on his feet. "But it just kills you," he told LePeters, "when they sit there, comfortable as warm bread, insisting they're telling it to you straight and you know damned well they're stinking up your good machine with a pack of lies. If they didn't pull that on you, you wouldn't have to lay a hand on them."

Violence was in the air, and even though LePeters was cordoned off both geographically and by the nature of his work, some of it drifted down the hall to him. One afternoon, a report came through of a hood who had remained beyond the law's grasp even though he had pulled off ten straight robberies of Chinese take-out restaurants. LePeters was horrified to see Teener himself, pared down to the merest suggestion of a man, start to flare his one nonplasticized nostril with a trace of his old pre-gadgeted ferocity. If the little chip of a detective hadn't learned humility, who on earth could be trusted. . . .

During one coffeebreak, LePeters went around the bullpen distributing the new issue of *Bullet-In*. Since taking over the sheet, he had instituted a Homicider's Crossword Puzzle and a new first-person feature entitled "My Favorite Shot" to be freelanced by a different heroic dick each issue. Gibney and Flamoyan winked at one another, and as a joke, suddenly shouldered LePeters away from his magazine cart and into a small interrogation room, then quickly locked the door, leaving him alone with a suspect. LePeters had never seen the man before, had no idea what he was accused of. He tried to get out, but then took a deep breath, switched personalities, and startled himself by how quickly he got into the swing of things. "Take your hat off," he told the suspect, a Negro with a flattened-out landing strip of a head. Uttering no word of protest, the Negro did what he was told. "All right, let's begin again," LePeters said, shouldering his way around the room, thumbs hooked into his belt. "I got an eyeball witness who'll swear he saw you there the day it happened. You jerk me off, you cop-fighting jive-ass, I'll frame your butt so good you'll do forty years in solitary. Now give it to me straight." To his amazement, the hardened suspect fell to his knees and started to cry, saying, "I didn't mean no harm. I whomped him around a little but I never thought he bust his head against no stove." LePeters felt giddy, as though he had flung a basketball the full length of the court—blindfolded —and seen it go right through the hoop. But at the same time he was horrified, his shoulders crushed with sorrow. "Shhhh," he whispered, kneeling beside the broken Negro. "I'm not a real dick. Forget what you just said and take my word for it, they don't have a thing on you." The Negro said that he had an apartment and that his rent was up to date. "I paid off a radio," he intoned, "I paid off a toaster, I got four more installments to go and I own my venetian blinds free and clear. What they want from me . . . I paid the doctor . . ."

Heartbroken, LePeters tried vainly to stop the man.

"I paid for the curtains," he wailed, doing a funeral dirge

now, "I give the pork man fifty dollars on account . . ."

Finally, LePeters clamped one hand over the Negro's mouth, cutting him off in mid-list. Then he shook hands with him, gave him a little hug, and rapped on the door, asking to come out. Flamoyan sprung the lock and LePeters emerged, toughly hitching up his pants.

"I think he's clean. I couldn't get a thing on him."

Doctor-Detective Worthway, with a great deal of time on his hands, had been watching the proceedings.

"You know what I said, about how there are phalluses and pussies around here, in roughly equal numbers?"

"I remember," said LePeters.

"You were just a pussy," said Worthway.

"That's from out here," said LePeters. "If you knew the entire story, you might change your tune."

The first month on Detectives' Hill went off without a hitch, too. There was not a trace of the East about it—but never in LePeters's life had he felt so protected. Great armadas of squad cars swept across the thin country roads. LePeters's family was almost obscenely safe. When he sent his daughter out to play with the other detective children, he was able to put her completely out of his mind, for a weekend if necessary. The police were everywhere. Never in history had a town been so thickly populated with dicks and ex-dicks. Let a man raise his voice to ask his wife for the catsup and bingo— a squad car was at the door, ready to begin an investigation. LePeters felt awful that he had no valuables to be safeguarded and that, in one sense, a great deal of the protection was going to waste. "Shit," went the motto of the town, "and you got a cop."

LePeters fully expected his windows to be smashed by long fairway drives on a daily basis and had cheerfully allotted money for the repairs. But a local ordinance gave him a great break, declaring that henceforth the beautiful course was out of bounds to golfers and was to be used instead as a bird sanctuary. Why, then, had the tortured Croats handed over the house on a platter? Surely they had known about the coming law. LePeters was edgy and fully expected the house to be revealed as having a thin, gelatinlike foundation and to collapse entirely one day, sucked into the ground without a trace. Still, he made midnight checks by flashlight, found it to be solid, packed with Slavic toughness. Financially naïve, he could not imagine his simply having gotten a good deal, the first in his life, to make up for all the times he had been bilked.

Deep in the back of his head, LePeters had counted on a bedroom breakthrough with his wife, Claire, on coming east. But the density of law-enforcing dicks somehow kept him in low sexual gear and he held back on his new ideas, a few involving Hindu unguents. He had a fantasy in which he tried something fancy and was immediately broken in on by bugging dicks who netted him and his wife and carried the carnally frozen duo in that style to headquarters to have the book thrown at them. For the time being, LePeters declared a sexual truce. Claire LePeters went along without comment, making her lean whiplike Minnesota body available to him for one or two positions at the most, but still electing to keep her lips private. LePeters stood pat; he had not yet gotten settled in the East, and this was no time to stir up the coals.

Never, on the other hand, had he been closer to his daughter, Jamie LePeters, a wavering, middle-of-the-roader when it came to gender. Since coming east, she had taken on a new, giggling sweetness around the mouth that LePeters found irresistible. Possibly stimulated by the move, and with time to kill before school began, she had gotten two new hobbies off the ground, coin and fish collecting. The coin array was pitifully slender, a handful of change, some of it from supermarkets. But she would show a penny that seemed run-of-the-mill to the coin-ignorant LePeters and say, "See this one. It's worth at least four thousand dollars, maybe more."

"Then how come they just gave it to you at the shoe store," LePeters answered, trying to prepare her for life's hardships.

"Because they don't know," she would say, and then tuck it gently into her little coinbox so as not to mar its enormous value. Her collection added up to around thirty-seven cents by LePeters's count and sometimes brought him near tears. He vowed to get her some from a faraway country like Uruguay, so at least it would have a little real substance. But according to his daughter, the collection was worth a king's ransom, at least fifty grand, and he let off trying to disabuse her of the notion. Some chance she's got, he thought, on life's highway.

To make her fish comfortable, she crammed the tank with scenic wonders, hobby equipment, assorted fish conveniences such as gymnasiums, until there was no room for the fish to swim. Unsure of their happiness, she would sit for hours, chin in hand, watching them and saying, "How do I know they really like it in there."

"That's with any pet," LePeters would say, comforting her with a kiss on the neck and wanting to marry her on the spot.

"One of them's a shark," she said to him one day, pointing to something that looked like a piece of black thread.

"Really," he said. "I didn't know they ran that small."

"They do," she assured him. "In a week, we'll need a whole room for him."

Twice a week, LePeters's sexually wavering daughter took guitar lessons from a local instructor named Ferrezano, who never let her near the instrument itself, claiming it was more important to get underway with a strong foundation. No dick himself, but with a great network of relatives who were, Ferrezano had once been in nightclub combos and spent half the sessions with his arm around the youngster, showing her framed pictures of himself, shaking hands with famous restaurateurs and bowling-alley execs, each of them inscribed "To Sal—You're the Greatest," then signed with names like "Chick" and "Matty." The remaining sessions, Ferrezano sat opposite the child and strummed tunes he had helped popularize during his heyday in the thirties, each of which, he felt, would have gone all the way had they gotten one lousy break. LePeters would ask his child if she were learning anything, to which she would say, "I'm getting the feel of it." One day, LePeters called the nostalgic Italian and said that at eight dollars a throw he felt his daughter ought to get more than strolls down memory lane, at least a chord or two. Ferrezano agreed and shortly thereafter, LePeters caught the youngster bent over the guitar, producing sounds by snatching at the strings with her teeth. The Italian told LePeters it was a new style of playing that was going to stand the entertainment world on its ear, an admitted orthodontia hazard, but in his view, well worth the risk.

"I'd rather she had a standard course," LePeters said.

"I'm only here to please," said Ferrezano. "We'll play it any way you want, fella."

Evenings, LePeters played Monopoly with his daughter, each trying desperately to lose so as not to hurt the other's feelings. If the youngster landed on Park Place, she'd say, "No, I don't want to buy it."

"How come?" LePeters would ask.

"Because you might land on it and have to pay me rent and I couldn't stand that."

"But you have to play tough. It's like life."

"I don't care. I'll only play if I don't have to take any money from you."

And so they silently changed the rules; instead of trying to crush the other player with property acquisitions, they strove instead to denude themselves of all money and possessions, to render themselves helpless and property-free as soon as possible in order to avoid giving pain to the other player.

LePeters made few friends in the immediate neighborhood, preferring to hang back for a while and get the feel of it. Although seeded thickly with law enforcers, there were pockets of non-dicks, too, particularly on his street, who had moved in because of the airtight safety of the area. Some of the non-dicks were plenty rough in their own right, not so easily written off. Down the street lived a pugnacious FBI man, a ten-year veteran of violent training on the federal level which should have been much tougher than the local brand. Yet all through LePeters's first month on the Hill, the fed had been working his way down the block, picking fights at every house and amazingly being beaten to a pulp at each stop along the way. An optometrist—on the surface an easy mark—had turned out to know Siamese foot-fighting and had easily downed the well-trained fed with a series of toekicks at the temple. Teased by the Hoover man, an ancient Talmudic Jew, bent over with learning, had suddenly flung off his tattered eastern European greatcoat and revealed himself to be not that old after all. Additionally, he had a terrific body, sleek, fatless, and sinewy, the result of four years of secret workouts in a local gym. Within twenty seconds he had pounded the surprised agent into submission. Sensing an easy victory, the fed had gone in after a slender interior decorator one day and guffawed loudly when a platoon of tiny, well-coiffed poodles greeted him at the outer hedge. But the dogs had turned out to be a rare and angry little breed, raised in lonely Kamchatkan outposts and known to dog lovers as "the barracuda of the poodle family"; forming what seemed to be a playful little circle, they suddenly yipped forward and within seconds had torn his ankles to shreds. One morning, LePeters saw the agent, flanked by two friends, disappear in the back yard of a nearby neighbor, then heard a series of timeless and profound groans. "Have you had enough," came the voice of the neighbor, Carmody, a higher-up in flexible packaging. LePeters was both terrified and curious, but hung back, figuring why get involved. Besides, the poodles had appeared and were circling close by, craning their short necks, trying their jaws. Finally, the fed limped out, supported by his two friends, his face white and contorted, still letting out groans as though from an entire childhood of stomach wounds. Later that very afternoon, bleary-eyed, poodle-torn, groggy from his nine-house drubbing, the FBI man walked by LePeters's house and said, "Hi there. Look, tomatoes have been disappearing from around my house. I don't say it's your daughter, but I just thought I'd mention it."

"Put that idea out of your head," said LePeters, blowing up his chest. "It's not her. Besides, what kind of greeting is that. You walk right over to me, a new guy in the neighborhood, and call his daughter a thief. Maybe if you changed your style you wouldn't get beat up so often."

"How'd you find out about that?"

"It gets around," said LePeters.

"Don't lean on me, fella," said the agent, but then he doubled over in a stray, leftover groan and LePeters helped him back to his house wondering what in the world was in it for the fed, what could he possibly be getting out of his surly, offensive approach to life. When the pain seemed to pass, the agent shrugged off LePeters and was able to continue on his own steam, affecting a highly exaggerated masculine swagger. LePeters returned to his own property, wondering if he could take the FBI man, even in his battered condition, and deciding that he probably could, although a great deal would depend on who got the better of the opening exchange of blows. He wondered if he could get him to let out those timeless and profound groans. It would hardly be worth it without them.

At the base of the residential area of Detectives' Hill, like a cheap ankle bracelet flung round its instep, was the town itself, mongrelized, uncertain in theme. Half the stores were country-quaint, relics of a time when police captains needed moustache wax and collar buttons; the other half were brazenly modern, in the postwar German industrial style. Flash fires, obviously attributable to no criminal element but to some peculiar, windswept natural force, had nonselectively torn through the area, burning out stores in a random pattern and giving the town the look of a brilliant mouth with many cavities. Following a mysterious local ordinance, all buildings, young or old, were leveled off at the second story. LePeters, in his first month, tried earnestly to work up a sense of kinship and pride in the town. A veteran of short stays in dozens of pinched-off little villages of the West, LePeters would have enjoyed planting his roots in one winner. It would have been satisfying, one day, to block the path of a smart-aleck reporter from the city and tell the brash young cub, "This here's our town. And we don't take too kindly to strangers." But that sort of local pride was rough sledding when it came to Detectives' Hill. Shakily orchestrated, packed with contradictions, it offered him no firm ground to stand on. Only at night did the Hill have a certain unity of theme. After dark, the emptied-out streets were lit by cold, high-intensity lights, noted for their ability to show up the smallest shred of criminal activity. LePeters enjoyed the town at these hours. On occasion, he took late-night walks, luxuriating in the plenitude of safety, dropping in at stores, many of which were run by retired dicks and stocked exclusively with items of Americana. The ex-crimebuster proprietors went in heavily for patriotic galas, and at the merest suggestion of some obscure national holiday, would race out to loop stars-and-stripes wreaths about the parking meters. During his nighttime strolls, LePeters invariably passed the single movie house, run by a one-armed war veteran and enthusiast of raucous prewar British farces, the more lightweight and scatterbrained the better. Seated in the ticket booth, the vet, particularly on slow nights, would pelt passersby with popcorn pieces; to those who complained, he would raise his prong in anger, point to it with his good hand, and holler, "Normandy." One night LePeters stopped a shower of it and decided he'd had enough. Ignoring the war-ravaged limb, he shouted back, "I was in the Korean show and went through plenty, but at least I don't go around making a career of it."

True to its shaky, divided identity, Detectives' Hill had stores that were either dick or non-dick in ownership. It occurred to LePeters that he had picked a town to match his own sectored-off face, but the thought was upsetting and he dropped it. In the latter category of store were a few run by ravaged, outcast proprietors along the lines of a trio of Negro cousins who were just setting up a stationery shop as LePeters moved in. Not really that thoughtful in the card-sending department, LePeters nevertheless dropped by one night to pick one up anyway, although actually to toss the fledgling Negroes some good-luck send-off business. He noticed each of the cousins had knobbed and bloated fingers of a kind he had never seen before; they might have been run through a special press, the price of a black store license. Using his great watery stumps, one of the owners wrapped LePeters's card in elaborate gold-embossed paper which had to be worth more than the card itself. Even someone financially naïve could see that was no way to do business; LePeters wanted to tell him his generosity was putting him on a downhill road. Even if he were suckering in LePeters to get a stranglehold on his future card-buying business, he was making a huge mistake. But Le-Peters kept silent; at least the Negro had the illusion of doing business. LePeters pocketed the magnificently wrapped card and gave the heavy-fingered owner a quarter above the purchase price.

"What's that?" the Negro asked, fingering the coin.

"A tip," said LePeters.

The Negro shrugged, sniffed at the coin with one widely flared nostril, and then tossed it into a Conquer Nephritis box.

LePeters had no all-out favorite store, but down the street was a general merchandise shop that came pretty close. Run by a cadaverous old codger in red suspenders, the store was crammed with corncob pipes, collar buttons, moustache wax, chewing tobacco, spats if you needed them, and spare parts for farm machinery, although LePeters had spotted no farms in the area. The old curmudgeon said the store dated back to the early days of the Morgans and Rockefellers. LePeters first stopped in for a fistful of cigars, and the old-timer said that at the turn of the century he had sold the very brand to a famed railway baron. "Well, make sure you're not giving me the same box," said LePeters, taking a stale handful. But he liked the old-timer, particularly since he had tested him early on girly-magazine policy and found the senior citizen a tower of discretion. His first day in the store, LePeters had gone to the girly rack and riffled through a few. Winking slyly, the old-timer said, "Guess I'll just tend to m'knittin'," and disappeared in the rear, allowing LePeters a clear and unembarrassed field day at the rack.

A mere two weeks after LePeters moved in, the old man slumped forward in a barrel of halibut bait and died instantly, hard-to-snuff-out scandals coming to light immediately about his having paid shapeless though hefty octogenarian broads to step in the back so he could have his way with them. Immediately thereafter, in moved the new owners, a dozen Dachau grads with habits LePeters found deplorable. Putting them through a girly-magazine test, LePeters stepped boldly up to the rack only to hear the Nazi-ravaged new owner announce to the jammed store, "We carry everything here for the gentleman who enjoys a good titbook." Items were suddenly given price tags that were not so much excessive as annoying, twenty-seven cents instead of a quarter, a dollar and three cents instead of a buck. Several times, LePeters had handed over a dollar bill, waited for change, and been asked, "Do you mind taking twenty-five pennies off my hands?" Once LePeters bought the Sunday papers and was about to leave when the Dachau man's wife flew out of the toy section hollering, "He's got a seventy-five-cent tube of moustache glue in his pocket that he wasn't going to pay for." Outraged, LePeters slammed his fist on the counter and said he had been coming into the store for years and had never been so insulted in his life. He realized that her paranoid personality might have been shaped by inhumane Nazi medical experiments, but for the moment, it didn't help. The storeowner calmed his wife, who apologized to LePeters and said, "All right, maybe you didn't take it, but you've got to admit that anyone who would steal from us deserves a good case of cancer."

"I don't have to admit that at all," said LePeters. "Particularly not for a nickel-and-dime offense. I think you're asking too harsh a penalty."

And then, with a certain First Family austerity, he said, "We don't do things like that in this country."

His face suddenly crinkling with kindness, the old Dachau survivor looked into LePeters's eyes and asked, "You're not by any chance related to a family named Feldstein?"

One part of LePeters wanted to give the man a hug; another part felt an electric coldness in the small of his back. Avoiding the man's eyes, he checked himself in an old country mirror and had a vision of his entire self splitting down the center, the halves declaring war on one another.

"What gave you an idea like that," he said, finally. "How could I be, with a name like mine."

The village came to no abrupt ending but tapered off, like a dead man's pencil scrawl, in an old railroad yard. A section of track that had once been a private line for the wealthy now led nowhere. Behind the yard was a bleak and ramshackle discothèque, spotlighted by the most powerful lights in town, in deference to its high crime potential. Outside, a cordon of dicks' wives, viewing it as a blot on the town, picketed in shifts, while two or three civil libertarians stood by and wagged their fingers in opposition. LePeters ended his nightly strolls at the edge of the railroad yard—and once, at a break in the shifts, he looked through the glazed windows and saw thick-waisted waitresses in tattered bunny suits serve drinks while an ancient go-go girl did last year's steps on a tiny platform. Huffed up, steaming, thickly visored, a motorcycle cop appeared in thunder and asked, "Everything all right, Mr. LePeters?"

"Tip-top," said LePeters. "I was just taking a walk."

"You know who I hate," said the cop. "I don't hate Eichmann. Oh no, not really. And I don't hate Hitler either. Not down deep. You know who I hate?"

"Who's that?"

"Anyone who does crime in the streets."

"It's getting to be quite a problem," said LePeters.

Such was life on Detectives' Hill, all very well and good, but where was the East? More cops, fewer hoods, brighter lights, a quarter of a pound more patriotism, and an extra peculiarity here and there—put them all together and they spelled one more town like all the others he had run across in his trek across the American heartland. One night, he told Claire LePeters he was going out for cigars; instead of walking, he took the squad, first checking the back seat, in accordance with a new regulation put through by Chief Guster, to see that no vengeance-seeking hoods were back there. LePeters drove for a while and then it seemed as though the squad were driving him, taking him past the boundaries of Detectives' Hill toward the great, definitely eastern metropolis that lay magnificently humped and crouched a couple of hours away. He was aware of what was happening, but let it happen all the same. LePeters crossed a thin, umbilical strip of road that tied Detectives' Hill to the main city road, and unaccountably turned on his police siren, switching on his rotating overhead warning lights, too, and covering the thin strip of road at 120 miles an hour; when he got to the city road, he quickly switched off all connections and went back to being an unmarked squad, except for the telltale police radio antennae. As he approached the first tentative outlines of the great city, LePeters felt a sweep of excitement at his shoulders, much like the first time he had looked at the Pacific. Now that's what I call East, he said to himself. No more kidding around.

Picking a softly lit street at random, he drove past several neighborhood cabarets, slowing down when he came to one called Ululu's, outstanding for its crystal and warm tones of orange light. He drove along, inspecting the façades of several others, but just as there is really only one special girl at the dance, he knew he had instantly become an Ululu's man. Somehow, on this night, he felt impelled to follow detective procedure more than usual, and parked his squad down the street and around the corner, stakeout style, so as not to alert the quarry to his presence. With only a few tables and many standees, the cabaret was thickly weeded with young men and women, all of them somehow casually comfortable and all the more graceful for their confined situation. LePeters suddenly felt self-conscious about his plain, detectivey clothes. Wide, loose-fitting slacks with a great floating sag at the crotch—that was the style around homicide bureaus. To be one of the boys, LePeters had always had his pants designed in this fashion. The Ululu's men were sleekly dressed in a continental style, and LePeters was glad to be packed in so that no one could notice and blow the whistle on his loosely crotched tailoring. Ordinarily, LePeters took seats in the rear of public places, with his back to a wall, detective-style, but at Ululu's he was grateful for any space at all; he stood near the entrance, gratefully hooked over in an odd sculpted posture. An attractive woman, expensively dressed and with tightly helmeted black hair, was hooked into him and asked, "What do you do for grins?" LePeters had never heard the expression before, but liked the eastern smack of it and filed it away, thinking he might try it around the bureau the next day. Instead of an answer, he asked, "Is Ululu a person?"

"You mean you don't know?" said the woman.

"This is my first trip," he said. "I saw the marquee and just fell in here."

The woman looked at him as though he had sent off a malevolent odor and then turned to some sort of bouncer, a squatly powerful man with great tumbles of black curls and a thinly fluted voice. "You should be proud of me, Yip love," she said. "I've been here for an hour and I haven't said shit, I haven't said fuck, I haven't said cunt and (spelling this last one) I particularly haven't said f . . . a . . . r . . . t."

In a clearing at the end of the bar sat a short fellow with long seal-black hair who seemed to shift sexes every thirty seconds or so in the drugged and heavily oranged light. It seemed to be required that new guests inch their way forward through the thicket of standees and plant a greeting kiss on the perspired mouth of the Eskimo host (or hostess, depending on when you got there). LePeters, still worried about his deeply dipped crotch, fought his way forward, and when his turn came, said, "Hi there, Ululu," and plunged in for a kiss. "*Buona sera*, baby love," said the Eskimo, and LePeters felt a sudden glow of real eastern acceptance. A magnificently dressed paraplegic dude clattered forward in a gaily decorated wheelchair, some pounding music began, and Ululu began to dance with him, raising his or her arms and throwing out lewd, perfectly timed pelvic shivers, while the Eskimo's dis-

abled partner aped the gestures above the waist and spun his
wheels wildly to keep in step. For that moment, LePeters
would gladly have changed places with the plucky, fun-loving
paraplegic, who was certainly having a better time of it than
many self-pitying able-bodied types around the bureau.
Working his way back to his original spot, LePeters brushed
alongside the most beautiful girl he had seen so far, a tall,
windswept, sorrowful child who seemed to move easily
through the crowd where others had been frozen in place. At
one of the highly coveted tables, a dagger-thin, polka-dotted
man played dominoes; barely looking up, he tapped the
empty seat and said, "Hey, Diane, slap your clit down here
for a second." The girl blushed for a moment, but sat down
anyway. LePeters was amazed she hadn't stormed out in a
huff. By sitting down, she had publicly acknowledged that
she had a clit. And she had taken the seat as instructed, too,
letting all of Ululu's know she had really slapped it right
down there. Boy, is this East, LePeters thought to himself. Now I'm really East. He looked at her and there was no
girl there, just a golden clit. "Guess who I'm sleeping with?"
she asked. The dagger-thin man had gone back to his dominoes and paid her no heed. "Don't you want to know?" she
asked. "Don't bother me with that shit," said the domino
player. LePeters would have given up home and possessions
to be in on such a conversation. The domino man told her of
several theatrical properties he had recently optioned. LePeters wasn't sure what options were, but loved the sound of
them and was certain that if you made a house-to-house
search of every western town he had ever lived in—throw in
Detectives' Hill as well—you'd never come up with a single
one. And here were several being discussed right in front of
him. On the spot, he thought of a play in which male and
female detectives are locked in a steambath; at the end of the

first act, it turns out to be hell. After the beautiful clit girl had swept on, LePeters, on an impulse, worked his way over to the thin domino player and told him the idea. "Would you option something like that?" asked LePeters.

"Quite frankly, I'm over-optioned," he said. LePeters was thrilled to be that involved in an option, even if he had been turned down on one. With weary eyes, the thin man looked LePeters full in the face for the first time and asked, "Are you an actor?"

My facial boundaries, LePeters thought. In the crush of authentically eastern excitement, he had forgotten all about them. The warm, cosmetically oranged lights seemed to have stripped five to ten years off several girls. Why hadn't they softened his scar down to insignificance. He felt exposed, a trapped thief, and would have much preferred to have his great floating dick pants held up to the crowd as an exercise in satire.

"I'm in crime," said LePeters, finally.

"I thought you might do character work," said the domino man and wearily asked the waiter for a mandolin. A small, quickly whirlpooling commotion began at the cabaret entrance. LePeters first noticed the wheelchaired dancer throwing punches, but they were hollow, rudderless blows and few paid any attention to them. A tall, confused executive type began swinging several attaché cases blindly about him; the black-helmeted girl screamed, "Shitfuckpiss . . . f . . . a . . . r . . . t" at him and then the powerful, great-curled man picked up the exec, held him above his head for one terrifying moment, and flung him easily through the front window. He went through with a tearing sound, rather than a crash, showering bits of orange glass in every direction, but also leaving a lovely halo of iced and shimmering orange stalactites where the glass had been. LePeters was terrified, but also felt it was quite the loveliest thing he had ever seen. For a moment, he wanted to go through himself, but only if he were given a written, no-injuries guarantee. All sound stopped but for the hum of the disabled man's wheels as he spun in a circle, pumping out futile blows. LePeters, feeling a need to do something, yanked out his badgette and showed it to the domino man. Then he pushed his way to the street. Bewildered, the attaché man sat on the concrete, covered with a rich brocade of lovely, delicate orange pieces; LePeters had expected the man to be decapitated, and was amazed that he seemed to have come through without injury. Much more panicked than the man, LePeters helped him to his feet, then began shoving him and saying, "Get out of here, run, before you get hurt."

"Now listen here," said the man, but LePeters, stronger at the moment than ten men, kept shoving him along; to insure his safety he would have flung the fellow through another window, but as it was, he finally whipped him around a corner until the man indeed began to run. Once, as a child, LePeters remembered seeing a huge drunken man on a subway platform, teetering along the edge as though he might fall in front of a train. Breaking from his mother, he had made a lightning dash to the man's side, shoving him alongside the wall and then easing him along to the street. His impulse then, as now, had not so much been for the safety of the man as to fulfill a mission that required him to keep terrible things from happening. He had always been at his toughest preventing fights, standing between men and refusing to allow them to punch each other.

The window man, catching some of LePeters's terror, had run off; as he disappeared, a thin threadlike line around his neck began to thicken, and he faded off, wearing a heavy blood collar. LePeters turned, as though to return to Ululu's,

but then walked swiftly to his car instead; with overhead
lights spinning dementedly, sirens screaming full blast, he
barreled through the parting traffic and raced all the way
back to Detectives' Hill, foot on the floor.

LePeters felt singed by his first contact with authentic eastern life; still, if that was to be the sum of it, of all seventeen
years of apprehension—a near-decapitation in an oranged
cabaret—he was willing to grab it and run. For the next
week, he plunged greedily back into homicide, his only concern that the man with the blood collar would waltz in one
day and finger him as a participant in the Ululu's window-
throw. LePeters took the experience as a warning—stick to
your knitting. For the next week he drew much closer to the
dicks, wearing the fattest, lowest-drooped slacks in his wardrobe; several of the dicks, the towering Gibney and the many-
gunned Medici in particular, mistrusted the standard armory
shells and preferred to pack their own. LePeters volunteered
to stay late one night and help them cram their bullets with a
special brand of powder, stealthily shipped up from Mexico
and known for its crazed, erratic, Gringo-hating impact.
When Flamoyan showed up with a fresh stock of Lone
Ranger jokes ("Meanwhile, back at the ranch, the Arabs are
eating their dates"), LePeters was the heartiest laugher in
the bureau. Flamoyan would point to a dick, hold his nose
with two fingers, and say, "Even his best friends won't tell
him." LePeters, not really loving the gag that much, would
cackle away, egg him on. These were his people. This was his
world, his work.

Medium-stalwart in most of his affairs, LePeters was a complete telephone coward. Good news generally came to him in face-to-face confrontations, on occasion in the morning mail. But the phone, if not his sworn enemy, was at best a fair-weather friend. Whenever he heard it ring, his first impulse was to fall back in a defensive crouch. In the new bureau, a step above the others in the violence department, the ring of the phone chimed in with the other background sounds of crime—police sirens, ambulance moans, the rattle of handcuffs, Gibney's cheerful whistle as he took his morning riffle through the sex photo files, the glum sound of recalcitrant cop-fighting suspects as Gibney and Medici took turns pounding them in the stomach for confessions—Hortham's loud lipsmacks as he toyed with an evidential bra—one chirping, thunking, metallic malevolent symphony of crime. On particular occasions, when LePeters's nerves were shot, the ring of the phone was a volley of bullets aimed for his stomach. The phone had always seemed so unfair to him—it offered no way to shoot back, no face to plead with, no lapel to hold, no throat to grab. Some claimed seriously to be able to tell the tenor of a coming conversation by the sound of the phone ring—for LePeters this was no great feat, since in his case, nine out of ten of the calls were losers. Not exactly easy behind the steering wheel either, LePeters saw his end coming while racing down a highway, answering a call in one of the newly installed car-phones.

In the new bureau, LePeters gave Teener the job of clearing his calls, his assistant acting as a tiny shield to deflect some of the gunfire. In among the telephone equipment Teener seemed right at home, a small mechanical adjunct to the wired network, a friendly little circuit-breaker. It was perfect having him in there. After all, wasn't his own little body governed by ticks and throbs, hums and buzzers? One morning a call came through, three quick ambushing bursts which Teener took without flinching. Seconds later, as though by delayed reaction, LePeters heard a twanging sound and saw his assistant drop the receiver, and then hold his middle, gasping, "Pins, needles, anything you got." LePeters cast about in vain for small metallic objects; finally, in desperation, he offered Teener a wad of bubble gum. Teener said all right, but would he please dry it off first to get it sticky. LePeters did so and gave it to his tiny friend who thrust it inside his shirt while LePeters modestly turned aside; soon Teener's breath came more evenly and he was able to straighten up. "That'll hold me till I get home," he said. "But it was goddamned close." The caller had been left strangling at the other end. LePeters told Teener to rest up and took it himself. It was Claire LePeters, out of breath, highly agitated: "Everything okay there?" she asked, "because it's not here. Here goes." She then told LePeters a strange story about their daughter's first day in school in the new neighborhood. She had taken the girl to school herself and let her wander among a large group of children who were milling about in the yard, waiting to go inside the building. A man who seemed to be the superintendent or principal then came forth, taking her by the hand and approaching the mother. He explained that there had been a mistake in the registration, that the LePeters's house lipped over by a few feet or so into another district which required that the child attend another school. Thereupon he walked with the two of them through the town of Detectives' Hill, beyond the railroad tracks until they came to the other establishment. In the yard were many more children than had been at the previous school, and all of them appeared to be Negroes. The superintendent had bowed low at the waist, saying, "This is your new school, Jamie, I hope you'll be very happy here," then shook hands with LePeters's wife, and went off with a little trot. "He just left us there," said Claire LePeters, "all alone in a sea of spades. You should have seen them, a whole swarm of them, as far as the eye could see. Then the bell rang and she got swept into the building with them, just like it was a whole black river. Anyway, she's in there now, if she's still alive. You better come right home and go get her."

"Just hang on," said LePeters excitedly. "Be right there." His wife's first words, when they were excited ones, usually threw him into a frenzy of action. Untypically, casting for straws now, he hesitated: "What do you mean spades?" he asked. "They were all colored kids?"

"All of them," she said. "Is that what you want to talk about now? You could have had her out of there by now."

"I just want to get my facts," said LePeters. "It could be important. Maybe there were just a lot of them and it just looked that way to you. There weren't any white kids?"

"I'm not answering that," said Claire LePeters. She skipped a few beats in silence and then said, "There were a few other things floating around that may not have been straight black. All I know is that you're not getting anything done."

"All right, then," said LePeters. "I'll be home in a flash. I assure you she's safe. What percentage would they have in harming her?"

◉

"They've thrown my kid in with a gang of spades," LePeters told Teener and then asked him if he would mind finishing up the day's clippings. He apologized for having to wish the job off on him, particularly on a day when his internal gadgets seemed to have run amok. Teener told LePeters to think nothing of it, to put the homicide clips out of his mind.

Pointing to his small joke of a chest, he said, "They slapped a new one in there over the weekend, transistor deal that come out of the space program. Does a whale of a job, but she tends to go off when you least expect it." The tiny detective's throbs and hums seemed to be ticking off at a smoother frequency and this soothed LePeters's conscience. He knocked on Glober's door and after a moment, his boss opened the door a crack, his breath coming in in great, winded blasts. Had he interrupted his employer at the height of orgiastic frenzy? LePeters was strangely unconcerned about the possibility; to a certain extent, he resented Glober's round-the-clock masturbatory carpet-rolls while he himself had to slave away on the clips with monastic dedication.

"Bruno, I've got a favor to ask," LePeters hollered through the door crack. "My kid's been mistakenly dumped into a spade school and I've got to go out there and straighten it out."

Strangling with interrupted lust, Glober, always generous when LePeters was in trouble, remained true to form: "Could you use a couple of bucks," he asked in syncopated gasps, "to smooth things over."

"I appreciate it, but I don't think it's a money deal," said LePeters. "Look, thanks for the day off and please, get back to what you were doing."

"What do you mean what I was doing?" asked Glober, still gasping through the door, but recovering quickly.

"What you were doing," said LePeters. "The work. I don't know why I put it that way."

Jumping into his overcoat, LePeters stopped momentarily at the door of the clippings department.

"Hey, Teener," he said. "Remember that house up on Detectives' Hill, the one I told you about. I said we practically stole it from this Croat family."

"Oh, yeah," said Teener, "I remember."

"Well, I just found out why we got such a terrific buy."

On the way down the hall, LePeters was stopped by Riggles of Polygraph who shouldered him inside the lie-box room and shut the door. "Just for a second," said Riggles, bolting the door. "I want to try something."

"Any other time," said LePeters. "I'm really in a hurry. I've got a spade problem with my kid and I'm taking the day off." But of all the dicks, LePeters had most respect for the gray-haired, constitutional-looking Riggles, a contemplative pipe-man, older than most of the dicks and possessor in the long ago of a correspondence-course law degree.

"All right, now," said Riggles, taking a seat behind his desk, "try something, preferably on the stupid side."

"I don't get your meaning. And I got to get the hell out of here."

"No, really," said Riggles, puffing contemplatively, a face from the ages of justice. "Scratch your head like a monkey, stick out your tongue."

"Wait a minute," he said, reaching into his desk. "I got a better one." He pulled out a little wraparound apron skirt, held it against himself, and did a little bump with it. "Do that," he said. "That'll be a good one. Go ahead."

Trying to conceal his disgust—after all, Riggles was the most serious of the dicks—LePeters grabbed the skirt and ticked off a couple of routine stripper movements.

"All right, now," said Riggles, sucking deeply on the pipe. "Now, who saw that?"

"What do you mean?" asked LePeters. "You saw it."

"Wrong," said Riggles. "A whole bunch of us did. C'mon out, fellas."

With that, a horde of detectives rushed in from the next room, Gibney, Kuens, Medici, Hortham, Flamoyan, even Sergeant Cartney of the Motor Pool Bureau.

"Hey, that's pretty good," said Flamoyan. "How about a little taste for Uncle Gus here."

"We were waiting to see your entire poon," said Gibney, poking LePeters in the ribs.

"It was the fish bowl over here," said Riggles with a distinguished senatorial chuckle, leading LePeters toward a tank in the corner of the room. "It's a two-way job we just got in. I just wanted to check it out. In the other room, they were able to see your every antic. I'm fighting to have one installed in every one of our interrogation rooms so that our suspects will never have a second's privacy. What a man does when he thinks he's alone is a tip-off to the guilty stuff he's pulling. Once you have the private stuff he's done, then you can put him on the box and really nail the bastard."

LePeters thought of his daughter, currently engulfed by spades, and her own fish box. He saw a picture of her staring at it, concerned for the fishes' welfare. Was someone staring back? Then it occurred to him that of all the dicks present, only the heavily armed Medici hadn't joined in the joshing. LePeters had said "spade." Was it possible that Medici had heard him and taken it to heart.

"What about my talking," he asked the Negro detective, as though in the interest of science. "Could you overhear that?"

"Not too closely 'cause of the fish bubbles," said Medici, doing some intense digging with a toothpick and not letting LePeters catch his eyes. "But don't you fear. I got the gist of it."

◉

Plunging into his squad, LePeters tore out to Detectives'
Hill, trying a few tentative siren blasts, but then holding
back. Trying to stuff himself with last-minute enjoyment before the roof fell in, LePeters turned on his normal radio and
blended it in with the detective alerts. "A light-skinned
Negro weighing approximately one hundred and fifty
pounds" . . . *Tell it like it is* . . . "wearing white sneakers
and a black fedora" . . . *What's it all about, Alfie?* . . .
"carrying a satchel believed to contain two thousand dollars
in U.S.C." . . . *Mah baby do the hanky-panky* . . . "believed to be armed" . . . Considering his daughter's plight,
swallowed up in a colored tide, LePeters was amazed he
could still eat up the essentially black music, and danced in
his seat as he slid through traffic in the squad. He drove directly to the railroad yard, bouncing his wheels over a few
disjointed sections of track and wondering if there were any
once hotly-juiced third rails among them with a few stray
leftover jolts to them. Squat and bleary-eyed in the sun, the
discredited discothèque was bare of pickets for the moment;
though it was a fraction past the noon hour, its walls
amazingly seemed to rock and bulge with music and good
cheer. Who were the revelers, LePeters wondered, with time
for discothèques in the midday sun? Some old blank-
socketed shells of cars were strewn about the railroad yard,
and LePeters wondered if people lived in them. If they did,
how long could they get away with it in Detectives' Hill—
neatness-obsessed and security-conscious as it was? A heavy-
set woman, easily a three-hundred-pounder, lolled against
the door of the discothèque, wearing anklets and snapping
off huge, proud gum bubbles. LePeters thought of Sissy

Glober, particularly as she looked on C-8. Though repelled by the comparison, one small strand of him wondered about the hefty gum-chewer and her sebaceous mysteries.

Damping down the thought, LePeters pushed on until finally he came to the colored school, amazed that he had never noticed it before, the one building in Detectives' Hill he had completely overlooked. It was one story taller than the others, too, having somehow been spared that slashing stroke that had leveled the others off at two. There were no children in the yard, but the building seemed grim and sullen. Was it screened by a thin, generalized film of colored-ness? Though the experimental playground equipment was dazzling in its fun-filled Scandinavian modernity—obviously a conscience-salving gift from wealthy liberal groups—pathetic inferior education seemed to be stamped onto the building, to flow from its concrete pores. LePeters took a careful breath, afraid to inhale, then galloped up the front steps. Inside, the building was choked and strangling with the smell of cleansers—God only knew what they were trying to cover up. On one of the corridor walls, LePeters saw a marvelous collage, tangled and swamplike, signed "Kenneth Carver Washington, eight years old." He loved it, yet wondered whether he was giving it extra points for its black origin. On second thought, he decided it was brilliant in any league. Chipper, brisk stewardess-type administrative assistants clicked through the halls as though it were a normal school. Peeking into one of the schoolrooms, LePeters, without surprise, saw that it was not as black as his wife had painted it, although it was black enough. A few oddly skinned youngsters were speckled here and there, South Americans perhaps. LePeters was impressed by the principal, a powerful-looking no-nonsense type of old, her short-cropped dyke's hairdo somehow reassuring. Each of the pic-

tures on her office wall showed her standing in front of different roller coasters, younger, smiling, and with a certain pride
of ownership. Had she once been an operator—and if so,
wasn't it a strange background for principaling. Still, it might
indicate a certain youthful zest, a clean, open, amusement-
park mind, not really that bad as a foundation for dealing
with children. As she spoke, LePeters became aware of background Morse code sounds. Shifting about, he looked for a
hidden device; had Teener stolen out of the bureau to back
him in a difficult mission? Then he realized it was in the
principal's speech, a dental flaw. "Pleased you could come
down, Mr. LePeters, dit," she said. "We like to think of each
youngster dit as a piece of untouched wood dit dat. They
come to us in that manner ditdatditdatditdat, and it is our
ditdat job to mold and shape this wooden object into a useful and much more than ornamental piece of society." Her
opening remarks concluded, the principal, almost with relief,
fired out a major all-out Morse barrage: Ditdatditdatditdat-
ditdatditdatditdatditdat. Waiting for her to wind up, LePeters, who'd taken a little Morse in the service, wondered if
the outbursts made any verbal sense and took a stab at deciphering them. Was she flashing a message back to some secret educational arm of government? When she had finished,
she smiled sweetly as though after a hiccough, and LePeters,
expecting to be cut down by another burst, plunged in and
said, "My wife and I didn't expect this kind of school and
quite frankly would like to get our little girl, Jamie, out of it.
I'm in detective work, we came from the West and didn't at
all have in mind her being around a general sense of poverty."

The principal said she understood, that the school admittedly had a few problems, but that allocation of students was
out of her hands, controlled by a board of town elders. Her

tone was remarkably codeless; perhaps when you got right
down to brass tacks with her, she dropped the Morse. Or was
she still involved with roller coasters, her voice coded at the
peaks, Morse-less in the valleys? LePeters thanked her, got
up to go, and saw his battered FBI fight-victim neighbor
stroll by and duck into a classroom. He seemed freshly
scrubbed and walked in a cloud of cheap yet briskly masculine after-shave lotion. LePeters asked what he was doing
there, and the principal said, "He's teaching the fifth grade
sex education. Some of the parents are kind enough to help
out ditdatditdatditdat. . . ." LePeters was chilled by the information. What kind of background could the pugnacious
fed have for the delicate handling of sex instruction? Unquestionably, the FBI had some sort of program, and chances
are it was straight and law-abiding, an unembarrassed, no-
nonsense, entirely wholesome approach to the dangerous
subject that skipped warily past all lascivious landmines. But
didn't the school know about the fed's lack of self-control,
the fights he'd had with everyone in town? Still, LePeters
thought, maybe he was good at it, all restraint in the classroom just as he was lacking in insight on the street. And he
had to admit he had not really pitched in and shored up
Jamie with any instruction of his own, although he sincerely
meant to get a good book someday and feed her a little to see
how it took. Then, too, perhaps the fed's presence meant his
own child attended the school, another white skin to help
shrink the preposterously off-balance percentages. He asked
the principal if this were true. "No, Sherry attends our other
school across town, although we'd love to have her." LePeters felt like blowing the whistle right then and there. That
was no deal at all, keeping your own daughter free and clear
while you slip off afternoons, scrubbed and well-groomed, to
feed sex to the spades. Unsteady on his feet and burning up

with annoyance, LePeters walked out of the principal's office. Pretty, white administrative assistants in tight, high-rumped dresses chattered by, hugging official papers to their starched bosoms, the best-looking wenches he'd seen around Detectives' Hill, easily pretty enough to be stewardesses on one of America's top airlines. An irritable-looking little girl strolled by, muttering to herself, miraculously white-skinned. LePeters recognized her from the general store, only daughter of the irritating Dachau owners. Far from pretty, her features were poorly matched, badly thrown together. She wore a giant, cheaply made Menorah candle souvenir on her bodice and whined to herself as she stepped into the principal's office. LePeters listened to her high-pitched nasal complaint: along with a batch of other students, she had been taken to a cereal factory on a bus—an educational trip—but had not been allowed to disembark. The children stayed inside while the teacher pointed to the building and explained how cereal was made. Then the bus returned to the school grounds. The principal listened to the child, then gunned her down with a burst of irritated Morse. When the Menorah child left the office, LePeters snatched her high above the ground, reached behind her knotted hair, and kissed a snow-white ear.

The city elders were housed in the town hall, easily the most patriotic building in a rousingly pro-American town. The lawn was thickly studded with statues and plaques commemorating the names of local infantrymen who had been wiped out in battle, sons of Detectives' Hill air aces who had gone down in aerial flames. LePeters ducked through what seemed to be a thick, billowing wetwash of U.S. flags, draped low in the halls and smacking against his face as he picked his way along. On the walls were still more flags, smaller but even more boldly furled, belonging to tiny Asian and South American countries, run by peppery little dictators who fiercely adhered to the American creed. LePeters stiffened into a martial parade-type walk as he marched through the halls; though he had logged three and a half years in the Army, he felt soiled and shabby, as though he really hadn't done enough for his country to justify holding his head high in a building of this sort.

His visit to the colored school had somehow been reassuring; for all of her coded style, the principal seemed dedicated to doing her best with the mess she had been handed. The scattering of light-skinned children and the one all-out white though Dachau-involved face had reduced the sting of his wife's picture of a coal-black situation. Then, too, the squadron of part-stewardess-type administrators would certainly see to it that nothing terrible happened—and there seemed to be no precociously developed black longshoremen types to wrest them to the ground for corridor rapes. True, the FBI man's presence as a sex counselor had been rattling, but his freshly scrubbed, briskly cologned look had taken the edge off the loaded possibilities of his unlikely role as a sex counselor. Still, as LePeters marched along to the Nathan Hale room, the early fears crawled back across his shoulders and all he could see clearly was that he wanted his daughter out of all that coloredness. A little was fine, even to be sought after, fifty-fifty workable. But a whole schoolful was frightening, out of the question.

A tall red-faced man, not so much fat as average weight but swollen with Dickensian floridness, stood outside the Nathan Hale, holding a great chart beneath his arm and breathing with difficulty, as though he had gone way over the line with smoking—and even if he stopped, it was too late to do him any good. He, too, wore a cheaply made Sabbath candle emblem on his lapel, making LePeters wonder if there were not a small basement-based Talmudic group cranking them out in a strange, fanatical opposition to the massive flow of Detectives' Hill Americana.

LePeters introduced himself, but the man, exploding with red-faced anxiety, seemed not to hear him. "They'll go for it," he said, brandishing the chart like a torch. "Bet your boots on it." The man said that he was Gordon Mendelowitz, a smoking-jacket tycoon who had become known in the clothing industry for his Humanity Fund, a box of money always near him in the factory so that his employees need never go to shylocks. When a worker required a touch, all he had to do was go inside the front office and hold up his fingers, to indicate whether he wanted a five- or ten-spot. One Puerto Rican cutter had had his hand mangled in a jacket-padding slicer and would invariably hold up six fingers, all he had. Mendelowitz said he loved to give him the business, saying, "Is that all you want, Perez? Six bucks? Or don't you really mean ten?" Several years back, at a factory party, a child had kicked Mendelowitz in the temple and though it seemed harmless at the time, the blow had somehow lowered his resistance and made him immediately vulnerable to an enormous catalogue of diseases, some of them exotic, more than a few circulatory, the full weight of them combining to lay him low in the prime of his career. "An explanation for the redness you see around my countenance," said Mendelowitz. Forced to retire, he had bought a house in Detectives' Hill, and despite the strain on his arteries, had spent long hours cooking up a new zoning plan for the school. "I want it so that the poverty low-income kids will be spread around, not too many of them landing in one school or the other."

"Then you must have kids in the poverty school," said Le-

Peters, thrilled to find an ally. "That's what I'm doing here. They have my only daughter down there and it crossed my mind that I might try to get her away from all that poverty."

"We don't move in for two years," said Mendelowitz. "That's when they finish up building our split. But I want to get things set up around here for when my daughter's ready. I'm positive they'll go for it."

LePeters suddenly felt remiss in his obligations as a dad. Here was Mendelowitz, concerned two years in advance for his child's welfare, even though the world might fall apart in the interim. LePeters felt he could certainly measure his love for his child against Mendelowitz's. But his expressed itself in vague ways, never charted and zoned. He was anxious to get a look at the plan, but Mendelowitz kept it tightly furled, Torah style, out of his reach.

"Maybe if I went in there with you," said LePeters. "Sometimes an extra person is good for support, even if he's just standing around." Used to holding out alone against unionized fury, the retired industrialist seemed to hear nothing. A door opened and clouds of thinly fluted gastric cigar smoke billowed forth. Mendelowitz, ballooning with anxiety, marched in, and the door of the Nathan Hale room closed on LePeters. Offended momentarily, LePeters saw that Mendelowitz was probably right in spurning his help. He knew nothing of the town, hadn't pored over the chart, was a stranger to its details. What kind of support could he lend, really. Barging in with a towering lack of information, he might even wind up offending the Detectives' Hill elders. Then they would really pour on the coloredness. He would let Mendelowitz go it alone. It took only one dick to frisk a man properly; the second was always thrown in and had to stand by idly, in the event of some extraordinary emergency, a waste of taxpayer's money.

Thinking it over, LePeters now saw that it was a stroke of good fortune to have an industrialist, however arterially scarred, presenting a chart on his behalf. LePeters had done no work, yet would be able to ride in on the man's coattails. In the corridor, he heard band music, then saw a trio of gray-haired dicks' wives, gotten up as a Spirit of '76 trio, parading through the halls to patriotic music. The flute player carried a tray around her neck of the type used by nightclub cigarette girls, only filled with Savings Bond applications. LePeters disliked intimidation of this sort, a crass use of patriotism to bludgeon him into a bond purchase. But after acknowledging the poor taste, he figured why not, he was patriotic too, a good American, why not spring for a bond. Tossing down $18.75, he got cheery cake-batter smiles from the wives and a large "Make Mine America, Sir" button for his lapel. Pinning it on, he saw Mendelowitz stagger out of the Nathan Hale room, holding his heavy heart and gasping for a drink. "I thought sure they'd go for it," he said, the once proudly detailed chart now crumpled in his hand. LePeters helped him to the water fountain where Mendelowitz tried to collect himself. After wetting his lips, the industrialist said, "I'll tell you the truth, I always look an event right in the eye, and never once in business did I try to see a half dollar where there was only a dime. Frankly, they shit all over my plan."

"I was glad you were going in there," said LePeters, "for my sake, as well as yours, but I honestly don't understand the extent of your concern. Why get involved now? You don't move in for two years."

"They'll go by like a flash," said Mendelowitz.

"Maybe if I'd gone in there with you," said LePeters, "and they'd seen there was another guy behind it." Behind what, though, he thought. He was zone-ignorant. Maybe there was no justice to the plan at all, even less than in the current scheme, although frankly it was hard to see how. In truth, LePeters cared little about zone justice and knew he was being blinded by one idea: to get his daughter away from all those spades.

"I'll tell you something else," said Mendelowitz, getting to his feet and unashamedly using LePeters's lapels for support. "Remember how I mentioned the kick in the head and how it was responsible for all the sickness?"

"I remember," said LePeters.

"Well, quite frankly, a lot of my conditions have come on as a result of getting involved in this goddamned colored thing."

One salvaging note, LePeters thought, is that at least I've got a new friend, even though real intimacy was out of the question until two years had gone by. Still, if Mendelowitz were not actually living in the town, at least he was heavily involved in its affairs. But how could LePeters be sure of the friendship? In his last look at Mendelowitz, the tycoon seemed to have become aloof, unseeing, remote, a tycoon once again, unwilling to associate with workers except for one or two benevolent appearances at factory parties. His chart now shamed and repudiated, perhaps he was going to revel in his two years of allotted color-free grace. LePeters thought of entering the thickly smoked room himself. But if the heavily fortified Mendelowitz had been laughed off, what would they think of LePeters, not only chartless, but lacking confidently tycooned eloquence? Of course his child actually attended the school: that might be worth a few points. Then again, it might make his case more suspect, all that personal involvement. For a brief moment, he thought of checking out the armory weapon assigned to him and coming in with guns blazing, saying *There's my argument.* In reality, his only hope was to be sincere, shoot straight from the shoulder. *There are, quite frankly, gentlemen, too many spades for me, and I want my daughter out of there.* But he lacked the ability to be straightforward. Somehow his divided face held him back, also his failure to avenge his dad, the secret ties to the name of Sussman. His peculiar work as a dick. All would put a devious tremble in his voice, make it hard for him to look the elders in the eye. So he turned tail and decided what's the rush. Perhaps he would do a chart, one just as good as Mendelowitz's, even better in a certain way because of the immediacy of his daughter's situation. Hateful as they are, you do charts anyway, if you love your kid.

Besides, there was no emergency. Only his wife's voice had made it one. In reality, his child was safe. And certainly there were fair-minded citizens in the town who realized the inequity of the zoning and who were working quietly behind the scenes, without fanfare, to rectify the imbalance. He wished they would tolerate a little fanfare so at least he could know they were there. Still, maybe there were even some oblique and temporary advantages to attending the school. He could vouch personally for the playground equipment, a dazzling fun-fested breakthrough in architectural design. Perhaps the town had guiltily thrown its best academic talent into the hopper, too, a salve for its conscience. Witness the teams of neatly rumped stewardesses who took care of administrative work, the principal herself, admittedly coded and flawed in speech, but a tower of sincerity.

These thoughts pacified LePeters somewhat as he strolled along Patrick Henry Hall, ducked beneath Farragut Arch, and noticed for the first time the main lobby Infamy Murals, huge crippled-fleet portraits, sketched in brilliant color short

days after the Japanese sneak attack on Pearl Harbor, by a
heroic naval artist with a shell-torn arm.

Thus far, LePeters had not witnessed the spectacle of his
daughter in direct physical contact with spades. Unwilling to
see her stroll out of the school in a river of them, he waited
for her now in the abandoned railroad yard; leaning on the
rotted husk of an old Buick, he was able to pretend for the
moment she was going to a normal school, like millions of
other American kids.

"How'd it go, sweetheart," he said to her, when she had
finally appeared. He checked her quickly for colored damage,
but she seemed to have come off all right. He inhaled around
her neck, too, instantly ashamed of himself for doing so, but
it was important for him to know if she had picked up a
Negro smell. All he could detect was a special russet-colored
fall fragrance she got each year just before the leaves came
down; that, and perhaps the slightest hint of the wonderful
corridor cleanser he had detected on his way to the principal's office. Had they given her a quick scrubbing down during recess to calm his fears and throw him off?

"A girl named Samantha burped on my books," she said,
tiptoeing along slices of railroad track.

"It could have happened anywhere," said LePeters, much
louder than necessary. "I don't care what kind of school you
were in. It could've happened in your finest private classroom. That's kids and that's America."

"I know, Daddy, except that I wish she'd stop."

"I'll take care of that," said LePeters. He would, too.
Armed with some very real fuel, for the moment he felt
strong enough to barge right into the Nathan Hale room and

drop it right in the elders' lap. "I'm not in here for spades," he'd say. "It has nothing to do with that. I just want my daughter out of the kind of school where they tolerate such a thing as book-burping."

"They give you any math?" he asked, gently easing her off the subject.

"Just stuff I knew," she said.

LePeters wasn't surprised. Even though she had attended only homicidally inferior schools of the West, it would take the colored school with its colored math at least three years to catch up to her level. Still, maybe that wasn't so bad. Standing out, as she obviously must, would give her a comfortable edge, an extra lock of confidence she might parlay into mastering tricky situations all through life. Perhaps she would be able to see all of life's difficulties as just a lot of easy colored math.

Strolling through the town proper of Detectives' Hill, they kept reaching out and touching each other, something they had done for years; in no sense were they intimate touches, but more along the lines of reassurance that each was still there and had not gone up in smoke. LePeters was fiercely protective of his daughter and for some reason thought now of her pathetic coin collection. There were few things that could drive him to violence, but if anyone were to touch it or steal it he would immediately get guns and come out killing. In a sense, he hoped someone would just try to steal a few so he could show how much he loved her by shooting the thief full of holes. But then he had a terrible vision of himself, hungry, destitute, taking the coins himself. Or even worse, not hungry, not destitute, but cashing in the poor coins to spend on a tropical vacation with a girl, a young secretary who had temporarily mesmerized him with a British accent.

What kind of terrible person was he to have such visions, he thought, and tried to tear them from his head.

Just outside the Negro-owned greeting card store, a colored child twirled himself on the patriotically wreathed parking meter and said, "Hi, Jamie."

"Lo, Edward," she said, as though he were a normal child. LePeters winced at his first eyewitness verification that his daughter was really in direct close personal contact with colored kids. Up until now, he knew only that the school was colored, that she was inside it, but there was a dreamlike possibility that they had put her in a special fenced-off capsule of whiteness.

"Seems like a nice kid," said LePeters, hurrying her along. He was somewhat surprised how casually she'd accepted being thrown into a colored world, but not entirely; children were like that. Glacierlike in her exterior, it would probably run bubbling through her blood and come out years later, hands clutching at the headboard of an antique brass bed, eyes hollow and starved, in puzzled search of a first orgasm.

Clear of the town now, Jamie LePeters began to run up the steep shinbone of a hill that led to their sun-dazzled house at the peak. Somehow it was homier now, open-faced, comfortable, its ridiculous price tag no longer a mystery. LePeters ran alongside her for a while, cheerfully confident about his heart. Cancer-shy and stroke-wary, he never gave that one organ a second thought, considering it tough as nails and good for at least a century if he could stave off other bodily misfortunes. As they neared his house, his daughter broke clear of him, and he took this well, too. If she had been a son, able to sprint out in front in that manner, he knew full well one part of him would have hoped for a complete stumble. He was terribly pleased to have a daughter and wanted to get

to the point where he would be off on business in Africa for
several years and then return to find her full-grown, ready for
love, and anxious to sit in elegant restaurants with her wandering roué dad and be filled in on wines with gray-haired
world-wise winks and chuckles. That would be quite a leap,
he thought, considering that at present he was a lesser dick in
a homicide bureau and his daughter alone in a jungle of
spades. Still, it was possible; he had a tough heart. Playing for
a last-place club, all he had to do was make his move. The
season was young, the pennant far off.

Watching his daughter skip through the front door, it
seemed that something about her was different. Blurred by
the hilltop sun, her bones seemed to have been reshuffled.
Had she become gangling and high-rumped in the Watusi
style? The very thought buried him hopelessly in the league
cellar.

Like a tripped landmine, Claire LePeters flew out at her husband as he walked through the door, and asked, "You get her
out all right?," then strolled to the window and reflexively
checked the horizon for low-flying Russian bombers. In the
years before he met her, she had logged half a dozen seasons
as a ground observer in a small northwestern town, filling in a
gap in the country's defense perimeter, while Pentagon sci-
entists struggled to make radar beams more low-slung and
flexible. These had been the blushed and golden formative
years of her teens and early twenties, which she had wrapped
in a parcel and handed over to her country, no questions
asked. LePeters wondered whether all those nine-to-five
shifts in lonely eyries, waiting coiled and tense for Red
bombers that never showed, had not contributed to a general

wired-up surliness in her makeup. He often felt that if only one Soviet bomber had wandered off course and appeared in view, it would have broken the floodgates of her tension, making her an entirely different person, much easier to live with. But would she be living with him? As an openhearted, easygoing girl, perhaps she never would have left her northwestern home to trail a lowly lieutenant, Sussman at the time, on a homicidal odyssey across the nation.

She was a tall and fair-skinned woman, rather plain-looking until those certain times when a blushed and oblique prettiness fell upon her, slanting across her face like a sudden lightbeam through a narrow windowpane. Bewildered, she would twirl about as though she were under attack.

"I couldn't budge the elders," LePeters said to her, "but I checked around; they've got a good staff and I assure you she's safe. The cleanliness in those halls would make you faint dead away."

"In other words, you're just letting her stay there with niggers, the only white child and it has to be mine."

"Shhhh," said LePeters, putting his hand over her mouth and checking to make sure the child was out of sight. He dreamed of fights starting that way, LePeters covering her mouth, his wife chewing his fingers, little growling nibbling bites; slowly they would up the erotic ante, and it would end in starved and frenzied bedroom madness—but for a long time it hadn't once gone that way for him.

"I don't like that word," he said. "You want to just introduce words like that in a marriage, out of the clear blue sky? I didn't say I'm letting her stay there. I just said there's no emergency. They got a helluva staff down there and when you look at them you see that they're just little kids."

"Little niggers."

"That's what you saw," said LePeters. "I saw kids of every

kind. There's a terrific little white girl from Germany I spotted in the principal's office. Take my word for it, there's enough money in the family to have sent her to the finest schools. Yet which one did they pick? I think there are a few sons of Indian diplomats down there, too.

"I really like this," he said. "You come from the West where they never had a colored person and suddenly you're hollering niggers. Since when do you know niggers?"

"I know shit," she said with more weariness than contempt. "That's one subject no one can lecture me about."

Years of living in a homicidal world had made Claire LePeters wary of going into halls and rooms alone, even when the house was filled with company. Now, as she went upstairs to bathe her daughter, LePeters roamed up ahead in a clear-and-hold operation, hollering out okays every few feet along the way. He went into his bedroom and idly began to sort his socks; although he had a bushelful of black detective anklets to work with, the most he could ever come up with in an evening was three matched-up pairs. Although she had fought him with a certain ferocity, she had never really gone for his throat and it was small potatoes compared to the anger of which she was capable. He'd calmed her down a little, but had he really calmed himself? He thought about private school, a murderous proposition on dick's pay, particularly since he had saddled himself with the expensive Croat house. Yet he knew that if he really wanted his daughter out of there, he would work nights as a private dick, much as he hated it, do anything, really, to get the money. In truth, he hated having her in there as much as his wife did, maybe more—colored smells, colored snot, colored God knows what else. Yet he could not bring himself to yank her out. It was not just a question of being paralyzed by indecision—he was a master of that game and would have spotted it a mile off. It was something more, buried in the rubble of his mind, that he hadn't bent down to pick around for. Elbow-deep in detective anklets, LePeters heard a buzz on the elaborately rigged-up intercom. Anxious to keep tabs on one another, the clannish Croats had turned the house into a wonderland of communications, making it possible to check on one another in its deepest reaches.

"Ken?"

"Yes."

"Come down and see a souvenir your daughter brought home from school."

Lost in a massive bathtowel, Jamie LePeters stood knock-kneed and drowsy beside the tub, her face hazily soft and beautiful with hot-watered near-sleep.

"Show your father."

A perfect bracelet of tooth-marks, high on the shoulder, a good enough impression for use in dental lectures.

"Who gave that to you?" he asked.

"Samantha, the girl who burped on my books. I forgot to tell you about it."

"Have you seen enough?" said Claire LePeters. He felt sorry for her whenever she was bent over tubs. "Poisoned nigger bites on the first day of school."

"It looks worse than it really is," he said.

"Then why don't you get your goddamned ass down there if you love them so much and leave my daughter alone."

Many times LePeters had boasted of his wife's strength, the way she stood toe to toe with him, traded him curse for curse. "I'm married to a real broad," he would say with a certain pride. Yet one day a friend from the West Coast showed up with his new bride, a small blond girl, worshipful, clinging—and LePeters almost died.

"I'm taking her out," he said now. "I never said I wasn't. I just claim that it doesn't have to be eight thirty tomorrow morning. It's still no emergency."

Nevertheless he dawdled. Although he had been inside the school, somehow the memory of its antiseptic corridors filmed over in his mind and he was more frightened of it than ever. Each morning he would walk her to the very rim of the schoolgrounds, and then, with his eyes closed, toss her in. Afternoons, he would take off early and fish her out, giving her an immediate damage check and then carting her off in the squad—an armory of safety to make up for the unprotected hours—to buy her massive stuffed animals, huge, ridiculous hippos and mile-high giraffes. One argument to his wife was that the education part was all that mattered; the home took care of the social graces. At the slightest sign of a scholastic deficiency, out she would go. Still, he took no chances and sat with her at night, drilling her on Wisconsin dairy farms, the population of Canada, lengths of the world's great bridges, topping off evenings with music appreciation, an hour of listening to rare sonatas and checking to see if she could hum them a little. All the while, Claire LePeters existed in a state of cold fury. "I don't know," LePeters said one night, "I think she's doing rather well. When you consider how panicky we were."

"All I know," she said, "is that I've got one daughter and she goes to school with niggers and no one else's daughter does."

Only on weekends, with his child roaming the ultra-safe

streets with sons and daughters of white dicks, could LePeters pretend all was well and there was no crisis. Late one
Saturday afternoon, he sat outside on his steeply inclined
lawn, rocks propped beneath the lawnchair to keep him from
plummeting to the bottom, when he saw the FBI man in bermudas leading Jamie by the hand across the street. Immediately incensed, LePeters ran down the hill with fists clenched
and said quietly, "The very first thing is, I don't care what
she did, take your hands off her."

The fed chewed on the suggestion a moment, then in a rea-
sonable manner said, "All right. I just don't think she ought
to be going around the neighborhood talking the way she
does."

"Don't ever put your hands on her again," said LePeters.

Wet-lipped, neutral-eyed, the fed nodded almost sweetly
and said, "All right, Mr. LePeters," and walked off, minus
his usual swagger. Claire LePeters showed up suddenly beside her husband. The girl skipped past the two of them singing:

> "Jive-ass mutha-fuckah
> Jive-ass mutha-fuckah
> Suck your butt, suck your butt . . ."

"The school anthem?" asked Claire LePeters.

"It's just words," he said. "Sounds. What does she know
about them. I'd just like to see that sonofabitch put his
hands on her again."

"I like the times you pick to get tough," she said and took
her first steps up the sheer slope of their suburban lawn.

◉

Several weeks after the school term began, an invitation came for a combination cake sale and PTA meeting. "Maybe if we showed up we could help the situation," said LePeters. "We never took an interest in these things."

"I'll go," said his wife. "Just get me a gas mask, and I'll be right at your side. That's just what I'm in the mood for, a little nigger cake."

The night of the meeting, LePeters went alone, pausing beneath the cold light of a bulletin board outside, still a little afraid of the school even though he'd walked its sterilized corridors. Huddled, shadowy figures carrying shopping bags walked through the front door on weary, spreading feet. LePeters strained his eyes, looking for white faces, the Dachau dad, perhaps a revitalized Mendelowitz. If a cluster of whites showed up, he would sail right into their midst and go right in with them. A taxi rolled up finally with, miracle of miracles, Mendelowitz holding an armload of new charts, not as large as the zoning ones, but more of them and each having a certain testiness to it.

"Let's go," Mendelowitz said, eager this time to have Le-Peters at his side. The two charged forward, LePeters feeling militant and dicklike, as though he were breezing in to make an easy pinch. Once again, as soon as LePeters got inside the building, his terror faded. In the auditorium, the meeting had already begun with five small colored children singing "Fly Me to the Moon," four of them routine, but one with a proud, rhythmic, deep-souled growl of a voice, heartbreaking at eight, good enough then and there to plunge right into show business. In the rear, a slender Negro with a fat man's head, prowled back and forth on drunken legs, hands clasped behind his back in the diplomatic style, stopping now and then to point to a choir child and say, "Now I know where she go. Now I know where she *at*." The other Negroes shushed him down with cries of "Shame." LePeters scanned the audience for white faces; he and Mendelowitz seemed to be the only ones, except for a classily dressed ascotted man in the front row who was more or less on the fence, colorwise, perhaps an Indian diplomat after all. LePeters savored the look of him, ammunition against his wife. When the singing was over, a pale-skinned man with rimless glasses swept forth and monotonously began to defend the Detectives' Hill school budget. He wore his dyed hair flatly slicked on his head like a single sheet of black wallpaper and droned out figures, allocations, disbursements, tertiary audits. It's lucky I'm here, LePeters thought. Otherwise he'd be cramming crooked figures down the throats of a bunch of poor spades. Maybe that's why he allowed his daughter to be dipped each day in spaded waters. Someone had to. But what did he know about budgets and allocations? When it came to tertiary audits, he was just another spade. He looked over at Mendelowitz who seemed poised, waiting to make his move, to pick his spot. Finally, the speaker said "conduits" and LePeters was thrilled to see the tycoon leap to his feet, shouting "Aha!"

"Aha, what?" asked the speaker.

"The conduits," said Mendelowitz. "Where do they go?"

"You want me to trace each conduit?" asked the speaker. "It would take all night."

"We got lots of time, haven't we, folks?" said Mendelowitz, sweeping his arm out to the assembled Negroes.

"Amen, brother," they said with heavy arms folded and sullen, righteous cranks of the head.

For the next several hours, the speaker sailed down conduits, Mendelowitz glued to his side, using his charts for a paddle. Each time they rounded a tricky bend, the two were at each others' throats; sometimes the audience Negroes backed up Mendelowitz, grunting "Sho" when he made a point; other times, to LePeters's amazement, they begrudgingly threw their support to the crafty school official. On and on through the night, they dueled on financial waters, Mendelowitz hurling out budgetary torpedoes while the school official shrewdly dodged about, failing to present his stern. In the front row sat a woman with crossed and swollen arms, and a button on her chest that said "Clarissa." For hours she'd sat without moving a hair, studying the speakers as they railed at one another. Finally she said, "They wastin' my fuckin' time," and got up to go. Many of the other Negroes got up and followed her out, their arms mysteriously crossed, too, as they paraded down the aisles. When the auditorium had emptied out, Mendelowitz charged forward to congratulate the school official, as though after a briskly fought tennis match. With one arm around the man, the tycoon said, "We're more or less on the same team." LePeters walked out by himself, a little disappointed that he hadn't gotten a shot at the cake. He had been anxious to sample a slice, actually to see if it tasted colored. Pleased that he had gone to the meeting, he wondered if he could honestly say he had helped forward his daughter's education. And what would he be able to bring back to tell his wife who was understandably upset about her daughter's unique situation? That colored parents were more concerned about budgets than whites? "You should have seen them," he would say, "fighting tooth and nail over allocations, looking into every dime. Down at the white school, they're probably relaxed and let every goddamned thing slide right through."

The instant he walked outside, he was afraid of the school all over again. The Negroes had scattered, groups of them climbing into old Packards. Though it was close to midnight, LePeters was reluctant to go home. His wife would be sleeping all the way over to one side of the bed, half of her dangling off the side as though to sprint off if he touched her. He wondered how she could sleep, dangling that way. She wore tight, constricting pants at night, too, a few sizes too small. He wondered if she masturbated. Years back, her coiled and whiplike intensity had taken the attractive shape of a frenzied sexual storm, sweeping away everything in its path, including LePeters. Once, when he was standing in a lonely eyrie with her, helping her watch for Red bombers, she had gnawed at him like a locust while he took the watch. Their way of sex, even then, was for one of them to gnaw and grind away, the other quiet, pretending not to be there, taking turns in that manner. Sometimes, signals crossed, they would collide in passion and look at each other in alarm and surprise as if to say, "You didn't tell me you'd be here." One night, he asked her if she ever touched herself and she had wheeled around, unable to catch her breath, her face a smear of angry tears. . . .

Now alone in the colored yard, LePeters walked up to the bulletin board and, in the cold, smoked schoolyard light, read a proclamation:

In an effort to forestall an epidemic of worms, each Low School parent is hereby instructed to implement upon his child a weekly rectal check, in order to ascertain early evidence of this condition. Cooperation is heartily endorsed by
Yours respectfully
The Elders

He had to reach up on tiptoes to read the announcement and wondered why it had been posted so high off the ground. Many of the colored parents were squat, had weary feet, and were hardly spry. They would have to lift one another up to get a good look at the announcement. Coming down on his heels, he felt a twinge beneath his legs unlike any sensation he had ever experienced. He paid only small attention to it until he started to walk; each step was like the breaking of great hot bulbs against his groin.

Hands were on him, tender and blistered, Negroes from a slow-ignition Packard.

"Somebody whomp him upside the head."

"No, he be from the cake sale."

"Where he live at?"

LePeters said he lived nearby, but that if they didn't mind to please call Detective Teener in the Thirty-eighth Precinct. He pointed to a police phone, attached to a telephone pole, and said it was all right to use it, not to be afraid, he was a dick.

"I ain't fuckin' with no poh-lice," said one.

"His chile go to your chile school," said the woman with the Clarissa button. Though her voice was gentle, in the cold schoolyard light her face seemed sullen, frightened, gray with bitter suspicion. Comfortable as long as he didn't move, Le-Peters watched her waddle off to make the call. The thought of being taken to his home never crossed his mind as a possibility. This was no time to be carted in by spades, broken-balled. Waiting on the sidewalk, LePeters chatted amiably with one of the Negro parents, a man with a beautifully clipped beard who carried a cane and aside from his color seemed in his erect stance, remarkably like a British colonial officer.

"They're doing a helluva job on the kids down here," said LePeters.

"That's right, they is."

"I can't think of anything they've overlooked."

"You ain't shittin' . . ."

Though he fell right in line with everything LePeters said,

the colonial stood up testily to his wife, the woman named Clarissa. An argument raged over the colonial's brother, a man who shined shoes, but only on the consideration that they be off the owner's feet. The woman said that considering the size of the family he had to support, he ought to toss away his pride and shine them off or on. The colonial backed up his independent brother, admitting that shining them only off cut down the volume of business, but in the overall, it was a neater, less distracting operation. "And say there panty-bloomers up top that shoe, how he going to concentrate. Go 'head, answer me that." The woman made a face and he said, "There your answer. He be trying to slick that shoe and all the while he be concentrating on her natural born ass. That's why he better working *off* the feet."

LePeters wanted no part of the argument, yet paralyzed, lightning ready to strike his groin again, he was imprisoned between them and felt compelled to join in. Taking up the woman's side, he said, "It seems to me it would be easier to keep a shoe steady if it were on somebody's foot." But the second he said it, he was ashamed of himself for joining in their pathetic argument of issues that were far out of his domain.

Much later, a squad slipped in quietly beside them, and before LePeters could find his voice, Teener and the towering Gibney, both working night shifts, poured out with guns raised, ready to cut down the cake-sale Negroes if they so much as moved a muscle.

"You're missing the point," LePeters said from the ground. "They helped me. My kid goes to school down here and I got a twinge as I was reading the bulletin board."

Teener tucked his gun away and with great charm apologized to the woman named Clarissa. "I'm deeply sorry for any inconvenience caused, madame," he said, with a sweeping bow, his behavior a far cry from the old days, before he'd become bullet-whittled and would have shot first and asked questions later.

Gibney, who'd appeared in violence, falling across the yard like a telephone pole, knelt beside LePeters, gentle now, a dick helping another dick, and asked, "Have you notified your loved ones?"

LePeters said no, but he preferred to hold off until he found out exactly what had gone wrong. The Negroes looked on forlornly as Gibney helped LePeters into the squad, Teener going along to offer token assistance; LePeters felt he might be dealing the black people a racial slap in the face; perhaps he ought to be going off with them to a colored hospital and be given a root cure instead of throwing in his lot with detective medication.

It was understood by the trio that LePeters would be wheeled off to an old and massive institution in the city, a favorite of the dicks and called in crime-fighting circles "Detectives' Hospital." Gibney said that if he ever had a bullet lodged dangerously close to his brain, he hoped he would be taken there where they knew how to deal with such things. As they approached the city, Teener's eyes began to jiggle about in his head and he asked LePeters, "Are you *sure* you want to go to Detectives' Hospital and not somewhere else just as good." LePeters saw no reason not to go; he was, after all, some kind of dick and even though he had not actually been bullet-riddled, the heavy saddlebagged feeling in his groin was not something he had invented. For the rest of the ride, LePeters could not find Teener's eyes. The tiny detective twitched about nervously and seemed to perspire for the first time. This was certainly dangerous for his internal mechanisms, yet on the other hand, perhaps it was a good sign, indicating that some of his glandular functions were in good working order. As they rolled into the admissions room, a nurse breezed by the agonized LePeters and hollered, "Detective Teener's here, everybody." Soon a great thicket of nurses and orderlies gathered round, plucking at him as though he were a commencement boy. "This is why I hate to come back to this place," he whispered to LePeters, at the same time flashing a strained smile at the group around him. The crowd parted for a beaming doctor who strolled in, clasped his hands together, and said, "My God, when I think of the mess he was when they brought him in here. Not much more than a little puddle, was he, girls? And look at the way he gets around now." Evidently, Teener had been the most difficult case in the hospital's history and each of the personnel was terribly proud of him. Each had a hand in turning him into an admittedly tiny yet completely functioning little human being. Still, LePeters thought it was shameful that they never let him forget it and made such a fuss over him.

"For Christ's sake," he said. "Give him some air. Don't you see you're embarrassing the hell out of him."

The crowd broke up and LePeters felt proud of the strength in his voice, doubly so because of his yet undiagnosed, mysterious, and, on occasion, fiercely painful ailment. In the car, for a time, he'd felt sorry for himself, a broken-nutted lesser dick with a spade-engulfed daughter, fleeing in terror from his wife. His positive action in defending his friend restored some of his confidence, in spite of the unknown medical terrors that lay ahead.

The doctor tore off a thinly polite smile and said, "What seems to be your difficulty?"

"I'm a detective, but I wasn't shot or anything. I was stretching and felt something give in my groin area."

The doctor told a nurse, all right, admit him, and walked off. LePeters thought they had better not be getting any gadgets ready and they also better make sure they knew what they were doing before slipping one in or he'd raise the roof and sue their asses off. Actually, if he were backed to the wall, he would not have minded having one attached if it were out where he could see it. But internals, carrying on where he couldn't watch them every second, were totally out of the question.

Teener produced a card and proudly told the admissions nurse, "I'd like everything on here, if you please," but the nurse without even checking told him politely that his hospital credit card had long expired. Embarrassed again, the little man said to LePeters, "Don't worry, when you get out of here, I'll buy you one of the greatest lunches in history, at any restaurant of your choosing."

LePeters said for Christ's sakes, to stop thanking him, a friend was a friend. "The boys will all be rooting for you," said Gibney, with his hat in his hand. When the two detectives left, the admissions nurse, in a new procedure, took prints of every kind—fingerprints, footprints, voice prints, and odor prints, produced by a bellows-like machine tucked up against one of his armpits.

"We love that little buddy of yours," said the nurse as she wheeled LePeters up to the ward. "He was the most cooperative little devil, although I guess he didn't have much choice considering the mess he was. Still, each of us had a hand in making him what he is today, and we're all proud of it."

"All I was saying is that you shouldn't embarrass him that way," said LePeters.

"You're one of the surly ones, aren't you," said the nurse, boosting him onto the bed.

Though it was late and the light was dim, LePeters could make out eight beds in the ward with a single TV set in the corner. Two elderly nightgowned patients were in a fierce wrangle over which channel to turn to. Afraid to get out of bed, LePeters leaned forward and shushed them down, saying, "Leave his on awhile, then turn to yours." Both appeared to be at death's door and LePeters thought they were insane to be using up their wizened reservoirs of strength in a senseless video debate. A lovely Swedish nurse, blond and braided, switched on an individual light, stripped LePeters down, and began to give him a tantalizing alcohol wash. She had a mysterious curve to her smile, and the cloth, edging closer to the source of his torment, was like a Scandinavian mouth. LePeters closed his eyes and wondered: Is it possible? Is it really going to happen? Then, as the cloth licked almost upon him, she tossed it to him and said, "I know what you want. Here, finish it yourself." LePeters, who had not been rakish for a long time, untypically said, "I'm weak as hell. But couldn't you, in the finest tradition of the nursing ideal, finish up for me."

"Screw off," she said, flicking off the light. A bit later, Teener's doctor arrived and LePeters, certain he'd be miffed by his downstairs defense of the little detective, perhaps employing radical techniques to get even, took a tough, what-the-hell attitude. "I know you're probably sore about what went on down there," he said, "but I acted in what I thought was my friend's best interests. I don't need any kindness or pats on the head. All I want is your medical skills, which I understand are formidable. I'm not afraid of anything you've got here, only check with me before you slip any of those newly developed gadgets in me."

"All right," said the doctor, evenly, not backing up, but not moving forward either. He examined LePeters briskly, then said, "I find you herniated and recommend attending to it first thing in the morning."

"So be it," said LePeters.

As soon as the doctor left, the Swedish nurse brought in a steaming tray of gourmet dishes, each one marked with a label: *Canapés Marquis à la Marguery, Bisque aux Oeufs Biarritz, Enchiladas Monterey, Salade Cathay*. At a signal, two other nurses breezed in from opposite directions with a dessert option of either *Cassata Permitana* or cupcakes with *Sauce à la Belle Indienne*. LePeters, who wasn't starved but could have used a cheeseburger, asked what was going on. The Swedish nurse pulled out a little card in her apron, then stamped her foot and said, "Oh shit" and admitted she'd mistakenly brought in the Hopeless Menu, an all-stops-out banquet for people with inoperable tumors.

"That's some goddamned mistake," said LePeters. "What if I just had to lie here wondering why you were giving me these things."

The nurse seemed shaken by her mistake and LePeters enjoyed having her on the run, wondering if he could parlay it into the complete rubdown he'd had in mind before. But he pulled in the reins and said, "All right, forget it. As long as you brought it, I might as well nibble on a few things." He gave her an avuncular tap on her behind which she accepted almost gratefully, a small price considering the enormity of her foul-up. When she left, LePeters nibbled warily, finally shoved the tray aside, afraid he would pick up a tumor if he stuffed himself. An old lady limped by in the corridor, peered in at LePeters, and said, "I finally read it and after the first few pages I threw it in the trash. You ought to be ashamed, penning such garbage." For a moment, LePeters felt amazingly guilty, sorry for the outrage he'd perpetrated. "And worst of all, it's against my people," said the crone. Recovering, LePeters thought, You can't argue with a crazy person, and said, "Millions loved it," then turned away and let her limp on, still outraged. Wide awake in the darkness, LePeters was able to make out the form of a white-mufflered man in the opposite aisle with a girl seated on his bed, climbing all over him with spidery caresses. For a moment he thought it might be the man who'd been thrown through the window at Ululu's, surgically collared up, his head tacked on by a slender thread. If so, his friend was probably the lovely clit girl, proving her sympathy by strapping herself to his side, loving his head back on. He wondered how they were able to get by the regulations, a girl in the ward all night, although he had to admit they were certainly quiet about it.

More wide awake than ever, and jealous of the clit girl, attached to the patient like a compress, he thought of sedatives and wondered if the doctor had not interpreted his tough stand as meaning he wanted no medications whatever, at the most a bullet to chew on during the hopefully minor surgery. If so, the doctor was certainly on the wrong track. Or perhaps the doctor, seeking revenge, had given him a reverse sedative, one that would turn him into the most wide-awake fellow in history through the surgery, making the minor sew-up comparable in terror to an eleven-hour open-heart marathon in a Leningrad lab. But then sleep came, like a blow on the head, the pill obviously tucked discreetly away in the *Enchiladas Monterey*.

It's all over, LePeters thought with joy as he awakened the next morning, but then he checked inside his gown and saw that not a finger had been laid on him. Still, he felt strangely light; the hospital with all of its surgical terrors was not nearly so violent as the world of homicide; herniated as he was, his wife could not, in fairness, expect him to do anything for the moment about his daughter's school. His limbs were springy and he wondered whether the Swedish nurse hadn't stolen in beside him during the night in a wonderfully openhearted dues-paying gesture. In good appetite, LePeters was slightly disappointed to see the nurse wheel in a lean, Spartan breakfast. Now that he was onto the Hopeless, and confident he was not considered to be within miles of that category, he would not have minded a shot at some of its early morning gourmet delights.

LePeters looked across the aisle and saw that the patient he'd wondered about was, indeed, the Ululu's window man. "Hi, there," he waved across.

"Hi, there yourself," the man waved back and thanked LePeters for helping him on the night he had been heaved through the nightclub windowpane. Then a cloud passed over his face. "You know I'm ashamed to show my face in that place," he said.

"You mean you want to go back?"

"How the hell can I?" he asked. "Once you pull something like that you're on Ululu's list and you never get a table as long as you live."

"I think you're crazy," said LePeters. "You could have been killed. If I were you, I'd stay a million miles away from there. How do you know it won't happen again, worse."

The man plunged his head into his hands. "I'm nothing without that place," he said. "And now I can't go."

◉

Though the man had collapsed in grief, LePeters couldn't resist asking him whether he'd had a girl with him the night before.

"Couple of actress friends," said the man, raising his collared head weakly.

LePeters thought sure then the man was crazy. With actress friends willing to love-spider him from dusk to dawn, and all the many places in the city to go, he had to insist on

one in which he had been cut to ribbons. Taking his eyes
from the man, LePeters wondered if he still wore the heavy
saddlebags; the schoolyard sensation blinked on and off like
an old traffic light, red for pain, green for clear sailing. In any
case, he was still bagged and wondered why the doctor
had not given the go-ahead on remedial procedures. As
though wired in on his thoughts, the Swedish nurse rolled
in and began to lather him up for a pubic shave. Lying back
in regal luxury, LePeters thought, at the moment, it was
easily worth a little minor surgery to get a Swedish lathering.
But then it occurred to him that there were millions of men
all over America who were being lathered in the normal
course of their workaday lives and didn't have to be wheeled
into surgery as the price of a good time. He felt a little sorry
for himself and promised finally to have a confrontation with
his wife, telling her to quit dangling from the far edge of the
bed, to come over to his side or at least meet him in the
middle, otherwise he would round up girls who would. Of
course, it couldn't have been any fun for her either, leading a
starved and dangling sex life. LePeters told the Scandinavian
girl she was easily pretty enough to be on magazine covers;
though she had been sitting quietly at the side of the bed,
legs plumply crossed, a sweet look on her face, she suddenly
wheeled about, angrily revealing far-from-perfect features
that would certainly collapse under the harsh scrutiny of
fashion-photographer strobes. "All right," she said, "get me
on one." Totally unprepared for the savagery of her response,
LePeters, in a thin voice, said, "I'll talk to some of my con-
tacts in publishing." Slowly regaining her composure, the red-
faced nurse sloshed him about in a quiet way until Teener's
doctor came in and said, "Towel him down, the deal's off."

"Phony bastard," the nurse said to LePeters as she dried
off the suds and then left in a huff. LePeters was amazed he

could ever have considered her face lovely enough to adorn covers of national magazines, locked as they were in fierce circulation battles. Fearing a misunderstanding on the doctor's part, LePeters said, "It isn't what you think. I never touched her although if you're looking for wild goings-on, you might put your head in here after dark when everyone's supposed to be sleeping."

Detecting a lack of interest on the doctor's part, LePeters said, "What do you mean, the deal's off?"

In a confession that struck LePeters as being remarkable in its candor, Dr. Jastro said that he had once been a real estate shark, known for his shrewdness in putting over fast-buck deals; only late in life had he undergone a massive conscience attack and switched over to the study and practice of medicine. Jastro admitted, however, that he still had some of the old vulturelike real estate hustle in him. Fast pitch, quick sale, turnover and on to the next pigeon. "Quite frankly," he said, "I may have tried to hustle you into an operation you really didn't need. But I'll be damned if I'll tolerate that in myself or in anyone I know. You're far from being in great shape, but I'm not cutting."

Though he admired the doctor's integrity, LePeters, in one quarter of himself, was a little disappointed. He had gone this far down the line toward the knife, why pull back now. Besides, he was counting on the recuperation period as a neat way to get away from his life, to think about the black school, to piece things together away from the violent world of homicide. Now he would have to dive right in, crotch pain and all.

"So that's it, eh," he said wearily. "Anything I should or shouldn't do?"

"Carry on as usual," said Dr. Jastro, suddenly hawk-faced

and talking out of the side of his mouth. "Only try like the dickens not to tilt."

Fat chance. He could follow instructions, walk the straight and narrow; but what if it was the world about him that did the tilting? He was sick to his stomach about his daughter's coal-black school; yet as a newly herniated fellow, never knowing when he would be hurled to the ground in pelvic agony, he felt more powerless that ever to do anything about it. Discharged now, he vowed to walk carefully, looking neither to the left nor the right, yet with his first steps, the ground beneath his feet seemed to angle off sharply, like the deck of a sinking liner. As he left the ward, a detective he didn't recognize, bullet-riddled, bleeding like a sieve, was being wheeled into surgery, pleading to have his Magnum .45 returned to him. Darkly handsome, he had the wet, limpid eyes of a killer, yet now they were filled with tears. Being taken off to face death, quite understandably he wanted a chance to protect himself, if necessary to shoot back. In the exit corridor, LePeters passed a room that said Violent Ward; a lovely socialite in expensive furs appeared, close enough for LePeters to smell peppermint-fresh breath; she must have been out on a frolicsome eight-hour pass and she stood on her toes, waving "Ciao, Benito" to a boyishly attractive lover, then was scooped up by two giant interns and carried off, heavy metal doors sliding behind her. Not a bad deal for Benito, LePeters thought, milking the juice of her capricious daytime pleasures, then letting the ward handle any irrational after-dark tantrums. Outside, tired hustlers in gray vultured droves circled glumly on the building limits, their aim evidently to grab up long-abstaining patients, newly sewn together, surging with new health. Teener and Gibney waited in a squad, and as they drove off slowly, Gibney pointed one out as Helena and said she was fond of detectives and liked to kid around by having them slip a pistol between her legs. "Loaded?" LePeters asked.

"Either way," said Gibney. Helena strolled by, faded and gold-toothed but with the remnants of a legendary body. "Like to crack some ice, boys," she said.

"We've hocked our pistols, haven't we, fellas," said Gibney, stopping the car. "Now beat it before I bust you, baby."

Still dangerously saddlebagged, and in no mood for lechery, LePeters was nevertheless fascinated by the hooker, particularly since he knew she had been thigh-gunned; he filed her away for future reference. "How does one keep one's wife from finding out?" asked Teener, more to himself than anyone. He had a troubled look on his face and his reaction to the faded joydoll interested LePeters who had always wondered about his friend's performance level, something to think about when you considered his machinelike predicament. Gibney stepped on the gas and LePeters thought back to the bullet-riddled dick who was being wheeled in for surgery, gunless and scared out of his wits. Almost as though his thinking had been broadcast on the police radio, Gibney said he had been having a hassle with his wife, who loved to go out to dances, certainly understandable when you considered the physical abuse she was taking in their crime-infested neighborhood. "Naturally, I don't move two steps without my hardware, and Peg's always complaining that when we dance close it more or less bruises her buns."

"Anyway," he said, opening his jacket, "we're going stepping tonight and I thought I'd come in with this. What do you think of 'er?" He showed LePeters a compromise gun;

encased as it was in a flowered evening holster, indeed it seemed small and polite, only medium deadly, capable of firing small, sociable, somewhat apologetic bullets.

"It's a good move," said LePeters. "I doubt she'll even feel it."

As they neared Detectives' Hill, LePeters thanked the two dicks and asked if he could please be dropped off a block or so from his house. "There's no need in frightening my wife," he said, but actually the short stroll was to test his hernia. First to greet him were the barracuda-like Kamchatkan poodles, wearing square metal boxes around their heads, like knight's armor, bigger than the poodles themselves; evidently the authorities had become tipped off to their ankle-slashing proclivities and decided to take action. LePeters's ancient rabbinical neighbor, with a body of legendary strength beneath his caftan, leaned across the fence and said, "How they hanging, Mr. Peters?" He wondered whether it was a casual remark, an attempt to bring his Talmudic past into line with the current beat or did he really know something about LePeters's condition? In that case his question could only be construed as random cruelty. Further along the road, the FBI man, giving his lawn a brisk crew cut, waved in a friendly manner and said, "Hope you're feeling in top shape." LePeters reflected on the irony of the two greetings. The ancient Talmudic scholar, a natural ally, had greeted him with crushing insensitivity; on the other hand, the federal agent, with a record of boorishness out to here, had crossed him up with kindness. At the door of his own home, Claire LePeters waited, edgy and nervous; starched and super-clean, a shower-taker who sometimes put in entire afternoons under the nozzle, she seemed nevertheless to have packed on an extra year of age overnight; and though he waited patiently, no beam of fresh midwestern beauty fell across her face, coming to the rescue. LePeters felt sorry for her and wondered if perhaps she needed him more than she realized. Maybe she felt she had pushed him into herniation. "I've got a great dinner ready," she said, and handed him a get-well card, one she hadn't had time to mail. It was a little on the formal side, the tenderest word being "dear," but still, it was a thought, and he melted. Though she kept her lips under wraps, he hugged her anyway and decided on the spot that if she ever had a slow-wasting disease, he would tend to her right to the end and never lay eyes on another broad until she was dead at least a year. In consideration of his hernia, she said "Jamie's been fine" and let it go at that, not a trace of spades in her voice. It made him feel like a heel and he flirted for a second with turning around and saying, "Look, you're right, I'm taking her the hell out of there tomorrow even if we have to teach her ourselves," but even if he had wanted to press it, it was the one button he could not find. Instead, he climbed to the second floor, taking the steps slowly, the worst enemy of herniated guys. His daughter was out playing in the neighborhood; over her bed was something new, a placard, saying "Welcome, Future Policewoman" above a picture of a rosy-cheeked youngster with whistle and club. In smaller type, down below, was a letter from Chief Guster, saying:

To be posted in the room of every progeny of a police officer and not to be taken down under any circumstances unless a written explanation form is filed with this department.

LePeters was terribly upset; hadn't his daughter enough
trouble keeping her head above water in a heavily spaded atmosphere? He had a vision of her now, fully grown, but with
a short dyke's haircut and stocky hips, giving out traffic tickets, then working undercover around public washrooms,
suckering sex offenders into indecent exposure. Where did
Radcliffe come into the picture and summers at the Sor-
bonne? He yanked the poster off the wall, but then he read
Chief Guster's message again and instead, shoved it way off
to the side behind her toybox, technically in her room but
where she would rarely if ever glance at the damned thing.

It was probably the same old homicide bureau, but limping
back this time, LePeters seemed to see it through smeared
glass, a dirty lens. In the hall, LePeters first ran into Detective Medici, holding a fat colored baby with fanged teeth and
a seemingly violent temperament. Craning his neck as
though on the lookout for infantile criminal activity, he
snapped his fangs in all directions, a dangerous, charmless tot
getting an early jump on homicide. "Ain't he cute," said the
proud Medici, showing him off to the other dicks. LePeters
extended his hand for a head pat and took two fangs in the
wrist. "Watch it there, boy," he said, yanking back his hand.
"Boy," said the enraged Medici, handing the baby to a passing dick, and feeling for one of his multiple guns. "He just
called my kid 'boy.' "
    "Not the way you think, for Christ's sakes," said LePeters.
"You ought to know I'm the last guy in the bureau to come
out with a racial epithet. I'll match my record against anybody. All I'm saying is that you ought to get him out of that

habit. For his own good. What if he were to bite a dog, for
Christ's sakes." Somewhat placated, the Negro detective
took his hand away from his holster. But LePeters wondered
whether deep in his heart, he had not indeed intended a
color slur after all. His nerves were probably cracking under
the strain of his daughter's enrollment in a coal-black educational institution. Making a silent promise to keep himself
in check, he met Medici soon after and maddeningly fell into
the trap again. Standing next to the dark sex-patroller at the
water fountain, LePeters sighed and said, "You know, I really
wouldn't mind carryin' my poor achin' feet on home."

Shaking his head with disbelief, Medici said, "What you
trying to say is you want me to take off my guns and go out
there in the alley with you. Is that it?"

"Never in a million years," said LePeters. "I know what
you're getting at, but believe me you're dead wrong. Try to
understand that I've been under a lot of strain lately, a new
hernia and a school problem, and as a result, all kinds of
things have been popping out of my mouth."

But his tongue kept playing tricks on him. "Frankly," Le-
Peters said, "I don't know where I'm at, sweetie-baby."
Medici took a long time to consider his next move. Finally he
hitched up his gunbelt and, with the smell of baby powder
on him, said, "Just watch your ass," and moved on. LePeters
recalled then that he had seen Medici good-naturedly exchanging racial slanders with other dicks.

Once, with a wink, he had heard Gibney say, "You know,
Medici, I wouldn't even really mind living next to you," to
which Medici good-naturedly responded, "You just after my
watermelon patch, babe." The secret was that Gibney and
Medici were both real dicks, brothers linked by a bond of
authentic homicidal fury. LePeters wore a baby badge and

had to remind himself that down at the core, he was no dick
at all.

Back in his office, LePeters noticed a sign on the bulletin
board:

> *Anyone caught making derogatory*
> *remarks about Detective LePeters's*
> *new hernia will be busted right*
> *down to patrol donkey.*
>
>   *Detective-Lieutenant Glober*

LePeters thought it was generous of his superior to think
of him. But was it, really? Maybe just being quiet would have
been a wiser course. In one sense, the announcement was a
bugle call, making his groin the center of a lot of unwanted
attention. LePeters thought he would talk it over with his
friend, Teener, but the tiny man seemed strangely aloof,
craning his head around nervously in a distant, private world.
LePeters's first feeling was one of anger. But he realized he
was overreacting. In his own mind, because of his friend's
size and mechanical makeup, he had not really assigned him
the right to have moods. But surely the tiny man still had
remnants of deep feelings and a perfect right to go into
harmless little tickered depressions just like anyone else. Perhaps the mood of the homicide bureau was catching up with
him. There had been a rash of unexplained, senseless homicides. Ordinarily, nine out of ten could be cleared on the
spot, a wino one block away with a dripping kitchen knife, a
dazed husband still standing over his wife's body with a
smoking gun. But the new ones that kept piling up were
clueless and unaccountably involved elderly men with grown
sons. Unable to stand up to the maddeningly sudden and

senseless shoot-ups, the sons kept calling up pitifully to ask, "Anything new on Dad's death?" One such grieving lad showed up regularly at the bullpen itself; one day, LePeters heard Gibney say to him, "If it's any consolation to you, kid, I know who killed your dad, only I'm not going to tell you." When the boy had left, LePeters, always wary about meddling in detective affairs, asked him, "How could you do that to the kid?"

"I got a pretty good hunch," said Gibney, "but not enough evidence to make a pinch. I figure I'll give the kid something to chew on."

"I don't see it that way," said LePeters. "I think it would be better to tell him nothing. This way he'll go crazy."

"Go fuck yourself," said Gibney, a remark that wounded LePeters terribly.

From long experience with homicide PR, LePeters knew that during a wave of uncleared homicides, his department would be the first to suffer; and sure enough the ax soon fell. LePeters caught the first hint of this when his immaculately laid-out clipping displays began to come back from Chief Guster's office with a note saying: "Don't bother me with this shit." Next to take it on the chin was *Bullet-In*, instructions rolling in to kill the red duotone that gave the pub its slick appearance. LePeters decided to tighten his belt and take it manfully. After all, physical composition was the last thing that made for greatness in a homicide sheet. He would ignore the handicap and work with more energy than ever, souping up the pale inferior-grade pages with whatever bold, fresh ideas he had on hand and bull his way through the economy wave. But there were other distractions. One day, Hortham of Micro-Analysis strolled by and told LePeters of a new weapon that had been picked up in a raid, one so complicated that no one in the department had yet been able

to figure out how to work it. "Hold on a second, I'll drag it
in." Hortham disappeared and soon came back shoving what
seemed to be a massive iron crab. LePeters thought he heard
a sound coming from the strange weapon but quickly realized
it was his friend Teener, ticking louder from the extra departmental pressure. "Fool around with it awhile," said
Hortham, "see what you think." LePeters walked up to the
fearsome weapon, but when Hortham went back to the lab,
he said the hell with it and returned to his desk. All through
the afternoon, he tried to work, but it was impossible to
concentrate and he kept peering over at the gun-crab to see if
it had moved. Once he touched it; it had the nyloned texture
of a great-snouted white marlin he remembered seeing on display at a Bahamian dock. He was amazed that Teener did not
seem to be in the least distracted, although when he thought
about it, his friend, of course, would indeed be fully accus-
tomed to complicated gadgetry. Finally, LePeters got up and
began to shove it back to the lab. For a moment, it seemed to
push back, but then finally he was able to move it along, pain
blinking in his crotch as he slid it down the hall. If it ever
went off, even one tentacle, it would probably blow him back
to the Far West. With one final shove, exhausted from nervous energy, he turned it back to Hortham.
    "You dope it out?" asked the lab man.
    "Not a nickel's worth," said LePeters. "If I were you, I'd
move it the hell out of here."

Since his hernia, LePeters rarely traveled far for his lunch
and took to eating in the detectives' cafeteria, situated in the
bureau basement and famed for its simple and honest fare—
beefed-up, thickly grueled soups designed to line a crimebus-

ter's stomach with homey energy; tough, springy meat patties
that would give a dick that extra bounce; pie slabs cut mas-
sively to anchor a man down during long investigations.
Nearby, and sharing the basement, was the detective firing
range; though LePeters had long gotten used to being sere-
naded by raucous bursts of lunchtime gunfire, he expected
one day to see a fusillade of bullets tear through the dessert
counter and hack down half a dozen of the bureau's finest
men in the flower of their careers. Only then, perhaps, would
the department see the folly of its building plan. On his first
post-herniated trip to the cafeteria, LePeters here, too, noticed a slight tilt in the atmosphere, a subtle change, although one that he alone seemed to respond to. In a policy
switch, paroled cons who had been working as waiters, had
all been tossed out, their places taken by an efficient team of
"oven faces," girls from a nearby home who had all at one
time been involved in various types of explosions. Hitherto
barred from public contact and no doubt grateful for the
chance at employment, the girls unquestionably performed
their jobs with more zest than the sluggish parolees. Some
had trim figures, bordering on the curvaceous, and leaped co-
quettishly out of the way as the good-natured dicks made
swipes at their behinds. LePeters's heart went out to them
and he was able to see the humaneness behind the new program; still he wondered about the advisability of allowing
them near food and found himself racing through his first
meal, anxious to tear back to his office and get to work. Polishing off an apple pie slab, he was soon joined by the puckish,
sharp-bellied Detective Flamoyan who had obviously read
and taken to heart Glober's hernia warning. "Not a word out
of my mouth about your nuts," he said, holding up a hand in
denial of mischief-making.

"I'm not that sensitive," said LePeters.

Flamoyan ordered some coffee from one of the girls and
got a courteous smile in return, stitched on and high to the
left. After a few sips he said, "Look, you remember the
trouble I've had coming up with a tag for you. Well, while
you were suffering in the hospital, it finally come to me, the
thing I couldn't put my finger on. Amazing how it's laying
right there under your nose and one don't see it."

LePeters sympathized and said he'd had the same sensation many times himself. "Anyway," said Flamoyan, dabbing
his lips and rising with regal majesty, "I have decided to call
you 'Izzie.' "

The name was ice water on LePeters's back. "I don't get
the connection," he said, but Flamoyan rose and began to
walk off in silence, a lord who had issued an irrevocable edict.
LePeters followed him out of the cafeteria, saying, "You just
pin something like that on a guy and check out with no explanation . . ."

"Take it easy, Iz boy," said Flamoyan, taking a satisfied
puff of a cigar and disappearing in the elevator. "I'M NOT
ACCEPTING IT," LePeters hollered out as the doors
closed. But LePeters indeed got the connection. It was an
extraordinary development. For eighteen years, he had kept
his Sussmaned past a secret, in many ways even to himself.
Unless his wife, acting under herniated stress, had irrationally phoned in the information, the only one who could possibly have blown the whistle was his boss, Glober, up until
now a model of discretion through all their years of hopping
from bureau to bureau. It was not a devastating blow, but
one he could easily have done without at the moment. He
saw, too, that he had made a mistake in getting flustered and
flying down the hall after Flamoyan. Perhaps the jokester
had been testing; if LePeters had been cool and simply answered back, "Fine, and I'll call you Irving," Flamoyan

would have seen he was on the wrong track. Now he knew he had struck paydirt and, before long, LePeters would be Izzied to death. He marveled at the skill of the detective in ferreting out his weak spot and then slamming him with it. Was it an instinctive feeling or was there something about his appearance that gave him away? LePeters went into the detective john and gave himself a thorough going-over, the first in a long time. He had taught himself to block out the scarred dividing line when looking into mirrors, to see the good in both sides and make believe it was all one big happy face. In the sallow light of the detective john, still smarting from Flamoyan's remark, it seemed to him that he looked a little Jewish on the left, although this was easily compensated for by what seemed to be a much larger Anglo-Saxon plain on the right.

But this was preposterous. Even Flamoyan, with his enormous thirst for insulting remarks, had no time to look for secret Semitic pockets on a man's face. Either it was a lucky stab, or Glober, in some inexplicable lapse of judgment, had spilled the beans.

Strangely unable to deal with his daughter's schooling, possessor now of an uncertain pelvis, LePeters felt that the last thing he needed at the moment was his old repudiated name, Sussman, bobbing to the surface. If Glober indeed had let it out of the bag, perhaps it was not too late for a retraction, although he was hard put to see exactly what form it would take. The following day, LePeters stood guard outside Glober's office, waiting for a chance to see him; at ten o'clock the door opened momentarily and LePeters thought he saw Sissy Glober in underwear perched cross-legged, in the Indian style, atop her father's desk while Glober studied her as though she were a new item of office equipment. LePeters

shut the door quickly and for a moment could feel only deep
pangs of erotic jealousy at the idea of having a lovely girl
right there in the typewriter position where you could reach
out at her with hardly a break in the workaday routine.
Shortly thereafter, the girl emerged, neatly coiffed and tailored, with no evidence of having dressed in a hurry. LePeters
was certain that what he had peered in on was simply a frank
father-daughter chat that he had seen in a tilted, badly fo-
cused manner. In a moment of harmless caprice, perhaps, she
had coltishly leaped up on her father's desk for a more trusting, head-on confrontation. Still, LePeters remembered her
C-8 pose and couldn't be sure. After waving his daughter off,
Glober tried to slip back to his office, but LePeters nailed
him and said he had urgent matters on his mind. Since coming east, Glober had picked up an ad-agency style. "I'll make
a rez," he said, "and we'll lunch it up." Locking the door
behind him, LePeters knew that once alone, Glober would
slap on colognes, arrange his hair in a casually rumpled style,
and then perhaps try to get in a quick session at the window,
spying on a corsetarium a block from the bureau.

As they strolled toward the restaurant, Glober said, "Look,
for Christ's sake, if it's about a girl, whatever you do, don't
break up your marriage."

"I wish that's what it was," said LePeters, whereupon
Glober told him about a wonderful nurse he had known
many years before who had almost come between him and
his wife. "As you know, Bess and I have stuck it out, and it
proved to be the wisest thing I ever did."

"But who knows," he said, as they neared the restaurant,
"maybe it wasn't. Therese was some girl. I'll never forget
her."

"Let's face it," he said, in a complete turnabout. "I did a

schmuck thing. I should have grabbed her and gotten the hell out of there while the getting was good."

The restaurant Glober picked was richly baronial, far from the bureau. By the time they got to it, Glober was sunk in depression about his lost love and called over a gypsy violinist, giving him a list of requests from half a dozen hit musical comedies of the past decade. As the violinist struck up a medley from the first show, Glober's eyes glazed over with the start of tears; it seemed a completely inappropriate time to talk about his own difficulties, and for the first half-dozen selections, LePeters kept a respectful silence. But halfway through "Wonderful Town," LePeters with some concern saw the entire lunch slipping away from him; touching his friend's forearm he said in a gentle voice, "I wonder if we could talk."

"Sure, Ken," said Glober. "But just remember, anytime you get a shot at happiness, grab it and run."

"That'll be enough, Carlos," he said, waving away the musician.

"Something's come up about my name," said LePeters. "It's been so long that you probably don't remember, but when we first met I was called Sussman."

"Of course I remember that."

"Check," LePeters said. "Well, anyway, it's a long dead and buried name, but I think it got out around the bureau and that's something I could really live without. Since you and Claire are the only ones who even know the name, I thought I'd mention it to you."

"And that's what you wanted to ask me about, is that it?"

"That's it."

"Let's order," said Glober, twirling his head suddenly and snapping his fingers for the maître d'. Patiently, LePeters sat by while Glober grandly ordered a seemingly endless list of exotic specialties.

"It's okay, because I plan to catch a light bite for dinner," he said.

"Okay, how about Sussman?" said LePeters. Glober suddenly ducked beneath the table, rustling around under the cloth for a while until LePeters, curious, joined him.

"I thought something was running around," said Glober. "I guess it was my imagination."

"I didn't see anything," said LePeters. "Not at a fine place like this. Listen, I have to put it right to you, did you say anything about my early name?"

"I may have," said Glober.

"What do you mean you may have? You either did or you didn't."

"All right, I did," said Glober, petulantly. "Are you happy now? Did you get what you want?"

"Then you did do it," said LePeters. Until this point, the idea of his boss and friend betraying him had only been the vaguest of notions, and in one sense, the luncheon had merely been a routine security check. The idea that after eighteen years Glober had suddenly and irrationally broken his confidence was beyond LePeters's comprehension. Adding to his astonishment was the fact that Glober now seemed annoyed at him.

"What in the hell did you do it for?" asked LePeters. "You know how touchy I am about the thing."

"I think you're crazy," said Glober. "You're much too sensitive about it."

"But don't you think it ought to be my decision? If I wanted to be Sussman, I'd have stayed Sussman. I'm LePeters now, for Christ's sakes, until you shot your mouth off."

"I don't think you're seeing it clearly," said Glober, starting his Clams Casino. "Listen, you have a point. I don't think we ought to discuss it now."

LePeters felt as though he were taking ineffectual punches at giant toy-store pandas. It crossed his mind, too, that perhaps there was some aspect of Glober's behavior he wasn't seeing clearly. Perhaps his boss had every right to come clean to the bureau about his employee's true identity. In spite of himself, LePeters began to nibble at his appetizer.

"I don't know, Bruno, I just think you should have asked me. How many people did you tell?"

"I can't remember," said Glober. "I sent out a few cards."

"Cards?" said LePeters. "What do you mean cards? Why did you do it that way?" The idea of small, expensively engraved Sussman announcements circulating through the bureau was maddening.

"All right," said Glober. "I admit it wasn't a wise idea, but it's done and I think you ought to go a little easier on me about it."

In a rush of self-pity, LePeters said, "Look, you've seen me limping around. One gust of wind catches me wrong and I'm wheeled into surgery. I've got a home situation with my wife that I don't want to go into at this particular lunch and the thing that's really driving me crazy is my daughter in a colored school. Even if I wanted to take her out, which I'm not sure of, I don't know where I'd get the money for private school. You know how they kid guys in the bureau. What in the hell did you have to pick this time to tell everyone that eighteen years ago I was Sussman." LePeters realized that he was throwing himself on Glober's mercy. But though the other man was taller, older, more successful, and possessor of a flinty, rocklike New England heritage, there was no one really there to throw himself at. Glober stretched his neck about, as though to catch glimpses of people in private restaurant booths, and then suddenly faced LePeters, his large blocked-off head streaked with sudden anguish.

"All right now, let me tell *you* something. A man stays in his office and keeps a chipper smile on his face and everyone thinks his life is rosy, right. Well, I'm through keeping up a facade and protecting the people around me. Eight years ago, I invested in a spice plant in the Carolinas, a can't-miss proposition recommended by the finest minds in the brokerage business. Well, two weeks ago, my agent calls and tells me that the goddamned thing is sinking into a swamp. Given every possible break in tax accounting, the best I can come out with is a ninety grand loss. That's if I'm lucky."

"You know what I earn?" asked LePeters.

"That's why you don't have this," said Glober. "This is big money I'm talking about."

Broken-balled, sexually starved, his daughter drowning in a messy school situation, and himself about to become the target of a wave of homicidal Jew-needles, LePeters nevertheless was confronted by a man about to lose a small slice of what was undoubtedly a massive fortune and asked to feel pity for him.

Strangely enough he did.

To his surprise, the torrent of departmental abuse never materialized. Flamoyan tried a few halfhearted mezuzah taunts, but along with the other dicks, he was too steeped in uncleared homicides to take time out for ethnic ribbing. One morning, Teener approached and said, "I just want to tell you I think your people are wonderful."

"What people is that?" asked LePeters.

"Your people," said Teener. "You know, the people of your heritage."

"I don't know what the fuck you're talking about," said LePeters, turning his back on the little man. All afternoon, he tried to keep up a spark of anger against the tiny man, but it was rough going. LePeters still felt the remark was in questionable taste: looked at another way, however, it was probably thrown out in a spirit of generosity. Late in the afternoon, LePeters couldn't contain his discomfort and hollered out, "I'm sorry I blew up. I just don't like to think of myself as having people. Anyway, your people are wonderful, too."

"I'm glad you come across with that remark," said Teener, who had obviously been stung. "And yours are *really* and *truly* wonderful."

Though his wife kept her school unhappiness on a low flame, LePeters, acting on his own steam, checked private schools in the area and found them all stuffed to the gills. Only one was a possibility, twenty-four miles from Detectives' Hill, and still under construction, although the headmistress assured LePeters that every effort was being made to rush it through to completion. One day LePeters waited for his daughter, far enough away from the Low School so that he couldn't see it at all; when his daughter came by in a swarm of pig-tailed colored girls, LePeters narrowed his eyes so that he could not quite see their faces and they looked like a happy multiracial group of the type seen on Brotherhood posters. Scooping up his daughter, he took her to his squad and the two drove out to the private school. The ride was through rich, greenery-laden country and the school itself was in a handsome estate

area, although LePeters, arriving at the site, couldn't see how
the builders could possibly finish it up in a day under two
years. At some future time the school would have a fine, rich
tradition, songs, flags, and statues of founders in secret arbor-
covered meeting places. But for the moment it was only a
series of great dirt pits, construction machinery standing
around idle and an occasional workman strolling along eating
a sandwich. As he parked the car, LePeters saw two little
white girls stroll by, arms around each other; that moment he
would have pledged away his next ten years' earnings to have
his daughter join them. An arm around her shoulder, he followed the strolling pair to the one existing building, a two-
story frame house that seemed to have been left over from
the torn-down estate and was obviously the classroom and
administrative building. Inside, two women waited, one
stocky, restless, bouncy on her toes, the other thin, unevenly
toothed, with yellow neurasthenic fingers she kept running
through her falling hair. "I'm Miss Latham, Danforth's headmistress," said the heavy-set woman, "and this is Miss Anthrina, our student dean." LePeters shook hands and presented his daughter who had brought along her guitar as evidence of varied cultural interests. LePeters asked her to play
a song and she did "Ferry Me Across the Water," strumming
the first half and then finishing up by plucking the strings
with her teeth, in the new style she had been taught by Ferrezano, the guitar teacher. She then produced her coin collection, LePeters feeling sorry at the moment he had not
really deprived himself and gotten her a few expensive cen-
tennial sets from newly emerging African countries. The
child then pulled out a furled-up drawing of a man holding
up a skyscraper and titled "Daddy." Embarrassed, LePeters
noticed that she had sketched in sex organs and with a
chuckle he took it back before the two officials could get a

good look. The headmistress, who had stood by with a patient smile, then said, "And now, Miss Anthrina will do the testing."

"You're not going to hurt me, are you?" asked Jamie LePeters, as she was led off to a separate room, to which the thin, nervous woman flashed a harsh, badly toothed smile back at LePeters.

Actually, LePeters was a little surprised they were going ahead with the test. The tuition was a couple of grand and considering the condition of the premises he would have thought they'd grab anyone, no questions asked. The headmistress stood opposite him, totally silent; a little edgy in her presence, LePeters said, "She's in a poverty school right now. I don't really care who goes there but I'd just as soon get her out until they do something about it."

Still facing him, the headmistress remained silent; LePeters was amazed at people who could tolerate long stretches with no conversation and chalked it up to some superior heritage. After fifteen minutes, the thin woman came out, holding his daughter's hand; going in, she had seemed shrill and abrasive. Now, she held his daughter in a tender, protective way.

"I'm terribly sorry, Mr. LePeters," said the woman. "But she could never keep up. She's at least a year and a half behind and it would just be a waste of everyone's time."

LePeters, startled at the rush of feelings that came over him, grabbed his daughter to him as though she had been in an accident. "Tell the truth," he said. "Is it because I'm a dick?" Unspoken was the thought that it might be something else in his background. His mother in the maid-recruiting business, his dead father's lowly furrier background. Was it conceivable that they had run a Sussman check?

"I assure you it's a purely academic decision," said the thin woman in a gentle voice, "for the child's own good."

"I'll tell you one thing," said LePeters, still hugging his daughter as though they were pedestrians in whizzing traffic. "She'll come out of this smarter than your whole school put together. I don't care what your tests show."

The headmistress remained silent, bouncing lightly on her toes. "The parents always feel terrible about this," said the thin woman, with what seemed to be genuine concern.

"Up your ass," LePeters said, but he kept it low, under his breath, so the child wouldn't hear him.

◉

Outside, in the construction area, a workman ate a hard-boiled egg, leaning on LePeters's squad. LePeters tore open his coat to show his badgette and said, "All right, move it, you bastard, or I'll lock you up."

"I've got orders that it's all right to do things like this," said the workman.

"Orders," said LePeters. "What orders?" But his daughter tugged at him and he got inside the car; the workman leaped aside and he tore out of the gate.

"I'm nauseous and why were you so mean," said his daughter.

"Daddies are when they're under pressure."

"Does this mean that I have to keep going to school with burnt toast?"

"Where'd you hear that?" asked LePeters.

"They call me white cracker so I made it up for them."

"The best thing is to ignore names, although I realize it's rough sailing."

"I don't know," he said a bit later, answering her question.

"Why don't you stick it out for a little while longer. They
look like a pretty good bunch of kids, very sensible. And Lord
knows the staff is probably one of the greatest in the country."

"Besides," he said, clinging to straws, "this early part
doesn't really matter. What counts is later on, when you get
into the college thing. That's really the whole number right
there."

Watching his daughter doze off, he felt as though a thick
net of sorrow had been dropped across the road and he were
driving through it. He wondered if the private school test
had not in some quiet way been wounding to her; to escape
she had gone racing into an anguished sleep. Surely she must
have sensed the contempt of the two teachers as she chewed
out a tune on her guitar and flashed her genital sketch. But
LePeters, to his amazement, noticed that a subtle change
had come over his sleeping daughter. Always marginally
sexed, even now she wore a Navy peajacket and a boy's base-
ball cap. But her high forehead and the giggling sweetness
about her mouth had taken on a new cast and LePeters was
confident she had been lifted gently but inescapably into the
female camp forever.

Inching his way painfully up to his high-peaked house, LePeters cursed the fates for not having made him a herniated fellow several months earlier. An uncertain pelvis would no
question have ruled out his purchase of the loftily situated
Croat dwelling; in turn, his daughter would have been comfortably situated in a snow-white classroom, wolfing down
first-rate education, not a spade within miles. That was no
bargain either, but at least then, with his daughter safe, he

might have felt like joining committees and arguing for a
sprinkling of colored children, easily as many as twenty per
cent, maybe more. At the top of the hill, his wife waited in a
skirt and blouse of blinding colors, like signal flags, visible for
miles. Years before, on her lonely Russian bomber-watches,
she had been required to wear graying, inconspicuous colors,
soft paisleys the brightest allowed. Now, as though to make
up for those camouflaged years, she put on skirts that dazzled
the senses, blouses capable of dealing out splitting head-
aches. It worked out well when she was gay, making her seem
a tasty tropical fruit salad. At other times, the colors served
only to call attention to her unhappiness, to fling her troubles
in LePeters's face. With his crotch blinking off warning signals, LePeters wondered what it was like for her, hanging
around all day in a high-peaked though furiously well-
protected home, waiting for a herniated pseudo-dick to roll
in the driveway. Though it was true she hid her lips and slept
dangling off the side of the bed in a sex-free zone, still she
stayed with him; a beautiful girl, one chamber of her seemed
confident that the rudderless LePeters, temporarily fenced in
but far from vanquished, would eventually chart a clear
course and lead the small family to glory. Had he ever shown
any equivalent trust in her? Years before, she had sung a few
notes over the phone to a talent agent and gotten a one-
month sight-unseen offer to travel the Rocky Mountain
states with a four-man combo led by a bass player named
Gomez. LePeters saw his wife becoming a tasty little treat
for the quartet and envisioned her being passed around from
musician to musician, Gomez getting the lion's share. Without waiting for the details, he torpedoed the plan. The turndown had come at a bad time for her and broken her wings.
Possibly, she had never forgiven him. Perhaps if he had let
her go, she would have charmed the Rocky Mountains, held

Gomez and the boys to a few late-night feels, and come home flushed with confidence, gratefully hurdling over to Le-Peters's side of the bed, maybe even pitching camp there for the rest of their days. And even if Gomez *had* slipped in for a tumble or two, by this time it would all have come out in the wash; and how puny it would have seemed vis-à-vis the life-time sense of triumph and fulfillment she would have acquired as a vocalist who had conquered the Rockies.

Waiting at the door, Claire LePeters said that their daughter's teacher had come to visit and was waiting inside. "You're the school expert," she said, with a wave toward the living room. "You handle it." Peering inside, LePeters saw that the teacher was a Negro and was angry at his wife for leaving him alone, but then calmed down when he noticed that she had at least offered him coffee and cake. Neatly dressed, the teacher seemed to be strangling in a tight white collar; he was terribly young, LePeters thought, a shade beyond his teens. He looked everywhere but straight ahead, some of his glances whizzing past LePeters's ears, none meeting his eyes.

"What's your name?" asked LePeters.

"Melvin," the man said, getting to his feet.

LePeters was crushed by the man's use of his first name in an introduction. Though awarded the rank of educator, evidently he still saw himself as a Red Cap or Western Union messenger boy. Small wonder Claire LePeters had fled. The thought of their daughter's precious educational future in the hands of a colored kid named Melvin, plagued by deep feelings of inadequacy, was too much for her. Still, the hang-up was a profound one, hardly the boy's fault, and LePeters took every precaution to be gentle, to avoid making it seem he was using a social edge.

"And I'm Ken," he said, shaking hands with the youthful educator and inviting him to sit down.

The teacher said he had been sent by the principal to rough in some of the areas that would be covered in the school year. "There was a feeling you'd be nervous," said the young man.

"Nonsense," said LePeters, holding up a hand in denial. "I liked the setup."

The teacher said they would be spending a great deal of time on the Founding Fathers, the writing of the Constitution, also furniture of the Georgian and Federal periods. Quickly setting up a slide projector and screen, he drew the blinds and showed LePeters color transparencies of decadent Italian castles built by doges, also handsome Louis XIV interiors. He switched slides then and LePeters thought he saw nude blonde volley-ball players with great figures. But it was actually a brilliantly carved winding staircase, gold-fleeced and fluted with a thousand piping cherubs. "This, of course, is my pride and joy," said the young man. "It's commonly thought to be the work of the Duke of Arvine. With the class's participation, I hope to demonstrate before we're through that it can be more accurately attributed to a hitherto unknown goldsmith named Lamento." LePeters wondered if Lamento were a colored guy. Also, if colored families were getting to see slides, too, or if it was a special show designed to throw the few white families off guard. "Then of course," said the teacher, "we cease all our other activities to spend a month on our term project. This year it's 'Paraguay, Past and Present.'" He switched off the projector and folded it into a preposterously tiny package. Still thinking of the private school, LePeters had listened only halfheartedly. But through his haze, it struck him that the young Negro had a

remarkable speaking voice, the words clear, beautifully artic-
ulated, not a trace of the characteristic Negro pattern to it.
In a move that was unusual for him, LePeters pointed this
out.

"You've got a helluva voice," he said, "and if you don't
mind my saying so, you don't sound colored. Not that it
would be bad if you did."

It was a risky proposition, he felt, saying a colored thing
directly to a colored guy—but to his surprise, the Negro met
his eyes for the first time, thanked him, and said he had
taken a course at college designed to root out Negro inflections in the voice. Through the use of taped recordings he had
gotten rid of many standard inflections such as "carryin' myself on down" instead of "walking over to" and "he goan"
instead of "he is going," "Oddly enough," he said with a
chuckle, "there's only one word in the language that still
gives me trouble. Guess which one. It will amuse you in the
light of your profession."

"What's that?" asked LePeters.

"Poh-lice."

"By the way," said the teacher, about to leave, "what are
the current opportunities in the detective bureau? It's for a
cousin who was wondering and knew I was coming over
here." The Negro said that his cousin had an ancient Assault
with a Deadly Weapon charge against him but had since
straightened out. "Would they hold it against him?" he
asked. "He was a mixed-up kid."

LePeters saw through the pathetically thin ruse. The
teacher was actually inquiring for himself, in the manner of
girls seeking abortion tips. Steeped in knowledge about decadent Italian castles, LePeters wondered why he would want
to give it all up for a life of crime prevention. What a shame
he had such yearnings instead of throwing himself totally

into a field in which he was so sorely needed. "Send me his name and I'll see what I can do," said LePeters. "Actually, though, the old rap might hurt him."

The teacher took his leave, saying he had to visit the Browns, a family nearby. "They're lovely people, I wonder if you know them. We have two of their children, Fanny Mae and little Eurethra."

"Now there's one," he said, with a snap of his fingers. "Before I went through Dixon Junior College, I'll bet you anything I would have said 'chillun.' "

"Sounds better the new way although I'm not sure," said LePeters. "And I'll give the Browns a buzz one of these days although we don't go out much."

When the teacher had gone, LePeters went upstairs to his daughter's room and, sure enough, found her knee-deep in clippings about Paraguay, smiling peasants offering their wares and troops marching in military precision, also a clump of hairy material, one of the main products for export. He wondered for the first time why she was being made an expert on Paraguay. At best, it was a country with only loose cultural ties to America. And one would be hard-pressed to make out a case for its representing a wave of the future. What good would it do her, all that Paraguay expertise. And why all the emphasis on Italian castles and exquisite centuries-old staircases and furniture? Were his daughter to mingle with wealthy circles, she might perhaps have some use for the know-how, but what Negro child in the class would come within miles of a Chippendale, much less a Lamento staircase. And he could not see why they were going so heavy on the Founding Fathers when, in the light of what had come afterward, one could have argued that they'd conspired to keep the Negroes lowly.

On reflection, the program seemed scattered, unplanned,

as though a special colored division at the board of education had decided to give them any old shit, as long as they stayed quiet and didn't go around knifing each other. But perhaps there was an aspect that LePeters had not seen clearly. The doge castles, after all, were college-level, so were Georgian furniture and obscure banisters. How many children would begin their careers with such in-depth knowledge of Paraguay? Admittedly it was a narrow specialty, but for that very reason perhaps key State Department vacancies were screaming to be filled. And what about businesses dying to open up the Paraguayan market but stymied temporarily for lack of personnel with a knowledge of the culture and national temperament? It was a far from sturdy conviction—but perhaps his daughter had been unable to cope with the private school exam because of its trivial concerns . . .

Downstairs, his wife asked, "How did it go at the private school?"

"I have a funny feeling she's over their heads."

He would have bet a week's pay on her answer: "That's because she's nigger-educated. Didn't you know that? A good solid nigger education automatically puts you over everyone's head." But she crossed him up by keeping the words silently locked in a small corkscrew of a smile. And it was far worse than if she had spoken.

Though he had sorely hungered for it, LePeters, since coming east, had had no contact whatever with his kin. He thought often of his gentle, perished dad, but with his pelvis a question mark he had no heart to pay a vengeance-seeking visit to Frickman Furs, especially since there might be some physical action involved in the confrontation. To find his mom, he would have to take a flight south, then track her down to flea-bitten motels in Georgia. Imagine his feelings if he actually found her in one, God knows in what condition. Only Uncle Fabe was a possibility, the sonofabitch who had callously wolfed down pails of coleslaw after his father's funeral. Though his burial behavior had been outrageous, still Fabe Sussman remained a close blood relation. So great was LePeters's longing to get next to one that he slipped away from his family soon afterward and paid a stealthy visit to the uncle he had gone around slightly hating. Fabe lived in a grim section of the great nearby city, one favored by elderly people of means who were at death's door. Going up in the elevator of his uncle's building, he told the doorman: "Six-H."

"Going to see Fabe Sussman?"

"Yes."

"I don't like his color," said the doorman, a shriveled peach-pit of a man who seemed far from in the pink himself.

Fabe Sussman rolled to the door in a wheelchair, LePeters immediately checking his color and not entirely pleased with what he saw. It was an in-between color, neither here nor there, far from pleasing but nothing to fall down the steps about either. Still, his father's brother had a cheerful, robust style and hollered to his wife, "Hey, Soph, come here and look at him. Look at this guy."

The wife came in and said, "Why didn't you visit before?"

"I just came in from the West," LePeters said. "And I'm still getting settled."

"Yes, but look at him," said the wheelchaired uncle. "Will you look at this guy. Look at the size of him. He's some guy."

"But he doesn't visit," said the wife. "So what good is it."

"There was just a little bit of money when we were kids," said Fabe, "so they gave it to me for college. Your father got nothing. Then, when I was setting up in business, your dad worked for me late at night, also for nothing. When the Frickmans found out about it, they almost threw him out of his job. They said he was giving me secrets, stealing for me. He was, too. Anyway, I don't want to talk business. I just want to look at you. I can't get over you. How are you doing, killin' 'em?" Leaning forward, with a wary eye on his wife, he chuckled and whispered, "I'll bet you're knocking off plenty of puss."

LePeters was astonished at his uncle's calm revelation of how he had swindled his father, more stakes driven into poor Bill Sussman's heart. Yet his uncle's open-faced admiration for him was so powerful and all-consuming that LePeters found it irresistible.

"I get my share," he said, returning the chuckle and lowering his eyes in modesty.

"And you're a detective, too," said Fabe Sussman, glowing with admiration. "Hey, Soph, I love this guy."

"Here," he said, pulling a wallet out of his bathrobe. "Take a few bucks. I know what you make."

"I can't do that," said LePeters, but the old man kept pushing it at him until finally he folded it quickly and put it in his pocket, more as a bond between them than because he wanted to take it, although admittedly it would come in handy. LePeters basked a while longer in the chuckling, convivial warmth of his uncle's pride, but knew he would never be comfortable if he didn't bring up the coleslaw accusation.

"I missed my own dad's funeral, Uncle Fabe," said LePeters. "But I must admit I was disappointed when I heard you ate a lot of coleslaw after it."

"Yeah," said Fabe, as close to solemnity as he'd come during the visit. "We used to sit around and eat it when we were kids.

"Hey," he said, brightening, "you want some now? Soph, send down for a pint of coleslaw. That's a good idea."

So that was it. The coleslaw eating had been a sign of deep affection and loss, a commemorative ritual linking the brothers through eternity. Terribly relieved, LePeters felt a great shower of tenderness for his broken uncle. He hugged the still robust invalid around his frail shoulders and had trouble hiding his tears. "None of that," said Fabe, brushing him aside. "We're guys."

"Are you sure you want the coleslaw?" asked the wife, about to use the phone. "A delivery boy just for that?"

"Maybe he wants some cold cuts," said Fabe. "That's a good idea. I'd do anything for this big, beautiful guy."

"It won't be necessary," said LePeters. "I don't think I could get anything down."

The woman walked up to him and, with a wagging finger and a harshly accusatory tone, said, "Why don't you come around to visit two old people?"

"I will, Aunt Sophie," he said, taking her around, too, and smelling old Turkish rugs. "From now on, I'm here every week."

Now that the painful coleslaw mix-up had been clarified, LePeters felt he could sit back and enjoy his new find, Uncle Fabe. In many ways, it was like having his father back, a boisterous, cocky, fun-loving version, daring where his dad had been timid, swaggering and hell-for-leather where Bill Sussman had been modest. And there was no way to resist the old man's sweepingly unashamed admiration for him. Fabe looked right past the thinness of his arms, his divided face and tattered groin, and saw only a big, beautiful guy from the West, plowing through forests of young girls, piling up landmark achievements in law enforcement. Just before he left, his uncle said he was going to pick up the phone and call Chief Guster, an old friend from the Western Front Club which annually rained gifts down upon disabled vets from Château-Thierry. LePeters said it wasn't necessary, that it was the last thing he wanted, but down deep he knew it wasn't the worst development in the world. Fabe was obviously a string-puller and LePeters envisioned him making a few moves that would quietly lift his daughter out of the colored school. Even in the cash department, he wasn't a bad guy to have around. Going down in the elevator, LePeters had peeked at his take and counted eighteen dollars. "How much did you get?" the doorman had asked, to which LePeters said, "None of your business." Other nephews had obviously trooped up to Fabe before, but doubtless they were on Sophie's side—and how many could possibly be huge, rugged dicks just in from the West? There would be other eighteens, doubtless a few hundred and thirty-eights, too, on important occasions, all of it adding up. Once Fabe's color improved, there would be nights on the town, too, ending up in discreetly elegant whorehouses, half the enjoyment of which would be the kidding around and playing piano with the girls in the sitting room, but not entirely ruling out a great piece of ass as the dawn came up. And not a prayer of any of it getting back either, because of the high prices and long tradition, high-ranking cops being in on it, too. They would all be taken care of by Madame Gladys who dated all the way back to Prohibition and had even been a great favorite of Diamond Jim Brady.

Hernia and all, LePeters seemed to have sponged up some of his uncle's zestful spirit and for several days walked about the bureau with a new bounce and cockiness. When Detectives Flamoyan and Hortham paraded outside his cubicle with a banner crudely scribbled "Yankel Go Home" LePeters laughed heartily and, in truth, felt totally untouched. A little later, LePeters caught up with Flamoyan in the corridor, leaned an elbow on his pointed belly as though it were a counter, and said, "I can wipe you out, you old fart, and you know it." Flamoyan looked grave and defeated and could muster only a "G'wan, you punk" as he moved off down the hall. There had been the usual joking, casual tone to the exchange but also a somber, dead-serious vein beneath; and it was the first time in LePeters's memory he could remember being unafraid of a detective's gun. Several days later, Teener took a call from Fabe while LePeters was out having a hearty detective's lunch. Teener said the old man had gone to the hospital for a routine checkup and hadn't wanted to bother LePeters. "All he said was 'How's that big, beautiful guy of mine doing?' "

"I wouldn't have minded talking to him," said LePeters.

The following day, LePeters got his chance when another hospital call came in. "How do you feel, kid?" asked Fabe. LePeters said he was on top, to which his uncle replied, "He's some guy," apparently talking to the others in his ward as much as to his nephew. A high, urgent, circulatory scream hidden in the ceiling of Fabe's voice gave LePeters some concern and he made plans to take his wife and daughter to visit the old man, either at home or in the hospital. But the next day, Fabe's wife called and, in a broken, agonized voice, said, "My husband's gone. You'll never visit now."

"Yes, I will," said LePeters.

"Oh no, you won't," said the widow. "I know the way these things go. Right now you think you'll visit, but you won't."

LePeters's grief had a slow fuse. At first he was only puzzled. But driving home, he began to rail at the fates for un-
covering a marvelous rascal of an uncle, teasing him with the
limitless possibilities, then whisking him away before a week
was gone. Whoever was in charge had some sense of humor.
For the second time in his life, LePeters skipped a momen-
tously important funeral, first his dad's, now Fabe's. Admittedly, the old man's courage had made a tremendous impression on him; at the edge of death, he'd found time to call
LePeters and ask how *he* was feeling. Even though he'd had
only the faintest brush with it, LePeters hoped that some of
his uncle's dash and confidence would remain with him. But
he had no heart to attend the funeral and then be tempted to
join in on yet another symbolic coleslaw eating. There was
too much death and violence in his own work around the
bureau; though he loved his uncle dearly and would have
given up a great deal to have him yanked back among the
living, let's face it, in death his uncle was just another stiff.
Each time he went to a delicatessen he would make it a point
to eat coleslaw with a special reverence, but he had no wish
to wolf some down after another funeral.

For a time, LePeters put in long hours at the bureau, manufacturing work where none legitimately existed. He even volunteered to beef up the skeleton crews that manned the
department on national holidays. One such morning, he sat
at his desk correcting spelling mistakes on multiple stab-
wound reports when Teener brought in Fabe's wife, wearing
widows' robes, shaking like a leaf, and looking as though she
had aged ten years in the two weeks since he had seen her.
She carried an attaché case and, like a traveling salesman,

snapped it open and laid several items inside on LePeters's desk. One was a glass figurine of a collie, another a letter-opener with Chinese carvings on the handle. Additionally, there were two piggybanks, some women's jewelry, a Benjamin Franklin half-dollar, and a combination paperweight and magnifying glass.

"These were all Fabe's that he used to tinker with," said the widow. "He wanted you to have any three."

LePeters grabbed the coin for his daughter, then settled on the carved letter-opener and the paperweight for his desk.

"I think you took the best," said the widow, snapping shut the case. She handed him some instructions for regular polishings of the letter-opener handle and then said good-bye. "I have to go around and see other nieces and nephews now. This is some job your uncle left me. But I loved him."

Teener, also working the skeleton crew, showed the old lady to the door; LePeters had been certain she was going to lace into him for missing Fabe's funeral and was grateful for being let off the hook. Examining his haul, he knew it was the thought that counted and that he was supposed to be touched at this symbolic representation of his uncle, all, in a sense, that remained of the rascally Fabe. Yet, in truth, he could not work up much sentiment over the miscellaneous items. The magnifier might be useful; no doubt his daughter would eat up the Ben Franklin half-a-buck. Then, too, the carved letter-opener probably had some real value, although it was going to be a nuisance to polish the handle on a daily basis. But for the most part, the next-to-worthless souvenirs served only to remind him how helpful his uncle might have been to him—say by slipping him a couple of grand that would allow LePeters to yank his daughter out of the colored school—although he truthfully could not swear he would have used it for that purpose. Just his luck that his uncle, out of some profound, deeply meaningful tie to LePeters, had slipped him the richly symbolical dime-store items while shoveling potloads of crass, feelingless money to other already wealthy relatives he had no love for at all. Feeling impoverished, LePeters went into Glober's office to steal some supplies, packages of paper, calendars, homicide report forms, anything that would make him richer than he was. Inside, Sissy Glober tested the carpeting in her stocking feet. She wore a short skirt, belted by a cascade of metal ringlets that tumbled to her knees. LePeters saw himself plucking at one and setting off a jangling alarm that would bring on a horde of detectives, guns at the ready, also Bruno Glober, generally reticent, but under the circumstances, sore as blazes. LePeters had known Sissy Glober since she was a child, but ever since seeing her bathtub nudes, he blocked out all other aspects of her personality and saw her only as the girl who had posed for C-8. "There's something about Dad's office," she said and then walked to the door, poking at it with her finger the way she might have tested meat for tenderness. Just before it clicked shut, LePeters saw Teener working furiously, as though he were filling in for ten men.

"I don't know about the door closed," LePeters said, expecting to be gunned down at any moment. He was amazed that instead of giving off a jangling alarm, her belt, when she moved, made only the softest of sounds, like crushed cellophane. "What do you think of this stuff?" she asked, putting her fist in front of his nose, then tightening it until he heard a cracking sound. Somehow, as though he had been waiting a lifetime to do so, he knew he was to inhale and did so deeply and obediently; the heating unit had been on all along, but he was instantly aware now of its high mentholated whine. Then the overhead magnesium lights seemed to drop down and he felt as though he had been smacked across his brow with a scythe. Reaching for invisible banisters, he fell to his knees, and put his head into her skirt. "What's going on?" he asked. "What is this?"

"I'll never tell," she said, but she stood by patiently while he used the laddered metal of her belt to get to his feet, climbing rung by rung. Or so it seemed. Easing him into her father's swivel chair, she sat at his feet and looked at him with enormous curiosity. The only word that meant anything to him was "slow" which seemed to come whispering out of the pores of the paneled walls. Through a mentholated veil he watched her hair spill out on his legs like a golden tent and felt a soaked and inevitable sensation, then saw her eyes again, this time happily demented. As though they had carefully rehearsed the next moment, she drew her legs up and sat before him on her father's desk while LePeters reached into his back pocket; as the veil lifted, he studied her carefully through Fabe's magnifying glass. His head cleared, and in a panic, he rushed to the door, opened it slightly, and looked out on Teener, the center of a one-man tornado of activity. He had never seen his little partner work so hard.

"You're very creative," she said, stretching out her arms as though she wanted to become permanently taller. "What are office affairs like?"

"Messy," he said. "Especially around homicide bureaus. Listen, what was that stuff? I've never run into anything like it."

"It's the sensual end, isn't it? You can get it from a druggist if he's a sleaze."

"It put me through the roof," said LePeters. "My only objection is the way you sprung it on me. I've just come off a hernia."

She walked up to him and kissed him the length of his boundaried scar; surprisingly, no one had ever done that before. "Your touch is most elegant," she said. "I've never had much luck with the callow."

He looked across the courtyard at the barred windows of the interrogation cubicles. Each day, as a child, he had passed a terrifying orphanage with windows barred in a similar fashion. Only once had he seen someone inside, a young boy. He had often wondered whether the entire orphanage were being run for the one lonely fellow.

Downstairs, a massive sea of new squads jammed the parking lot.

"Put it out of your mind," he said, fluttering one of Bruno Glober's towels to clear the air. "That's all I'd need is to get into something now."

Driving home, he wondered whether Teener had sniffed up to the door and figured out what was going on inside. With the benefit of new chemicals, it would take someone like Hortham of Micro-Analysis around twenty seconds to examine Glober's office and fill in the details. Still, realistically speaking, his crime had not been that great. For all he knew, Sissy Glober might have been discreetly magnified by every detective in the bureau. The experience had caught him off guard and been disturbing, but it also lingered; somehow, the soaked and mentholated sensation in Glober's swivel chair struck him as being peculiarly eastern, as though he had finally been initiated into the mysteries of the Atlantic Coast. Or at least one of them. He could have kicked himself for not extending the haze a few minutes longer and getting Sissy Glober to do C-8 for him. As long as she was up on the desk already.

Hawk-eyed in the daytime, LePeters was relatively blind at

twilight. Sliding into his driveway a bit later, he thought he saw a side of beef hanging from the limb of his front lawn dogwood tree. Thinking it was a strange way to make meat deliveries, he climbed the lawn, and when he got closer he saw that it was his daughter, hanging in a jackknifed position, her hands and ankles all tied together. "It was Samantha," the child said, through angry tears. "She could have killed me."

"How long have you been up there?" asked LePeters, trying to work the knots apart.

"Almost a week," said the child. "Wait till I get her for this."

LePeters had no luck with the knots, but then thought of Fabe's orientally carved letter-opener, and whipped it out. Dull as it was, it did the job and LePeters got his daughter down. His wife ran out on the lawn with a flaming shishkebab implement and said, "What happened?"

"Samantha lynched me," said the girl, running to her mother. "I want her lynched back."

"I do, too," Claire LePeters said quietly. "I really do."

"It wasn't exactly a lynching," LePeters said, "but it was no joke either."

"Aren't you going to get her?" his wife asked. "Aren't you going to at least do that?"

"Of course," said LePeters. "You think I'm just going to stand around."

Heading for the town on foot, LePeters thought how lucky it was Fabe had willed him the carved letter-opener. At that moment, it had been better than having a couple of grand in cash. But he didn't believe it entirely and wondered why he couldn't have had the money *and* the opener. There was no doubt that Fabe's seemingly worthless souvenirs were coming in handy, though. Who would have dreamed he'd have made such use of the magnifying glass, for another example. As he walked through the deserted streets of Detectives' Hill it crossed his mind that if he hadn't magnified Sissy Glober, perhaps his daughter would not have been beefed to the tree limb. LePeters dreaded the thought of going on a house-to-house search of the Negro section for the child. Much to his relief, he saw a guilty-looking black child leaning against a car husk and eating a Hershey bar in the abandoned railroad yard. "Are you Samantha?" he asked as he approached. She said nothing, but when he got within a few feet of her she suddenly dashed off, bobbing up and down behind different rotted car shells. He saw now that she was the child who had sung "Fly Me to the Moon" so beautifully during the Negro cake sale. "I just want to talk," he said, lumbering after her with blinking pelvis. She stopped finally and waited for him, as though all she had wanted to do was demonstrate her superior speed. She was tall and wiry, yet it seemed amazing that she had been able to tie up his daughter to the tree limb, and he decided she must have gotten some help. He really had meant to talk quietly to her, but when he had her cornered, his eyes rubbed over with fury and he picked her off the ground, saying, "What'd you have to do that for. You could have killed her." Then he began to run across the railroad yard with her, in the direction of the low-income Negro housing project, beyond the colored school. Not really sure what he was going to do with her, he stopped at the edge of the railroad to catch his breath, still holding the child and wondering whether he were carrying about a potentially great rhythm and blues singer who would bear the scar of this experience forever. What about his daughter, though, who was bound to carry a scar or two of her own?

She made a great fishlike leap to get free and LePeters heard a familiar cracking sound in his vest pocket. My God, she put one in my pocket, he thought, as he released the child, sunk to his knees, and for the second time that day felt himself enveloped in the mentholated haze. He held the mystified child's ankles, fought against touching her elsewhere, and whispered to the grass, "Suck, oh suck, suck, suck." He stayed that way, on hands and knees before the child in a bundled penitential mound, begging forgiveness until the veil before his eyes lifted.

"I heard that," the child said, finishing her Hershey bar and making no attempt to run off. "I'm telling my daddy soon's he get home."

"You didn't hear anything," LePeters said, getting to his feet.

"Hell, I didn't. I heard you say you wanted to feel my butt."

"You imagined it," said LePeters. But he was frightened and asked, "When's your dad get home?"

"I don't know. He left six years ago. But he comin' home soon."

"Don't say anything to anyone," said LePeters. "And we'll forget the other thing. Only try to play a little more nicely with my daughter. Don't you kids know any girls' games?"

◉

Claire LePeters waited for her husband on the front lawn. "Did you find her?" she asked.

"Yes," he said. "I got it straightened out."

"What's that funny smell on you?" she asked.

"Hernia medicine. I didn't realize it was so strong. Her father's out of town, but I settled the thing. I don't think we'll have any trouble again."

"But what did you do? Did you bring in the police?"

"That's not necessary. Not for kids. Anyway, I got it straightened out."

"I can just imagine."

Late that night, LePeters tiptoed into his daughter's room and examined her body. Her wrists had red marks on them, her ankles even fainter ones, but otherwise she seemed untouched by the experience. As the night went by, she had a way of easing out of the blankets as though she were coming from a toothpaste tube. He shoved her back gently and thought for some reason of the colored-school worm check, wondering whether his wife knew about it and had given her one. He considered doing it as she slept but somehow felt certain that several white ones would dance forth to tantalize and mock him. How could he stand up to his wife's case now? No matter how attractive a face you put on it, his child really had been hung from the bottom branch of a dogwood tree. What if he had arrived an hour later? And where, incidentally, were the vaunted Detectives' Hill police who had a full report on it every time a leaf fell. Maybe they were good at everything but lynchings. Perhaps all this had nothing to do with his daughter attending a colored school, but where could he find evidence that it was everyday stuff at white schools, too? Besides, he had no heart to make such a case, to trample on Claire LePeters's objections and offer exquisitely thought-out reasons why the lynching would build his daughter's character. He didn't believe it himself and felt as though the Croat foundation was weak after all and he was sinking into the ground along with the handsomely modernistic house. He started to move toward his bedroom, but he smelled a faint wisp of the mentholation from his coat and walked downstairs to the garage instead. Reaching into the glove compartment of his squad, he took out the Sissy Glober nudes and looked at them through Fabe's magnifier. He took a long time to work up to C-8 and when he got to it, he inhaled his jacket and tried to get himself back into the mentholated haze, back into the soaked swivel chair, into the photograph itself. Then he put the pictures back and went up to his wife, undressing and slipping into bed. He was amazed that anyone could sleep at such a precarious angle. Moving to her side of the bed, he fitted himself against her and kissed the back of her neck which he had always found heartbreaking and innocent.

"What is it?" she said.

"It's Kenny," he said. "I'm restless."

"Then where's your technique?"

Leaning forward once more, he bit her ear gently and said, "You're a lovely woman."

"That's no technique," she said, sitting up crossly. "That isn't anything."

"Look," he said, turning on the light and putting on his robe, "I'm getting the hell out of here. I've been trying to pretend that great things are happening on all fronts, but let's face it, they're not. I've got to get away and think things over before it all goes down the drain."

"And you're going without me?" she said, startled. "For the first time?"

"I'm going alone," he said. "Without anybody. I'm tired of spades. I'm tired of homicide, and getting into the sack with you every night is no prize package either. I've been doing something wrong and I just want to get by myself and figure out what it is.

"Besides," he said, hauling out a suitcase he'd kept from his Army days, "I want to rest up my hernia, too."

PART
TWO

PART TWO

PART
TWO

⊙⊙⊙⊙⊙

DRIVING TO THE AIRPORT, LEPETERS FELT AS
though he were wearing a steel harness, forged in guilt. For
seventeen years, all through their bumpy homicidal caravan
across the country, never once had he dreamed of leaving his
wife's side; now that they had arrived east, he had thrown up
his hands and impulsively flashed off on a luxury vacation,
leaving her stranded in a high-peaked Croat house, their
daughter crushed below in a black stampede. Secretly, he
hoped that, thin shoulders and all, she would somehow rescue the situation; then, suntanned, pelvically sound, he
would arrive home and find his daughter casually attending a
bone-white school, the colored days tucked away like an evil
memory. Together, they would enter a full and rich new
phase of life. But in truth, how could Claire LePeters achieve
such a miracle when he had snatched their savings for a fun-
fested individual vacation and left her with only a couple of
bucks?

   As long as he was doing evil things, LePeters figured he
might as well shoot the works and had allowed Teener to

hire an expensive limo to take him to the airport. As he drove, the driver threw back his head and regaled the detective with fundamental truths about domestic relations. "When Harry Homeowner arrives after a rugged day at the office, he wants a smile and a good dinner. But let's say Mary Housewife has had her own problems. Perhaps Sally Schoolchild has been home with a cold. Or Nora Neighbor has been giving her a hard time. How can you expect her to pretend nothing has happened?"

Snow had flurried up thickly across the windshield, and twice the driver had overshot the airport entrance. They were late for the flight, and LePeters pictured driving around for hours in a white maze, then arriving late and being penalized the full price of the round-trip airline tickets; agonizingly he would have to slip back to Detectives' Hill, penniless and untanned.

"Forgive me for interrupting your story," LePeters said, as they overshot the entrance the third time, "but I think Danny Driver ought to pay attention to some of these signs."

Earlier that day, LePeters had been nervous about asking Glober for time off. Like a fighter doing pre-bout warm-ups in his dressing room, he had revved himself up at Teener's desk.

"I need to get away," said LePeters. "Things are coming down on me."

"I've been kind of crowded myself," said the little detective.

"Even in the best of marriages, it's good to get a little distance on occasion."

"You can love your wife all you want," said Teener, "but people have to get away from each other."

"I was thinking about some island," said LePeters. "In the south where it's warm."

"Just this morning, on the way to work, I thought, it would be nice to get away to an island. I've had my heart set on going to one in the south."

"You're saying the same things as I am," said LePeters.

"What the hell do you mean?" said Teener, in one of his rare spurts of anger.

◉

LePeters found his boss astonishingly generous and understanding. But what was there to be astonished about? He had been so busy envying Glober the mysterious wealth he had accumulated in homicide, the private office and hand-sewn suits, that he had overlooked the fact that his boss always came through for him in the clutch. In seventeen years, Glober's only possible breach of form had been the recent distribution of cards saying LePeters's real name was Sussman. Even in that case, perhaps in some mysterious way LePeters did not yet understand, Glober had been doing him a favor. More to the point, what had LePeters done for his boss, except to peer treacherously between his daughter's legs with a pocket magnifier? In Glober's own office, as though to rub it in. LePeters vowed that as soon as things straightened out for him, he would have the Globers over for a delicious meal, one that would certainly be paltry by their standards but at least heartfelt.

Not only did Glober grant LePeters the time off, but he also said he would get him a reservation at a private fishing club on a small and wonderful island in the south. "A few dicks vacation there now and then, but it's beyond the range of most."

LePeters would have preferred an island that was completely homicide-free, but the private and exclusive part sounded appealing and he pumped Glober's hand in gratitude.

"Don't mention it," said Glober. "Just bring me back a couple of colognes if you think of it." Just before LePeters left, Glober, as a seeming afterthought, closed his door and asked LePeters if he would mind telling him the names of various girls he had laid over the seventeen years they had been together.

"You know, around the bureau. You tell me yours, I'll tell you mine. One for one."

"There haven't been many, really," said LePeters. "I've stuck pretty close to home."

"I've got to hand it to you," said Glober. "You're a close-mouthed guy." But as LePeters backed off toward the door, Glober snatched his arm and said, "Next time I see you, you're not getting off so easy. You're definitely telling me. I got a hunch we've been screwing a few of the exact same broads."

LePeters had planned on traveling alone, on getting away from every trace of his homicidal life. Yet for the moment, he considered asking Teener to come along with him. So small was his friend in both stature and personality that it would be like having a companion and at the same time being alone, the best of both worlds. On the other hand, there was always the possibility of Teener being unable to adapt to a tropical climate and of having to be shipped back in a box as a series of broken parts. LePeters decided it was not worth the risk.

As LePeters entered the terminal, a nest of kneeling press photographers banged flashbulbs off in his face and a pad-carrying reporter dashed up to ask, "How would you describe your trip, Detective LePeters, business or pleasure?"

"Strictly pleasure," said LePeters. He spotted Teener near a newsstand and asked him, "What is this?"

"Isn't it great?" said Teener, smiling toward the photogs and slipping the words from the corner of his mouth. "I arranged it through a contact. Releases will go out to Detectives' Hill and surrounding areas and there'll be coverage at the other end."

"What the hell good is it?" asked LePeters, but when the reporter asked him if he were going off on an extradition case, he had to admit that in a small chamber of himself he enjoyed being the center of all the press commotion.

"No comment," he said, in fulfillment of a lifetime ambition.

"That's all for now, boys," said Teener, waving off the photographers and popping a cigar into his mouth. A handsome airline executive, immaculately decked out in a braided uniform, stepped up to the detective pair, did a heel-clicking bow, and then asked LePeters to put all of his luggage on the scale. Earlier, Teener had told him he had a contact at the airlines and to be as liberal as he liked about packing; LePeters had brought along his entire wardrobe, including old suits and bathrobes he would never be able to use in a million years. The executive, after another bow, took LePeters's newspapers and magazines, also a small handbag, and asked to see his wallet. He hefted it, as though to check the weight, then flipped it over his shoulder onto the groaning scale.

"What happened to your contact?" LePeters whispered to Teener.

"I don't understand," said Teener, flushed, colorless.

"There must have been a crackdown. But believe me, heads are going to roll."

LePeters begrudgingly paid the massive overweight charge and walked to the cordoned-off passenger section; in a great wash of alcohol, a disheveled gray-haired man smacked his wife across the mouth several times, drove his toes into his worshipful little boy's rear, and kept zipping and unzipping his own fly. LePeters's first reaction was to feel great sympathy for the youngster and to wonder whether he, too, by taking a luxury vacation at the first sign of winter, wasn't smacking his wife around and booting his child. An immediate danger was that the man might smash out a few windows in mid-flight and send them all plummeting to the ground. "Let me handle this," said Teener, hitching up his specially made little trousers and sweeping up to a stewardess. "You're not letting a guy like that fly, are you?" he asked.

"The captain's got his eyes on him," said the girl. "If he reaches a certain level of violence, we won't carry him."

The man evidently never reached that level and was permitted to board, still smacking his wife about the head and flailing out after his cowering but devoted child. LePeters said good-bye to his little friend and took his seat, immediately disappointed by the stewardesses; expecting winners, instead he had gotten a grim and tattered batch, still a little cute, but for the most part, worn down by long, depleting court battles over their right to hang on to jobs in middle age. Some had recent hysterectomies and still wore surgical and orthopedic appliances, but were dressed in short skirts and did winsome little curtsies to keep up an illusion of cuteness. One seat ahead, a woman with heavily caked-up layers of facial makeup told a story to her seatmate in an almost parodied Brooklyn accent, making it hard for LePeters to concentrate. He found her style vulgar and was about to ask her to quiet down when he became strangely fascinated by the story. A woman had recently lost a husband named Buddy, and though she had many chances to go out on dates, she refused them all, still deeply devoted to the memory of her late husband. Though Buddy had been a racetrack gambler and general wastrel, he was also kind and affectionate and the woman simply could not get over the hurt of loving him. Then there was Ramona, a lovely teen-age daughter who had been deeply devoted to her father and who barely spoke at all now. "She just walks the corridors," said the Brooklyn woman in her thick accent, "wearing her nightgown, holding a teddybear, her eyes as big as this." LePeters slowly and curiously became enmeshed in the story; when he heard about Ramona, a racing fire engine of sympathy screamed through him. He wanted to go to the woman and tell her he understood how she felt about Buddy, the depth of her love, how she would never quite get over him. As for Ramona, he longed to gather up the mysterious girl and hold her forever, marrying her if she liked, or even marrying her mother just to have Ramona around where he could always look at her. He would have done anything to be with Ramona at that very moment, to catch her in his arms as she tripped through the midnight corridors with puzzled star-crossed eyes. He wondered if the Brooklyn woman would yield her phone number and decided to shoot the works, leaning forward and saying, "Do you think Ramona will pull out of it?"

"I'd lay ten to one against," said the woman, "and who asked you to listen."

"I knew you wouldn't understand," said LePeters. "A type like you. How a perfect stranger could become deeply involved with lovely generous people, even though they're only characters in a story.

"Just forget I said a word."

From the air, the island seemed to be divided into two sections, one packed and humming with activity, the other sterile, orderly, somewhat deserted. Off to the sterile side was Glober's fishing club. "Glad you decided to camp with us and not in Jigtown," said the desk clerk as LePeters signed in. Behind the registration counter lay a huge soaked fish that might have been an old drunk sleeping off a night on the town. Its expression was sightless, astonished, as though it were baffled at the turn of events that had led it to a hotel check-in counter. "What if I were to silverplate the bill," said the clerk, "mount it up and ship it to you with a tag, saying 'Caught by Detective LePeters.' At only a modest fee. One of our guests flew the coop and stuck us with it."

LePeters said he would prefer to pass it by and moved off toward his room.

"Even if I promised not to tell anyone you're a cheat?" the clerk hollered after him. The assigned room was on a balcony overlooking a courtyard-harbor in which boats pressed their snouts against the hotel foundation. The arrangement seemed to invite guests to leap directly from their rooms to the decks below. It struck LePeters that he might be the only guest in the hotel, but as he approached his room, a tall, distinguished-looking man with a solemn expression and gray, juridical ringlets in his hair came by. Beside him was his wife, a small, dried-out woman in a festive tourist hat. At first glance, LePeters knew that she would have a nickname along the lines of "Poppy" or "Cappy" and the reputation of being a regular gal and a great sport. The man said he was a mid-western attorney, and then, as though he were being harshly cross-examined, began to squirm a bit and to say, "I specialize in one form of law. It's a little unusual. I feel we're breaking new ground.

"Well, hell," he said, going completely to pieces, "someone's got to defend these people." Drenched with sweat, he went on to say that he represented the publishers of such magazines as *Haughty Whip* and *Painful Bindings*, his job being to sweep into communities in which the publications were banned, beat down injunctions, and get them right back on the newsstands.

"Actually," he said, still squirming, "the fiction's not that bad and I for one think the movie reviews are first-rate. And you'd be surprised, the editors aren't monsters, either; some of them are sweet guys, and if they were standing here, I assure you they'd blend right in with the three of us."

LePeters maintained a juridical silence of his own and quite frankly enjoyed the spectacle of the man strangling himself with guilt.

"A lot of people get our books mixed up with the spanking pubs," said the attorney, "*Bottoms High* and *Backside Smacks*. That's where your real filth is and I wouldn't touch them with a ten-foot pole. I think it's damned unfair, don't you, hon, but when the authorities start sweeping they use a big broom and we get lumped right in with them. Well, aren't you going to ask if I get to meet any of the girls? That's what everyone wants to know."

LePeters decided to be charitable. "Do you?" he asked, breaking the silence.

"Nary a one," said the attorney. "I'm interested in the field only from a legal standpoint."

With that, he snapped open the door next to LePeters.

"Oh, by the way," he said, one arm around his withered wife in the ironically fun-fested hat, "I'd like you to meet my wife, Grace.

"Back home, folks like to call her ChiChi."

◉

After taking a refreshing nap, LePeters, anxious to get started on a suntan, yanked open the closet door to get his swimsuit. The door was a connecting one between two rooms; inside, the woman named ChiChi was tied to a chair; dressed in simple, unembroidered dimestore underwear, she still wore the gay frolicsome tourist hat. Withered and dried out in the alcove, her body seemed surprisingly supple in the dim hotel lamplight. Her husband, bare-chested, in Bermudas, stood over her with a whip; on the dresser pointed at them, was a small Japanese camera, its shutter clicking off shots at twenty-second intervals.

"Hi, there," said the attorney, embarrassed but obviously trying to make the best of it. "We're doing a little freelance for *Painful Bindings*. They pay fifteen dollars a shot on acceptance and another ten on publication. What the hell, we've got the in, why not take advantage of it?"

"I'm sorry I just walked in," said LePeters.

"Yes," said the attorney, "and you're probably making some kind of moral judgment about what you're seeing, too. Even though it's just a harmless little thing we do to fill in the time. And even though I set the thing up so that ChiChi's face never shows.

"Well, let me tell you something," he said to LePeters with biblical wrath. "If they ever put my little old gal's face in the book, I'd go up there and tear the walls down."

⊙

That afternoon, LePeters looked up Benjamin R. Boners, a retired General Assignments man and friend of Glober's who had quit the department to roam the islands. LePeters found his man at the docks, a cocky little fellow who walked with a proud, bandy-legged nautical strut; after introductions, the two charted a small boat from a Negro skipper, the idea being that they would circle the island, relax and perhaps do a little casual fishing, but only if the spirit moved them. Some ten miles offshore, the shallow waters were crowded with sunken liners, their prows sticking out of the water like kitchen knives. LePeters had romantic notions about bearded imperial Spaniards, clinging to storm-tossed decks. "When'd that one go down?" LePeters asked the black captain.

"Let me see, that one over there went under last Thursday and that bugger bust wide open last Saturday night." His fantasies up in smoke, LePeters nonetheless found that the clear and open seas filled him with a need to speak only of essential truths.

"It's being a dick and yet not being a dick," LePeters told his ruddy little friend. "I think that's really at the heart of what drove me down here. I figure I got to go one way or the other. Then everything else falls into line."

Picking up LePeters's mood, Boners's eyes squinted with mariners' wisdom and he began to speak of his early days as a charterboat captain and fisherman on the China Coast. "Nothing would please me more in those days than baiting a big hook with ballyhoo, sailing out past Hosea's Lighthouse and waiting for Mr. Marlin to stick his nose out of the water and take his afternoon tea. Sometimes I'd take a pair of JiJi girls along and we'd cut a few didoes right out there on deck, staring up at the ten-foot waves and listening to the Honolulu weather bastards tell us we were sailing fair and moderate seas.

"The sea'll take a lot, my friend," said Boners. "She'll let you trim your pencil in the hold, turn her back while you're smoking boo, and she don't give a hoot about your pedigree.

"But you just cross her once," said Boners, leaning forward to thump LePeters's chest, "and she'll crush your little poppies." LePeters was charmed by the ex-dick's yarn-spinning style and had settled back for another serving of it when the Negro captain yelled, "Hey, Homicide, we got company. Come here and give me a hand." While the two detectives were chatting, the skipper on his own initiative had baited a line and apparently hooked a massive fish. With a bowlegged strut, Boners ambled forward to help, but for some reason the Negro shouldered him aside, saying, "Not you, you'll bust your ass." He handed the pole to LePeters who, despite some embarrassment for his friend, held on as instructed. "I'll circle round so's she'll wear herself out," said the skipper. The pull was tremendous and LePeters was surprised at his own excitement when the fish broke water in one great-snouted leap. After twenty minutes, the fish showed no sign of tiring. The Negro took over the pole and LePeters grabbed the wheel. Still offended by the mysterious rebuke, Boners sulked in a corner of the boat, his head in his hands. Half an hour later, the fish seemed peppier than ever. The Negro had the line and it was hard to tell who was pulling what, when LePeters saw Boners march to the rear of the boat, yank out a pistol, and with perfect aim drill two shots through the fish's head.

"What the fuck'd you do that to the fish for?" said the skipper, holding a suddenly slack line.

Boners cooled his gun, then slipped it back in a concealed holster.

"I don't take shit from fish."

◉

Startled momentarily by the gunfire, LePeters nevertheless was ready to back Boners all the way. A young detectivey swagger came over him of the sort he never experienced around the bureau; indeed, he wished he had taken along a gun so that he could rip off a few rounds in support of his gutsy hell-for-leather little friend. The skipper was quite irritated, but decided to bring the bullet-riddled fish into port anyway, in case some native wanted to buy it for meat. Rolling up to the dock, with the tough little ex-dick at his side, LePeters felt for a moment that he and Boners were back on the China Coast, the most feared twosome west of Macao. Anyone who called them fags had half an hour to get out of town. On the dock itself, a contest seemed to be in progress, each fisherman standing proudly beside his top catch of the day. Reading one another's thoughts, the two detectives picked up the great headless fish, carried it to the dock's edge and dumped it at the judge's feet.

"There's the winner," said Boners, wiping fish blood from his hands.

"Who says?" an angry participant shouted. "That's just a mutilated turd."

"My friend says," said LePeters, snapping up the trophy, anxious for a brawl. "And he's got a little surprise under his coat in case there are any arguments."

◉

Still milking the triumphant mood, the two detectives took their trophy into the harborside bar of Jigtown's main hotel and had it filled with rum, each taking comradely swallows until they had worked up a good buzz. The bar was filled with Negroes, some of them whipped and despondent islanders, another group well-dressed business types who seemed to be in from the States. The unexpected swarm of blacks made LePeters wonder about his recent but now seemingly total involvement with Negroes. For forty years, they had existed only on the outer edges of his life. Suddenly battalions of them had come trooping down upon him and seemed to dominate his every breath. For half a dozen years, a Negro cleaning woman had come twice a week to LePeters's boyhood apartment in Jersey, going about her business without a word to anyone in the family. It was known to LePeters's parents that she had a son in jail, but they scrupulously avoided ever mentioning this until one day Flo Sussman casually asked, "How's the kid doing?"

"I was waiting for that," said the cleaning lady, leaving her scrub brush and getting to her feet. "I was waiting for you to say one harmful word about that boy of mine." With that she rammed her cleansers into a massive shopping bag and swooped out the door, never to be seen again. In grade school, LePeters had two Negroes in his class, one a piano-playing prodigy who was always ushered forth in immaculately starched dresses to play assembly marches. Great things were expected of her on the concert stage, but though LePeters kept one eye out for news of her fame, none ever seeped through to him. He had always felt a bit uncomfortable about this, as though one fluttering reed within him would never be entirely stilled until Alice Roby broke through to philharmonic greatness. The other Negro was a slender, somewhat sluggish youngster capable of taking dozes

on his feet; nonetheless he frightened LePeters, who was certain the sleepy style was a decoy and that, if pressed, the
youngster would be capable of coming to life and slashing
LePeters to pieces with fierce, rhythmically ticked-off welter-
weight combinations. One day they fought in the schoolyard
and LePeters was astonished to find the boy as listless as
ever, barely able to protect himself. The youngster, too,
seemed embarrassed at having let LePeters down and said
that he really was a good fighter but that he was always tired
from not getting enough to eat. Not only that but his mother
often kept him chained to a bed, sometimes for days at a
time. LePeters was moved by the disclosure and vowed to
himself that they would become fast friends, keeping in
touch throughout life, both rising to the tops of their profes-
sions, achieving leadership and then coming together one day
to settle a tangled, hate-filled racial dispute, drawing upon
their boyhood friendship to ease the settlement. But the boy
came to school irregularly, and finally not at all. LePeters
heard he had developed a chest disease and had to move
down south. In subsequent years, through college, the Army,
in the small towns that marked his odyssey across the West,
Negroes were only vaguely in the picture, small, punctuating
way-stations on his trip toward middle age. At his college
dorm, the black cook had singled out LePeters, known then
as Sussman, for once-a-week servings of what she called "Jew
Balls," highly spiced, hotly noodled concoctions that seemed
to combine the essence of all Negro and Jewish cooking. At
an Army dance concert, a colored trumpet player with dark
glasses and a goatee had amazingly pushed his way across the
floor to shake hands with LePeters, inspecting his palm immediately afterward and saying, "There's a lot of Jesus,
Moses, and John in that handshake, m'man. Sincere." Once,
in an Army gym, LePeters had gotten into a one-on-one bas-

ketball game with a Negro, who was clearly superior to him, scoring twenty goals before LePeters had bagged his first. With a pain in his chest, LePeters asked to be excused, but the black athlete refused to let the game end and long into the night kept racing proudly past LePeters to pump in baskets, his score mounting into the hundreds. That was the extent of his involvement with black people; a casual brush here and there, a speck of trivial activity in the corner of his eyes. Now, ironically, a black world dashed down upon his head, colored cops, spade hoods, dark teachers in a coal-black school. Of all the islands in the great Atlantic, he had singled out one for tired colored businessmen.

◉

Almost as though he were tuned in to LePeters's thoughts, Boners said he would tolerate a man regardless of color, "but only up to a point."

"What point's that?" LePeters asked, with a small edge in his voice. Sensing his friend's irritation, Boners said, "I don't know what that point is. I guess you might say I'm a great friend of the colored man."

The bartender, who had been grim and sullen, suddenly leaned forward and said, "You guys go for a little clean pussy?"

Without waiting for an answer, he told them to spin around, not making too much fuss, and they would see the girl he had in mind. Across the road, they could make out a plump, light-skinned native girl, hanging out wash on the second-floor balcony of a run-down building. The dicks smiled at her and she returned the gesture with an unevenly toothed grin of her own. "Now there she is," said the bartender, taking a photograph out of his wallet, "and this is what she looks like." The girl in the photograph was slender and festive as she skipped through a meadow, joyously gathering flowers. Additionally, she had red hair and a kind of wild Irish coltishness about her.

"You sure that's the same one?" LePeters asked.

" 'Fore she got sick," said the bartender. He then went on to say that she took immaculate care of herself and was the cleanest girl on the island. "You make the gratuity deal with her yourself," said the bartender. "I just like to see the kid get herself straightened out."

The girl in the picture seemed a far cry from the one on the ledge and LePeters wondered if it was possible they were the same doll; before he could make up his mind, Boners had hopped down from the barstool and in his cocky, bandy-legged China Coast style was walking across the street. LePeters noticed an enormous curved tooth hanging from a chain around the bartender's neck and wondered about its significance. He imagined tribal dances and sacred white-killing blood oaths around secret, darkened Congo campfires.

"What's the tooth all about?" he asked the bartender.

"A customer give it to me," he said. "It come out of one of them cereal boxes."

LePeters sipped his rum and before he knew it, Boners was back, cockily hitching up his pants and leaping up on the stool. It seemed to LePeters that he had operated with incredible speed. "How'd you make out?" he asked his friend.

"Like a dream," said Boners. "You see, I could tell she was eyeing me, all the way from that balcony. Otherwise, I wouldn't have made my move. Anyway, it was just like I expected, clear sailing.

"Most important of all, she didn't take a dime."

A bit later, when Boners had left him, a Haitian firedancer

leaped up on a stage to entertain the visiting black businessmen. Her act involved starting small fires about the room by
spitting gasoline on the floor, shouting "Olé!" and then erotically damping them down with her behind. LePeters found
himself idly speculating on how the act would go in a big
eastern nitery. At the same time, it occurred to him that he
was missing a great bet by not moving into the heart of Jigtown where all the action seemed to be. Off to one side and
paying no attention to the gasoline dance sat an attractive,
heavy-chested young girl and a small, cranky-looking insect of
a fellow, in heated colloquy over what LePeters could have
sworn was her menstrual cycle. Never in his life had LePeters
spoken menstrually to a girl; indeed, Claire LePeters had
often said that was one of his great failings, turning a deaf ear
to her monthly travails. Whatever the case, he would have
given plenty to be in on this particular discussion and asked
the bartender if there was any chance of an introduction to
the couple. "You don't seem to understand," said the bartender. "I am dedicated to the destruction of everything you
own, the burning of your home, the wiping out of your property and the killing of your loved ones. The only reason I'm
talking to you at all is that you seem to be a sweet guy." The
bartender said, however, that he was interested in designing
clothing and would introduce LePeters to the couple if the
detective, in turn, promised to set up a job interview for him
at some topflight East Coast wholesale house. For a second,
LePeters was tempted to arrange something for the black
bartender at Frickman Furs. Considering all the blood his
dead dad Bill Sussman had poured into the company, the
least Frickman could do was grant fifteen minutes to a friend
of LePeters, even if they predictably wound up turning
thumbs down on the hostile islander. But the thought was
complicated and unpleasant; warmed by the rum and a bit

footloose on his first solo vacation, LePeters decided to take on the couple alone.

He felt a little funny about approaching the only Caucasian couple in the Jigtown bar—white, when the chips were down, going to white. There were some black women scattered about the room, but LePeters had long since faced the fact that colored girls, though he took his hat off to them and wished them well, were simply not fascinating to him. Nowhere within him could he find the slightest trace of interest in exploring their dusky Congo wonders. Casually drifting over to the white pair, he said, "I don't see any point in not laying it right out on the table. I'm a lonely fellow, down here on a vacation, and I thought I might horn in on your conversation." LePeters took the girl's generous smile as an invitation to sit down; the ill-tempered fellow, however, tossed LePeters a cynical Middle European look and as though to show his displeasure began speaking to the girl in an obscure Spanish dialect. LePeters, a French major at college, felt totally closed out but could have sworn that little menstrual sparks kept flying out of the Latin chitchat, evidence that they were still hammering away at the same trickily erotic subject. After a while, the girl sighed, having apparently arrived at some delicate impasse, and produced a rubber ball, suggesting that they all have a catch on a small strip of beach alongside the Jigtown bar. As they stepped outside, the girl's friend suddenly grabbed off a fistful of LePeters's waist fat and said, "What do you plan doing about this?"

"Put your mind at ease," said LePeters, patting him on the head to remind him he was a little fellow. "Down just a bit deeper, I'm hard as a rock. And I'm in detective work."

LePeters detected an appealing deep-forest fragrance as the girl glided past him, her hair long and thick, her body a fraction short of being absurdly voluptuous. She had on a bathing suit that was modest and dated and seemed to have been chosen in some preposterous hope that by wearing it she might miraculously avoid trouble and pass as a girl with a normal body. She belonged to that species of overbrimming creature LePeters had been running into throughout his life; automatically he would consider them beyond his reach, quickly rationalizing that he really liked springy, coltlike women with no bosoms to confuse him and complicate matters. She had a sturdy, dutiful style of throwing the ball, and LePeters thought of women of the hills, great-haunched and natural, carrying urns to the tops of mountains, cooking lamb racks over an open fire, later making sturdy, tradition-bound love to their warrior husbands; the kind of woman who at the same time was fully capable of slicing off a pecker if her mate so much as glanced at another girl of the hills.

Her friend, humpbacked and tentacled as he was, had a surprisingly sure-handed way of swallowing up the ball and reminded LePeters of legendary playground athletes who were blocked from big-league competition either because of asthma or moms who insisted they first get a toehold in the dry-goods business. LePeters, not really that good as a catcher, had developed a compensatory loose-limbed, easygoing loping style and a gracious big-league chuckle of surprise when he dropped balls—as though he was so preoccupied with overall style and attitude it was understandable he might let a few get away from him. There was a definite competitive thread to the catch, the insectlike fellow giving LePeters tough throws, LePeters fine when the ball was in front of him, in deep trouble if it were thrown over his head. Since childhood, he'd had a fear of turning his back on the ball, convinced that if he did he would wind up in a deep mountain gorge, covered over with bones. It was a tense catch for a while, with, no two ways about it, the girl as a prize, but then the sun took over, slowing them down, spinning them lazily around, tying them together in a slow and sensual triangle.

The girl did a mock collapse in the sand and LePeters fell down beside her as though he were joining a partner in some strenuous activity for a well-earned comradely rest; actually, it was in the hope of a lucky brush against her deep, conservatively supported bosoms. She had a marvelous forest dampness about her, forcing LePeters, who felt like a heel for doing so, to think of his wife Claire who'd never once broken into a sweat. It was a semi-joke between them, his wife turning up her nose at his armpit stains and saying, "Pretty girls don't do that." In what was unquestionably a dig at LePeters, the girl's spindly friend said, "I might as well go up and get the bed ready for us." Whatever the ploy, it worked and LePeters was sick to his stomach at the thought that they actually lived together.

"One bed, eh?" said LePeters.

"Um-hm," said the girl.

"For the two of you . . ." said LePeters.

"That's right," said the girl. There was some tease to her attitude, but she suddenly frowned, as though she were both concerned about LePeters and dissatisfied with a style she'd been trying out, one that had turned out to be completely wrong for her.

"Nothing happens, though," she said. "Victor can't actually do anything. It's very sad. I lie there, you know, sort of Venus de Milo, and Victor studies me."

"And you let him?" said LePeters, slightly relieved, but still plenty sick, too.

"Oh God, you should see his face. He really wants to," said the girl.

LePeters felt a momentary twinge of sympathy for the obviously troubled Victor and thought of summoning him
forth for another catch, dropping a few balls intentionally to
shore up his tattered virility. But it was only a twinge. Who
was he to feel sorry for anyone. After all, take a peek at what
Victor was getting—dark forest-scented night-long figure
studies, broken up by earnest menstrual confabs. Compared
to his own setup, having to tackle the iron-willed, iron-
girdled Claire LePeters, Victor was on easy street.

The girl said she was Ellen Rosenberg, previously Ellen
Cunningham whose engagement to a monied Rumanian had
been broken off by a jealous, meddling, prospective mother-
in-law. At a party, the old crone had waggled a gray finger at
Ellen and whispered to her son, "For my money, she looks a
little Jewish." On the spot, in a lightning move that was totally untypical of her, she had become Ellen Rosenberg, as
though to say, "They want Jewish, I'll give them Jewish."
How ironic for LePeters who had once been a Sussman. Here
on a faraway island, basically set up for vacationing black cor-
porate types, he had chanced upon a girl who in a sense had
eagerly snatched up the very Sussmaned past he had self-
consciously rejected. Her story, as told, was a clear and open
road, but LePeters soon saw that it was lined with regularly
spaced sexual booby traps that both thrilled and terrified
him; whether they were designed for that purpose, he wasn't
one to say. Only twenty-two, she had tried many careers,
including the airlines which she finally had to quit because
the takeoffs and particularly the landings were almost un-
bearably sensual for her. One pilot in particular had a flying
style that really gave her the works. "Each time we came
down, in Kansas or someplace like that, I'd get, you know,
wet. And then in the lounge, Ned would always wink at me

and say 'How's your doo doo.' " Much as he enjoyed it, the
story struck LePeters as being overwhelmingly vulgar and he
made a note to tell her, once he got to know her better, not
to spin off the yarn on such short acquaintance and if she
absolutely had to, to leave off the "doo doo" tagline.

After the airlines, Ellen Rosenberg had finally decided
that she was truly gifted in working with her hands. "Watch
what I can do with a simple handful of sand." Gathering up
a damp clump of it, she molded it a bit, whistling happily as
she worked, and then set it down beside LePeters with enormous pride. It had the shape of a bowl to LePeters and did
not look richly crafted, although he conceded she may have
been after some subtly primitive pre-Columbian values he
was powerless to evaluate. "There's a job in an ironmongery
when I get back to the city," she said, "three Armenian
brothers. It's going to be grab-ass, grab-titty from the second
I get there, but it's a wonderful chance to learn about kilns."
LePeters wondered about the sexual shafts that wormed
their way into each of her stories and adventures: on the
credit side, she did not toss them off with any particular re-
lish and seemed wearily resigned to that side of her nature, as
though she were dealing with a facial tic she had no power
to control.

A great wolflike dog shambled over to them and LePeters,
a little nervous, shoved him about playfully, saying, "There
you go, fella" and "What you want, boy" more or less to
show Ellen Rosenberg he was an outdoorsy guy. But the dog
had a lazy, stoop-necked determination to its movements and
LePeters suddenly realized it was fully capable of pulling his
throat out, leaving him dead in the middle of the barren Jigtown beach. How could he rule this out as a possibility. After
all, it was a foreign dog. What could it know about LePe-

ters's wife, his kid, his overall responsibilities back in the States. Not that it would think twice if it were fully informed.

"You fool around with him for a while," he said, turning the animal over to Ellen Rosenberg, "I've been having a little trouble with the old kidneys." It was a cowardly thing to do, but the truth was, even though he was attracted to the girl, she was still a fairly casual acquaintance and if it had to be him or her he was picking himself. Casually jogging back to the hotel, he found the john and pretended to take a leak, then peeked out of the window to see how things were going. When he was sure the dog was gone, he put on a look of disappointment, then trotted back and said, "Where'd he go? What did you do, chase him off?"

Ellen Rosenberg worked on her bowls. Completing a row of them, one more clumsy than the other, she looked up and said, "You were scared shitless, weren't you?"

It was the kind of remark that should have shattered him. As it was, it was no caress, but perhaps because of its directness and the gentle way she said it, it didn't bother him that much either.

"I'd take on a horse, a bull, anything. In my work, I come up against some pretty crazy guys, Mexicans, all kinds. There's something about dogs, though, quiet ones like that."

"Let me touch this," she said, running her hand the length of his face-dividing scar. It was another gesture that should have sent him through the roof—even Claire LePeters had been trained to pretend it wasn't there—but after a little shiver, he relaxed and let her play with his scar, even though he was so self-conscious about it that part of the reason he'd come to the islands was to get a suntan so it would blend in more with his face.

"Look at this," she said, delightedly running her fingers

along the extra folds of his stomach. "Will you just look at this!" Though she had practically made a public announcement that he wasn't sleek-waisted, once again, for some miraculous reason, he wasn't disturbed.

"Anytime I make the decision, it comes right off," he said.

"You're not used to being touched, are you?" she said, returning to her bowls.

"Not true," he said, lying through his teeth. "I get touched plenty."

A black ice-cream vendor strolled by and said, "How about a popsicle, grandpa, and one for your daughter?" Though the vendor, kidding or not, had drawn attention to the vast age difference between LePeters and Ellen Rosenberg, once again he found himself reacting with outrageous good-nature, buying a couple of ice creams and sending the black peddler off with a healthy tip. "Listen," LePeters said, with a hitch in his voice and fearful of a turndown, "what about some dinner later on?" Looking down at her handicrafts, Ellen Rosenberg touched her fingertips against his and was silent for a moment. It was a small gesture, but it seemed binding and eternal and would have been more so if they had happened to be shy young Czech lovers in a meadow.

"Listen," she said, finally, still looking at the bowls, "even though our fingers are touching, I don't know about dinner."

"How come?" asked LePeters.

"I can't hurt Victor," she said, "and besides, I've got delicate tissues."

How much had happened, really. Not that much. For all he knew, Ellen Rosenberg, delicately tissued, menstrually trou-

bled, might never show up in his life again. Pared right down
to the core, all that had gone on was a little innocent finger-
and scar-touching on a deserted beach. Yet LePeters felt like
the worst rat in the world for selling out his kid and Claire
LePeters, a preposterous notion when you consider that his
wife kept her lips in hiding, her body dangling light-years
away from him, and in so many ways was telling him, sexually at least, to get lost. Only once in his married life had
LePeters strayed and at that it was one of the feeblest mean-
derings in the book. One weekend, Claire LePeters flew off
to show Jamie to her lonely western parents. LePeters,
attending a Friends of Turkey get-together alone, quickly
fished a desirable redhead from the throng of politically ori-
ented merrymakers. "Anything goes," the girl had said, as
she took LePeters on a guilt-ridden ride to a hotel she was
particularly fond of, "except one thing. I don't go for one-
night stands." Keeping much of himself cordoned off, out of
bounds, LePeters made love to her and even had a few kicks
along the way, but then let her know by his attitude the next
morning that she had just let herself in for another of that
most dreadful of all experiences, the one-niter. LePeters took
showers around the clock, then went to pick up his wife and
daughter at the terminal, the little girl seemingly baffled by
his presence. "Who that man?" she said, pointing to LePeters, who was convinced that despite his spotless condition
and the child's almost ridiculous youth and innocence she
had somehow been able to smoke out the redhead.

Not that he had done that much straying with Ellen
Rosenberg. What troubled him was the speed with which his
feelings about her had gone galloping on ahead. On Detectives' Hill, he had spoken of feeling hemmed in, frustrated,
having to rest his hernia. Had he really gone off in search of
an Ellen Rosenberg who could turn a spotlight on his facial

scar, cackle openly at his extra fat and get away with it because in some way she indicated that she cared about him.

LePeters was somewhat bruised by Ellen Rosenberg's dinner turndown; yet only three hours later, he found himself
freshly showered, dressed to the nines, sitting at the same bar
and thirsting for new Jigtown adventures, all probably attributable to the amazing effects of a single extra-dry Gibson on
a tropical isle. But then immediately and heartbreakingly, he
saw Ellen Rosenberg being swept off to dinner by the desperately unattractive Victor, after tossing LePeters a halfhearted
wave. Would the keenest of observers have guessed she was a
girl who only short hours before had affectionately fondled
his scar? LePeters spent the balance of the evening hanging
around with Boners, then moved his bags to Jigtown's main
hotel and went to bed, unable for the life of him to figure out
if he was having a good time. On the one hand, his face had
become quickly bronzed, a trait that ran in the family, any
member of whom had only to poke his face up at the sky to
come away with a thrilling suntan. While others raced off for
costly Florida vacations, LePeters remembered kindly old
Bill Sussman, his departed furrier dad, slipping off to a bench
behind a deserted stadium, then returning in an hour or so
with a rich tan that would have been the envy of royalty. As a
child on the beach, LePeters recalled his mom, Flo Sussman,
urging him to "move up a little closer to the sun," a totally
unnecessary piece of advice since Bill Sussman had passed
the knack for instant tans along to his son. Not a bad legacy
when you consider that the best some kings had been able to
do for their offspring was saddle them with tragic blood diseases. At the moment, however, his fresh suntan was of little
use to LePeters who was aware of great sheets of loneliness
pouring down upon him in the lonely oceanfront hotel room.
Back on Detectives' Hill, even though it would have taken a

carefully planned commando operation to slip through
Claire LePeters's defenses, at least she was there, across the
bed, and he could hear her breathing. And if his wife kept
him affection-starved, there was always Jamie, good for at
least a dozen hugs and kisses on the nose before she finally
settled into sleep. An ace up LePeters's sleeve was his knowledge that no matter how low he got at night, a single glimpse
of morning light was enough to change his mood dramatically, to induce a great yelping leap of the heart totally out of
proportion to his situation, which was usually no bargain.
But that knowledge helped him only slightly as he tossed
about and fought for sleep in a lonely Jigtown hotel room,
one that had no doubt been slept in by a long procession of
fun-seeking colored executives before him.

Early the next morning Ellen Rosenberg pounded on LePeters's door and proposed an exploratory hike to the island's
interior in search of ancient caves and rare government-pro-
tected vegetation of spectacular beauty. LePeters hollered
back okay, even though his head was clouded over and he
knew it would be at least an hour before he could be the
slightest bit romantic and charming. He joined her in front
of the hotel and found her barefoot, peasantlike and fra-
grantly damp, even before they had done any strenuous hiking. As they set off, she said she had packed a lunch of
chicken sections and Russian dressing and insisted that you
could eat tons of it with not the slightest risk of getting
paunchier. LePeters noticed that she walked at least three
steps up ahead of him and could not help wondering if this
were some sort of sexual signaling in the way of restless female gibbons at the peak of the mating season. "The reason

I'm staying up ahead," she said, "is that outside my high school one day, an old guy leaped out of the bushes and snapped my pants." LePeters did not mind the three-pace separation and rather enjoyed watching Ellen Rosenberg weave provocatively on ahead of him, although from time to time he closed the gap for a folksy affectionate tap on her behind, as though congratulating her for her sturdy, uncomplaining hiking technique. "If I were interested in a fellow," she said, tossing the words back over her shoulder, "he would have to have a philosophy, so I could sit around at his feet a lot." The remark put a certain amount of pressure on LePeters who was fully aware that he had no formal attack on life, although he had made many serious promises to himself to take some time off and get one set up.

"Quite frankly," he told her as they entered a dense and thickly overgrown section of the island, "I'm a little suspicious of guys who can just toss one off in a neat little capsule. Nine times out of ten they don't hold up." But there was something loose and freewheeling about his mood as he slipped along behind the thinly skirted Ellen Rosenberg and he decided to take a shot at one. At worst, she would wheel around in disgust and jog back to Victor for an afternoon figure study, a dark prospect, but then again, nothing to make LePeters blow his brains out. He told her he was a dick and had often wondered why he had ended up in that particular game since when he thought about it, it was probably more than an accident. Otherwise, why would he have stayed at it for seventeen years when with no great effort he might have been able to make a mid-career switch to children's ready-to-wear. "I suppose," he said, "there's a part of it I like. The closing in on people, the look in their eyes. If you have a choice, it's just so much better than being closed in on.

"There's an awful lot to dick work we're so close to we can't evaluate it," he said, more or less in summary. "I have a hunch that years from now, they're going to feel that it was really an art form of a kind, maybe the only real one of the sixties. The way they finally saw the beauty in soup cans and cereal boxes."

"That's it?" said Ellen Rosenberg.

"That's it," said LePeters.

"That's your philosophy?"

"There's more to it than that, but it would take years to go into it. Why, anything wrong?"

"No," she said, slowing down and dreamily trailing a naked toe through the underbrush, "except that it's going to take a little getting used to." But she let him catch up with her and put her damp hand in his; they trudged along in step now, and LePeters was able to see that in the way of philosophy all she was asking for was to be thrown a bone.

As they neared the interior, they began to climb a hill, Ellen Rosenberg steering them along with great confidence and expertise as though she were in her own back yard. Spotting a swarthy type in a wide-brimmed hat who appeared to be a forest ranger of some kind, Ellen Rosenberg gave him a cheery wave and said, "That's Hernando, care to take him along?"

"What do we need him for?" LePeters asked.

"We can sort of fool around with him," she said. "He doesn't have that much to do." LePeters conceded to himself that it must have been lonely work Hernando was up to, and indeed wondered what it would be like to be in charge of keeping an eye on what was probably the world's only exclusively colored wildlife preserve, unless you wanted to get into Africa, probable home of pithecanthropus man. Still, LePeters at the moment saw no need for deep involvement with the fellow and told Ellen Rosenberg he would prefer to pass the ranger by. If he were after that kind of tomfoolery they might as well go back to Jigtown and scoop up the unpleasant but at least more familiar Victor. "You seem to know your way around these parts pretty well," said LePeters, as Ellen Rosenberg snaked along the narrow almost hidden jungle paths. "Ever been here before?"

She said that indeed she had covered the same terrain previously, but only once, with an aging retailer, who had skipped away from his wife for a solo celebration of his seventy-fifth birthday. "No grabbies," she said. "We camped out and it made him feel like a million to have a young knish sleeping at his feet."

LePeters wondered how she had gotten into the racket of shoring up the confidence of not especially distinguished fellows. To attract her, all that seemed to be required was that a fellow be tremendously down on himself. What could possibly be in it for her, Florence Nightingale to the emotionally shell-torn. Just LePeters's luck, he had probably gotten to her when after buoying up the battered egos of a long series of retailers, she was about to swerve off in another more profitable direction, one that would insure her a bigger slice of the emotional pie.

When they were almost at the peak of the hill, Ellen Rosenberg plopped down in a small clearing and broke out the chicken sections, dipping them in the Russian dressing and falling upon them with luscious, finger-licking, natural-woman gusto. LePeters saw what she was up to but had to be honest with himself and admit he was on the fence about that approach to eating, one part of him preferring a more demure dining style.

Later, when it was dark, they reached the top of the hill, LePeters tired and in something of a lustful turmoil after a day's worth of following the sturdy and hypnotically sensual hiking movements of Ellen Rosenberg. Each time he made an outwardly playful yet actually dead serious attempt to hurl her to the ground beneath a shrub, she would leap nimbly out of his reach and switch the subject to ceramic urn-baking or world peace. At the top of the hill, she pointed out what appeared to be an inn, one she had no doubt visited with the ancient retailer. To get to it, they crossed a bamboo bridge, LePeters taking deep swallows of the thick, fragrant tropical air though far from certain it was the best thing in the world for his lungs. Overhead, the birds let out frightened, demented shrieks and might have just gotten word that the world was crazy. Waiting at the end of the bridge was an elderly couple who greeted them in harsh Germanic accents, the woman taking Ellen Rosenberg off in private, no doubt to inquire discreetly about the elderly retailer. Putting an arm around LePeters's shoulder, the innkeeper led him to the edge of a cliff where he waved at the rich valley below and said, "These are my hills, this is my valley. Here I have found peace." The fellow said that he and his wife were indeed Germans and had slipped out of Berlin and headed for the islands in 1945, just before the roof fell in on Hitler.

"What'd you do in Germany?" asked LePeters.

"I was a Nazi," said the fellow, indicating that he had been indirectly responsible for the deaths of at least three Jews he knew about, possibly two others, but not more than six altogether. The fellow's remarks were made with a certain candor, which LePeters could not find it in himself to label "refreshing." He came within a hair of telling the innkeeper to proceed with caution, that he had once been Kenneth Sussman, but he held off, probably because he had always felt that any reaction to the death camps short of blowing up the entire planet was cheapening.

"I wonder if you and the young lady intend to spend the

night?" the old fellow asked. The remark caught LePeters off guard and for some reason he began to slap at his leg as though a small boy had accidentally shot an arrow into it. But then Ellen Rosenberg darted by and said of course they were, they wouldn't consider staying anywhere else. Counting the birth of his daughter, the massive carton of candy bars he had won for a school-safety jingle contest, and a handful of other triumphs, LePeters had to consider this one of the six great moments of his life.

The innkeeper couple invited them in for a simple meal that consisted of a series of humbly prepared dishes, the couple eating with bent-backed pilgrim gratitude and savoring each bite with religious awe. It occurred to LePeters that they had plenty to be humble about. What was the spare diet supposed to do, make up for Dachau? In the middle of the meal, after making an honest attempt to get some enjoyment out of a humble mound of mashed potatoes, LePeters finally slipped his plate beneath the innkeeper's nose and said, "Listen, don't you have any salt or pepper around here? Garlic, anything. I can't enjoy these the way they're set up." He stood up and put his jaw close to the German's, and Ellen Rosenberg, sensing it wasn't table spices he was upset about, scooped up a bottle of homemade wine and led him outside, singing operatic selections in a voice that was only fair and doing mock ballet steps. It was a tipsy, carefree style, LePeters sensing it may have been a coverup for nervousness. The cabin she took him to had no electricity, no blankets or bedding, no light except for a spear or two that came through the trees from the stars. LePeters lay back on the mattress and lit a cigarette, as though he were about to play a scene he had been through a thousand times. "What am I getting," she said, "Paul Newman?" She took off her blouse and, with her breasts heavy and free, walked across the cabin to the window, as naturally as if she were alone and tidying up her room at Sarah Lawrence. LePeters tried without success to whip down the impulse but could not help thinking of Claire LePeters, naked for a flash and then making squealing leaps beneath the covers, the whole idea of exposure a painful ordeal. And it had nothing to do with her body which, in some quarters, would have been considered thinly spectacular. Damp and honied, Ellen Rosenberg sat beside him and attempted to bring up urns again, but LePeters cut her off and said, "I just want to tell you that what you did was lovely, that walk across the room."

"Listen, it wasn't that easy," she said. "I was scared out of my wits."

Hugging her in the near-darkness, LePeters knocked over the wine bottle which shattered in thousands of pieces, almost as though it had been ground down by a machine. Since they were both barefoot now, it was as though they were surrounded by a dangerous glass moat, sealed to the bed until daybreak when, with luck, they might be able to pick their way to safety. "Schmuck," said Ellen Rosenberg, sitting up with real irritation, a remark that injured LePeters but not that much since she timed it with a light caress of his shoulders. A few inches of wine remained in the jagged bottom of the bottle and they took turns sipping from it, despite the possibility that at any moment their lips might be slashed to ribbons. It had not seemed to be on his mind at all, but LePeters suddenly drew back from Ellen Rosenberg, took her by the shoulders, and said, "Look, you're a good kid, but everything isn't what it's cracked up to be. I'm down here alone, but I've got a wife and there's a kid in the picture, too, one I'm crazy about. As a matter of fact, I'm in the middle of a devil of a school problem and probably ought to be back there dealing with it. I just thought you ought to know some of this stuff."

Until this moment, Ellen Rosenberg, despite the nude walk across the room, had given no clear evidence she wanted to be made love to. For all LePeters knew, what she had in mind was a retailing night at the foot of the bed. But now, after waiting only one short, breathless beat, she threw her arms around him and said, "Oh, my God, why didn't you tell me?" plunging her tongue down his throat, a place where not that many tongues had been.

"Hey, wait a minute," said LePeters, struggling free. "What about your tissues?"

"They're not that delicate," she said, pressing him back on the bed and tearing at him like an animal.

LePeters woke to find Ellen Rosenberg unaltered, a carbon copy of the girl he had gone hiking with the day before. Naïvely perhaps, he had expected to find some sharply visible change in her—or, for that matter, in any woman who had been made love to, the way you would expect a prairie woman's eyes never to be quite the same after an Indian raid. Although he had capitalized on the results, he was still baffled by her behavior. When he had appeared to be a foot-loose, vacationing fun-seeker, with no apparent ties, she had found him interesting, yet warily kept him at arms' length. The second he let slip that he was hopelessly chained to a marriage and a kid, she had torn his clothes off. Basically a child of the forties, LePeters had expected the opposite. As they trooped back to the hotel, Ellen Rosenberg, perhaps sensing his puzzlement, explained that with a single fellow,

her instinct was to be tentative and cautious, under no circumstances to sleep with him on the first date. In the case of
a married man, there was little need for coyness. "Are you
kidding," she said, as they held hands on the way to Jigtown.
"If you told me you were tied down, I'd have balled you in
twenty minutes." Ironically, LePeters would have bet twenty
to one that throwing Claire LePeters and his kid on the table
would have blown the whole ball game.

Buoyant, cheerful, Ellen Rosenberg mapped out plans for
the week that included glass-bottom boats, trips to neighbor-
ing islands and a look-see at a revival meeting right in the
heart of Jigtown. Another fellow would have thanked his
lucky stars and dug in for the week, tried to stretch it into ten
days, then, with his lips sealed, headed back to his family and
kept the undemanding Ellen Rosenberg as a twice-a-week
cupcake on the side. Not LePeters. He was still a novice at
philandering and even as they neared the hotel he could feel
himself backing away. All he could see was that he was deep
in one mess, why start another. This in spite of the fact that
the soft and trusting Ellen Rosenberg had been nicer to him
than any woman he had known. By the time they reached
Jigtown, the separation was complete and LePeters had
come up with a solution to the delicate situation: he would
say good-bye, pack his bags at mile-a-minute speed, and hotfoot it the hell out of there while the going was good.

In her hotel room, Ellen Rosenberg plopped down on her
bed, face in the pillow, and asked LePeters if he knew anything about lower-back massages.

"Not that much," he said. "Look, I just got word that they
need me back at the bullpen."

"Word?" she said, sitting up. "How'd you get word?"

"They got it to me. Anyway, I have to hightail it out of
here and thought maybe I could see you back in the city."

"Sure," she said, rather forlornly, hands clasped between her legs. She took a quick and pathetic sniff of her shoulder as though it might be her perfume that was driving him off.

"Look," he said, patting her thick hair and wondering if it would be a horrendous breach of character to slip under the covers with her for a send-off tumble, "it's got nothing to do with you. You're a terrific kid.

"Take my word for it," he said, one foot out of the door now, "if it wasn't for business, and believe me I'm in a crazy one, wild horses couldn't tear me away from this place."

It was Boners who took LePeters to the airport. One spin-off benefit of being in crime work was the wonderful sense of kinship that existed between dicks around the world. Let a Chicago man show up in New York on an extradition case— or even in some one-horse town in the Far West—and he could count on being given the red-carpet treatment: top eats, a visit to the standout joints, and a chance to shoot the breeze with fellows who spoke the same language. As they neared the terminal, Boners slipped LePeters a tiny locket that was meant as a going-away present. It had a scroll inside that said:

A VOMITING AMERICAN

- *I vomit from those Americans who've lived off the fat of this land yet go around p--ing and moaning and wanting change.*
- *I vomit from those who would take guns away from Americans and not let them shoot freely when in their hearts they know it's right.*
- *I vomit from those who would not obey every*

law, since, after all, what are laws for.
- *I vomit from those who place little stock in
  personal cleanliness, going around with messy,
  greasy, unruly uncombed hair and dirt under
  fingernails that were given to them tidy.*
- *Finally, I vomit most from those who have the
  gall to say that God is laying down on the job.
  If you vomit with me, accept this scroll.*

Benjamin R. Boners

In truth, LePeters could think of few if any of the precepts
he agreed with. Yet he decided there was no point in getting
into a heated point-by-point debate with the retired dick and
winding up his vacation with more strain than he had come
down with. So he thanked Boners and pocketed the gift,
which he had every intention of dumping as soon as he got
off the ground. The odds, after all, were only slight that he
would ever have to face Boners again, say, at a convention,
and be asked to whip out the locket as evidence that he had
gone around treasuring it. LePeters made a mental note to
send the fellow a box of chocolate-covered cherries once he
got back to Detectives' Hill. And as long as he was at it, he
might as well send one to Ellen Rosenberg. Then, with a
final wave to the misguidedly patriotic dick and to the island
in general, LePeters mounted the gangplank and took his last
look at Jigtown.

Mouthless, with only tiny smoked holes where the eyes and
nostrils had been, the mummied child crossed the lawn to
LePeters. Great crosses of adhesive patched its face and the
hands were outstretched, beseeching, a sleepwalker wheeling

through a radioactive dream. With a slight, embarrassed smirk, the Negro girl named Samantha circled lazily on a bike. For his brief idyll with Ellen Rosenberg, LePeters had been fully prepared to accept bearded, wrathful vengeance from on high; nonetheless, he was startled by its swiftness and the direct no-nonsense nature of the blow: his daughter involved in a fight-to-the-finish washroom razor brawl with half a dozen older and better-coordinated colored kids. Burned out, directionless, the plaster child groped across the lawn and the feelings inside LePeters's wrecked chest were beyond pity; one part of him wanted to crush the child like a paper cut-out, throw it away and start a new one. On his knees, LePeters put his face in the grass and heard his daughter say, "Did it work? Did I really fool you?" He looked up and saw her peeling away the bandages until her straw-colored curls tumbled free. "Tell the truth," she said, "were you scared out of your wits or were you just making me feel good?" LePeters said that indeed he had been frightened but that it was not a good idea to go around doing that to people. "You pull that on older folks, for example, and it might be lights-out for them, then and there. I wasn't referring to someone like myself particularly." LePeters, however, was thrilled to see his daughter and had no heart to go on with the gentle scolding. Instead, he heaved her up in the air, enjoying the special children smell of her, and gave her a good bite in the stomach, realizing with a certain sadness that he'd have to stop those before long since they would be open to question when she got a bit older.

Claire LePeters came across with a surprise kiss and said that the school had been making its own movie, one about contaminated meat. "She's a slice of over-the-hill calves' liver or something. I saw a little of it and it's really not that bad; they do it dressed as puppets and when it's finished they ship it around to depressed areas, maybe even India. She's always play-acting now. That's what the bandages are."

Warily, Samantha came close and said, "The other kids can't act shit compared to your daughter, Mrs. LePeters."

LePeters's wife asked the colored child if she wanted to come in for something to eat; Samantha said she wouldn't mind a liverwurst sandwich but preferred having it thrown out the window to her. Entering the house with his arm around his wife and daughter, LePeters could have sworn he smelled a hotly spiced dish that was a favorite of his, even though he had only eaten it once. A cook of astonishing inventiveness, Claire LePeters smothered him with frustration by offering up adventurous ground-breaking culinary treats a single time, instantly growing bored with them and never whipping them up again. There had been a particular concoction, prepared for him in early marriage, that had driven him wild. In a vain attempt to flatter another serving out of her, LePeters gave the dish an exotic French label, one that worked his wife's name into it and made it sound as though it were a famed specialty at Le Pavillon. Only now, seventeen years later, with the guilty fragrance of Ellen Rosenberg still touching his skin, had the taste-treat made a return engagement. Slapping together a heaping liverwurst sandwich, Claire LePeters wrapped it in tinfoil and wafted it out the window; the three then sat down for the first time in ages to a heaping family dish of *Emince du Boeuf à Claire LePeters Marengo.*

Though LePeters had enjoyed himself in the islands, he regretted the time he had spent away from his daughter, just a few days but ones that could never be replaced. He wondered, too, about the exact chemistry of the relationship between them; how could he describe it other than to talk about hamburgers, ferris-wheel rides, card tricks, plenty of squeezes, and a story he had made up about a guinea pig that becomes a Hollywood star, turning its back on its loved ones, but then getting lonely, renouncing its phony friends and going back to its original owner, a detective's ten-year-old daughter. Surely there had to be much more between a father and a little girl—who couldn't be counted on to remain little forever. After dinner, LePeters headed toward her room, determined to make every second with his daughter meaningful since in a mere seven years or so she would be leaving for her freshman year at college and it better not be a colored one. Upstairs, LePeters saw immediately that he had not done enough for her room; if she had to go to a terrible school, at the very least he could have provided her with expensive mohair rugs, world atlases, terrific bookshelves, and warm, indirect lighting. Not sure how to get things started with her at the moment, LePeters began with a big hug and then ran a finger along the books in her library, surprised at the titles he came across. He could have sworn that on many occasions he had carted home batches of sturdy children's classics such as *Dombey and Son*. Yet for some reason, all she had held on to was a little shelf of books that included *The Life of W. C. Fields, Believe It or Not—14th Series, Getting to Know Kenya*, a karate handbook, and *Shark!!!* Still wondering what she was doing with such a strange and heartbreaking little library, LePeters asked his daughter how she was getting along at school. "And not only that, but how have you been doing generally?"

"Fine," said the little girl.

"But how are, you know, things?"

"There are some things I can't tell you, Daddy. You might get mad."

"Me?" said LePeters, pointing a finger at himself in surprise. "You've just insulted your dad." He then went on to tell her that even though he might come off as being on the stiff side, there was actually very little in the way of human behavior that could throw him off and certainly nothing from his own kid. "In the kind of work I do," he told her, "I get to see most everything." Then he sat back and braced himself for what he was sure would be a parade of youthful sexual shenanigans that would seem grim and consequential in the child's eyes yet with a little luck turn out to be innocent. His daughter, come to think of it, was the same age as a girl named Sheila who had once invited LePeters, and presumably other fellows in the neighborhood, up to her apartment for regularly scheduled shower-curtain peeks at her newly sprouted pubic hair. Shortly afterward, her dad had been trundled off to prison on an embezzling charge, an event most of the neighbors pounced on as the key to her dark behavior. In this day and age, of course, shower-stall treats would be considered small potatoes. No matter, LePeters thought, just so long as I don't hear she's gone the distance.

"Remember the viaduct on Collins Avenue?" the little girl asked.

"I sure do," said LePeters, who remembered it only too well, a shakily constructed bridge at the foot of Detectives' Hill, dizzying to the eye, that arced its way uncertainly over a whizzing parade of traffic below.

"Samantha and four other kids dared me to go out on it, hang by my legs upside down and spit at the cars below. I said I wouldn't, so they did it first and then they pushed me out on it. I was scared out of my wits because if I fell I would crack my head open and be dead. That was one of the things we did. Then we went over to the sand pit near the new housing project where a colored kid was killed last year. He tried to yell for help, but it was probably just glub, glub, glub. Anyway, there's a vine you can use to swing over it that makes you miss the sand pit by a few feet. So when the workmen weren't looking, we tricked them and took turns swinging on the vine. You feel like Tarzan. It's really great up there. I can hardly describe the feeling, like a king, although no one wants to fall off and wind up dead like that poor colored kid. Imagine how his parents feel."

Sitting cross-legged before him, as though she were entertaining at a campfire, Jamie LePeters then launched into a whole series of hair-raising adventures she'd had in her father's absence, each involving some death-defying walk along a building ledge, a stroll through a fire-condemned school that might collapse at any moment, or a game played in an abandoned railroad yard on a section of third rail everyone was sure didn't have any voltage left in it. Each of the yarns hit LePeters like a battering ram. "What did you do that for?" he would say in shock or "Why weren't you careful?" More often he would simply make an *ummpph* sound that only seemed to spark her into some new spine-tingling anecdote in which she escaped death by a whisker. LePeters had to laugh at himself for his fears of pre-adolescent orgies. How happily he would have grabbed one now in place of the shockers he was being treated to.

"I've really had some terrific adventures," she said. "That's one thing this neighborhood is great for. One of my greatest was when Samantha took me to see where she lives. You should see what goes on there. Around thirty little kids in one room with snot hanging down and garbage all over the place. I don't see how she gets her homework done. And this drunken colored lady with a big belly in the middle of it on an old mattress. What eyeballs she had! She called me over and gave me a quarter and said it was because I was nice to Samantha. Was I scared when I went over to her. We went outside and three Puerto Rican guys started to beat us up, but then Samantha got some bigger boys to chase them away. We went over and hitched a ride on the back of the new ambulance with the driver not even knowing we were hanging on to the back of it with one hand. If he ever found out. Then it was dark so I came home, right past the plasterer who always throws rocks at me and tries to hit me on the head. Someone ought to tell him not to do that. In certain ways that I can't explain, I really love to live around here."

"Listen," said the exhausted LePeters, who'd been glued to her side through every viaduct leap, a step behind as she made her fire-condemned rounds, "let's make a deal."

"What's that?" she asked, fully awake but getting into her pajamas anyway.

"From now on, we won't have any more of these little talks."

Emboldened by the unexpected lawn kiss from his wife, LePeters, after saying good night to his daughter, walked across the hallway, hoping for a long-awaited bedroom breakthrough. Claire LePeters had not exactly greeted her husband with a brass band, but on the other hand she had seemed genuinely pleased to see him again. Maybe that was the ticket, scoop up all of their savings, take a ruthless annual vacation in the sun and let her see if life was any bed of roses

without him. Inside the bedroom, the two lamps gave off a
sour, pornographic haze that was disappointing to LePeters,
who was touchy about such things and had been known to
storm out of award-winning restaurants that were poorly lit.
He preferred a warm and oranged feeling. On the plus side of
the ledger, Claire LePeters was tastily curled up on his side
of the bed, which was foreign territory to her. He hung his tie
on a closet rack, one that he had built in general shop as a
teen-ager and still displayed proudly as his only mechanical
triumph. Then, to allay Claire LePeters's fear of being spied
on, he made sure that all doors, windows, and wall cracks
were totally sealed off so that no intruder had a chance of
getting a peek at them unless he were willing to gamble on a
desperate, helmeted kamikaze plunge through the ceiling.
Glancing over at his wife, LePeters thought back to the high-
lights of his intimate life with her, two occasions in particular
when the normally quiescent Claire LePeters had unaccountably flown into tornadoes of sexual abandon. The first
involved a night when the two were forced by bad weather to
spend the night in a ninth-rate fleabag hotel in the redlight
district of a hell-for-leather western mining town. The second came three weeks before the birth of Jamie LePeters
when his wife's kindly obstetrician had put a firm veto on
anything but the most casual of bedroom high-jinx. Both
times, Claire LePeters had turned demented, famished, almost lunatic in her craving for him. Now, back from his vacation and with the smell of the islands and the appeal of the
stranger about him, LePeters felt he might be in for a third
historic session. For an unbalanced second, he was tempted
to tell his wife about the pleasant one-shot experience with
the gentle Ellen Rosenberg. As his friend and lifetime companion, she would chuckle gently and both would enjoy the
harmless little adventure together, seeing it in perspective as

an innocent lark that under no circumstances would be repeated. But even LePeters, a novice at dilly-dallying, saw that this could be suicidal. Instead, he decided that without revealing their origin, he would trot out a few of the potentially valuable new moves he had picked up in Jigtown. The Rosenberg girl, perhaps because she was delicately tissued— or was it because she had learned there was no way to mold a classic urn in a day?—had been a great one for going slow. In their single night together, deep in the Jigtown interior, she had demonstrated to LePeters the exquisite rewards involved in wandering lazily around the corners rather than tearing on ahead at breakneck speed. Now LePeters set about trying a few of the new foot-dragging procedures on his wife. Quickly, he saw that they were not going to send her through the roof. But she did seem to appreciate his sudden inventiveness and more or less watched him with a certain pleased alertness, as if delighted by some neat plot twists from a movie-maker she had once enjoyed but long since written off. LePeters recalled some early times when she had cried bitterly and pointed a guilty finger at him for not "giving" her an orgasm, as though it were his responsibility to leave the bedroom and come dashing back with one on a tray. He had long since seen through all that and realized that unless she kicked in a bit it was no go. On this occasion, typically, she fell a bit shy of the finish line, but seemed pleased and relaxed, happy she had gone along for the ride.

"You certainly are a different person," she said, when LePeters appeared to have run through his repertoire.

"It's the getting away," he said. "It really clears the cobwebs." And then, to her enormous surprise, LePeters confidently grabbed his wife a second time and trotted out a few new turns he had slyly been keeping up his sleeve.

As a boy, it always thrilled LePeters to learn that he was sick, since the days at home meant delicious toast and juices and round-the-clock radio shows, brilliantly balanced between adventure and homespun comedy, ones that he could listen to until he was blue in the face. The first day back at school was another matter; inevitably, the class, in his absence, would have lurched off in some dramatic new educational direction leaving sick boys who had missed the first day of patient explanation to be crippled in their comprehension of the subject for all of their days. Returns from summer camp were also trying times for LePeters. As he shyly wandered back to the local drugstore, someone would dash up and ask, "Have you seen Gribbins?" and then begin to howl with laughter and astonishment. Gribbins, who had gone off to camp as a spindly boy, easy to beat up, would then make his entrance, having mushroomed into a huge, powerful dinosaur of a fellow, raging with strength, so great in the chest and arms his legs could barely support him. "That's nothing," someone else would say. "Wait till you get a load of Whitey." At which point there would be a general sucking in of breath as a second behemoth lumbered into view.

Now, returning to the bullpen, LePeters was exhilarated, since it meant he was going back to the comfortable ritual of his desk and clippings and glue pot and the solidarity of familiar faces all tied together in the same homicide game. Had he been a full-fledged dick, no doubt he would have felt even more of a sense of belonging. He also braced himself for what he was sure would be an onslaught of staggering changes that had taken place in his absence. Sadly, he realized that the changes would not be boyhood ones; even if

Teener had been force-fed with special Japanese nutriments, there was no way for him to have sprouted six inches into a newly muscled teen-ager brimming with health. Inevitably, LePeters would learn that a dick he was fond of had been lured into a subway by a streetwise punk and stopped three in the chest. Or that another friend, having succumbed to the pressures of homicidal pursuit, now popped glycerine tablets into his mouth as a fresh cardiac patient.

First to greet LePeters was his friend and sidekick, Detective Teener, who had a sweet tooth for departmental gossip equal to his own. Extending a bullet-whittled hand, Teener sat at LePeters's desk and told him that indeed there had been an office heart attack, the unfortunate fellow being the bureau wiseacre, Detective Flamoyan. LePeters was genuinely sad but also a little pleased, as though there were a certain number of attacks to be had and Flamoyan's coronary meant there was one less around for him. Almost on cue, Flamoyan appeared, breathing heavily, and said that after a night of drinking he had awakened at four in the morning to a terrible pain in his chest that wouldn't go away, a definite heart attack. "My way of dealing with it was to get dressed and drive to the beach, where I ran seven miles on the sand until I was almost unconscious. Then I went back home and sank back into bed, completely exhausted."

"Did it go away?" LePeters asked.

"No, it got worse," said Flamoyan. "Next time it happens to me I'm not going to do any heavy track work. I almost killed myself."

A conspicuous change was the addition to the homicide public relations staff of Sissy Glober as a full-time worker. Installed by her dad at a desk directly opposite LePeters's, she now sat reading back issues of *Bullet-In*, her long legs drawn up and her thinly covered crotch on full view from every conceivable direction and possibly visible to ships at sea. LePeters, trying to be businesslike on his first day back, made wild gymnastic cranes of his neck to avoid her legs, but was always magnetically drawn back to them and wound up having to take a diversionary stroll through the bullpen with Teener at his side. Though he dearly treasured them, LePeters had always felt that such displays by girls were freakish one-in-a-million accidents. Now he wondered if by some slim chance Sissy Glober had an inkling of what she was doing. If so, did it give her some pleasure, perhaps make her feel she was symbolically screwing all law enforcement in America.

LePeters took a look at a new homicidal electronic system that had been installed so that people whose husbands and wives had been axed to death could, with a single phone call, be sure of having a pair of dicks at their side within a matter of minutes. But the system seemed to puzzle the pair of old-time dicks in charge of it; dazzled by the maze of electronic circuitry, they scratched their heads in confusion while a third dick patiently explained to a woman on the phone that the quickest way to get something done about her slaughtered husband was still to come down and make a personal complaint, and if at all possible bring the remains with her and anything else that might serve as a clue. Otherwise, she would have to wait until the baffled dicks got the hang of the confusing electronic callboard.

Though the bullpen was rarely a totally festive place, LePeters, on this occasion, was aware of a particular veil of glumness that hung in the air. Teener said he knew exactly what LePeters was talking about; indeed, the pall that lay upon the bureau had made his job as arrangements chairman of the annual Homicide and Aggravated Battery Gala almost impossible to perform. Teener said the atmosphere was unmistakably a result of the capture of a fellow who had been

responsible for the bureau's most heinous unsolved crime—
the gunning down of a slew of fathers of teen-age kids. The
guilty party had turned out to be a member of the homicide
team itself, a hitherto trusted, old-line dick known for his
soft, casual style around the bullpen, all in marked contrast
to the savagery with which he smashed the heads of law-
violaters. LePeters now understood the black and bitter
mood of the bureau. Nothing was more likely to bring a
dick's world down upon his head than the knowledge that
one of his own kind had turned homicidal. LePeters had seen
the bureau's toughest operatives, men who had long gone
past fifteen kills, practically weep with rage and confusion
when a colleague joined the opposing team. Perhaps each detective had a horrible fear that deep in his own recesses there
existed a tiny homicidal button that might one day get itself
pushed. Whenever a rogue law-officer case turned up, dicks
would walk about for a few days in a grim and sullen mood,
often getting it out of their systems by rounding up marginally suspicious types in cafeterias and using their bone-
bangers to drum some sense into their heads. But the emer-
gence of a renegade cop case seemed to drive other dicks
completely up a wall. Such a man appeared to be the sky-
high Detective Gibney, an ace vice-squadder who at the moment could not seem to make peace with the latest case.
Hunched over in a corner of the bullpen, almost as though
he had been institutionalized, he wept bitterly and smashed
his fist against the bench, saying over and over again, "The
poor miserable cocksucker. How could he be so stupid,
stupid, stupid."

"Easy now, fella," LePeters said, laying a consoling hand
on the distraught dick's shoulder.

"No, no, no," said Gibney, brushing LePeters aside.
"Never mind easy." And then, with a fresh gush of tears and

one loud, bitter, terrifying wail of sorrow, Gibney completely mystified LePeters by howling, "I just wish to God it had been me."

Half to escape the thick and mournful atmosphere and partly to worm his way back into his boss's affections and make up for the time he'd spent in the sun, LePeters returned to his desk where, for a moment, even Sissy Glober's expansively crotched legs seemed a little on the somber side. LePeters wondered if she had more of the sensual mentholated material either in her desk or on her person—and if so, was he slated to get another crack at some. He checked then to make sure no one had been tampering with the contents of his desk, particularly some of the pictures of high-rumped Senegalese teen-agers he kept hidden beneath a few innocuous Involuntary Manslaughter forms. Glober, LePeters's long-time boss, then slipped in, with an anguished, hunted look on his face. LePeters assumed his superior, too, was depressed about the captured rogue dick, but then he realized it was only Glober's preposterous self-consciousness about coming in late. Even though Glober had risen to great though mysterious heights of wealth and prominence and, indeed, become head of all homicidal public relations, he suffered enormous pangs of guilt about showing up a few minutes after the correct punch-in time; he was the boss and LePeters an employee, yet he had been known to throw himself at LePeters's feet in pleas for understanding. Now, red-eyed, ashen-faced, Glober looked as though he had already put in a tortured hour framing a lateness excuse. Slinking along toward his office with his collar turned up, he did a last-second pivot and made for LePeters's desk, where he grabbed his assistant's lapels and said, "Look, for Christ's sakes, it happens. The most well-meaning of guys can miss a train . . ."

"Of course," LePeters said, resisting the temptation to exploit his boss's misery.

"Thanks, fella," said Glober. "I knew you'd understand."

Instantly cheerful, Glober called LePeters aside and said he had decided to give him a key to his private john. The two of them would be the only ones in the bureau allowed to freshen up in there, relieve themselves, and even knock off the morning paper. LePeters had not exactly been craving a key to the clean little handsomely mirrored bathroom and, indeed, would much have preferred a boost in salary, but he thanked his boss nevertheless and was quite pleased. However, the second Glober handed over the key, LePeters noticed a change in his boss's behavior. Immediately, Glober began to give him suspicious over-the-shoulder looks as though fearful that LePeters was going to spend all day in the john and he wouldn't be able to get in. LePeters tried the john an hour after getting the key, locking the door behind him and feeling an immediate temptation to use all of Glober's cosmetic and pharmacological equipment, even to dab on some of his special prescriptive skin creams. To be on the safe side, he decided, however, to make his first visit a quick one, rinsing his hands off, running a comb through his hair, and calling it quits. As soon as he left, he ran into Glober who'd been pacing up and down outside the door. "You sure took your time, fella," said Glober, giving LePeters a nasty chuckle and then slamming the door in his face. All that afternoon, Glober kept giving LePeters funny looks; on each of his visits to the private john, he would smile thinly and sarcastically at his employee as if to say, "I hope you don't *mind*." At the end of the day, LePeters, a nervous wreck, walked into Glober's office, tossed the key into his boss's lap and said, "Listen, I appreciate what you did for me, but I really think I'd rather use the old john. I feel a little confined in this one."

"All right, all right," said Glober, throwing up his hands and turning his back to LePeters. "But sometimes I don't understand you. I try to do something for you and I wind up getting shit thrown in my face."

◎

With two ducats to the Homicide and Aggravated Battery Gala tucked into his wallet, LePeters sat in the squad and angrily gunned the motor, annoyed at Claire LePeters for hanging him up and angry at himself for not saying the hell with her and heading for the bash alone. Twice he tore out of the driveway and circled the block, but could not get himself to blast off toward the highway and wound up slinking back into the driveway to wait some more. At least an hour late, Claire LePeters looked sensational when she showed up and LePeters knew, from experience, that she would tower over the other dicks' wives in loveliness. A girl of many appearances, her face on this occasion had something coin-stamped and ancient about it; dark and sullen, she might have been glimpsed turning a corner in sixteenth-century Florence. Still, all this was hardly an excuse for the offensive lateness and for not even offering an apology. He'd like to see some other dick's wife try to get away with a stunt like that. She'd wind up having her head slapped in, maybe even pistol-whipped, lying on the floor and begging for forgiveness. Only once had LePeters tapped his wife on the jaw and indeed she *had* wound up on the floor whining for forgiveness. But LePeters had been shocked by his uncivilized behavior and before he left for the bullpen the next day had dropped a note of apology on her dresser; soon they slipped back into the old setup, with Claire LePeters keeping him hours late for appointments.

Teener had booked the party into the ballroom of a clean but second-rate hotel near the bureau, one that was known for giving hefty rake-offs on affairs that were police-involved. LePeters half expected to slip in unnoticed and pretend that he and his wife had arrived hours before but had spent a long time wandering about romantically on porticoes. As he entered, however, he saw that the dicks and their wives were all hungrily crouched over near the buffet table, watching the door and ready to spring at the refreshments the second LePeters arrived. "They're here," someone hollered, the moment LePeters and his wife were in the door, at which time the crime-fighting couples flew at the table and began to stuff themselves with cheese dips and hefty little squares of pizza. "Jesus, were you late," said Glober, not making things any easier for LePeters. "You hung us up in the worst way."

Trying to make himself comfortable, LePeters glanced around at the dicks' wives and was, as usual, startled by some of the extraordinary match-ups. There was simply no way to know a detective in his daily crime-fighting routine and be able to guess the kind of woman he had taken as his lifetime partner. A lean, toughly romantic law-enforcer might turn up with a huge cowlike creature, while some slovenly ham-handed nose-picker rolled in with a bride of ravishing fairness. As though aware of the tremendous inequities, each dick seemed a bit awkward and off-balance with his wife at his side, as though he had been caught in the locker room wearing flowered bikini underwear. LePeters had known Gabby Glober for many years, a square-shouldered, chatty little rascal able to whip up a charity function at a moment's notice; many considered her peppery style to be responsible for Glober's meteoric rise to power and affluence. A surprise to him, on the other hand, was Detective Gibney's teammate. The giraffe-like vice squadder had often spoken of his wife as having been raped, battered, and buggered repeatedly as a result of living in an extremely high-incidence crime neighborhood. Expecting a despondent and sniveling creature, LePeters was startled when Phyllis Gibney turned out to be a fair-skinned, green-eyed Irish wench, quite robust and voluptuous, as though the violations of her body and spirit had worked inversely to make her a staggering beauty. Another shocker was Teener's bride. LePeters didn't have the faintest idea of the kind of girl who would take a shine to his bullet-whittled little friend. The last person in the world LePeters expected to meet was Deborah Teener, an attractively thin and horn-rimmed lovely with an unmistakable whiff of Radcliffe and coming-out parties about her.

His own wife, while holding her own in the loveliness stakes, put him right in the soup by saying to Chief Guster, "We've heard you make twenty-three thousand a year. I think it's unfair that you make that much while we only make eighty-five hundred. You should make more than us, but not that much more." LePeters could hardly believe his ears; putting the most attractive face on the outburst, his wife's remarks could only be considered to be unspeakably rude and uncalled for. Not only that, but they were a little Jewish. To pull this at a time when LePeters's early name, Sussman, was now a matter of common knowledge around the bureau was unconscionable.

"What'd you have to hit him with that for," he said, taking Claire LePeters aside.

"Fuck him," she said.

"Easily said," said the irate LePeters. "Meanwhile, I'm the one who has to work for that man."

◉

Teener, who had promised that Lawrence Welk and Louis
Armstrong would be on hand to entertain, called the group
to attention and said he was sorry but that both luminaries
had phoned at the last second to say they had come down
with viruses and couldn't make it. As a last-minute substi-
tute, Teener had gotten hold of Dr. Paul Jixen, who agreed to
serve up a short talk on "Tolerance for Sexual Deviates"
("but only up to a point, and what point is that, may I
ask?"). The group listened politely, the sole exception being
Detective Flamoyan, who at one point got to his feet with a
potted palm branch shoved between his legs, giving a brief
comical illusion of apelike indecent exposure. Glober, in
charge of the next section of entertainment, began to play
the first of thirty taped recordings taken in evidence from the
exclusive digs of a famous entertainer whose aorta had been
slashed by an unknown assailant. Each of the recordings featured the sighs and moans of starlets who had been to bed
with the noted homicide victim, totally unaware that an expensive German-made recorder, buried in the mattress, was
secretly taking down their most intimate murmurings. At
one point it had been felt that the horny tapings would lead
homiciders to the identity of the murderer, but when that
approach didn't pan out, the tapes were kept around the bureau for recreational purposes.

Before starting in on the moans of a particular starlet, the
famous entertainer would reveal her name, saying, "My
night with Angie Farmer . . . and what a lulu it was." This
was certainly an insensitive way to handle the material, but it
did add enjoyment by enabling the listener to put a particular set of moans together with the face of some delightful

newcomer to the screen. After a dozen or so girls were heard from, some of the wives excused themselves, in polite outrage, and went off to another room to chat among themselves. LePeters, a visual man when it came to porno material, listened only halfheartedly, joining the other dicks in a hearty guffaw now and then to show he was one of the boys. At one point, Claire LePeters nudged him and said, "Isn't that your dad's voice."

"Don't be ridiculous," LePeters said, but then he listened hard and, indeed, the delirious sound of a starlet in heat seemed to have segued into the clear and unmistakably high-pitched tenor sound of Bill Sussman, doing an early Jerome Kern number. It was one LePeters remembered him singing at parties when he was a boy and his furrier dad was still in the prime of health. What in the world was his departed dad's voice, so painfully familiar to him, doing in the middle of a homicidal starlet taping. LePeters immediately sought out his boss, Glober, who was standing near the punch bowl and on this occasion did not even bother to feign innocence.

"I know, I know," he said, "I spliced it in. Go ahead, kill me."

"Where in the hell did you get it?" LePeters asked.

"Is that really so important," said Glober. "Is that what we really need to know. Look, I couldn't resist it. When was the last time you heard your dad sing?"

"Oh, I don't know," said LePeters. "Ten, fifteen years ago, when he died. But I sure as hell didn't want to hear it in there. How could you do such a thing."

"Tell me, wise guy," said Glober. "How'd it make you feel?"

"Funny," said LePeters. "A whole mixture of things. I wanted to cry. I don't know what I wanted to do."

"That's what I mean," said Glober, as though the argument was sealed. "Don't forget," he said, with an avuncular arm around LePeters's shoulder, "I had a dad, too."

"Is my father in any more of those?" LePeters asked.

"Just the one you heard."

"Well then do me a favor," said LePeters. "Don't do any more things like that, okay?"

"Anything you say, fella."

◉

"What do you think of what he did?" LePeters asked his wife, when he had returned to his seat.

"I don't think he did you that much of a favor."

"I'm not sure you're right," said LePeters. "But he definitely should have checked with me. I probably would have wanted to listen to it, but in a more private setting."

◉

After the tapings, the dicks and their wives sat down to a light supper which quite remarkably featured clams on the half-shell, pâté de foie gras, and imported bottles of red wine. LePeters was quite proud of his buddy Teener for serving up such exotic fare, right in the teeth of his certain knowledge that the dicks, to a man, were beer and meat-and-potatoes lovers and had probably never tasted wine before. No doubt the finishing-school-oriented Deborah Teener, who stood by with a certain shy authority, had a hand in the preparation of the menu. LePeters couldn't help wondering what the aristocratic charmer saw in his friend, a fine fellow, but in so many ways just a little junkheap of a man. To his knowledge, Deborah Teener had met her husband *after* he had been whittled down by gunfire. Perhaps he was attractive for representing the total opposite of every value she had been brought up to cherish and admire. Or was it sheer sexual fascination . . . some machinelike component within him that enabled the little guy to maintain his virility long into the night, indeed through entire seasons of love-making. . . .

◉

The dicks, who needed no certification of their toughness, somehow were in particular awe of the wine, sitting about nervously, unable to leap in and enjoy their dinners. But then the hard-as-nails colored dick Medici broke the ice by shouldering his way through to the table, rolling up his sleeves with great ceremony, and swilling down a glass of the delicate French import in one gulp. Everyone applauded, several of the dicks calling him "Pierre" in jocular reference to his continental manners. Poking a playful elbow into his ribs, the lush Phyllis Gibney said, "You certainly do have a lot of suave." The dicks then dug in with a will, although LePeters did overhear Hortham of Micro-Analysis say, "I sure could use a pair of Frank Sinatras with music," hash-house lingo for frankfurters and beans.

◉

Opposite LePeters sat a fair-haired, heavily holstered dick LePeters had never seen before. Apparently wifeless and keeping somewhat to himself, the stranger nevertheless seemed to jump awake whenever Claire LePeters pulled out a cigarette, immediately on hand with a lighter and on one occasion overturning a tureen of soup in his haste to accommodate her. LePeters's wife smiled shyly, appreciating the gallantry and paying no attention to the great puddles of lobster bisque all around her and the fact that Detective Hortham's wrist had been scalded in the hubbub. The fellow introduced himself simply as Chico and said he had been with the bureau before LePeters joined up but had retired to go into film-making. He had developed a way of shooting films from the waist in the same manner as a dick would use his pistols for a close-in gun battle. As hard as he tried, LePeters could not seem to get a clear look at Detective Chico's face; indeed, he thought it might be the harsh hotel lighting that was giving him trouble, although he had no such problems in seeing the other dick faces. In LePeters's eyes, the fellow had a strange weather-vaning look to him and seemed to flash back and forth from Negro to white, never stopping long enough to be categorized in either camp. What was clear beyond doubt was his strong interest in Claire LePeters. On hand to serve up the gourmet meal were four auto-thefters temporarily on probation. Midway through the supper, while serving a tray of croissants, one of them slipped Claire LePeters a quick goose, trying to make it seem accidental and to blend into the overall festive atmosphere. Long before LePeters could react, Detective Chico smashed a wine bottle and waved the jagged ends in the sneaky auto-thefter's face, getting across to him that if he ever tried that number again he would have his nose sliced off. Dazzled by the fellow's quick reflexes, LePeters found himself offering lights to other wives about the table, even those who'd obviously sworn off smoking years back.

After the meal, the auto-thefters cleared away the tables, put on tuxedo jackets, and began to play selections stolen from the old Glen Miller band in its heyday. Quick to hit the dance floor was Detective Medici, whose lovely, dignified, high-yellow wife at first protested, saying, "I'd rather refrain from such exertion" but soon joined him in a frenzied, buck-toothed, leg-flinging, panty-flaunting salute to the great jit-terbugging craze of the forties; each time they broke, Medici, employing a much cooler dancing style, did a neatly timed dip and fired off a few shots from his service pistol. When other crime-fighting couples moved out on the floor, Detec-tive Chico sidled over and said to LePeters, "May I borrow your damsel?" He then led Claire LePeters forward and be-gan to do a graceful yet slightly effeminate handkerchief dance that might have been practiced by fisherfolk on some obscure Aegean island. A strong dance-floor leader, Claire Le-Peters for years had waged grim and silent ballroom battles with her husband over who was to do the leading. One day, midway through a slow foxtrot, LePeters said the hell with it and never danced with her again. On this occasion, Claire LePeters at first giggled at Detective Chico's obvious feminine dancing posture, but then found herself drawn in-evitably into the dance, taking up the handkerchief when it was passed to her and soon matching her partner step for fatalistic step.

Glober, a man of hair-raising directness, saw LePeters staring at the couple and said, "How are you and Claire get-ting along? For example, what goes on between the two of you in the hay? You don't have to tell me if you absolutely don't want to."

"I absolutely don't want to tell you," said LePeters. "We're getting along fine."

"It all goes back to the old bedroom workbench," said Glober. "That's where the trouble starts."

Glober then filled LePeters in on Detective Chico's background, saying that he had not actually resigned from the bureau, so much as he had been eased out when his kill total got ridiculously out of hand. The city was evidently

awash with the vengeance-seeking sons and other relatives of
people he had gunned down for the slimmest of offenses.
And though Detective Chico would never admit this, the
reason he had gone into film-making was that much of the
work was done abroad where he was more or less beyond
the reach of people who were after his hide. A bit later, Detective Chico brought back Claire LePeters and said he was
deeply interested in LePeters's career and would like to
spend some time studying his clipping displays to see if there
were any money-making film ideas in them. A commotion
then broke out, with the hotel owner screaming at Teener
and insisting that the little PR man had cheated him out of
his payment for staging the affair. While Teener sweated out
the man's curses, his wife, cool and aristocratic, scribbled off
a check and handed it to the fellow as though she were paying off a gardener and telling him his services would no
longer be required. "Thank you, hon," said Teener, jumping
up to give the finely bred Deborah Teener a peck on the
cheek.

Later, as LePeters started up the engine on his squad, a
hand shot in through the window, Detective Chico giving
Claire LePeters a final light for her cigarette.

"Thanks," said LePeters, as his wife fumbled about for a
filter-tip. "We've got an automatic lighter in the car."

"I thought you might be stuck," said Detective Chico,
weather-vaning from black to white in the darkness. "And
listen, I really am interested in your career and seeing if we
can get together on a flick."

"I don't think I'm cut out for that medium," said LePeters. "But I do appreciate your interest."

They drove off. Claire LePeters put her head against him,
cozily drunk. He remembered a night when, as a lark, and
perhaps at some desperate sexual dead end, she had taken off

her panties and driven with her bottom exposed to the other drivers flashing by on the highway. On that occasion, LePeters found himself enjoying the daring stunt, especially since there was no way for other motorists to interfere by, say, snatching at her through the window.

Now, as they moved closer to home, LePeters turned on the radio and enjoyed the feel of his wife nestling up against his shoulder.

"He's pretty attractive, isn't he," he said, as they flashed along the blackened highway.

"Who's that?" she asked.

"The movie dick," said LePeters. "You know who."

"You think so?" she said, squirming closer to him. "I really hadn't noticed."

Thus far, his daughter had logged almost a full year in a colored school and LePeters was proud to announce there wasn't a mark on her. To look at Jamie LePeters—clear-complected, bright-eyed, smart as a whip—no outsider could possibly guess she was being educated in almost total darkness. Not for a moment did LePeters think of allowing her to continue in this manner, but he had begun to think in terms of rounding it off at one year; although he would never admit it, way down deep he was starting to consider two. His wife was the ticket: so long as she didn't rock the boat too vigorously LePeters himself was in no great hurry either to make a convulsive move away from Detectives' Hill or take on the back-breaking expense of a fine private school.

One day, after an exhausting drive from the bureau back to Detectives' Hill, LePeters passed his daughter's school chum Samantha, sitting on a railroad tie, cramming great quantities of what appeared to be marshmallow fluff into her mouth. On closer inspection, it turned out to be bars of cooking starch that weren't even candy-flavored.

"Don't you know you shouldn't do that," LePeters hollered out of the window. "You'll ruin your stomach."

"Nah, this good for you," said the little girl, who had a kind of tall, angular cuteness about her, despite the hairraising sordidness of her upbringing. The starch certainly wasn't her fault. Eating it was no doubt part of some cottonfield superstition passed along through generations of Mississippi relatives.

"Listen, don't give any to Jamie," said LePeters. "Okay?"

"She been in the city fahv times," said the little girl.

"What do you mean?"

"What I said I mean," said the little girl, leaping about from tie to tie with the grace of a future Olympic competitor. Though she was capable of perfidious deeds, something in the child's innocent, offhand style told LePeters that every word she'd spoken on this occasion was gospel. Oddly, what bothered LePeters was not so much the picture of his daughter being passed around by small urban packs of flophouse degenerates, but the fact that something was going on that he didn't know about. Fortunately, Jamie LePeters bore a striking resemblance to her mother rather than her dad, especially around the eyes and cheekbones. Still, she had come from him; he saw her as a chip of himself the way that useful household objects were lucky spin-offs from the space program. So how could something be going on inside of her that he didn't know about.

Determined not to pounce right on her, LePeters let dinner go by in silence and even played her a few games of boxball and Ping-Pong, although on this occasion, he kept the scores tight before letting her blast him off the map.

"Are you sure you've got me all tucked in," she asked later, a little girl who liked to be sealed into her bed as tight as packaged Swiss cheese.

"I'm sure," said LePeters, stooping to kiss her. "Listen carefully, since I'm only asking you this once. Are you a girl who's been in the city five times?"

"I knew I'd be found out," she said, sitting up with clenched fists. "All right, who's the rat that told you and I'll bet I know who it is."

"Totally unimportant," said LePeters. He said the squealer's identity wasn't the point at all, so much as the fact that when kids from the country fell into the hands of city types who were just waiting for them, tragic things could happen. He was a bit skimpy on the details. The city was great, said LePeters, and someday she would certainly be allowed to swarm into it and take it by storm. But only later on, when she was ready to handle it. As he spoke, LePeters realized two things: one was that the child had not really roamed through the city but had merely touched down at the terminal for the adventure of it and immediately scrambled back on the next train to Detectives' Hill. The second was that if the city was so great, why hadn't he been taking advantage of its many cultural wonders, just waiting to be scooped up by a father and an alert child. Immediately, LePeters got tickets for the ballet and made reservations at a fine gourmet restaurant; on the weekend, all dressed up, he flashed off to the great eastern metropolis with Jamie at his side. Midway through the ballet, LePeters bought his daughter some chocolate-covered peanuts and said, "Well, are you loving it?"

"What are you asking me that for," said the child. "This is all your idea."

"I don't follow you," said LePeters. "It's for the two of us."

"Well I would never pick this," said the child. "This is for you."

After a disappointing dinner at which the child hated the hamburger because it wasn't skinny and didn't come on a bun, LePeters said, "I don't understand you. You're in the greatest city in the world and you're not loving it."

"Because we're doing all the things that you love. I want to keep doing them because I don't want to hurt your feelings, but I don't actually love them that much."

Later, they passed a drugstore that sold nose putty for actors. Suspicious of the types that hung around the place, LePeters warily took his daughter inside where she tried some on and bought a pound of it with her own allowance. "Now I'm having a great time," she said, slapping some on and getting ready to startle passersby with her new nose. "That's the single best store in the world. Can we come back to it every single week without fail?"

"It's just a novelty," said LePeters. "Wait and see how you get tired of it."

LePeters nonetheless entered into a compact with his daughter in which each week they would troop into the city and ignore its great feast of cultural splendors; instead they would spend their time digging into the shrapnel and debris of the city, outcast streets and alleys lined with forlorn merchant mariners, grave and ancient hookers. As far as LePeters was concerned his daughter could have dug up the identical treats right outside the colored Low School at the foot of Detectives' Hill, and saved a lot of bother. But Jamie LePeters didn't see it that way, loving the city visits and starting to race on ahead of LePeters as soon as they got near the worst sections of it. Their first trip, inevitably, was to the nose putty store which was also good for stripper equipment

and costumes left over from bedraggled musicals that had
closed out of town. They would then make an odyssey
through coin shops, stores that sold old trombones and ones
that featured surgical equipment, although LePeters was
afraid of the latter and would not let his daughter go into
them no matter how much she pleaded. As they traveled,
they would eat a fragmented meal that began with a few
pizza slices, continued along with orange drinks and french
fries, and tapered off, an hour or so later, with great bags of
hot chestnuts, one nibble of which brought back LePeters's
entire boyhood. Jamie LePeters's favorite store of all, one
that was saved for last, was a cavernous dustbin of a ware-
house that specialized in ancient issues of *Coronet* and *U.S.
Camera*, also early Batman comics that had risen tremendously in value. "Whatever you do," Jamie LePeters made
her father promise, "don't tell a soul about this place. I know
what happens. Once word gets out, every kid in the country
will be in here buying the issues that I want." The visits were
not exactly crammed full of excitement for LePeters. Sensing
his fidgetiness, the proprietor of the store, a man with a cra-
tered face, would try to perk him up by feeding him publishing tidbits. "You can't move the forties' *Geographics*," he
would say. "Not when you got books out there with girls that
spread. Maybe I should get into that."

"Stay out of it," said LePeters. "Anybody can make a buck
that way." But was his advice really sound. On Saturdays,
Jamie LePeters appeared to be the only customer at the back-
number magazine store. She was an excited one all right, but
LePeters had to wonder how it was possible to keep such a
business running, especially since there was no evidence
things picked up during the week. One day, LePeters stood
over his daughter's shoulder and told her that he had owned

many of the comics she was poring over right now, some that
he had bought for himself, others he had gotten from a feebleminded boy named Alfred Reitler, who would give his
away after a quick flip-through. "And you didn't save them,"
said Jamie LePeters, angry and near tears. "They would have
been worth millions by now and you could've given them to
me, especially if you had kept them in cellophane. Why'd
you do it, Dad?"

"How could I know?" he said.

"You should've known. Do you think you could find them
now?"

"Where would I look?"

"That means I'll never have them. . . ."

As they made their weekly odyssey through grim, shell-torn
sections of the city, LePeters kept a wary eye on his daughter,
always on the alert to intercept some weirdo who might
make a grab for her. But he could only watch her just so
carefully; inevitably, during the brief moments his back was
turned, there would be some outrageous commotion with his
daughter the center of it. On one occasion, LePeters stopped
for a cigar, telling his daughter he would only be a second.
Several beats later, sensing trouble, he stepped outside and
saw huge throngs of concerned people, cops racing, wrecked
cars strewn about, his daughter up on a horse with a
mountie. This was the story, as closely as he could piece it
together: Jamie LePeters had playfully winked at a passing
Puerto Rican woman; feeling insulted, the woman swung an
umbrella at the child, missed and hit a salesman who'd
stumbled blindly out into traffic causing a four-way collision.

"That's my daughter," said LePeters, pulling out his badgette and showing it to the mountie.

"What's this?" the mountie asked, fingering the little
metal insignia.

"My tin," said LePeters. "I'm connected with Homicide."

"Looks like it come out of a toystore," said the mountie,
handing back the badge and then passing down Jamie LePeters.

"Let me ask you something," LePeters said to his daughter, as he hustled her away from all the trouble. "How'd you
manage to start all that in so short a time?"

"It wasn't my fault," said Jamie LePeters. "You can't expect me to just be a statue."

LePeters reminded her that they were late for the movies,
two ancient Laurel and Hardy's, dredged up by a movie
house that ordinarily showed cycle-bum flicks. "And incidentally," she said, suddenly brightening, "I had no idea you
were famous."

"I'm not," said LePeters.

"Oh yes you are," she said. "The way that cop just let you
go when you showed him who you were. You're famous all
right.

"I've got a famous dad."

◉

One Saturday morning, to vary their pattern, LePeters insisted they go to the zoo. The previous week, his daughter
had discovered a wondrous store that sold promotional eight-
by-ten glossy pictures from early Hollywood extravaganzas,
the owner promising to set aside a special group of Victor
McLaglens if she got there early on the next visit. "There's

probably no point in even going there," said Jamie LePeters, as they made a quick pass at the snake house. "I'm sure they're all gone by now."

"We've got plenty of time," said LePeters. "I'm sure you're the only little girl who wants them."

"Are you serious," she said. "Do you know what they're worth?"

As they wheeled out of the zoo, Jamie LePeters suddenly shouted, "Hey, there's Mommy." LePeters looked up and indeed saw Claire LePeters, wearing a peasant blouse and skirt and cavorting along a rock formation; close behind, attractively decked out in casually youthful denims, was the forcibly retired Detective Chico of the Homicide Gala. Spotting her husband and daughter, Claire LePeters danced down from the rocks and as she approached, LePeters became aware of a special private fragrance of hers, one he remembered from the Far West when he'd first known her, and it appeared each year, on schedule, almost to the day. "It's here again," he would say, inhaling her and trying to get as much of it as possible into his lungs. "Your summer smell." Now, for the first time in many years, the fragrance was back but mystifyingly out of season. Remaining on the rock mound, Detective Chico waved to LePeters and then got down on all fours, pretending he was an animal and inviting Jamie LePeters to come after him in a make-believe hunting game. LePeters stood alongside his wife, watching the game out of the corner of his eyes; finally he jumped up on the rocks and caught Jamie in his arms, tickling her in a special way she complained about but secretly loved. Taking a section of what appeared to be normal rope out of his pocket, Detective Chico amazingly balanced it on the tip of his nose. "Did you really do that?" asked Jamie LePeters. "How did you do that?" Before Detective Chico could answer, LePeters hoisted his daughter up on his shoulders and galloped around in a circle like a mad pony; high on the rocks, the two homiciders carried on a grim and silent duel, matching each other game for game, LePeters finally pulling the child aside and spinning off a hastily constructed story about trolls.

"That's a terrific little girl you've got there," said Detective Chico.

"We think so," said LePeters.

"I myself never had any children."

"What a coincidence," said Claire LePeters to her husband. "The way we just ran into each other. We're going to just walk awhile and then I'll see you both at home."

"Great," said LePeters. "We've got a few stores to go to."

Claire LePeters and Detective Chico then walked off, keeping a gap of about eight feet between them so that no one would ever guess they knew each other. Cavorting about on the rocks, the film-making homicider had appeared to be unmistakably white, settling once and for all the question of his mysterious flickering skin pigmentation. But now, as he faded off on the horizon, he quite irritatingly was again black, not as the ace of spades, but definitely on the colored side.

"How come everybody was suddenly playing with me?" asked Jamie LePeters.

"Everybody suddenly felt like it."

"Mommy certainly has a nice friend," said the child.

"He's Daddy's friend, too," said LePeters. "Not just hers. And I'm not so sure about the nice part. It's too early to tell."

◉

Giving his wife and the film-making homicider every possible benefit of the doubt, LePeters still came off feeling a bit queasy, as though he had just taken a rough wind-tossed flight across the Southwest. There were too many unanswered questions. Let's say Claire LePeters had just bumped into Detective Chico in the park, a one in a million shot, but still possible. What was she doing in the city to begin with and how had she gotten in without LePeters's squad. Shouldn't she have been back on Detectives' Hill, thinking up a suppertime treat for her husband and daughter when they pulled in after their doomsday odyssey of forlorn sections of the city. In all fairness, they would hardly come in famished, but they would certainly have been able to handle a refreshing light bite. Three weeks had passed since the Homicide Gala; had she taken other rocky zoo strolls with Detective Chico or had this been the first one.

In Claire LePeters's defense, not once had her husband asked her to come along on one of the weekly pilgrimages. But in a sense, he felt he had been doing her the favor of a lifetime. The trips no doubt brought LePeters and his daughter ever closer together, but apart from that aspect he would not have wished them on his worst enemy. Most of them involved standing around in cold, dusty stores that handled preposterous lines of merchandise, and not even a shot at a cool extra-dry Gibson to settle him down and make things seem a little brighter. He knew Claire LePeters pretty well and would not have wanted to see her face in the back-number magazine store while Jamie LePeters took hours poring over ancient issues of *Strength and Health*.

Determined to root out a few answers, LePeters ran into a new phenomenon. Ever since his brief island idyll with Ellen Rosenberg, his wife had begun to meet him halfway on the bed, dutifully if not zestfully succumbing to his nighttime advances. Now Claire LePeters entered a mysterious new period marked by a long numbing silence on her part; though she walked about normally and her great eyes practically screamed out entire speeches, all actual language remained deeply corkscrewed in her mouth; it seemed it would take a bottle opener with great hydraulic jaws to pry out a single sentence. No matter what lively conversational openers LePeters tried, all he got back was the ghostly echo of his own voice. During meals, in answer to his request for salt, pepper, and other light spices, Claire LePeters dealt out a series of "mmmmms" and "unnnnnhs" as though a forceps had torn the tongue from her throat.

With the center clogged and no particular passing game worth mentioning, LePeters decided to try for a few yards by slipping off tackle. Instead of making bull-like charges at her soundless barricades, he invited her to take a stroll down to the village one night to catch a ninth-rate private-eye movie. In good times, it would have been the kind of throwaway evening Claire LePeters enjoyed, although he wasn't sure she would now. Throughout the flick, LePeters would keep up a running commentary, pointing out flaws in the investigation procedures that no Hollywood hack could be expected to know about.

With a silent nod of acquiescence, Clarie LePeters made arrangements for a local babysitter to show up, a granitelike ex-soothsaying Polish woman of terrifying reliability who would actually stand guard at the bed with stocky arms folded until Jamie LePeters slipped off to sleep. While packs of local patrol cars regularly zipped by to ensure their safety, they made their way to the center of town, LePeters pointing out how great it was to have a movie house that you could actually walk to and why that was one reason it would be tough to leave Detectives' Hill. As a reply, he got only the soft clip-clop of Claire LePeters's fashionably sturdy imported Italian clogs. At one point, they passed a dark, thickly hedged area, the only possible place in all Detectives' Hill where there was even the slightest chance of being assaulted, although, no doubt, any intruder would have been corralled by twenty dicks before he'd had a chance to sit back and gloat over his triumph. Crossing this section, LePeters half-hoped someone would plunge out of the bushes and leap on Claire LePeters, forcing some kind of verbal rise out of her. By the time they reached the movie house, Claire LePeters's silences had truly become much noisier than actual talk, so thunderously loud that at one point he felt he had to hold his ears to keep them from bursting. By the time the credits appeared on the screen, LePeters felt he could no longer take it and whispered, "Listen, I have to have a little feedback from you." Claire LePeters made a "shhhhh" sound, indicating she wanted to get involved in the film. "For shame," said a gum-popping woman two rows back, her massive thighs propped up against the seat in front of her. "I'm as much for quiet as you are," LePeters hollered back, thinking this was a maddening reversal of roles since he was the one who generally shushed movie mumblers, particularly during sensitively made European imports in which every nuance counted. On the other hand, during B films it was his feeling that anything goes.

When the film was over, they walked in silence to the Dachau-run general store to pick up an armload of preposterously priced home-furnishing magazines; on this occasion, price was no object and LePeters would have happily shelled out a king's ransom to jog his wife into a little lively chatter. Behind the counter, the proprietor, a survivor of the hell camps, beamed at them and said, "It's nice to see a Jewish family stroll in here once in a while. In this town, we're only eight per cent."

"We're not that Jewish," said LePeters, quickly checking to make sure there wasn't anyone around, particularly some member of a law enforcement agency.

Staggering out in a floor-length skirt, the proprietor's wife said, "You'll be good and sorry for that remark someday." Then she went down to the basement, still smarting over deep, war-torn psychic and physical wounds that would proabably never mend.

◉

Sure enough, a local cop, paging through *Field and Stream,* lifted his head and said, "The only thing I've got against Jews is the synagogue duty I once pulled out on the Coast." He said that he had been assigned to guard a temple in a city of the West, the only building for miles around in which you got buffeted on all sides by chilling winds. "Anywhere else, the churches, even the African consulates, you got a little protection, but not in front of that temple. I froze my nuts off and I'll never forgive the Jews for that."

LePeters, a cop, too, in his own right, felt he didn't have to sit still for any guff from the lowly pavement-pounder.

"Don't you see that it's not their fault," he said, coming to the defense of his long-dormant faith. "It was the building department that set it up that way."

Not happy with either the store or its ownership, LePeters yearned for the old days—even though he had just gotten in on the tail end of them—a time when moustache wax and collar buttons were on sale and, as a shopper, he didn't have to feel that the death camps were his fault. Wandering toward the back, LePeters was surprised to come across Gordon Mendelowitz, the tycoon who had bravely tried to shove an equitably drawn-up zoning plan down the elders' throats, one that would have given both his own daughter and LePeters's a fair shake in the colored and white department. Once hale, fit, and ready to tackle the world, Mendelowitz now appeared to be bent over, defeated, a shadow of himself. With palsied hands, he stood in the near-darkness wrapping packages while his equally whipped but apparently devoted wife handed him pieces of string for his bundles. "How are you doing?" LePeters asked, shocked at Mendelowitz's condition, but still glad to see his one-time zoning ally. "I haven't seen you in a dog's age."

"Don't ask me anything," said Mendelowitz. "I'm supposed to go about my business and not get into anything sensitive."

"He's had a lot of attacks," said Mrs. Mendelowitz. "The least thing upsets him."

From what LePeters could gather, the once forceful industrial giant had been so thrown by the almost insanely unfair school setup, he had suffered a total collapse, having to give up the strain of industrial warfare for the most menial of jobs and damned lucky at that to be able to hold one down. LePeters felt terribly sorry for the man but at the same time a bit strengthened himself. He was not exactly setting the world on fire, but at least he had not gone under and so far as he could judge had plenty of vinegar left. The elders had disappointed him, but they had not chased him out of the ball park, even though, in truth, he wasn't the one who had to troop into the Low School each day and be surrounded by black school chums as far as the eye could see; any suffering LePeters was doing, in the education department, was by proxy. At the same time, LePeters was terribly impressed by the loyal Mrs. Mendelowitz, who had stuck by her husband instead of heading for the hills the first time a medical cannon was fired. Though she was no doll, LePeters, for one brief moment, felt he would have traded places with Gordon Mendelowitz, just to have a devoted woman at his side who would at least talk to him when he had things to get off his chest. But on second thought, he wasn't sure he would want to go that far.

"Listen, drop up to the house sometime," said LePeters. "We'd love to see you."

"We'll have to take a rain check on that," said Mrs. Mendelowitz, not only talking but doing her husband's talking, too, to save him the strain. "Gordon has to go easy on the night air."

As soon as they got back, Claire LePeters flew into the bathroom, padlocked the door behind her, and began to take a shower of such intense heat that jets of steam shot through the keyhole, smoking the bedroom mirrors.

"What do you need it so hot for in there," LePeters shouted, at his wits' end over his wife's peculiar behavior. "Look, will you say something. If it makes you more comfortable, say it right through the door. I'll hear you."

Finally, Claire LePeters broke her verbal fast, although LePeters could very easily have done without her opening lines. "All right, I've been having an affair," she said. "With the fellow at the zoo. Do you feel better now that you've wormed it out of me."

At the very word "affair," LePeters felt his entire life turning on a dime; it might get better, chances are it would get worse—but it would never be the same again. Confused about Daylight Saving Time, LePeters's daughter was under the impression that not only did you have to wind the clock back but you also had to do the things you did before all over again. At the moment, LePeters wished he could drop back an hour and read from another script, one in which the word "affair" never got said.

"How long's it been going on?" he asked, as though it were a virus that could be checked at an early stage.

"Three weeks . . ."

"How many times a week?" he asked.

"What are you doing, filling out an application?"

"This is fucking serious," he shouted. "I'm plenty sore about this. This is no more kidding around . . ."

"All right," she said, as though counting on her fingers, "let me see . . . two . . . no, make that three times a week."

Convinced there was some standard way to react to affairs when you ran into them, LePeters was anxious to make sure he got the procedure exactly right.

"I see," he said cautiously. "Do you like it?"

"Jesus," said Claire LePeters.

She raced out of the bathroom then and LePeters got his first look at her in the light of this new revelation. A towel flapped loosely about her and she seemed unconcerned about whether or not it covered her; this in itself was different, as though she were much more free now, a woman of affairs. Apart from that, she seemed solemn, pornographic, a little shorter, and at the same time light and bouncy on her feet. That's the way his wife looked when she was having an affair.

"I'd like to get to the bottom of this," said LePeters.

"What bottom?" she said. "I'm having an affair. That's the bottom."

"It certainly is," he said. "How could you do this right in

the middle of the colored problem we're having. Couldn't you wait till we'd cleared it up. Is that what you do when your kid's in a colored school. You go out detective-fucking."

"You've just ended the discussion."

With that she leaped into bed, LePeters hopping right in after her as though he were chasing her down a street. He put his arm on her shoulder now, not at all sure if you were allowed to do that when your wife was having an affair. Of course you were allowed, but was it the right way to go. Torn between murderous anger and a need to be a man of the world, LePeters went the gentle way and said, "Look, you started it, it's over, now you have to stop it."

"I didn't start it. He called and asked if I'd like to see the rushes on a new lesbian picture he's shooting. We watched them at his place. Then we had some tea and he ordered me to take off my clothes. So I had to take them off. In a way it was wonderful."

"He *ordered* you," said LePeters. "Don't I order you to take them off. You keep them on."

"This was different."

"Right this second if I ordered you to take them off what would you do?"

"It's late."

"That's what I mean."

"He said he wanted us to become a man–woman film-making team, if it was okay with you."

"It's not okay with me."

"He said he wanted to come here, arm in arm with me, and ask you to understand. If you wanted to punch him in the mouth, he wouldn't even defend himself, although he's plenty capable of it."

"Tell him not to show up," said LePeters.

"Listen," she said, sitting up, pleading, gentler than he remembered her ever being, "I'd want you to come to the house for dinner, anytime you wanted. You're a wonderful father."

"Listen," said LePeters, already picturing himself squeezed out of the house he had started to love, Detective Chico sitting in his favorite lounging chair, even slipping into bed when Jamie LePeters fell asleep. "None of this is going to happen. Call him right this second and tell him it's all over and not only that but it probably never happened in the first place."

"I can't call him now. He's out shooting scenes for his lesbian flick. I'm helping with the costumes."

"Well, call him in the morning."

"I'm not sure I can."

"You can," said LePeters, turning his back to her and pretending he had a real chance to go to sleep. "The whole trouble is you haven't tried."

The whole idea of actually getting in even a short doze was a cruel and preposterous joke. LePeters tossed about, broken-faced, a twilight stirring in, of all places, the polar edges of his groin. It fit together perfectly now, the lights for Claire Le-Peters's every cigarette, the feigned interest in LePeters's homicide clipping displays when in truth they were probably the last thing on earth Detective Shithead cared about. And LePeters would continue to call him Detective Shithead, too, whether he liked it or not. The inventive tricks and zoo games for Jamie LePeters, all shrewdly designed to get her ready for a new dad. That'll be the day, thought LePeters. If it ever came to that, he'd sneak her away as far as Trieste and put her in a Trieste school.

Why in the world did his wife have to do this to him when they were getting along so nicely, especially since he'd brought a whole carload of new tricks back from the islands. And why did she have to select Detective Chico. He might have been able to understand the president of a plastics company or a renowned violinist. But another dick? As far as he was concerned, the film-making didn't count for much; if Chico had any real skill as a cinematographer, it certainly hadn't surfaced in the way of any public reputation. If he ever got some decent reviews for his work, LePeters would die, but he'd have to concede it might make a difference. Flailing about and fighting for sleep, LePeters kicked a hard object and fished out a cute little toy pig with a revolving head.

"What's this?" LePeters asked, poking his wife.

"What's what?"

"This," said LePeters. "Say, did he give this to you?"

"Is that what you want to know at this hour? Yes, he gave it to me."

"And you put it right in bed with me. His toy."

"All right, I'll give it to Jamie."

"You're not giving it to Jamie. When did you come up with this kind of cruelty."

"Will you let me sleep."

LePeters searched about for ways in which he had fouled up and perhaps unconsciously driven her into Chico's arms. Maybe it was his handling of the colored school. Although all the returns weren't in quite yet, Chico might very well turn out to be officially colored. There was a definite tie-in there. Maybe she was saying, in essence, you want colored, I'll give you colored. But if this was Claire LePeters's way of forcing the kid out of the school, it was no soap. She could take on the whole Marine band and he wasn't going to be stampeded on that one. He just wasn't going to do that to

the colored people. Could the whole thing possibly be a simple matter of economics? Considering his wife careless and
slipshod about money, it was LePeters who suspiciously held
sway over the family finances, such as they were. Each time
Claire LePeters needed money, LePeters cautiously doled
out a couple of bucks pointing out, on occasion, that it was
hard-earned detective's pay and to go easy with it. Who
knows, perhaps having to ask him for touches every few minutes and never having even a small wad she could call her
own was humiliating. So painful she didn't even want to talk
about it. LePeters felt he was on to something now and
tapped her on the shoulder once again.

"What is it now?"

"How'd you like your own checking account?"

"Right this second?"

"No, in the morning. We'll set one up."

"That would be very nice."

"Terrific," said LePeters. But seconds later, once again he
was sunk in a gray and boundless sorrow. What he'd really
wanted to hear was that she would never see Detective Chico
again, was sorry she had ever started with him, and would
sign a sacred oath that there would be no more Chicos for
the rest of her days. How could he get her to say something
like that.

In the morning Claire LePeters set a princely breakfast before him, one featuring hot buns, cereal cooked to a perfect
consistency, and coffee richly brewed, the work of an impec-
cable housekeeper and from all outward appearances a devoted bride. LePeters wasn't fooled. If she thought that was
going to cancel out the tempestuous affair with Detective

Chico she was way off base. He dug in anyway, since there was no point in wasting it and no way to tell if it was the first in a series of great breakfasts to come or just a one-shot treat to cool him off. After Jamie LePeters had gone trotting off to the colored school, his wife said she had called Detective Chico but that he had insisted she come in and tell him the news to his face.

"I feel I have to do it and was wondering if I could borrow the squad."

"What about me?" LePeters asked. "How'll I get in?"

"You can either take the train or why don't you take the day off?"

"I don't know if I want to give you my squad," said LePeters.

Half an hour later, Claire LePeters was dressed in a dignified tailored suit and hat, as though she were going off to meet a principal. She stood in the driveway, looking up at LePeters who was framed in the kitchen window, jiggling the car keys; he felt as though something terribly profound was happening, and that years later he might regret bitterly this handing over of what he sensed was a vital piece of himself. On the other hand, his wife was suppliant, pleading; wasn't it just a matter of doing something kind for a desperate fellow human being? That was another way to look at it. He chucked the keys out of the window. "Thank you, darling," she said, snatching them like an experienced shortstop. "I just have to get this done and then I promise I'll make it up to you."

LePeters busied himself with little diverting tasks, taking a long time to brush his teeth and remembering a time when a

childhood dentist named Rodner had actually smacked his
face for having perfect contact points and not making a big
enough fuss over them. "I see one mouth like that in fifty,"
said the excitable Rodner, "and you just sit around taking it
for granted." Then LePeters paid some bills, feeling a little
thrill of accomplishment as he wrote out the checks, as
though each one represented the staving off of some disaster.
Every settled payment made LePeters feel cleaner and gave
him added strength which he sensed he'd be needing and in
any case couldn't do him any harm. Feeling he had to do
something with his hands, LePeters went to work nailing up
a banister for the attic, probably to show Claire LePeters
that he was just as mechanical as any other fellow. "It's what
you want to do with your time," he had said to her when she
frowned at him for not being handy. "I can be the most mechanical guy in town if I want to be. But I've got other things
on my mind." In all honesty, what were the other things?

By midday, LePeters began to get restless, realizing that he
had allowed himself to be chained to the house. When Detective Chico got a load of Claire LePeters in her tailored
suit, no question he would try to talk her into one more for
the road. And what guarantee did LePeters have that she
would decline. He cursed himself for handing over the squad
and, for that matter, handing over Claire LePeters. Right
this second they were probably listening to some mood
music, the bastard having ordered her out of her tailored suit.
LePeters tried to picture Detective Chico's apartment. No
question there would be out-of-focus stills from his films that
any idiot could take but that Claire LePeters would be
tricked into thinking were arty. And weapons, too, planted
all over the place in case one of the vengeance-seeking relatives of people he'd frivolously knocked off in the line of duty

ever showed up. It wouldn't be a bad idea to round up a few; they could all move in on Chico together before he hot-footed it off to Europe or somewhere to make a film.

Late in the day, Jamie LePeters showed up, surprised to see her father at home.

"What are you, sick, Dad?"

"No, I just thought I'd take a day off once in a while."

"Great," said the little girl, whipping off her coat. "Now we can play thirty games of boxball."

In no mood for games, LePeters cut her down to three which he played in a haggard, mechanical style, not using any of the tricks he occasionally trotted out to dazzle her.

"I don't think you're trying, Dad," she said. "You told me you were an Olympic boxball player."

"I was," said LePeters. "But I was feeling tip-top in those days."

⊙

It was LePeters who fixed dinner for his daughter, bread-sticks and clam chowder, a favorite new combination of hers. Only several weeks before, he had introduced her to the joys of breadstick eating, saying that he would have to butter them for her since only one man in a hundred could do this properly. Even if you were born with a gift for it, it took years of training to perfect the art. Then, he had sliced off a surgi-cally precise sliver of butter and begun to apply it in a care-fully evened-off coat, finally passing it along to her with great ceremony. "There you are," he'd said, sitting back in tri-umph, admiring his masterwork, "a perfectly buttered bread-stick."

"And it's delicious, too," said Jamie LePeters, taking the

first bite. "Do you think I'll be able to do that someday?"

"It's possible," said LePeters. "They say it runs in the family."

On this occasion, Jamie LePeters lined up the butter and breadstick box, sat down in the tiny dining alcove LePeters also used for a study, and got ready to be startled by another of the amazing rituals. "It's all set up, Dad," she said. "I'm really going to watch you this time so that someday maybe I'll be able to do it, too."

"Why don't you try it now," said LePeters. "You're old enough to start doing some of these things yourself."

"Are you serious? I'd never be able to handle it the way you do."

"Just slap it on," said LePeters. "I'm sure it'll be all right."

By midnight, Claire LePeters still hadn't either shown up or called. How the hell long was it taking to say good-bye to the sonofabitch. LePeters had half a mind to go after them, but how could he go anywhere without his squad. He had never realized quite how important the squad was to him, even though it wasn't particularly souped up or weighted down with detective equipment. Even if he had the car, where would he look for them in the great city with its millions of hiding places. Chico was certainly smart enough to be unlisted and holed up in a place where none of the legions of people who were after him could track him down.

Finally, the phone rang, LePeters pouncing on the receiver as though he were strangling a long-necked bird. "It's me," said

Claire LePeters calling collect. "I thought it was the least I could do."

"You could have done more than that," said LePeters. "You could actually be here. Is the affair over?"

"I'm not sure," she said. "He's in the next room. He threatened to talk to you on the phone but I wouldn't let him because I don't want trouble."

"When can I expect you to get your ass back here?"

"You've just put your finger on one of the reasons all this is happening. He would never say a thing like that. Besides, I can't leave because he has us all boarded up."

"All right, get him on the phone."

"I'm not doing that. He's in there with the film-cutter who also sleeps here and has the job of guarding him night and day."

"I thought he's so tough," said LePeters, sensing a momentary advantage.

"He is," she said. "He showed me X-rays of a fellow he beat up recently in an argument over a cab. He said I should tell you about them."

"All right, where are you?" he asked, remembering an ax he'd bought to chop down a diseased peach tree and never used again. It probably wasn't too dull and might be useful hacking his way through Chico's boarded-up doors. If that didn't work, he'd borrow a piece from one of the dicks and shoot his way through.

"I can't tell you," she said. "It would be letting him down."

"But you're allowed to let your husband down, right. Okay, answer me one thing. Did you screw today?"

"You would think of that. We just held each other, which is something you wouldn't know about. I was too aggravated for the other."

"All right," said LePeters, slightly relieved. "Get home. I could do without this type of phone bill."

"I'm all boarded up."

"Put him on the phone."

"Something terrible will happen."

"Something terrible already has."

"I have to hang up."

"Don't hang up."

"I have to."

"I'm not very proud of you, Claire."

"I'm hanging up."

Alone and sleepless at three in the morning, LePeters was aware of the powerful stillness of Detectives' Hill, a definite plus most of the time, but no advantage when your wife was boarded up romantically with an ex-dick in a great and massive city, humming with activity, fifty miles away. He thought of swallowing a pill, but was deathly afraid of getting hooked on them and preferred taking ten or fifteen short dozes during the day at his desk to get the last night's sleep back. The phone was one link to the outside world, but who would he call at this hour? His mother was a possibility, but he had no number for her and, unquestionably, her colored maid-recruiting bureau in the South would be closed for the night. And even if he could get through to her motel room in Birmingham or Jackson, how would that look, a detective calling his mother to hold his hand over a marital squabble. And after years of not talking to her. Gordon Mendelowitz, no stranger to sorrow, was a definite possibility, but a call at this hour might just drive a final nail into the sickly tycoon's coffin. On an impulse, he decided to call Detective Teener, his faithful sidekick at the bureau, and a man apparently bent on doing favors for LePeters, who so far had never asked him for any. "What's up," Teener asked in an alert, suspicious voice.

"A thing involving my wife," said LePeters. "I had to talk to somebody."

"Listen, I can't speak now," said Teener, guardedly, as though he were glancing over his little shoulder.

"How come?" asked LePeters.

"We're having some people over."

"At four in the morning."

"They're very rich," said Teener.

"I see," said LePeters.

"I have to get off," said Teener, hanging up softly and not even adding a "Sorry, fella" to make LePeters feel a little better. Evidently Teener only liked to help a guy out when no help was needed. Later in the day, he would come rushing over to LePeters with a case of bourbon or a crateful of sweatshirts that LePeters could have dirt cheap, even though he didn't need them. What was he doing entertaining rich people at four in the morning? No doubt, they were the socially well-connected Deborah Teener's friends, people who had long since chucked the clock out the window and could operate pretty much on their own frivolous schedule. But Teener was still a dick who had to keep regular hours; not only that, but most of him was machine-made and he was not exactly overbrimming with health. He had better watch himself if he knew what was good for him. LePeters made out a list of people he could call—Glober, Gibney, Doctor-Detective Worthway, even Medici in the totally black section of the city—except that once he had the list he tore it up and felt no need to use it. He sensed there was a chapter coming up in his life in which he would have to be alone;

now was as good a time as any to start getting used to it. He went outside and stood on the lawn for an hour or so, at times getting up on his toes, as though by really squinting his eyes and trying very hard to do so he could actually penetrate the haze and see his wife and Detective Chico in the huge, pulsing city fifty miles away.

◉

From the bedroom window, LePeters watched his dazed and forlorn wife stumble out of the dawn. He wondered if he had slept at all and, if so, for how long. It would help him to know how many dozes to take during the day. He was as happy to see the squad roll in the driveway as he was to see his wife. But then he noticed with horror that the entire side was battered in. It was as though his own face had suffered the damage.

"How'd it happen?" he asked her as she staggered past him.

"I don't know. I was upset. Chico leaped behind the wheel so it would seem as if he was driving."

"Did you get the other fellow's license?"

"Please," she said, walking past him to the bedroom.

LePeters followed her in and whipped his best suit out of the closet, a gray-striper he had picked up in a store that catered to retired outfielders who were now restaurateurs. Then he began to slick his black shoes to a blinding shine.

"Where are you going?" she asked, checking her eyes to see if any wrinkles had shown up.

"I got a little affair of my own going," he said. "One I didn't tell you about. A young kid. And I'll tell you another thing. I'm not paying a quarter to get that squad fixed. You can hand the bill over to Detective Shithead and let him worry about it."

◉

Returning to the bureau, LePeters shouldered his way through a pack of "autograph hounds," small-time hustlers and con men with plenty of time on their hands who hung around dicks, in combined adulation and contempt, like flies on a horse's tail. "Here comes some big heat," one of them said as LePeters approached. "Let him through." The dicks were tolerant of these pests, since it had been proven that anyone of them, at a given time, might cough up a vital piece of information on some brutal, unsolved slaughter. He went upstairs on the bullpen elevator, specially padded so that a suspect might not cheat justice by bashing his own brains out on the walls. Taking his place on the coffee-wagon line, Le-Peters picked up a prune danish and coffee, deliberately passing up the departmental favorite, "a yid (bagel) with cream cheese," demonstrating that those who might discredit him for being a Sussman were actually more Jewish in their ways than he was.

Catch a dick in a serious moment and he would say he had chosen homicide investigation because the taking of a human life had to be the gravest crime of all. Yet the dedicated dicks thought nothing of interrupting their holy missions with at least twenty breaks a day for delicious little snacks. After polishing off the light bite, LePeters walked into the bullpen to watch the "Stars of Tomorrow Show," a regular nine o'clock lineup in which young hoods who had been apprehended by the nightshift dicks were paraded about so that their mangy faces could be recorded in each dick's memory, for future reference. "Take a good look at these boys," said Detective Gibney, as he steered the motley group of "new faces" around the bullpen. "They're two for a nickel now, but every one of them will definitely be a killer before he gets finished." The hoods were then herded off to be booked, and LePeters headed for his desk, knowing full well he would not be able to concentrate on his clipping displays, but thrilled that he was so good at his job he could fake it for a while and no one would know the difference.

Everywhere he looked, LePeters thought he saw a satisfied detective with a lovely, devoted wife and a cozy little home to go back to, with only an occasional case of flu and maybe a splinter that was hard to remove to mar his life. He knew better, of course, but that was the way it seemed to him. Still annoyed over Teener's middle-of-the-night rebuff to him, Le-Peters nonetheless collared his little friend and gave him a nutshell summary of what he considered his wife's treacherous behavior and the pickle she had gotten him into.

"See those," said Teener, in answer, pointing to a great batch of unopened correspondence on his specially made little desk. "They're alimony letters from my first wife, Patsy."

With a spiteful little smirk, he added, "I'm not giving her a quarter."

When LePeters first met Teener, he had seen him as no more than a pitiful little heap of gadgets with barely a breath of life in his lungs. Now he was turning out to be quite a rascal. Not only did he have the lovely and socially well-connected Deborah Teener in tow, but he had also put a first wife under his belt, not to mention three cute little girls, born of the marriage.

"Don't you have to pay?" LePeters asked. "I thought they come after you."

"They're not getting me," said Teener. He then described a plan that he would put to use if things got too hot for him. He and Deborah Teener would fly west and take up residence with some Cree friends who were still technically part of the Indian nation, living on land that was illegally seized from them. Teener had been advised that this residence would make him alimony-safe; whatever the case, any resultant litigation could be tied up in court for years. During all that time, the first Mrs. Teener would not be able to count on receiving a thin dime.

"But what about your first wife?" LePeters asked. "Is it that she's rich and you feel she doesn't need it?"

"No, she's starving," said Teener, crossing his arms. "I just don't pay alimony. I don't like it. Don't care a bit for it, never have."

"And your three little girls?" LePeters asked, with a particular stake in this matter.

"I show up on all holidays wearing a fake beard and with a bushel of presents on my back. I give them to the girls and they think I'm just an old teddy bear. That's the way I want them to think of their father. That's all they need."

Teener said all this with that same look of determination he must have had on the fateful day he'd been whittled down to his current size by hoodlum gunfire—and LePeters would not have wanted to be in the shoes of any ex-wife trying to get a quarter out of him. But what did Teener's tough alimony stance have to say to him. Very little, he concluded, since divorce settlements were still a long way off, and in any case, he couldn't picture himself being that tough on Claire LePeters, even though she seemed at the moment to be heartlessly driving a stake through his chest. There was always the chance that her romp with Detective Chico had nothing to do with LePeters and was merely a desperate way

of filling in some deep-seated womanly puzzle piece; ultimately it would all redound to LePeters's benefit and their
shared happiness. But why couldn't she hurry up and fill it in.
And what if LePeters wasn't around to enjoy the gravy. Always sensitive to his employee's moods, Bruno Glober, the
public relations top dog, soon had a sympathetic arm around
LePeters's shoulders. "Sorry you're down, boy," he said. "I
want you to know that you're as good at your work at fifty
per cent as most fellows are when they go all out.

"Still," he said, grabbing his topcoat and beckoning LePeters to follow along for lunch, "we do have to get that other
fifty per cent out of you."

No question about it, Glober had always taken LePeters's
welfare seriously to heart. Yet there was also a part of him
that enjoyed seeing someone other than himself in hot water.
And Glober was never one to close his ears to a good lip-
smacking story. As LePeters worked his way through the
painful series of events, it was all Glober could do to keep
from tossing in little cries of "Gleeps!" and "Hot dog!" After
hearing his colleague's story, Glober immediately advised Le-
Peters not to get divorced and then said that his way of dealing with marital pressures was to have a delicious thirty-year-
old girl installed in a $750-month high-rise apartment in the
city and to visit her two to three times a week, always showing up with a gift; on Christmas, he would spring for a really
outstanding one such as a fur coat, a white Honda, or a $500
non-refillable lighter that you simply throw away when it's
out of fuel.

"And it works," said Glober, "I swear to Christ it works."

"You know what I make," said LePeters. "It's totally out
of the question for me. Besides, how does that get my wife
back?"

"She'll come back," said Glober. "And you'd be surprised,

when you commit yourself to something like this, the money just falls in naturally.

"Listen," he said, "you've probably seen my chick around." He then described a girl LePeters recalled as working in the Auto Theft Division, rather shopworn but possessor of one of the most profoundly sculpted behinds in town.

"You know Betsy," said Glober. "Tell the truth, you ever gotten into that?"

"I've never even spoken to the girl," said LePeters.

"I'll bet," said Glober, with a sly smile. "You did slip in there, didn't you? I can tell. I've always had the feeling we've been knocking off some of the same puss.

"Listen," he said, his mood changing gradually and becoming ever more grim, "I don't mind spending a total of nine thousand a year in rent money plus all the other money on coats and then another guy sneaking in there for a slice scotfree. Just because I spend all that dough it doesn't mean I own the girl."

Then he bared his teeth and put his jaw right up against LePeters's.

"I just think I'm entitled to know about it, that's all."

Deriving little solace from his boss, LePeters, late in the day, sought out Doctor-Detective Worthway, one of whose functions was to cheer up depressed dicks whose work had gotten the best of them and who were right on the edge of nervous breakdowns. LePeters had not seen too much of death, but he had seen a little of it. It wasn't handling the stiffs themselves that got detectives down; they were dead already. It was mostly the atmosphere of death that caught up with them, the actual smell of it in rooms where there had been a slaughter, the bloodstains and, particularly, the accusatory looks from unappreciative relatives of the deceased, glaring murderously at investigating dicks who were only trying to be helpful. Often it would be the vengeful eyes of an arrested killer, staring back through the cell bars, that would drive a depressed homicider into the arms of Doctor-Detective Worthway. "He had no right to look at me that way," a dissembling dick would say to the psycho-homicider. "I couldn't stand it. All I was trying to do was cleanse society of him." Worthway didn't see too many marital spats; with rare exceptions such as Teener and his socially prominent new bride, most dicks were married to worshipful ex-manicuresses and hairdressers who stuck by their men through thick and thin and always had a hot beefed-up dinner ready for them at the end of a tough day on the streets. Not to mention cozy slippers and a TV set tuned in to exactly the right series. (Surprisingly, it would turn out to be a crime show, although you would think the weary dicks would have had their bellyful of homicide at the end of an eight-hour shift.)

"What are you getting so excited about," said Worthway, after LePeters had laid his story out on the table. "She got a little hungry so she went out for a light bite."

"Terrific," said LePeters. "What am I supposed to be, yesterday's string beans? There was a little cupcake down in the islands who thought I was pretty tasty."

Hauling down an anatomy book, Worthway turned to a rather lasciviously drawn sketch of the female parts and, using a pointer, said, "Here's where you touch. Did you touch any of these?"

"I touched them all," said LePeters.

"And she didn't go through the roof?"

"Nope."

"Then something's definitely wrong. Listen, you better make a move or you kids'll probably split up."

"I am making a move," said LePeters. "I'm talking to you."

"That's not enough. What's this fellow's name?"

"Detective Shithead."

"His real name . . ."

"Chico . . . I can hardly get myself to say it."

"You've got to start saying it."

"What will it accomplish?"

"It's a step. Remember, he's a person, with needs and hopes and aspirations of his own. All right now, does he give her any gifts?"

LePeters remembered the toy pig with the revolving head that Claire LePeters had thoughtlessly placed in the center of his bed, her cruellest act so far.

"A few," said LePeters.

"My advice is not to trade him gift for gift. You'll just be playing his game. If you absolutely can't stand it and have to give her something, get her a towel or some other item for the house.

"Now I'm going to tell you something that'll really hand you a laugh," said Worthway, chuckling to himself in anticipation of the insight he was about to feed LePeters. "He's really much more interested in you."

"How do you figure that?" asked LePeters.

"I've seen a lot of this," said Worthway. "You watch and see. It's really your ass he's after and not your wife's."

◉

Though LePeters respected Worthway's Heidelberg background and training, he had trouble swallowing the last little tidbit he'd handed out. It was true that Chico had expressed a serious interest in LePeters's homicide clipping displays, but surely that was only the thinnest of decoys. And if indeed it was LePeters's ass he was after, why didn't he come right out and say so instead of involving the innocent Claire LePeters. LePeters would simply tell him nothing doing and suggest that he be on his way, back to his more freewheeling film world where that kind of thing no doubt was everyday stuff. Late in the afternoon, when it was time for the graveyard shift to take over, LePeters stayed at his desk, chilled and lonely, envious of the detectives who were going home to warm firesides and affectionate wives who would stand on their heads to make their husbands happy. Since hoods and other suspects tended to be home in the evening, most of the desirable pinches were made on the late shift. Still, it was mostly bachelors who took the graveyard since late-night stakeouts were totally disruptive to normal life, and meals in particular would often come down to stale coffee and cold beans in all-night hashhouses. When he was alone at his desk, LePeters fished Ellen Rosenberg's number out of the phone book and called her at the ironmongery; even though he hadn't seen her for a month he hadn't the slightest doubt that she would be all ready for him, happy to make an immediate and massive rearrangement of her life that would fit him in for a large slice of her time.

"I'm happy to hear from you," said Ellen Rosenberg, who seemed to have one foot out the door, "but I have a dinner date tonight."

"What did you do that for," said LePeters, who nonsensically felt betrayed.

"It's just some pissy little guy who's been coveting me. I couldn't get rid of him."

"I don't like to do that to a person," said LePeters, "but maybe you can duck out on him."

"I'll see what I can do," said Ellen Rosenberg.

They made plans to meet at an out-of-the-way diner on the edge of the city, one that had warm lighting and served drinks and also delicious, hot, open roast beef sandwiches. Once the date was set up, LePeters felt almost dizzy with furtiveness, slinking over to get his coat and then pulling his collar up to hide his face as he slipped out of the bullpen. He walked in shadows, peering back over his shoulder every now and then, fully expecting a car to slide by and nail him before he got to the diner. Nail him for what? Compared to the enormity of Claire LePeters's transgression, his was a mere flyspeck. All he was doing was going off to meet Ellen Rosenberg and he hadn't even met her yet.

Unlike girls from summer camp who became dogs when you saw them in the city, Ellen Rosenberg looked lovely in a full orange sweater, having gained perhaps thirty per cent in appearance since the shift from the colored island. Picking up his clandestine style, she clasped his hands across the table and they looked deeply into each others' eyes. A waitress named Sophie took their drink orders and began to treat them as though they had been having these secret rendezvous for many months. "You kids," she'd say, with feigned irritation and a little crank of her head. "Honest . . . the way you carry on." LePeters quickly told Ellen Rosenberg the story of his faithless wife; halfway along, he was overcome and shocked himself by actually crying so that a few tears fell into his cantaloupe. It was a risky thing to do. Ellen Rosenberg would have every right to mark him down as a weak sister; on the other hand it would demonstrate deep feeling and a sense of humanity. Whatever the case, she seemed to like it and leaned over to give him a kiss on the neck. "Don't you worry about it," she said. "It's just a little cockydoody thing in your life." She was a great girl all right, but LePeters couldn't help notice that she would react to almost every crisis with a "shitty" or a "pissy" or a "cocky-doody." Thus far, it was his only criticism of her, but it was rather a grave one and there was probably no way to get her out of it. Clutching her hand, he led her off to the squad, feeling dark and windswept, the whole city driving against them. "Ain't love grand," the waitress hollered after them.

"You just need someone to be nice to you," said Ellen Rosenberg, huddling against his shoulder. "And I came along."

"Where to?" he asked, once he was behind the wheel, thinking how strange and disturbing it was to see someone in Claire LePeters's window seat, even though he was still mad at her for getting the side bashed in. "Let's go visit my folks," said Ellen Rosenberg. She said there was a strong tradition of taking care of men in her family and she wanted LePeters to see it in action. "On four occasions my father almost drowned and my mother swam out and rescued him." It was too early to actually meet them so once they got to their destination, a friendly little community on the outskirts of the city, LePeters and Ellen Rosenberg took up a position behind a hedge, the one where an old man had once jumped out and traumatically snapped her panties. Peering out in the moonlight, LePeters first saw an elderly gentleman relaxing in a reclining chair while a stocky woman served him what appeared to be bowls of stew. "Mom and Pops," said Ellen Rosenberg, who then pointed out her older sister, a cheerfully buxom girl who was giving backrubs to a young man at the opposite end of the lawn. LePeters was able to see immediately what she was getting at. It was a lovely scene to behold and he wondered if he was destined to get in on some of it. Once again, it was unfair to do so, but LePeters couldn't help recall Claire LePeters's stockbroker dad tripping over an extension cord and her mom cackling with glee at his clumsiness instead of running over to see if he'd broken his leg. "My wife's from another tradition," said LePeters, still feasting on what he saw beyond the hedge. "She's probably very beautiful," said Ellen Rosenberg with amazing generosity. "Not right this second," said LePeters. They drove then to Ellen Rosenberg's apartment and went upstairs in an elevator that was choked with dozens of homey but conflicting cooking smells. The apartment itself was quite modest but also astonishingly clean and thunderously self-sufficient, everything in place right down to the last washcloth. Ellen Rosenberg got out of her dress and hopped into a boy's undershirt and tight boy's bluejeans, a treat for LePeters who went wild over this style of dress on girls even if it marked him down as a clear-cut fag. She then showed him some new work she had been doing in iron and glass which he tried to love but found just as dull as the sand bowls in Jigtown. "Maybe I'll take one off your hands," he lied, "if the price isn't too out of line."

"Doody," she said, with a laugh. "They're not good enough to be sold and you know it."

Why did she have to say things like "Doody," the fastidious LePeters wondered. If it was a delayed reaction to early training, couldn't she come up with a more charming way of being rebellious? Stripping the issue from his mind, LePeters unzipped her boy's pants and they made love, but not before she had personally taken off his shoes and propped him up on her bed with pillows, making sure there wasn't the slightest wrinkle in the sheets that might disturb his comfort. "Now slow," she said, running her fingers over him in that deliberate urn-molding style he'd found so agonizingly pleasurable in the islands—while at the same time realizing it wasn't the only game in town. As hard as he tried to lose his footing completely and tumble freely into oblivion, he could not

help keeping one hand on the guard railing, so to speak, because he still didn't feel comfortable about staying out the
entire night and figured on getting back to Detectives' Hill
around three in the morning. "I know," she said, when it was
around that time, "you want to get back."

"Just a habit," he said. "Listen, was it good?"

"Was it good," she said incredulously. "He wants to know
if it was good . . .

"Jesus," she said, with a strange little shiver.

"I see," said LePeters, who still wasn't sure if it was good
but hoped it had been so profoundly fine as to be beyond
comment.

Sulking for just a moment about his premature departure,
she suddenly leaped out of bed, tied an apron around her
plump, naked haunches and began to whip up a batch of
scrambled eggs, along with toast and hot coffee, whistling as
she worked and pretending it was breakfast time even though
he was lighting out in the middle of the night. Wolfing down
the eggs, LePeters had to wonder what in the world was
wrong with him. He was propped up in a beautiful, great-
breasted young girl's bed, eating a *Life* Magazine fold-out
color-spread breakfast, prepared by her own hand. He had
been made love to in regal fashion. If he decided he was in
the mood for two hours of frenzied nude Gypsy dances, she
would be happy to oblige him. Let's say it would amuse him
to see her dangle from the window ledge by her thumbs. Out
she would go, no problem at all. Another fully orchestrated
slow-motion tumble in the hay? All he had to do was ask.
How come none of this was enough for him?

◉

This time it was LePeters who slipped into the bedroom late at night under his wife's baleful glare.

"And you stayed out this late?" she said, surprising him with her concern.

"Yes," he said. "I had a date. How's your affair?"

"Fine," she said.

"I can't for the life of me see why you'd settle on a fellow like him," said LePeters. "If you'd come up with some kind of substantial guy maybe I could understand it."

"I don't know," said Claire LePeters, suddenly friendly and intimate, as though she was sharing confidences with a sorority chum, "it's some of the things he does. For example he hasn't bathed since he met me. He wants to keep the scent of me on him as long as possible."

Stunned, LePeters quickly retaliated by saying he had been out with a very young girl. "Boy, was she young," he said. "I'd forgotten what it was like to be around a person that lean in years." He had no way of measuring the effect on her of these remarks. Maybe they were damaging. All he knew is that no matter how hard he came down on the young references, it was a drop in the bucket compared with the image he now had to contend with of Detective Chico, whirling through the streets, sniffing gratefully at his arms, intoxicated with the magical fragrance of Claire LePeters, for seventeen years his beloved wife.

In the weeks that followed, they waged a grim and silent duel of affairs, matching each other indiscretion for indiscretion. They saw each other on the fly, LePeters coming when his wife was going and vice versa, tossing each other tantalizing bits of information, such as "We were at the Italian street fair yesterday. Don't miss it," to which the other would reply, "Wow, we were there two days ago." Both would then grin perversely at the near-collision and the bloodbath that would no doubt have occurred if the two couples had spotted each other at the Italian gala. To his knowledge, Claire LePeters had been sucked naturally and mindlessly into the wild liaison with Detective Chico. His own fling was much more calculated. No matter how hard he tried to lose himself in the cozy, voluptuous, plumply pillowed world of Ellen Rosenberg, he was always aware that his main objective was to match his wife screw for retaliatory screw. It certainly wasn't the fault of the Rosenberg girl, who did everything but bring the Sunday paper to him in her teeth. Not only that, but she seemed to become lovelier each day and he was confident that if he ever decided to pack it in and return to Detectives' Hill on a permanent basis, a line would form on the right to sample that haunting deep-forest fragrance that had traveled so well from the islands (even though her legs were slightly bowed, a feature that hadn't shown up in Jigtown). Though she kept mum about it, Ellen Rosenberg was no dope about the substantial pocket of coolness in LePeters's nature. Late one night, LePeters lay back comfortably on Ellen Rosenberg's convertible couch-bed, nibbling on a huge batch of freshly prepared hot popcorn, whipped up specially for him. Up on her toes, she entertained him with naked semiprofessional ballet postures, the phonograph turned up full blast to a Bach oratorio. "Oh, farty," she said, suddenly, snapping off the record and caving awkwardly into a sofa.

"What's up," said LePeters.

"You're really not here," she said. "You're miles away."

"Negative," said LePeters. "I'm here and I'm all eyes and ears."

"No you're not," she said. "If you were really with me you'd have me next to a high-powered lamp and be poring over my private parts for hours and hours with a look of love on your face."

"Where's the lamp?" said LePeters, totally sincere. "I was going to do that but I just hadn't gotten around to it."

"That's all right," she said, running her hand through his sparse hair, LePeters miraculously not minding that massive sections of his scalp were being laid bare by the rearrangement. "If you were truly available, you probably wouldn't be half so attractive."

◉

If LePeters spent more time in bed with his wife and Detective Chico than he did with Ellen Rosenberg, Claire LePeters certainly was no small contributor to this state of affairs. She kept the fires of his imagination going by thoughtlessly leaving fluffy little gifts around the house, lovingly served up to her by Detective Chico. Cheap but charming Japanese fans and adorable amusement park stuffed animals. Also clipped-out fragments of verse that LePeters would love to have reminded her that Chico didn't write. And you didn't have to be a particularly gifted fellow to clip out someone else's. "If music be the food of love, play on" was the only line in all recorded poetry that LePeters knew by heart. He was a good memorizer and if he'd wanted to put his mind to it he could have picked up reams of it, but what in the world would have been the point.

One night Claire LePeters took both his hands in hers and led him gently toward a couch. Sensing a plea for reconciliation, LePeters charted out all his moves in advance: straight-backed, aloof, he would listen to her with a certain patrician coolness, but then he would suddenly capitulate, giving her a tremendous hug and telling her—with great insight and mastery over primal vengeance-seeking urges—that as far as he was concerned nothing had happened. And if a little something had gone on, great, they would simply use it to build a better future.

"Chico's confused," she said, with one stroke throwing his entire strategy down the drain. "He doesn't understand for the life of him why you haven't moved out yet."

"Well I'm sorry if I'm not moving fast enough for him."

"He says that if he were in your boots he would have either moved already or thrown me out on my ass."

"Does he know that as far as I'm concerned he's a dead man?"

"He says you don't mean it when you say things like that. He says what you really mean is that you'd probably like to fuck him."

"You picked yourself quite a charmer."

"Dr. Worthway agrees that there's something going on between the two of you."

"You saw Doctor-Detective Worthway?" LePeters cried, invaders crossing his last frontier.

"The day I cracked up the squad. I was all upset, so Chico took me to see him."

"And he saw the both of you?"

"Yes."

"That's got to be an all-time low."

"I understand you saw my wife and the shithead the other day," said LePeters, barging right in on the bureau shrink the second he got to the bullpen.

"You're lucky I've got a light day," said Worthway. "All right, I'll see you. Yes, I saw them."

"What'd you do that for?"

"Sometimes you learn more from the wife."

"And what's this about how I'm interested in Chico."

"Well, how about that," said Worthway. "What would you think of a nice, juicy detective's ass?"

"I thought you're supposed to be on my team," said the shaken LePeters. "Is that how you're helping me."

"It's something we all have to face. Facing it, we move on."

"And you actually saw Chico, too. That's the part that would really hurt."

"You're quite right," said Worthway. "It wouldn't have been proper to see him at this stage. I made him stand in the doorway and promise not to listen in."

LePeters felt he could take all the punishment the world wanted to dish out, but if it was affecting his kid, that would be it right there and someone would have to pay through the nose. There was no way to tell just how much of this was hitting Jamie LePeters. She saw her mother and father less and less. When LePeters was on his way at some odd hour, she would ask, "Where are you going?"

"To meet a friend," LePeters would say.

"A nice one?"

"A great one."

"Where does Mommy go?"

"You'll have to ask her."

And then the child would ask no more, going off to clean out her fish bowl or to sort out her terrible coins, presumably contented. But there was no way to really tell how much of this was getting through to her. Bruised by her father, sold down the river by her mom, there was a chance that in years to come she would trust neither man nor woman and be able to relax only in the company of French dwarfs. When LePeters and his wife were away, she was amply taken care of by the devoted, heavy-armed Madame Chav, who never let her take more than two steps before reining her back to safety. When LePeters asked her to take good care of the child, she would answer only with stolid, reliable cranks of her head. The only line he had ever heard her speak was, "I *love* that child," which came out like a terrifying Polish oath. One day, LePeters learned that her devotion to the child had actually led her to the lengths of climbing into bed with her, after she was asleep, to see that no intruder sneaked in there to do her some harm. Here, LePeters put his foot down. "I don't want her in the sack with my kid," he told Claire LePeters. "I don't care how much she loves her."

"All right, I'll tell her," said Claire LePeters. "You pick the funniest times to assert yourself."

One day, the last person in the world LePeters needed on his hands came rolling into town—his mother. Not only that, but she crossed him up by appearing as an entirely different kind of mom from the one he remembered. After Bill Sussman hit the dust, a victim of overwork and a double-cross by his bosses at Frickman Furs, LePeters remembered his mother turning bitter and leathery, striking out after money in any way she could get her hands on it. She had gone into one of the lowliest rackets of all—the recruitment of poorly educated colored southern teen-agers for low-paying jobs as domestics up north. That certainly wasn't the kind of behavior he respected, and in the years that followed, he had more or less washed his hands of his mother, deciding to get along without one. Now, ironically, Flo Sussman had turned up at the most troubled time of her son's life and gave all evidence of having become a sweet, little, gentle old lady, with no more axe to grind, content to nibble happily at whatever remaining crumbs life had to throw at her. "I just wanted to tell you I'm here," she said to him in a telephone call. "I've moved into a tiny apartment where I don't bother anyone and I just go about my business, thankful to God for the air he gives me to breathe. I don't want a thing from anyone. I just want to enjoy these last few years and if anyone else has a lot of money, they're welcome to it."

The sudden arrival of Flo Sussman with her new life-style caught LePeters off guard. Even though she'd asked him for nothing—except a quick visit if he had the time—he was too busy being aggravated to fit a mother into his scheme of things. Still, her gentle, almost shy manner on the phone aroused certain courtly feelings within him; he felt an urge to go to her and put a protective arm around her frail shoulders, even if it was only for a short time.

One night, he stole an hour from his time with Ellen Rosenberg and drove out to the dilapidated, crime-infested section of the city where his mother had taken a cheap apartment. On the way, he thought of some of the terrific things she had done, such as flying out to his Army base and buying a car for him, a lovely little two-seater Ford, the first he had ever owned. Even though every officer on the base drove one and he was embarrassed about having to chisel rides all the time, he had still lacked the nerve to shell out all that money for a single item. Flo Sussman planed to his side and bought it with hard-earned dollars of her own. Not only that, but she stuck around until he got the hang of it, fearlessly sitting next to him while he learned to shift gears on icy, fog-bound country roads of the Pacific Northwest. Her only reward had been a couple of delicious officers' club fish dinners and whatever meager time he could spare her.

○

As LePeters parked in front of the grim apartment building, his mother was waiting for him in the street, immediately making a big fuss over the squad, which he had made sure to have washed for the occasion. "They gave it to me at Homicide," said LePeters. "No they didn't," said Flo Sussman, "you were never with the cops and they didn't give you any cars." LePeters then remembered that his mother had never acknowledged his work as a homicider; as far as she was concerned, he was in retailing. It wasn't that she was ashamed of his work. She simply didn't want to know about it.

As far as being any kind of a temptress goes, Flo Sussman, coming down the stretch toward her seventies, had given up the ghost. She wore a lovely little old lady's shawl and had gracefully allowed her once brilliantly dyed blond hair to turn to a silken natural gray. She also wore a low-slung little old lady's dress which modestly covered her still magnificently shaped legs to the ankles. Overcome with sentiment, he gave her a wonderful hug and allowed himself to be led into the corner soda fountain and shown off to the owners. LePeters soon was able to see the full dimensions of her current life; long hours of loneliness, a few trips to the store to see some live faces, then back to the apartment to sit in a rocker and think about a dead husband, lost days, lost opportunities, not with bitterness perhaps, but not thrilled about the sum of her life either. He felt a sudden obligation to send

her down to the island of Jamaica for a few months in the
sun and some laughs, but realized this was next to impossible. If he could not afford a noncolored private school for his
kid, how could he justify sending his mother on a luxury
jaunt to the Caribbean? As they took the stairs to her fourth-
floor apartment, Flo Sussman, winded, stopped on the landing for a moment to catch her breath. "Don't feel you have
to do something for me," she said, with that uncanny ability
to ferret out her son's thoughts. "I mean that. I'm just tickled to death to be alive."

Immediately after Flo Sussman had moved in, her apartment had been broken into twice, and as a consequence, her
front door was now covered with a sea of multiple locks.
"But it's all right," she said. "Nobody touched my person
and maybe they won't break in again." LePeters hoped the
sonsofbitches would try it just one more time, while he was
there, so he could show them what happened when not only
a defenseless old lady was on hand, but also a grown
homicider.

Looking around, LePeters saw touching mementos of his
past, particularly a Coney Island boardwalk picture of his father when Bill Sussman must have been forty, his own age.
He studied the picture carefully to see if Bill Sussman had
more or less hair than LePeters had now at the same age.
There was no way to tell, since his father had worn his
combed back in an honest, unashamed manner while LePeters didn't dare do that; never had he taken a straight, un-
blinking look at his own hairline except maybe once or twice
after showers. Flo Sussman asked her son if he wanted any
refreshments, and then produced a glass of rubbing alcohol
for him; after one distasteful sip, he realized she had mistaken
it for a fresh glass of club soda. Not wanting to ruffle her, he
quietly poured the lethal liquid back into its container. But

not before he had seen clearly that gorgeous legs and all, his mother was turning senile; the best course might very well be to scoop her up and carry her off to live in his house on Detectives' Hill where someone could keep an eye on her. He cursed himself for not being married to a girl who would understand the need for such emergency measures. If his mother ever died from accidentally swallowing some floor shellac, then he would really light into Claire LePeters and certainly ban her from the funeral. Maybe even divorce her on the spot.

For the moment, sadly enough, vacations in the sun and a move to Detectives' Hill seemed to be out of the question. But he clenched his fists and swore that at the very minimum he would definitely buy her an air-conditioner and at least get a little freshness into her scrubbed but dank little apartment. Even though Bill Sussman was long dead and gone, the tiny apartment reminded LePeters of his good-natured father who had never harmed a soul. If the old man were still alive, LePeters was sure his folks would be living in big, sunny quarters with plenty of fresh flowers around; there would be family gatherings that LePeters would be invited to, not to mention his daughter, Jamie. They would be thrilled to have her visit, too. He got angry at Frickman Furs all over again for the way they had treated his dad. Slipping his mother a folded-up twenty, he could have sworn he heard her say, "Well, that'll really help" before putting it in her purse. Even if she did, the mild sarcasm was certainly forgivable; it was remarkable she was taking things as well as she was. "I think I'm about ready to pay a little visit to Gus Frickman," LePeters said to his mother.

"I won't allow it," his mother said, aware of the menace in his voice. "They're dirt, they always were dirt. Fine. Let them be dirt."

"Things are different now, Mom," he said, not sure what he meant but certain about the strength of his emotion. "People aren't allowed to get away with things anymore." Then how come Detective Chico was getting away with slipping it to his wife?

"Promise me that whatever you do you'll be careful," said Flo Sussman, sounding exactly like the mother of his childhood.

"I'll be all right," said LePeters, kissing her extraordinarily fine-spun gray hair and slipping her another ten. "Gus Frickman's the one who's got to watch his step."

That was the detective in him talking. No hood in the world could ever get away with telling a dick to "take it easy," with its implication of possible weakness. "*You* take it easy," the dick would fire back with blood in his eyes, holding the man with his gaze until the fellow shrugged his shoulders and said, "Okay, okay, *I'll* take it easy."

Leaving his mother's apartment, LePeters had one idea locked in his head: he had to settle the score with Frickman Furs for the disgraceful way they had dealt with his dead father. It was convenient, too, since he had just so much anger within him and for the moment it meant he would not have to worry about dealing with Detective Chico, a much tougher nut to crack, with one of the all-time kill records in the history of the bureau to his credit. It wasn't just Detective Chico alone, either; he had to start facing the fact that Chico and Claire LePeters were a team and it would be difficult to argue that he had lured her into the arrangement against her will.

For the moment, what he had in mind was a direct assault on Gus Frickman. This time he was not going to be charmed or soft-soaped out of it either. If Gus Frickman turned out to be a fellow in his nineties and had to be wheeled out to see

him, too damned bad. He wasn't going to listen to any baloney about how nice it was that he had turned out to be such
a fine fellow, and a homicide detective to boot. And they
were not going to buy him off with any diversionary roast beef
lunch either, no matter how delicious. He would simply look
them straight in the eyes and ask them to account for their
treatment of his father. And if they didn't come up with
some pretty smart answers in a big hurry, he would let them
have it both barrels and not blink an eyelash.

He didn't waste much time. The next morning, he looked
up Frickman Furs in the phone book and took half a day off
from work. In case he had to get hardnosed, he put a Swiss
Army knife in one pocket and a length of basement pipe in
the other, both taken from a sleepy-eyed but extremely violent local street-gang leader. He took a bus to Frickman Furs
and as he neared his destination, he noticed with nostalgia
that the businessman pedestrians became not only older but
also more old-fashioned, wearing wide slacks, white socks,
and fedoras, entire streets full of Bill Sussman types. Getting
off the bus, he spotted a barbershop in the Frickman building and it occurred to him that Bill Sussman had probably
hopped in there for his trims. No doubt he had traded views
on life with Sal Medaglia who'd seen a side of his father that
LePeters didn't know about, a Bill Sussman who perhaps felt
that wives could be a pain in the ass and a man had to have a
cupcake on the side. A luncheonette on the corner looked as
though it had been there for a long time. Bill Sussman had
probably eaten his favorite dish there, mushroom and barley
soup, and for all he knew had grabbed himself a handful of
many a plump Italian waitress. Did the elevator man who
took him to the thirty-fourth floor know his father? How
about the switchboard operator whose eyes opened wide
when he said he was Detective Kenneth LePeters, son of Bill

Sussman who used to work there? She was stocky and a bit over the hill, but must have been quite a number when his father was still in the picture. What if he found out that Bill Sussman had knocked her off a couple of times in the stock room during boisterous Christmas parties? Instead of Gus Frickman, a thin, heavy-lipped colored man came out with a cap in his hand and stood before LePeters with his head lowered, unable to meet his eyes. "I'm Check," he said. "And your father was sure a nice man." Deep in the rubble of his mind, LePeters remembered his father referring to a fellow named Check who was not too heavy in the brains department, but strong as an ox and willing to go to the moon for him. Check stood before LePeters in the supplicant's position, as though he was willing to leave Frickman Furs on the spot and put himself totally at LePeters's disposal. But what could LePeters do with him? He had no need for a man around the house and certainly couldn't afford him, even though he got the impression that Check would work for a pittance. Maybe there was a way to use him to bring down Detective Chico, particularly if rumors of Check's strength were valid. But all of this was farfetched. Not knowing how to deal with the situation, LePeters grinned, tapped Check on the shoulder with affection, and said, "Great." Shyly, and mercifully, the fellow shuffled backward into the cutting room, his place instantly taken by a trio of Frickman Fur bosses. They were led by ancient Gus Frickman, whose eyes were coated over in a heavily fleshed and sinister manner. LePeters realized suddenly that he was blind and consciously took a deep breath as if by doing so he could fill himself with new toughness. If they thought a little blindness was going to scare him off, they were slightly off base. Bill Sussman had lost not only his vision but everything he had. If he could be reached, wherever he was, LePeters was sure he would have jumped at the chance to come back on earth, even as a blindie. At Gus Frickman's side was "Bucks" Frickman, his son, who had gotten the nickname when it became evident that he was going to take over his father's monied position at Frickman Furs with great ease and absolutely no opposition. Also on hand was another old-timer named Allan Jory, who had been screwed by the Frickmans along with Bill Sussman but had outfoxed them by piling up millions on the grain market. Amused, they kept him around and let him be some kind of partner, even though he didn't need a cent of the money. This was the trio that confronted LePeters and asked him to come into the showroom and have some tea. Now that he had seen them he was sure that physically, at least, he could take them. Gus Frickman, sinister as he looked, was, of course, helpless, and Allan Jory, for all of his ruddiness, was an old man and would probably go down without much of a struggle. Bucks Frickman, a younger fellow, was another story, but LePeters felt he could be handled, particularly with the element of surprise; and of course it would be no contest if he brought his Swiss Army knife or the length of pipe into the picture. It seemed unlikely that the confrontation was going to go that way but you never knew and LePeters checked his pockets to make sure the weapons hadn't dropped through the lining.

"Awfully glad to see you, Kenny," said Bucks Frickman, who was evidently going to be the spokesman for the trio. "We hear great things about you." Suntanned, with a chipper smile, he had the reputation of being a charm boy and had filled his father with pride by opening up several territories to chinchilla that old Gus Frickman had never been able to crack. The suntan was a fresh one, as though he had just planed in from Florida where by all rights LePeters's mother, Flo Sussman, should have been.

"Don't he look just like 'Sussy,' " said Allan Jory, who for all his accumulated millions, struck LePeters as being a sycophant. Sussy, indeed. Where did they come off calling his dignified father, long departed, by that name. Just once, he'd like to see them throw a "Sussy" at him. They'd never know what hit them. Still, he had to admit that the nickname, for all its irreverence, bespoke a certain casual locker-room familiarity. They must have known his father pretty well, had plenty of laughs with him. For all LePeters knew, his father had called old Gus Frickman "Fricksy" or something along that line. Whatever the case, these speculations weren't getting him any closer to the goal-line. Gus Frickman's only reaction to the proceedings was to clear his throat and hoist a giant wad across the room where it lodged silently in the expensive carpeting. This was evidently a privilege he enjoyed because of his rank in the company and his physical debility. The disgusting action passed without comment. LePeters decided to go right for the throat.

"How come you guys screwed my father?" he said to the three men who were arced around him in a semicircle. Gus Frickman immediately hoisted another torpedo across the room while Allan Jory yanked out a clipper and began to trim his fingernails. Only Bucks Frickman held LePeters's gaze, as though he had been expecting the question. "Now look, Kenny," he said. "Let's get something straight. Nobody screwed your father. I know how your mom feels and I'm sorry about that. But we loved your dad and we were all damned sorry when he died in more ways than one. We lost a wonderful co-worker and a wonderful friend. Now that's just the way it was. When my father lost his sight, your old man became a father to me. He taught me the business and, believe me, I never forgot it. When he died, I felt it was the worst thing that had ever happened to me."

"Sure," LePeters said, convinced of the young man's sincerity yet hating to give in. "Then how come you screwed him."

"All right," said Bucks, "let's hear it. Right out on the table. How did we screw him? You tell me and I'll fix it, once and for all."

Completely on the defensive now, LePeters felt dizzy and asked to be excused for just a second. Allan Jory led him to the washroom where he threw some cold water on his head. Spotting a telephone, he called his mother. "Listen, Mom," he said. "This has to be a short one. I want you to tell me exactly what they did to my father. You know, down here at Frickman."

"What they did to him . . ." his mother sighed. "How they treated him. The promises . . . the treatment . . . I wish I had words. I'm an old lady."

"I know you're old, Mom," said LePeters, "and I sympathize with that. But you've got to tell me exactly what they did. Otherwise I can't operate."

"Just like that," she said. "You want to know everything . . . a whole lifetime . . . in two seconds. You know how many books I could write . . ."

"Okay, Mom," said LePeter's. "I think I got the idea."

Indeed, LePeters had gotten the idea before he'd even made the call. The truth was, instead of being a furnace of hell for him, Frickman Furs had been his father's lifeblood. The three men he had always thought of as vultures, and that included the sightless, disgusting Gus Frickman, were in reality his buddies. The real hell for Bill Sussman had been his home and the tough, ever-complaining Flo Sussman. Frickman Furs, where he had pals, where he could kid around, where he could pinch a showroom girl on the ass, was his playground, and the supposedly tough grinding hours he had spent on the job had actually sustained him, given him extra years to live. LePeters believed Bucks Frickman when he said that Bill Sussman had been a father to him. LePeters had been away all those years, first on Army duty, then making his odyssey across the nation, hopping from one homicide bureau to another, never bothering to fly back and see his dad. No wonder his father had taken on another son. As far as the big "screwing" on the part of Frickman Furs, the chances were that it had never existed. If they hadn't paid Bill Sussman a king's ransom every week, maybe he didn't deserve it. Who told him to work for the same company for forty-five years? Was anyone blocking the door? If he was any kind of tiger, all he had to do was walk across the hall and work for Burroughs Furs at a big increase or a partnership. Or start his own Frickman Furs. For that matter, was anyone keeping LePeters chained to his job in homicide clippings display? Years later, would he blame it on Glober and ask his daughter Jamie to go down and see him in the spirit of vengeance?

The great "screwing" of Bill Sussman, LePeters saw clearly, existed entirely in the head of his mother Flo Sussman, who had chosen to anchor the family's heart and soul to an enormous fraud. The hours spent at Frickman were the happiest of Bill Sussman's life. If someone had once promised him some extra dough someday that was part of the game. LePeters knew full well that if money were the issue Bucks Frickman was completely willing to settle that matter right on the spot.

"Well, what is it," the Frickman boy said, when LePeters got back from the washroom. "We gave your mother a check. Do you want me to make out another one? Hell, I'll send her one every week. You want her in Florida, I'll take care of that, too. I just want to settle this thing once and for all and clear the air."

"It's settled," LePeters said. "You don't need to send her any money. I ought to be able to take care of that myself. I just had to come down here."

"Will you shake my hand," Bucks asked him.

"Why not," LePeters said, giving him a firm clasp, and patting old Gus Frickman on the shoulder at the same time.

"Tell the truth," Bucks Frickman said, with the cheery smile that had helped him open up new chinchilla territories. "Did you bring your gun along?"

"Damn right," said LePeters, patting his coat pocket. "I never go anywhere without it."

The black and thickly polluted air of the fur district seemed fresh and crisp to LePeters as he walked out of the Frickman building, feeling cleaner and hundreds of pounds lighter than when he had arrived. It had taken him more than a decade to make the trip and the great thing about it was not so much that a central lie of his existence had been eradicated, but that it was over and he didn't have to go back and do it again. Normally, his impulse would have been to flash out to Detectives' Hill, scoop Claire LePeters up in his arms, and shout the good news to her. Before he had walked a block, he realized with sadness that this was impossible since at the moment she was probably either trying some new and gymnastic bedroom stunt with Detective Chico or auditioning dykes for one of his second-rate films. He could scoop the buxom Ellen Rosenberg up in his arms and tell her the news, but it wouldn't be the same; with all her warmth and generosity, she did not have the background to understand the significance of his triumph at Frickman Furs. Although half the day was shot, LePeters felt funny about missing an entire twenty-four hours of homicide and headed back to the bureau. In the anteroom of the bullpen, a notorious armed robbery repeater announced to the assembled dicks that he had decided to go straight and never pull another stickup again. Unescorted, he had strolled into the bullpen to declare that his days as a criminal had been wasted ones. "Surely there must be a more satisfying life than this," he said. "Constantly being hunted down like a dog. Well, I'm one fellow who's had it up to here." Several wise old bull dicks winked at each other, knowing full well this was a sure sign that the fellow would be pulling another job before the week was out. The most widely discussed homicide, at the moment, was a "Gold Coast" affair, involving a beautiful young heiress whose assailant had killed her by stuffing a massive potato up her rectum. By the time LePeters arrived, the evidentiary vegetable had already passed through Micro-Analysis and was being tossed about by several of the younger dicks in a bullpen game of touch football. As LePeters made for his desk, the quarterbacking Detective Flamoyan heaved him a slot pass over the middle which LePeters caught easily, immediately starting downfield and warding off tacklers. Only after he had trotted the length of the bullpen did he realize that he was carrying the celebrated anal spud. Casting about for a patsy, he spotted a visiting private eye who had first called the case in to the bureau and tossed it right over to him. Since homicide detectives considered themselves the elite of the law-enforcing profession and were terribly contemptuous of "mongrels" and "door-knockers" it was absolutely the right move on LePeters's part.

Returning to his desk to sort out the day's homicide clip-

pings, LePeters turned his thoughts to the outrageous ways
men often picked to mortify one another's flesh. Certainly
the rich girl ass-killing was one of the weirdest he had run up
against. There had been no "defense wounds" reported on
the slain heiress, which meant that she had been taken by
surprise; the assailant might have been a trusted family friend
or suitor who could have been playing gin rummy with
her when the idea flew into his head of coming at her with
the giant vegetable. How was it possible to develop such hate
for a woman? As down as he was on Claire LePeters, he
could never see himself taking a potato to her—although
admittedly, he had often imagined his wife going up in
flames aboard an inferior airliner—and having to scrape
through life without her, a feat he was sure he would be able
to manage.

Late in the day, LePeters punched out and decided to take in
a movie; since it was an odd hour, he had the entire theater
to himself and was able to enjoy getting involved in the
affairs of the two carefree American lovers in Rio; still, he
ended up feeling gloomy since he had to get right out of their
lives at the end of two hours while they went on to have
more fun. Afterward, he pulled up his collar and slipped
through the streets toward Ellen Rosenberg's apartment,
warily looking back past his shoulder lest someone spot him,
although he still didn't have the faintest idea who he was
worried about. All he knew is that he was terribly concerned
about being nailed in the act of visiting the sensuous Ellen
Rosenberg. Each time he approached her apartment, LePeters could have sworn he spotted a mysterious tee-shirted fellow slinking suspiciously down the hall as though he had just

left her front door. He told himself it was only the pale, fragmented hallway light playing tricks on him. On this occasion, once again LePeters thought he saw the same fellow emerging from Ellen Rosenberg's pad. But he was certain it was no apparition. In fact, it was unmistakably the humpbacked, tentacled fellow named Victor, who had been so surly to him in Jigtown and who was on record as having conducted many a nude figure study of Ellen Rosenberg, although presumably he had stopped right there. Marching into the apartment, LePeters found Ellen Rosenberg foaming over with a headful of shampoo lather; immediately he hit her with his suspicions about Victor, whom she had promised not to allow any more studies of her body, even though the sessions had supposedly been innocent, stopping short of actual body contact.

"Okay," Ellen Rosenberg confessed, "so he lives down the hall and helps me shampoo my hair. Big deal. Doody."

"And I suppose that's all he does," said LePeters, throwing out a "dummy line" in the style of an interrogating dick who pretends to have more information than he actually has. As so often happened during an actual grilling, the bluff produced the biggest haul of the day. "I didn't even feel anything," said Ellen Rosenberg, collapsing in tears. "It was over in a few minutes and I never stopped washing my hair."

"Your body is so precious to me," said LePeters. "And you just hand it over to any creep who lives down the hall. Don't I please you? Is there something I don't do?"

"It's just a little trick he has toward the end. He gets an extra minute or so out of it for both of us. Other than that one thing, you're ten times better.

"Look," she said, angry for the first time since he had met her, "let's just be together while we're together and the rest of the time let's leave each other alone."

"I'm not sure I can work it that way," said LePeters. With a single yank, he tore off her robe and swept her off to the converta-couch bed. "All right," he said, tearing into her body, "what's the trick?" Through the next frenzied ten minutes or so, she cried constantly, but after he had drawn away, she said it had been absolutely the best of all times for her and she felt closer to him than ever before:

"Me too," said LePeters. "And I'm not a bit angry. The only thing is, I'm not going to be seeing that much of you for a while."

"How come," she said. "I just finished saying it was the best time ever."

"I loved it, too," said LePeters. "But I've got to take some time off and spread myself around a little."

◎

Though LePeters had reacted savagely to his wife's dalliance with Detective Chico, miraculously, he felt no equivalent bitterness toward Ellen Rosenberg. In a curious way, he was grateful to her. What he had done was to shift over from an unhappy, tightly manacled dependency on Claire LePeters to a much more pleasant but also suffocating reliance on Ellen Rosenberg. Now that the Rosenberg girl, to a mild degree, had joined his wife in selling him down the river, he felt a curious shiver of freedom. What he sensed he wanted to do was to find out a few things about women, a group he knew painfully little about when you consider that he had been married to a member of it for seventeen years. But was a housewife who could find happiness in the arms of a film-making ex-homicider representative of her sex? And what about the gentle Ellen Rosenberg and her strange and rather coarse preoccupation with cockies and doodies. LePeters thought back to his previous experience with women and realized that it had been patchy and remote; it was as though he had only gotten to snatch at them through the windows of an erratically scheduled train. Somehow his adventures seemed to have involved him more often than not with feebleminded girls, cross-eyed, doomed, and a second fellow, taken along for courage. On one occasion, both he and a boy named Schildkraut, later to become a fabled knitwear executive, had spirited a slow-witted janitor's daughter up to an apartment fire escape, there to plant her between them and triumphantly join hands beneath her panties while the sensuous feeb bubbled slightly at the mouth and cocked her head romantically at the moon. Let a girl's I.Q. travel past 75 and she was out of bounds for LePeters. At summer camp, it was a sluggish bawd named "Brown Betty," smelling of cake batter, who had presented herself nightly to LePeters and Hans Oppenfeld, his refugee roommate, to be traded back and forth between them, while they both lolled about in thinly scooped jockstraps, neither daring to leave the other alone with the heavy-hipped baker's assistant.

Later, at college, LePeters began to work alone, but to be on the safe side, stuck to feebs, taking up with a dowdy corpse of a town girl named Dots who could be undressed, puppetlike, in bowling alleys, trucks, even on buses, without uttering a word. Though the rumor was that she was "crossboned" and could not actually be entered, one night, on the floor of a deserted gym, LePeters worked his way through to victory and may very well have been the first to do so.

If LePeters's girls were not graceless slothful types, inevitably they would turn out to be impossibly beautiful, romantic ones, designed to be silently and sheepishly adored and perhaps kissed a bit but never slept with. For many months, he traveled each weekend to a candy-covered village

where he would sit and worship a lovely yellow-haired rich
princess of a girl, luxuriating in his pain, never daring to
touch her, though on one occasion she put his tense hands
between her legs and said with some pique, "I thought you
were supposed to be fast." Each evening of his visit, her
wealthy merchant father would take them to a handsome
hilltop restaurant where LePeters would ask only for soup,
thinking it would be ungracious of him to order a full meal
and that the way to make a good impression was to eat like a
bird, thereby taking it easy on the old man's pocketbook.
"Will that be all?" the surprised waiter would say, to which
the girl's father would reply, "He's on a diet." One day, predictably, LePeters received a letter from her saying she could
no longer see him since she was going steady. LePeters remembered her other boyfriend as being a slight chipmunk of
a fellow who blew a whistle and yanked down on an imaginary toilet chain each time someone else at a party had
something to say. LePeters loved the pain of the rejection,
though admittedly he did dash off a note saying, "Are you
sure you want to go through with this."

Such was LePeters's life with girls, prior to Claire LePeters, the one exception being a wiry, late-inning entry from
Texas who was pure as the southern skies when approached
head on, but allowed all hell to break loose if slipped up on
from behind. Once LePeters caught on to the required strategy, he settled in for two months of furious bronco-busting
passion. As long as the frenzied activity took place behind
her, the attractive rascal was able to turn the most prim and
respectable face toward Dallas society, as though all back-
door shenanigans were being conducted by some shameless
and invisible twin sister. Tired of looking exclusively at her
spinal column and exhausted by some of the extreme postures required, LePeters finally decided he'd had enough of

the strange affair and literally ran away from her one night,
the disappointed wench following in tears, hollering out, "Is
it because I'm not a Jew?"

That took in the lot of them, a long series of occasionally
cute but doomed and voiceless feebs, a scattering of story-
book princesses way beyond his grasp, a reverse-pattern Texas
nympho, and except for a few unexplainable nights of bliss,
seventeen generally deprived years with Claire LePeters. Not
much of a scorecard for a fellow who had been on the scene
for four decades. With a wife who had made herself unavail-
able to him (though plenty available to Detective Chico),
LePeters was hardly in an enviable position. Yet for the program he had in mind, he wasn't that badly off. Responsible,
as he saw it, only to his daughter Jamie, LePeters was free to
sail out into the world of girls, young and old, and to scoop
up as many as possible, examining them from every angle, in
a bold attempt to make up for all the years in which he had
stuck close to home. Never mind this business of seeing all
women in one woman's smile. When he looked at Ellen Rosenberg's tits, he saw something absolutely first-rate, but that
was all he saw, one girl's tits. He wanted to look at fourteen
sets, then perhaps return to one. To get his new campaign off
the ground, LePeters cast about for someone surefire and
came up with the tiny-skirted Sissy Glober, daughter of his
boss, who several months before had introduced him briefly to
a strange, soaked, and mentholated below-the-belt world in
her father's very office. One night, LePeters stayed late and
nervously asked her for another snort of the crushed mystery
capsules she had once waved beneath his nose. Pouting a bit,
Sissy Glober said she had taken up with a group of vending-

machine repairmen and where had LePeters been all those months. But she fumbled with her hair, her eyes began to burn and before long they were in Glober's locked office, Le-Peters stretched out widely on his boss's Naugahyde couch, Sissy Glober at his feet, yellow-haired, demented, meticulously attending to him like some wet and marvelously schooled secretary of the flesh. Thus they entered into a limited compact in which the Glober girl would drain him nightly of his tension, making love to him more elaborately only on those special nights when the vending team was on an out-of-town delivery. For LePeters's part, he used Sissy Glober, almost as a gambler's stake, to catapult him into a massive network of further adventures. It mattered little if on any given night, things did not work out. With the Glober girl beneath his belt, it was as though he was playing with someone else's money and could not lose. What he had was not so much affairs as a series of affairlets, brief, tense, sexual interviews which he would cut off suddenly so he could dash off to conduct another. As a forty-year-old homicider with a boundaried face and not that much cash to burn, LePeters was afraid at first that he would have trouble corraling even one woman no less a truckload. Yet he soon found that by fixing his standards below the starlet level, he was able to recruit a small army, having to schedule them at a hectic, frenzied pace and not able to settle into any one situation—which fortunately was the whole idea of it. The main point was not to miss anything. In deep, hand-holding, nose-to-nose colloquy with a smoldering switchboard operator, LePeters would suddenly excuse himself and dash off to a street-corner rendezvous with a salty assistant bookkeeper in the city comptroller's office. Victorious in working his hand beneath the jumper of a topflight cocktail waitress (one with modeling aspirations who swore she'd only left the lounge with a total

of three ad execs in two years) LePeters would suddenly gun
the squad, drop her off on a corner, and tear across the city to
meet an over-the-hill action painter with an intriguing con-
tessa's style. With the newfound guile of a city planner, he
scheduled girls for every spare second of his time, squeezing
two in at his lunch hour, quickly bowling over Sissy Glober
after work, then wedging as many as three in of an evening
and even catching one on the fly when he slumped into a late-
night diner, exhausted, on his way back to Detectives' Hill
for a catnap, aware that even if he wasn't having much fun,
he was building up impressive numbers.

Early on, he learned to say as little as possible and to let
the girl discover that he was the missing puzzle piece of her
fantasies. If she were looking for tough and hardboiled,
LePeters was her boy. Let sensitive be her game, enter LePeters. After a fast getaway in which he virtually blackjacked
his quarry into a date, LePeters kept mum, leaning heavily
toward one tight-jawed, weatherbeaten expression that indicated he had been through quite a bit in his life but was
made of grizzled stuff and preferred not to take the easy
course of fobbing his troubles off on someone else's shoulders. Occasionally, he dropped hints of a faithless wife, an
approach which to his amazement failed to chase away a single candidate and indeed went over quite well with girls
who'd had some brush with education. Other times, he spoke
sparingly of fantasy, reality, and the nature of existence, hint-
ing with furrowed, sleep-worn eyes that he knew volumes
more than the few interesting notions he was allowing to
leak out—a routine that scored mightily with receptionists.

At all times in his life LePeters was easily able to lie back
and mentally thumb through every girl he had known, no
great feat since only a handful had to be accounted for. One
day, he realized deliriously that he had lost count and imme-

diately came down on the brakes, allowing himself the luxury of an entire three-day involvement with a tempestuous thirty-year-old ex-child actress who made him leaf through clipping files of her early triumphs, then took him to bed on a pile of old props, convincing herself that sleeping with LePeters was in some circuitous way going to get her back on Broadway. There followed an entire week with a confused poetess that ended bizarrely with LePeters falling off her bed in the dead of night and crushing a cat, the girl farting uncontrollably and making LePeters swear at scissors-point that if he ever wrote a novel he wouldn't put that in. Quickly he took up with a fashion photographer's assistant who protested, seconds after he met her, that she didn't want to get involved, but soon resignedly led him to her loft, telling the slack-waisted, thin-armed LePeters: "It's criminal to waste a beautiful body when you run into one." One night, when LePeters assumed she was in the throes of animal lust, he realized that she had him fixed with a baleful camera's eyes. "In and out, in and out, that's all it is to you, isn't it?" she said. "It's a lot more than that," he insisted, but that was all it was with her and he took it as his cue to move on. Before the sun set on another day, LePeters hooked up with a confused third-rate debutante, who quickly invited him to a "very special party." Arriving in innocence, LePeters found people dashing up to shake his hand, including the girl's parents, just back from Marrakesh, and saw that the party was in his honor, its purpose to announce his engagement. Realizing he had failed to tell the deb he was married and was even a dad, LePeters slipped out quietly at the height of the gala, but not before he had skimmed off his biggest coup to date, a sharp-nosed Egyptian typist whose intimate parts proved to be spellbindingly lovely in their symmetry. All through life, LePeters had accepted the popular magazine thesis that love resided in the spiritual and one torso was as good as another. Now he wasn't so sure. Once he had the Cairo charmer in tow, LePeters settled in for his longest tour to date, spending hours enjoying her classically shaped loins, a miracle of construction that might have been fashioned by prize-winning engineers, fresh from a triumph in Hungary involving lovely cantilevered bridges that were designed to join East and West together. At times LePeters felt he was being selfish about his find and longed to invite the staff of *Scientific American* to enjoy it with him. He soon came away with the thesis that perfectly matched, convivial temperaments were relatively unimportant and that perhaps exquisitely carved genitals, molded to legendary perfection, were enough to keep a couple together on life's highway. With no fund of anecdotes to amuse him, a slight lisp, and the annoying habit of showing up in wide-brimmed picture hats, this flower of the Nile might have seemed a bore. LePeters nonetheless took great pleasure in the knowledge that his latest and greatest owned perhaps the most exquisitely shaped pussy in the Western world.

At one point, LePeters had felt that affairs could only be ended by the slamming of a door, angry words, or a desperate leap through a window—and that ex-girls, when run into accidentally, were either to be ignored or given surly looks. Now, LePeters strangely felt a debt to each girl he had known and would not have minded running into a few of his old childhood feebs. He would give each one a hug and ask her how she was getting along. One day, he found himself on a high, pointed rock with Ellen Rosenberg, exchanging soft kisses in the snappish early winter cold. "What have you been having, affairs?" she asked, not scolding, simply curious. "A few," said LePeters, "and yourself?"

"I'm marrying Victor," she said shyly, a prospect that somehow warmed him and made him want to hold her close. "But listen," she said, scribbling on some paper. "Here's the number where we're going to be living. Call me—in case you want a little free titty."

However crudely expressed, it was a lovely and generous proposal and who knows, one that might very well come in handy on a rainy day. After he left her, he glanced rather dramatically at the paper and decided to crumple it up and throw it away, not without an awareness that it may have been his finest hour.

For all of his hectic, demoniacally paced social life, LePeters, though it be five in the morning, always managed to hotfoot it back to Detectives' Hill, where he would touch base by making sure his daughter was snugly and soundly asleep in her bed. Never once had he seen the sun come up in a strange girl's arms. Then, too, in some miraculous way, he made sure that his work as a homicider did not suffer, continuing to earn every bloodstained dollar that came his way. Weekends were thrown over entirely to Jamie LePeters, a cordon sanitaire of devotion in which he saw to it that his daughter had a fine time, no matter how haggard or sleep-starved he felt.

LePeters waited, although never entirely sure what he was waiting for. Probably some changes. Deep in his heart, no doubt he longed for Claire LePeters to grow bored with Detective Chico's childish Aegean handkerchief dances and come racing back to her husband, ready to resume her housewifely duties on a much more stable basis. Perhaps one day she would become aware of LePeters's rascally new style and confidence, a change that could only have been born of vast experience with a sea of delicious young cupcakes. Instead of being irritated, she would find her husband irresistibly engaging and long for a taste herself, before she got any further along in years. Somehow, for all of his rich new adventures, there was no way to transfer his newfound poise to any romantic dealings with Claire LePeters. Put to the test by his wife, he sensed that he would revert to being the old LePeters, self-confident only when dealing with girls who were slothful, had one floating eye, and couldn't fight back.

Changes did come about, if not in the heart of Claire LePeters, at least in the town of Detectives' Hill, sudden and dramatic ones that almost convinced LePeters that the waiting game was the desired one—and any attempt by man to tamper personally with his fate would only screw up the works. One day, a massive, sprawling family of bone-white Carolinians, trucked in by the town elders, took up residence on Detectives' Hill, registering eighteen children at the Low School, and in one stroke dramatically changing the racial balance to an infinitely more attractive white-to-black ratio. LePeters could only guess at the forces that had caused this puzzling change of attitude on the part of the town board. Perhaps the sight of the pathetic Gordon Mendelowitz, who had sacrificed a healthy heart to the cause of true integration and was now a broken man, had moved them to pity. Maybe his own frustrated attempts to communicate his misery had gotten through to the previously rigid, faceless, granitelike educators. More likely, it was pressure from on high, a curt manifesto from statewide officials instructing them to put up or close up. Whatever the case, no longer could LePeters in fairness declare that his daughter attended a straight colored school. As for the newly trucked-in family itself, they were a swarming group of mangy, gnomelike, bent-legged individuals who seemed to have existed since birth on poverty diets doled out by welfare groups and who had somehow converted this inferior fare into a stunted, mongrelized form of strength. Known as the Sapphires, they settled into a great, shambling clapboard house, paint-peeled and weatherworn, assigning a pair of starved and bloodthirsty hounds on long chains to guard it night and day, letting out hair-raising and wounded howls whether anyone approached or not. Mixed in with the dog howls were night-long screams of outrage that curled through the town, as Mo Sapphire, titular head of the family, used a belt to flay his stoutly angelic wife, a woman whose lungs reportedly were tissue-thin and who lived a pace or two from death's door. Soon afterward, Mo Sapphire and his ferretlike pack of starved adult kin began to show up on front doorsteps, demanding odd jobs which the Detectives' Hill residents were only too eager to supply. Obviously, if the Sapphires were refused they would beat it back to the Carolinas, returning the Low School to its all-colored status. LePeters himself weighed in with a leaf-raking assignment for Mo Sapphire, which the mangy family head performed sloppily, leaving behind a mysterious garage smell that took months to get rid of. Arrogantly, he demanded six bucks for his labors, which LePeters cheerfully doled out to him, the fellow going off chuckling as he counted the bills. LePeters did a little chuckling himself since the price was a steal and in his way he had helped preserve the delicate school ratio. Before long, a great termitelike swarm of Sapphire kids began to roam through the neighborhood, pecking, sniffing, finally devouring much that lay in its path. Temporarily allied with LePeters against the onslaught, the FBI man across the road suggested he give lessons in front- and back-stranglehold to Jamie LePeters. "Number one she'll be able to break the back of any kid her size, number two she won't have to, and number three it's good in deep-water drowning situations, too." LePeters thanked the fed, but decided he didn't want his daughter to get into any of that. Instead, he gave strict instructions to the stalwart Madame Chav that his daughter was to be kept in the house whenever a Sapphire came into view. True to her style, the devoted Polish sooth-sayer-turned-governess spent many sentrylike hours standing on the lawn, massive arms folded, ready to resist any Sapphire who came into view. Soon, mysterious fires began to break out in the community, along with clusters of child molestations, hitherto unheard-of on Detectives' Hill, known throughout the nation for its classically crime-starved conditions. Before long, household after household began to report the theft of tapestries and rare Chinese vases, almost unquestionably traceable to the Sapphires, who brazenly allowed the Oriental masterworks to show through the windows of their rat-infested domicile, even though they looked totally out of place. Still, no arrests were made, the Detectives' Hill police having evidently been given strict orders to give the Sapphires as wide a berth as possible, so as not to upset the attractive Low School ratio. No longer was it possible to walk the streets of Detectives' Hill in safety since there was every chance of being clubbed on the head by a marauding gnomelike little Southerner, operating in total confidence that there would be no interference by local dicks, pledged as they were to a strict "hands-off" policy.

In the face of the Sapphire deluge, Jamie LePeters stuck to her black friends who, compared to the invading newcomers, were settled Main Line residents of Detectives' Hill. Drawing closer than ever to the wild, free-spirited Samantha in particular, she managed, in some youthfully naïve way, to fluff off the fact that her friend had once given her bone-deep bites about the shoulders and on another occasion hung her from a dogwood tree like a side of beef. A chain-smoker at ten, constantly in hot water with the law, the black child cut entire weeks of school, stole tires from new Cadillacs, spat at cops, and generally became increasingly bold in her dangerous exploits, yet Jamie LePeters grew fonder of her by the day. "I can't help it, Dad," she said. "I know I could get a goody-goody friend that you would love, but there's something about Samantha." One day, the deprived black child's fortunes took an outrageously dramatic turn. Mysteriously absent for many years, her "real" parents, the Simmonses, suddenly showed up on Detectives' Hill, the father, Jacob Simmons, Esq., a tall, dignified, world-renowned herbalist, known internationally for his work in bringing nutritional solace to the needy in fledgling underdeveloped countries; the mother, Bess Simmons, a lovely fair-skinned coloratura soprano who had captured the hearts of Central Europe's opera-loving community in the early thirties. Snapping up a huge Dutch Colonial several hundred yards from LePeters's home, a prime slice of Detectives' Hill real estate, the Simmonses took immediate claim to their child, the style-conscious Bess Simmons outfitting her in the finest Saks Fifth Avenue had to offer, and then whisking her away for a fortnight of skiing at Klosters, there to mingle with leading lights of the international smart set. Whatever opposition there was to the black purchase of a fine home in the hitherto exclusively white section of Detectives' Hill melted quickly in the light of Jacob Simmons's international prestige and reputation. No sooner had the new family settled into their home and arranged the servants' quarters than important positions on various town councils were thrown open to Jacob Simmons, not the least of which was a seat on the elders, something that not even Gordon Mendelowitz, at the height of his tycooned power, had been able to wangle. Somewhat puzzled by the Simmonses' apparent lack of concern for their daughter for so many years, LePeters at the same time was proud of his town for opening its arms to the elegant black family; he felt personally enriched by the fact that they lived a stone's throw away and that their daughter was a long-time playmate of his own child. "How do you like how rich Samantha just became," Jamie LePeters said. "I certainly hope she remains a terrific kid." After all the years of neglect, the child herself seemed dazzled by the sudden rush of attention, but then settled comfortably into her new status, going easy on the bubble-gum-chewing, not spitting at people, and making a spirited attempt to cut down on her nose-picking. Though they had outfitted her in regal splendor and swept her off to famed ski resorts, planning future trips to Nice and Baden-Baden, the Simmonses seemed mysteriously content to let Samantha continue her classes at the inferior Low School. As it turned out, they had never actually examined the school proper. One day, the Simmonses arrived for a visit, took one horrified look at the Sapphires, and plucked their baffled daughter out of her classroom, immediately putting their house on the block and never again being seen within a thousand miles of Detectives' Hill.

Late one night, LePeters arrived home to find his bedroom empty; it was supposed to be empty since his wife was generally off in the city banging Detective Chico, but on this occa-

sion the emptiness was profound and came at him like a
scream. A possible explanation was that Claire LePeters had
suddenly gotten very neat, but LePeters checked her cabinet drawers and found them pretty well cleaned out. After
satisfying himself that his daughter hadn't checked out, too,
LePeters summoned Madame Chav, not afraid to disturb her
since she never ate or slept and if she did it was in stealth.
"She's gone off on location, to help shoot a picture," said the
ex-soothsayer. "But don't worry, I love your child and nobody's going to lay a hand on her."

"Where's the picture being shot?" LePeters asked.

"I'm not allowed to say. But I know where she is and can
get in touch with her if there's any trouble."

"What do you mean you can't say," said LePeters. "Aren't
I the one who pays you?"

"I'm supposed to keep it secret from you. But if you go
somewhere I'll keep it secret from her, too. That's the way I
work."

"I'm not going anywhere," said LePeters.

Returning to his bedroom, LePeters knew that if he
looked in the mirror he would find himself a little stoop-
shouldered. Never before had his bed seemed so empty, even
though he could hardly say that it had been filled up with a
loving wife over the past years. Now, it was as barren and life-
less as the desert. It was one thing for her to be locked in
unthinkable postures in the great city nearby. But to be on
location, a never-never land where all normal authority was
suspended, except for the director's, God alone knew the
things she would carry on there. He had to give her credit—
just when he thought the cupboard was bare she would think
up another shocker. For all he knew she had checked out
forever. He looked through her closets now, to see if she had
left anything worth coming back for. There were some ex-

pensive beaded sweaters and a handsome gown or two. Of
course she would be back. No woman in her right mind
would abandon things like that forever. Reassured, he lay
down on the vast bed, amazed at his powers of adjustment.
Ten minutes before, if you had told him he was going to be a
fellow with a wife off screwing on location, he would have
been horrified. Yet now he was one, and although he didn't
feel like a million there wasn't a chance in the world he
would blow his brains out either. He seemed to have a
bottomless capacity for feeling a little sad, but it was clear
that he was a survivor, too.

The chances were that he was even going to get a little
sleep.

As always, LePeters found comfort in the detectives' bullpen. The next morning, he took a fresh look at these folksily
violent men and wondered what he saw in them. Was he
really so different from them? And if indeed he was an outsider, how come he had kept his nose snubbed up against the
homicidal window not for an understandable nine months or
so but for seventeen long years? Almost to a man, these were
stocky, bullnecked, soup-eating fellows who wore sacklike,
deeply dipped pants, skinny ties, and white workmen's anklets over thick Irish ankles. For the most part, theirs were the
simple virtues—a man put in thirty years on the job, bowled
a bit, told a few fag jokes, watched the late show, had a faithful wife, and loyally practiced sex in one position, leaving the
tricky stuff to foreigners. The flag gave a man goosebumps,
and anyone who didn't like the country was invited to get the
fuck out of it. Old age? The time for a tidy pension, a neat
front porch, and friendly once-a-week beer parties with a few

choice old cronies to rehash great shoot-ups of yesteryear and agree that the country was going to the dogs. Enough remaining muscle to punch some greaseball in the snoot in case he got smart. And what was a man's most solemn hope? That when he finally got laid to rest there'd be someone around to deliver that most sought-after of all homicidal accolades: "By God, that fella was a good dick." And what about LePeters, who as a young man had read *Moby Dick* in one sitting, practically in one position, sprawled out on the New England coast so that he could taste and smell the brine of the book as he raced like a madman through its pages. Most of the time he was a little upset about something, but when he wasn't, a running clip of speculations glided through his head like blips on a radar screen. Hadn't he thought of death and infinity, wrestling with the precise structure of time until his teeth ached and his eyeballs, like tiny runaway planets, did backward loops in his head. If this were true, why had he spent almost two decades as a stranger among homiciders?

Who, exactly, was he kidding? Could he actually say that his heart was quiet when he heard "The Star-Spangled Banner" or saw the Marines storm a beachhead on a late-night Iwo Jima movie? When some dick proposed that we settle our differences with the Red world by "lobbing a few into the Kremlin men's room," wasn't there one slender pocket within him in which for a frozen instant the question was asked, "Why not?" LePeters had cop in him all right, more than he liked to admit. After all, wasn't it until recently that he'd been a little edgy about anything other than the traditional eyeball-to-eyeball confrontation in the hay? His heart went out to black people, killers and saints alike, but what about that fractional component within him that got a brief shiver of pleasure when a barefoot, defenseless Negro got smacked in the head until he confessed a phantom crime.

Sporting a "baby badge," safe in a demilitarized zone between dick and PR man, he could enjoy the parade of slaughter that marched before him, at the same time clucking his tongue and deploring the homicidal violence of it. It was a neat juggling trick, but after seventeen years of pulling it off, his arms were getting tired.

Late in the day, LePeters took the steps two at a time to Chief Guster's office, aware that for a change he was going to do something instead of waiting patiently for new sections of the roof to fall on his head. Stooped over and alone in his modest office, Guster wheeled about when he heard LePeters approach, at the same time zipping open his fly. LePeters approached cautiously, afraid the chief might have turned senile and was about to shoot him a toothless cackle, then hose him down with an old man's pecker. Pointing to the truss that he wore, the chief said, "This is where I keep the lettuce." A stack of crisp twenties was folded beneath the device and LePeters was relieved to see that the chief was only demonstrating a new technique of keeping money out of the reach of late-night muggers. Threatened with a bashed-in head, Guster would simply toss the fellow a wallet containing a couple of bucks and some easily replaced identification, his big loot safely tucked away in its pelvic hiding place. "It's a neat dodge," said LePeters. "I'll probably try it sometime." It always surprised LePeters that Guster was so kindly in his style. One might have expected the bureau chief to be the most vicious and remorseless of all homiciders. Yet Guster was known to be a terrific charity buff, a sucker for any needy minority group looking for a touch. He also took shoe shines all day long from a small colored boy whether he needed them or not, to make sure the kid had plenty of business. Even the truss trick was basically peace-loving and defensive. It was this style of Chief Guster's that made it somewhat easier for LePeters to speak.

"What's on your mind, fella?" asked the chief.

"Sorry to come barging in on you like this, Chief," said LePeters. "But there's something on my mind. I've been kicking around homicide bureaus for seventeen years now and it's occurred to me that I've never really been part of the action.

"I think it's about time I became a real dick."

PART
THREE

◎◎◎◎◎

TRUE TO HIS COMPASSIONATE STYLE, CHIEF
Guster took LePeters's years of fringe homicide work into
account and after blinking at the age requirements, slipped
him into the detective training course, a one-month program
that included classroom skull sessions, heavy work on the firing ranges, on-the-job field trips with seasoned homiciders,
and sessions at the morgue learning to relax around stiffs. In
among high-sideburned, heavy-necked young pups, LePeters
at forty had a few things going for him. Like an aging hoop
star in his last great year, he was slow to get down court and
had little elastic in his legs. Nonetheless, he wasted few mo-
tions, looked carefully for openings, and when he saw one,
took his shots with great deliberation and rarely missed,
breaking open many a ball game. Another valuable playing
card for LePeters was his faithless wife, off on location with a
film-making stud. In a strange way, this deceived state gave
him enormous powers of concentration, a rigidly tunneled
vision that served him well at such critical times as the first
fifteen minutes of viewing a fresh homicide victim. After all,

if he let his thoughts wander, inevitably they would collide with his wife and he didn't need that. Better to keep his thinking bull's-eye straight. This power of pinpoint thinking was enormously useful on the firing range, a place where breathing, control of the stomach muscles, and an almost Zen-like ability to close out the entire world except for the center of the target were much more important than aim, good vision, and young, coltlike muscles. Young dicks in training, their minds no doubt on pussy, had a tendency to trigger-jerk their .38's, to more or less jump the gun. LePeters, his thoughts for the moment as sanitized as those of a Ganges holy man, squeezed evenly, building up a record for accuracy that had old-time range men buzzing. On the difficult pop-up targets or "Hebes in the Weeds," a form of shooting that tested judgment, a fledgling dick more often than not would fire brilliantly but recklessly, gunning down a silhouette he was later told was only "some poor innocent guy taking a leak in the bushes." A split-second slower to fire, LePeters made sure to slaughter only kill-crazy pop-ups who were unmistakably bent on homicide.

Thus, LePeters's comparatively advanced years and his faithless wife combined to form a cementlike mixture that firmed up his spine and pulled his character together. Slowly he developed a clenched and measured new style, hesitating before he spoke, looking at the world with dead eyes—the ideal point of view for a new dick. Early in the program, as a test of nerves, trainee dicks were exposed not to an autopsy, which was small potatoes by comparison, but to a mummification case, considered, in LePeters's bureau, to be the worst of homicides. Such victims, who were either hung, or hung themselves, in the fierce wind and moistureless open air, often wound up thirty feet long and had to be carried in by a team of four instructors and displayed not in the morgue,

which was too confined, but in the basement level detectives'
bowling alley. A single glance at the poor endless beanpole of
a victim was enough to make three out of four young dicks
hit the dirt in a swoon. Viewing his first mummification case,
LePeters chewed hard on a strip of Dentyne yet kept his feet.
Using his new, streamlined thinking style, he allowed himself only a single speculation: that the fellow had probably
been a short guy who'd finally, in death, been able to reap a
kind of vengeance on the big boys who had always towered
over him.

In the many-tentacled world of homicide, fledgling dicks
soon moved toward specialties. Some were obviously going to
become "hardware freaks," experts in locks, windows,
murder weapons, an ability to determine how killers gained
entry, what road they had used to clear out. Others moved
toward "clockwork," zeroing in on time questions of all
kinds, terribly useful in the solution of crimes. When did the
dicks arrive? At precisely what time had the homicide occurred? When did "rigger" set in? LePeters saw quickly that
his strength as a homicider was going to lie in this ability to
"read a body." Quite early in his training he subscribed to
the golden rule of homicide: "A dead body is your best
friend." That is, stiffs, instead of being justifiably furious at
having been knocked off and clamming up, were more than
cooperative during investigations, and in a sense, had plenty
of life left in them. Most inexperienced dicks first checked a
dead man's face, falling for the old saw that somewhere in a
victim's expression was a mirror reflecting the one who'd laid
him out. Early on, LePeters saw that faces were invariably
neutral and somewhat benign, as though the victim were in
great shape and didn't have a worry in the world. Contrarily,
hands were a thousand times more expressive, sometimes de-
fiant, often still terror-struck, on rare occasions gently be-

mused. It was more difficult than most murderers knew to
slip a weapon into a dead man's hand in the interest of steering investigators around to suicide as a motive. On no occasion would a stiff grab a gun firmly; more often than not it
would let the weapon dribble free as if to say, "Not on your
life, buddy." Very often, hands told the entire story. On one
occasion, late in the training, LePeters accompanied a seasoned old pro to the scene of a homicide and noticed that the
victim's hands seemed to be formed in globular shapes, as
though describing a girl with great bazooms. LePeters
pointed this out to his instructor and indeed it eventually
turned out that a gorgeous heavy-chested wench had been an
accomplice to the crime. Grateful to LePeters, the old-timer
rewarded LePeters with a beautifully decorated rubber sheet,
standard equipment for every homicide squad car and used
to cover bodies in the streets so that irate store-owners could
never complain that their business was being chased away.
LePeters was amazed not at how easy it was to snuff out a
human life, but what a major problem it turned out to be. It
took a keen marksman to kill himself with a bullet in the
heart, shots often caroming around the rib cage like runaway
pinballs and landing with relatively little damage on the
other side. A detective who'd had a bullet whistle through
his ticker had been known to walk a mile to his squad, tell a
few jokes to his sidekick, go out dancing that night, and ex-
pire hours later after enjoying a terrific night's sleep. Was
there a better example than Detective Teener, LePeters's
sidekick? Rarely had a dick been so pared down by gunfire,
yet there he was, cavorting about with a hot little second
wife and getting along just fine. Once dead, the body was far
from finished, too, and LePeters wondered at the way nature
had conspired to help a stiff fight back and put homiciders on
the trail of the sonofabitch who did him in. Dragging along

massive concrete blocks, a slender drowning victim would eventually come bobbing to the surface, brimming over with evidence. A limepit case would be discovered months after death, in relatively great shape, having used the lime as a preservative. Most remarkable of all was man's prostate gland. In an effort to eliminate all traces of sex and age, racket men would toss their victim into a shack and burn it to the ground. Yet the prostate never burned. Though all about it lay in cinders, the stalwart little gland would inevitably be found, vigorous, unvanquished, in mint condition, ready to sing to the high heavens about the victim's age, sex, and other evidential goodies.

LePeters kept a loose-leaf scrapbook of homicidal nuggets that might someday be useful in turning the tide of a difficult investigation. He noted such apparent trivia as the fact that it was easy to misjudge the weight of a drowning victim. Puffed up to Macy's Thanksgiving Day float size by long exposure to the water, a victim might actually tip the scales at a svelte 110 pounds. Then, too, it was wise not to stand around and leisurely smoke a cigarette while a man was drowning, confident that he'd show his face three times before going down for keeps. Many victims went down once and stayed down, particularly if they were of Italian descent. Though it was certainly tempting, a detective must resist taking mugging Coney Island–type pictures with homicide victims, since hammy poses such as these often showed up in the tabloids and were bound to throw a dick's integrity open to question. It was important to keep all notes in a loose-leaf scrapbook so that the pages pertaining to a particular homicide could be dragged into court, and the rest of the book left behind. Many a dick, who'd taken his entire notebook along, had been embarrassed on the stand when a sheaf of wild Havana orgy shots had tumbled to the floor, thereby throwing his testimony "down the toilet," to use the courtroom phrase.

As LePeters got deeper into the course, he became even deadlier with his gun, keeping it in what appeared to be an oversized, stiff-leathered, frontier-type holster. Though younger dicks sunk fortunes into velvety baby-leathered rigs and appeared to be "well-hung," LePeters knew that in a tight situation a .38 might stick in a soft holster and result in one dead homicider. Creakily stiff, polished leather, for all of its old-fashioned appearance, meant a smooth, reliable draw. On the range, LePeters employed a relaxed style, casually slipping his free left hand into his side pocket and being hooted down for shooting like a dude. Yet LePeters had learned, by instinct, that a pocket hand provided the steadiest anchor for dead-eye firing. Before long, one by one, the younger dicks, envious of LePeters's astonishing scores, begrudgingly took up the deceptively dandified style.

LePeters took his gun everywhere, never comfortable unless he felt the friendly unbalanced weight of it against his chest; he was delighted when holster friction began to wear out the lining of his best suit jacket, a trademark of the experienced homicider. Finally, he understood the typical dick who felt like half a man without his weapon and even went to the lengths of wrapping it in cellophane in the morning so it could be worn in the shower. LePeters, along with the other dicks, was scornful of "grease jobs" or foreign-made guns, treasuring his all-American Smith and Wesson .38. As a younger man, freshly bar-mitzvahed, LePeters had kicked off each morning by solemnly winding the sacred phylacteries or "tifiln" around his arm until he finally grew bored and stored them away. Now, each morning, he leaped out of bed and put in twenty minutes of "dry-shooting" in his bedroom, propping up two or three radical quarterly magazines as targets, in the prescribed manner. What a distance he had traveled.

As the end of the month drew near, LePeters, though a loner through the program, joined the younger dicks in speculation about the nature of the final exam, different for each group of graduates. One morning, LePeters sat in class, idly jiggling a few cartridges, while an instructor lectured about statements from dying victims. "A deathbed statement is admissible as evidence," said the experienced old homicider, "but the well-trained dick takes all precautions to make sure that the victim goes ahead and dies. Otherwise, he'd be laughed out of court." As he added a few notes to his bulging loose-leaf, LePeters saw a little old lady walk into the classroom, dust around a bit and then slip out. "How many of you noticed that poor little old lady?" the instructor asked. Before any of the dicks could raise their hands, he was passing out papers and saying, "If you didn't see her, you are out of luck. She was your final examination." Designed to test the dick's power of observation, the test consisted of twenty-five multiple choice questions, and one essay, all involving the little old lady's appearance, her rights if she were a homicide suspect, how to conduct an investigation if she were a victim. Momentarily panicked, LePeters saw the entire month of hard work going down the drain. He thought back to his senior year at college when he had literally fainted over an economics final in which the entire exam hinged on a knowledge of grange organization. He actually knew the answer cold, but the possibility that he might not have was too much for him and had knocked him out of the box. But this was a different LePeters. Loosening his collar, sucking in his breath, LePeters waded in and startled himself by how much he remembered about the little old lady, her swarthy complexion, her sarcastic expression, the distinctive little old lady smell of her. Quickly gathering confidence, he flashed through the multiple choices, rapped out the essay and was the first to finish; with enormous cockiness, he sauntered up to the front desk, tossed his paper at the instructor and asked, "What else you got?"

Always, when it came to homicide, there was more to learn. At graduation, Inspector Horton, the guest speaker, took the occasion to tell the group about certain homiciders who'd foolishly thrown away half their careers stubbornly waiting for murderers to return to the scene of the crime. "What we've learned is sometimes they come back and sometimes they don't. The intelligent homicide detective goes back to the scene of the crime and hangs around for twenty minutes tops. If the murderer doesn't show up by then, the chances are he is staying as far away as possible, and is ashamed of his deed. *Wouldn't you be?*" On that note, the guest speaker yielded the dais to Father O'Neill and Rabbi Workman, a team of bureau chaplains who led the group in a wrap-up prayer, asking the Almighty to grant the new dicks strength in dealing with that oldest and rottenest thorn in the side of man—crime.

Jubilantly, the spanking new detectives clapped one another on the back and trooped up to Chief Guster's quarters, there to be welcomed aboard individually by the kindly old chief and handed that most cherished of all homicide emblems, a freshly engraved detective's tin. Waiting his turn, LePeters felt warmly relaxed, as though he'd put a couple of Gibsons under his belt. At one time, the inner circle of homicide had seemed an impregnable fortress, approachable only by those with the proper birthright. Through fierce application and a flexing of those muscles available to him, he had managed to breeze right through the course. He wondered what other unthinkably difficult skills he might be able to master. Could he build a cabinet? Pilot a salvage ship through the China seas? Why others, and not LePeters? Though half of his life had gone by the boards, he saw now that it was an inferior half and that the remaining section might very well turn out to be terrific.

"Congratulations, m'boy," said the chief, rushing forward to shake his hand. "You're an old one, but by God, you're a good one."

"Thank you, sir," said LePeters, taking a seat in the warm armchair opposite the old man's desk. Rummaging about in a bag of tins, the chief finally came up with the one that had LePeters's number on it. "There y'are, fella," he said, handing over the gleaming emblem, "wear it proudly. I wish that just for a minute I could change places with you."

Accepting the badge, LePeters breathed on it, then rubbed it down with his sleeve to give it an even higher shine. Then, after fitting it momentarily against the inside of his wallet to see how it would look there, he tossed it back in the startled chief's lap.

"What's the matter, son? Did I give you the wrong one?"

"It's the right tin," said LePeters. "But I'd be a hypocrite if I wore it. I'm interested in homicide all right, but not *that* interested, and the truth is, I'll never be a dick.

"I just wanted to see if I could become one."

It took very little time for the news of LePeters's startling rejection of the tin to sweep through the bullpen. Later, Le-

Peters was to learn that while the majority of the dicks were all for shooting his nuts off, still others looked at his behavior with a curious, begrudging respect, as though he had done something that had certainly flashed across every detective's mind once or twice. A provision of the law was that any man who had been a dick would be allowed to retain his weapon for a full three years after retirement—and that went for men who'd been dicks for as little as an hour or a day. In other words, LePeters. Later that afternoon, as he sat emptying his footlocker in the bullpen, Detective Flamoyan, a representative of the dicks who were out to get him, slipped up behind him.

"Hello, Izzy," said Flamoyan.

"Hello, schmuck," said LePeters.

"Cute," said Flamoyan. "I just want to tell you that there'll be a lot of guys coming after you. Maybe not now, but sometime, no matter where you go. Keep an eye out over your shoulder."

"Terrific," said LePeters. "I got a gun, you got a gun. We're even. I know how to use mine. Just make sure you know how to use yours."

◉

Before the week was out, LePeters found out who his friends were, Teener setting up a delicious little farewell supper for himself, Glober, Sissy Glober, and the gloomy Mailroom Sal, getting each one to deliver a testimonial speech in order to make it seem like a much bigger affair. Not much of a speaker himself, LePeters kept his remarks almost ridiculously brief: "Thank you all very, very much." Yet he received a tremendously warmhearted ovation when he took his seat. Leading his long-time employee aside, Glober handed over an astonishingly generous check for six months' wages—out of his own pocket—and asked LePeters how he would like to continue working for him in the international slacks business. At last LePeters knew the secret of Glober's tremendous affluence. In addition to his homicide PR work, he had been heading up a worldwide slacks network. "I'm not sure what I'd like to do," said LePeters. "I'm going to take my time before I jump into anything."

"What's wrong with the slacks business?" said Glober, who was evidently very touchy about his profitable sideline. "Do you know how many forces have to be put in motion to create a single pair?"

"I'm not being critical of it," said LePeters. "I'm not going to do much of anything for a while."

"It was good enough to get you that six months' pay, I notice," said Glober, slinking back to his seat, deeply injured.

"Don't let him frazzle you," said the lugubrious Mailroom Sal, putting a limp arm around LePeters's shoulder. "Listen," he said, handing LePeters a folded-up five-dollar bill, "I'd like you to have this."

"Five bucks?" said LePeters. "I can't take money from you, Mailroom." For all LePeters knew, the dejected fellow lived in one room somewhere and the sawbuck might represent a significant part of his rent.

"I want you to have it," said the clerk, "for never once chewing out my ass on how long it took you to get your mail."

"All right," said LePeters, "but I won't enjoy spending it."

Stooping down, LePeters put his arms around his old buddy, Detective Teener, in a farewell embrace, cheerfully accepting it when his tiny sidekick handed him a bill for half the cost of the testimonial send-off. Sitting down for a last brandy, LePeters was thrilled beyond words to see three of the bureau's toughest homiciders—Gibney, Hortham, and Medici—roll in to say good-bye to him.

"Say, intellectual," said Medici, tapping his holsters, "anybody gives you any hard shit, you tell him to come around and see us."

"I really appreciate that," said LePeters. "But I can take care of myself."

"Hey, that's right," said Gibney, with a chuckle, "our boy is now a genuine headbuster."

"It's no joke," said LePeters, and there must have been something in his tone that made the laughter die down.

◉

Later, Sissy Glober said good-bye to LePeters in her own way, silently leading him back to her apartment, which seemed to have been prepared in advance with incense and lighted candles. It was a tiny humpbacked little shell of a place with a single window that looked out on the lush gardens of a monied landlord who lived below. The daughter of a wealthy man herself, and no doubt able to afford sumptuous quarters, Sissy Glober had obviously taken the tiny pad as an exercise in character-building. LePeters waited expectantly for the first crush of mentholation, but she kissed him instead and asked him if this once they could try getting by without it. As a specially planned send-off treat, she poured forth a section of dialogue he recognized as having been yanked whole from a horny little paperbound sex book, written in the spirit of the new publishing freedom. "Oh, God, my darling," she said, spinning out of her clothes, "what are you waiting for? When are you going to ram your steaming joystick into my quivering expectant little honeybucket?"

"I wonder if you'd mind holding off on that," said LePeters.

"But I thought you'd love it," she said, momentarily crushed.

"I thought I would, too," said LePeters, "but I guess I don't."

Undrugged, far from her father's bullpen office, LePeters at first felt awkward making love to Sissy Glober—as though he had gone back to work without his socks. But he reached for her nonetheless, and it turned out to be a profound experience for her, one that ultimately brought her to tears.

"Is it because we're saying good-bye?" he asked a bit later, balancing her on his lap and feeling little or no pressure on his knees.

"Absolutely not," she said. "I was just thinking how happy I am that I'm not in love with you."

Though it had taken LePeters seventeen years to get out of homicide, adjusting to his new freedom took him about two hours. Fresh life filtered into his legs and the air he breathed swept much deeper into his lungs, as though he had cut out smoking after a lifetime of it. First to receive the news was his daughter, Jamie LePeters. He knew it would frighten her a bit, but felt it was all right since there was nothing to be frightened about.

"You mean you don't have a boss?" she said.

"That's right."

"Is it all right not to have one?"

"It seems to be."

"Holy mackerel," she said, spinning about in astonish-

ment, "a father without a boss. That's really amazing. Where
do you get the money now?"

"I don't know."

"Don't we still need some?"

"Yes, we do."

"And you're not worried about it?"

"Nope."

"Holy mackerel, you're not even worried. Then I guess I'm
not either."

For several days, LePeters's main activity was sleeping late;
he would trick himself by setting the clock for his old wake-
up time of seven o'clock so he could wake up and feel glum
and despairing, then realize he was a free fellow and sink
back down for hours more of carefree morning sleep. He also
took the squad out to the highway and watched the bumper-
to-bumper parade of infuriated fellows on their way to the
city, LePeters himself comfortably sailing along in the opposite lane. There was no gloating to any of this; it was as
though he was thrilled to have recovered from a disease and
felt compelled to return to the hospital and visit with friends
he had left behind. For forty-five years—until the day he had
been carted off in an ambulance—Bill Sussman had sprung
out of bed at seven sharp each morning, then dashed down-
town to slave away until dusk in the chilly Frickman Fur
vaults. LePeters had carried on the family's workbound tradition. But it was terribly important for him to know that a
fellow could actually quit his job and be idle for a while and
not have an avenging eagle swoop down between his shoulder blades and hack him to the ground.

For all of his new freedom, LePeters knew it was just a matter of time before he would have to track down his wife and
get her to stop fucking. In so many ways, he could see that
her activities had nothing to do with him. Did they interfere
with his wonderful morning sleeps? Did they stop him from
loving his daughter with new vigor now that he was a relaxed
dad? An entire city filled with charming cupcakes lay at his
feet. Did anything keep him from sailing in on daily visits
and scooping them up, one by one? The main trouble with
his wife's affair was that it seemed to make his life sloppy and
LePeters was basically neat. One morning, he opened his
eyes at eleven and called Teener at the bullpen, seeking out
information on Detective Chico's film, particularly where it
was being shot. "Incidentally," said LePeters, fearful that his
call might be misinterpreted, "I didn't call you to show you
that I can sleep late and you're not allowed to. Actually, I've
been up for hours."

"I'm glad you said that," said Teener. "Frankly, I thought
you were showing off a little."

A mine of information, easily a match for the bureau files
in that respect, Teener quickly came up with a charming
young film-buff acquaintance who would not only be able to
help out LePeters but would also gladly slip him a piece of
ass; in her world, it would represent no more than a handshake.

"I'm all right in that department," said LePeters, "but
thanks all the same."

LePeters met the film-oriented wench at a small bar called
Truffaut's, a hangout for heavily mustachioed splicers and
cutters whose names, though little known to the general
public, were fabled in the vagabond world of thinly budgeted
art films. Waiting for his contact, LePeters became aware of
clusters of lovely, hollow-eyed, long-haired girls who were

obviously film freaks; totally unaware of their stringy, no-
madic beauty, they seemed content to gather in crumbs of
cinematic wisdom from several sandaled fellows whose sole
claim to celebrity was that they had once been assistant stu-
dio men on an obscure Bergman documentary. LePeters had
to wonder where Claire LePeters fit into this world. Aware
that much of her life style had been shaped by Ann Ruther-
ford and Kathryn Grayson (his big influence was Richard
Conte), still he could not place her in this atmosphere of
Godard festivals and furious debates over Chabrol's clear-cut
debt to the genius of the early Joseph von Sternberg.

Idly, LePeters studied the expresso machine, imagining
himself taking Chico in ambush by toppling the great, boil-
ing, castlelike structure down upon his head. Before long,
Teener's friend arrived, a wistful little moppet who had obviously turned up for an entirely different kind of rendezvous.
Clasping hands with LePeters across the café table, the film-
haunted youngster told him she realized theirs was to be only
the briefest of idylls. "I know, my darling," she said, "you'll
spend a week with me, who knows, perhaps a month. Then
back you go to a life that can't possibly include me. I'll be
terribly hurt for a while, but then I know I'll recover. There
will be friends, distractions, my job—and before long, it will
pass and I'll be my old self again. So don't worry, foolish
puppy, I understand that I can only have you for a short
time. But don't you see, it's worth it to me. Joanna is a big
girl now."

"I don't think Teener explained this correctly to you," Le-
Peters said. "I'm very anxious to get a lead on my wife right
now. If this were any other time, I'm sure we'd be able to get
into the other."

"I see," she said, biting her lip. "Just let me sit here a moment, darling, and then I'll be all right. It's all so new to me."

Once relieved of her romantic fantasies, Teener's friend turned out to be briskly efficient; after a few inquiries at the café, she traced Chico's film-making troupe to a deserted strip of beach several hundred miles away, one that was ideal, according to the Truffaut's bunch, for shooting bleak and lonely scenes of alienation. LePeters gave the girl a beaded purse he had bought in advance, also a peck on the cheek which she accepted bravely, holding her fingers to the kissed area and closing her eyes in a beatific style.

Now that LePeters was about to barge in on his wife and Detective Chico, he was amazed at how casually he was able to go about his business. Perhaps the sudden new involvement in film made him feel that this section of his life was being recorded on camera and that if things did not go exactly right, a patient producer would allow it to be taken out and shot again. Whatever the case, the next morning he packed a small bag, at the last second taking along a hot-orange bathing suit that was uncomfortable to wear but gave him a great silhouette. Swinging the squad out to the highway, it occurred to him that however unpleasant it might be to have to seek out a wife and break up her affair, it was still a shade better than having to roll in for a nine-to-five shift on homicide. Ordinarily, LePeters on long drives made sure to stop every fifty miles for hot, reviving cups of black coffee whether he needed them or not. On this occasion, he breezed right along and made the trip in one clip, arriving shortly after noon in the deserted beach community Chico had chosen for shooting key sections of his flick. Famished, he pulled the squad alongside a tiny diner where a single customer, obviously attached to Chico's technical crew, held forth on a favorite theme, the shortsightedness of Hollywood execs that forced gifted fellows such as himself to have to labor away on tiny-budgeted flicks in deserted beach resorts. "All those worthwhile ideas pullulating before their eyes and what do they go ahead and shoot . . ."

"Dreck," said the counterman, right on cue. Polishing off a BLT down with plenty of mayo, LePeters walked toward the beach and spotted a giant, multi-tiered children's slide, the most fearsome he had ever seen. Though it was out of season and the amusement treat was boarded up, LePeters felt compelled to take a try at it; climbing the fence, he raced up the stairs and reached the top tier where he was able to see Chico's film-making troupe far in the distance. It was a fine view and, of course, if the movie-making ex-dick had any sense he would have been up there with LePeters, angling in on the action for a brilliant zoom shot. Using his jacket for a seat pad, LePeters took the great billowing slide in half a dozen thrilling downward ripples, saddened that it had to end so quickly. Stealing cautiously along the dunes, he drew near to the assembled crew and realized that although he was still several hundred yards away, his shadow had fallen across the set. Any lighting man worth his salt would have spotted it immediately, but these were ill-paid Gypsy types who for all of their artistic claims were obviously sloppy craftsmen, and no one on the set seemed to notice LePeters's elongated, spearlike silhouette. As he approached the grouping, LePeters had felt very much the outsider; now he realized that he was to be part of the picture. Though the shadow was totally an accident, LePeters was sure that at some later point Chico would no doubt claim it as his own, a symbol calculated to

drive home his theme of looming industrialization. Quietly
moving still closer, LePeters, out of some deep-vaulted instinct, had a sudden craving for movie candy and wished he
had brought some along. Soon he was able to make out
Chico, wearing dark glasses, a suede vest, and open-toed san-
dals, the very model of a New Wave director. At his side sat
Claire LePeters, neat, secretarial, her hair in a bun, looking
more briskly efficient than he had ever seen her look before.
He had fully expected to see her taking part in some orgiastic
beach scene involving bored young Italian fastbloods and was
frankly a little disappointed at her dignified role. He also felt
a wave of tenderness come over him and longed to run over
to her and give her a big hug. No doubt it was her efficient,
responsible style that did this to him. The scene being filmed
involved two dykes, one of them tripping dementedly along
the beach and being caught up suddenly by the second who
was to grab her by the shoulders and try to knock some sense
into her silly little head. Dissatisfied with the way it was
going, Chico temperamentally kicked up sand and insisted
the dykes take the scene again and again. No doubt he would
soon have the reputation of being a hard taskmaster, one
who would step on anyone who got in the way of his quest
for perfection. As far as LePeters was concerned, it was just
an old Jennifer Jones sequence, with a dyke inserted in the
place of a young John Payne-type lover. What really made
LePeters mad was that his wife, clearly one of America's great
Jennifer Jones experts, was patiently taking notes, as though
Chico's scenario represented fresh story-telling. Leaving the
protective, softly bosomed dune, LePeters got to his feet,
took the standard foul-shooter's deep breath, slipped one
hand in his pocket in the dude style he had helped popularize
around the bullpen, and shot two toes off Chico's open-
sandaled left foot, one for each month the ex-dick had spent

banging his wife. In a curious way, it was as much a reaction
to the pretentiousness of the film as it was to the fact that
Chico had stolen the heart of Claire LePeters.

He sat in the squad beside the lunchstand, waiting for anyone who wanted to follow him, but no doubt waiting for
Claire LePeters in particular. She showed up a bit later, out
of breath, crying about the blood and the carnage and how
awful it was, but he noticed she had a little flowered suitcase
in her hand and seemed all set to pop in beside him. When
he failed to open the door for her, she spoke to him through
the driver's window.

"I can still hear the shot," she said. "I have a feeling that I
always will."

"How come he didn't come after me?" LePeters asked.
"How come nobody did? I was sure there was going to be a
lot more."

"He told them it was an actor. Then he told me that he'd
get around to you, but that right now he didn't want to be
involved with the police. That was very smart of you."

"I was just playing it by ear."

Slipping two richly silken hand-painted ties out of her suitcase, she formed a saleswoman's demonstration knot in one
and said, "I know these are going to be hard for you to wear,
but I honestly bought them just for you. At a little shop that
caters to the film crowd."

"You're right," said LePeters. "I don't think I'll be able to
get much use out of them."

"You don't see it at all, do you?" she said, her hands wilted
as though a cake she had struggled with had been spoiled.
"That all of this was just for us. So I could be a better wife."

Oddly enough he did see it. Still, there was a momentum to his life now and there seemed no way for her to get in step with it. So he gunned the motor and patted her on the head, and she cried out: "What am I supposed to do?"

"I can't help you on that," he said, and drove off without her.

◉

He showed up at the Low School next. He could easily have waited until the afternoon session was over, but it struck him as being terribly important that he actually march in while classes were in full swing. He took up a position at the end of the corridor, and before long a swarm of children came down the halls, the newly trucked-in Sapphires neatly seeded in among the black youngsters to give the enrollment its first true melting pot appearance. Before long, Jamie LePeters turned up, at the end of a line of little black girls who did rhythmic dance steps as they paraded by, stopping every few beats to brandish stiletto-like hatpins at a thicket of hostile Sapphires who cautiously kept their distance. "Hi, Dad," said Jamie LePeters. "This is a new thing we thought up to help us gain respect. Don't worry, I would never use it on you." Without a word of explanation, LePeters took his daughter by the hand and led her through the front entrance, the scholarly teacher named Melvin hard on their heels. Assuming she had been injured in a crippling corridor fight, Melvin waved a sheaf of insurance forms in their direction and shouted out that it was probably just a test of strength. "You get a lot of that at this age."

LePeters had his daughter far beyond the school grounds before she realized anything unusual was going on.

"What's up?" she asked finally.

"I'm taking you out of the school."

"Just like that. Are you sure you're allowed to?"

"I'll check on it later," said LePeters.

"You may not be allowed to," said his daughter. "Not just like that. Anyway, what are we going to do?"

"I thought maybe we'd take a trip."

"A trip," she said. "Are you kidding. We can't do that. What about my room?"

"Your room will be all right."

"I've got fish in there."

"We'll take them along."

"I can just see that, checking into hotels and going to restaurants and never sure that they're having a good time. How do I know they'll love it?"

"They'll love it. I promise you."

"Hey, maybe you're right. Okay, Dad, let's go."

A NOTE ON THE TYPE

The text of this book is set in Electra, a Linotype face designed by W. A. Dwiggins. This face cannot be classified as either modern or old-style. It is not based on any historical model, nor does it echo any particular period or style. It avoids the extreme contrasts between thick and thin elements that mark most modern faces and attempts to give a feeling of fluidity, power, and speed.

This book was composed, printed, and bound by
H. Wolff Book Manufacturing Co., New York.
Typography and binding design by
Bonnie Spiegel